LYCAN KING'S CAPTIVES

Lycan King's Reign Duet
Book 1

JESSICA HALL

LYCAN KING'S CAPTIVES
Copyright © 2024 by Jessica Hall

ALL RIGHTS RESERVED.
No part of this publication may be reproduced, distributed, or transmitted in any form or by any means, including photocopying, recording, or other electronic or mechanical methods, without the prior written permission of the publisher, except as permitted by US copyright law. For permission requests, contact Jessica Hall.

The story, all names, characters, and incidents portrayed in this production are fictitious. No identification with actual persons (living or deceased), places, buildings, and products is intended or should be inferred.

Edited by Jaime Powell
Format & Inside Layout by Patrisha Badalo (Art Muse Graphic Designs)
Cover Design by Hannah Sternjakob

LYCAN KING'S CAPTIVES

Chapter One

Sienna

The ice cold air has me rubbing my arms as I walk home from the club. Snow settles on the ground, and it gives the illusion that there is beauty in this city. That is a far cry from the truth. Creatures that used to live only in horror movies and storybooks choose this time to come out and play, hunting their unsuspecting prey for fun. This city is not safe at night and is ruled by Lycan King Rehan. Humans like me are mere pawns to him. Despite this, I am apprehensive about Prince Xandros's succession, considering the whispers of his depravity. God only knows what new hellscape we'll be in once he takes over from his father.

My house is on a derelict street that runs along the forest which borders the city. The only street light that works is by the burned-out house next door, its faint orange light flickering in the darkness. As I survey my surroundings, goosebumps rise on my arms, and my neck prickles with the feeling of being watched. I pick up my pace, trying to slow my heavy breathing, which is making smoke clouds in the icy, chilled air.

I never used to do late shifts, always ensuring I was home before dark. With my uncle's debt hanging over my head and the threat that comes with it, I've been pulling extra shifts. Finally, it has paid off. I hope he hasn't skipped on another bill for me to cover. When the house appears, a slow dread comes over me at the prospect of entering the decaying weatherboard house. The paint is peeling, the windows have splintering cracks, and some are even boarded over to stop the cold air from getting inside. This place has more cracks, creases, and wrinkles than Mrs. Morris's face, and that old witch is past a hundred.

Approaching the porch, my boots crunch on each step, the holes in the bottom of my boots filling with ice-cold snow, making my teeth chatter. Carefully, I dig my keys out, trying to make as little noise as possible, praying my uncle has passed out or, if I'm lucky, has dropped dead so I don't have to look at his evil face again.

The old door, which is barely held on by the flimsy bent hinges, creaks open, and I curse under my breath before popping my head inside the door. The old box TV is playing with no sound, and I thank whoever's watching over me that he isn't awake, knowing he would shake me down for my tips.

Stepping inside, the stench of stale beer and cigarettes lingers in the air. The horrendous odor reaches my nose, and I fight back the urge to cough or gag, maybe both. I hold my breath, hoping not to wake him, and my grip on the old rattling brass handle shakes. I used to sneak in the back door; however, it's now boarded over from repeatedly being kicked. There is always someone looking for Uncle Sven. He's a ghastly man, despicable, and, unfortunately, my only family.

Ten days and I can finally leave this place, or so I hope. I've been saving for two years to buy my ticket out of here. My ticket is only a fancy way of saying I've been saving up to pay the seekers to smuggle me out of the city via the old tunnel system that was used when the war happened. Their escape through the tunnel system inadvertently left them vulnerable when the exits were blocked. They now heavily guard it. No guarantees; still, it's worth attempting since my future choices include remaining here with my uncle. The king leaving me in my uncle's care for years is punishment enough. I don't think I can endure another nineteen years with him.

I spot my uncle passed out drunk as usual, beer bottle dangling precariously from his fingertips as he slouches on the couch. Once, he could have been described as handsome; the years, though, have not been kind to him. His stained white shirt stretches over his massive beer gut. The filter on his smoke creates a ghastly stench as it burns. Hopefully, the bastard sets himself on fire and saves me from having to listen to his incessant whining about how raising me ruined his life. Closing the door, I grit my teeth at the sound of the lock clicking in place.

Every floorboard is written in my head like a blueprint on which were safe and which ones creaked. However, the beer can was not part of the blueprint in my mind as it crunches under my boot. I cringe, glancing at him. He huffs, the cigarette falling from between his lips onto his white-stained shirt.

I try not to laugh as I sneak to the stairs, taking them two at a time, when I hear his frantic slapping and whiny ass voice when it burns through to his flesh. As I reach my bedroom door, the glass coffee table littered with cans rattles. I suck in a breath and step inside, only to stop in my tracks. My room has been upturned, the drawers strewn across the floor, and my clothes scattered everywhere. Even the mattress leans against the window. No!

I blink back tears, daring to look at the corner where my chest of drawers has been knocked over and pulled apart. My stomach sinks, and I race over to it, ripping it out of the way to find the floorboard where I kept the box containing every cent I had now empty. I pull the last five-dollar bill out, which is barely recognizable since he's burned it.

A deep, menacing chuckle causes me to turn and see my uncle leaning against the door. A beer can in his hand. "Think you can hide money away from me!" he yells.

"That was mine. You had no right to go in my room,"

"No, right? This is my fucking house, you ungrateful brat,"

"That I fucking pay for; I pay the bills, not you. I am the only reason there is ever food in cupboards or the fridge. The power is on because of me!" I scream at him. I had been secretly saving for two years. For two years, I have put every spare bit of cash I've had in here. And it's all gone. That was my ticket out of here, and he stole it.

"Well, I owed Mal. It's fine. He'll let you pay the rest off," he says with a shrug.

"You piece of useless shit!" I yell at him in a fury. He's pushed me

Lycan King's Captives 3

too far this time; that outburst seems to push him when he tosses his beer can and storms into my room. I shriek, jumping to my feet.

His fingers tangle in my hair as he rips me backward. My head bangs loudly off the stained floorboards. I groan, opening my eyes only to see his foot coming toward my face. Quickly I roll, his foot stomping the ground where my head was before I turn, kicking his bad knee. He grunts, dropping to the ground, and I snatch my bag, racing for the door.

His ear-piercing screams yell at me to stop so he can kill me because that will really make me want to go back. My boots thump loudly as I race down the stairs, jumping when I am near the bottom before bursting out the front door, only to stop dead when I remember it is night time.

Now what?

I try to catch my breath, and I can hear him making his way after me, leaving me no other option than to leave the porch and the safety it offers—which is none—therefore, my chances are better inside this house than out of it. But inside is an ass-kicking I don't want.

Inhaling sharply, I pull my hood up to protect myself from the icy breeze and hope nothing is lurking in the shadows.

Every noise has me jumping as I navigate through the snow-covered city. Abandoned houses and burned-out cars line the sidewalk through this side of town, setting me more on edge whenever I hear a noise. This is a hunting territory for those caught in the streets at night.

At this time of night, most humans ensure they're indoors, tucked safely in their beds, and here I am, walking the streets, trying to get to Tasha's place while praying I am not eaten alive, gang raped by werewolves—seeing as those bastards are pack creatures—or left dead on the sidewalk drained of my blood.

Nearing the end of the suburb, the roads begin to clear of rubbish, and streetlights come into view. I glance toward the huge sky-rise buildings where Tasha lives, gulping down the dread, knowing I am going to have to try to pass through the city that comes alive at night with the most sinister monsters. With my head down, I pick up my pace, cutting through the next alleyway and coming out behind the main drag. Noise surrounds me, and I focus on my breathing, needing to keep my heartbeat low to ensure I don't entice a vamp to feast on me.

Bright lights cover all the shop windows. Billowing smoke pours from the restaurants, and the cloying scent of death fills the air, along with the screams of those inside the darker establishments—the clubs and bars that go from family-friendly during the day to dark and sinister at night, catering to those who prowl and hunt.

Alcohol is potent in the air, along with the odor of old blood, when I almost let out a shriek, nearly stumbling over a man's body lying in the street. His throat is ripped out, and the bite marks on his neck tell me what happened. A feeder; a human who voluntarily becomes a juice box for the vamps since their bites are addictive. Panic sets in as I draw closer to where I work, knowing it is the most sinister place in the city. It functions as a regular family welcome club and gambling house by day. By night, its character changes significantly. It's an auction house. And not the sort where you buy antiques. It's the place that sells lives and skin.

It sometimes makes me wonder how my uncle survives out here among these monsters when he gambles, and how he hasn't been killed for his so-called bad luck on the tables. It could be his awful odor; maybe they fear he'd be as unpalatable as he smells, and that's how he's survived.

Moving closer to the edge of the sidewalk, I try getting around the massive crowd lined up out front, only to be stopped by a hand grabbing hold of my jacket.

"Mm, I smell fresh meat," a voice sneers beside me, and my feet falter. Looking upward, I gaze into the eyes of a man who sends my blood cold. Werewolf. His leering gaze roams over me, and I suck in a breath.

"What's a pretty little thing like you doing out here? Want to meet my pack? I know they'd love to play with you," he purrs, and I gasp, stumbling back. His eyes sparkle and flicker at the movement as he stalks me.

"Run, little girl, nothing I love more than a good chase," he threatens when a hand grips my arm; I'm ripped away from the man and turned to face another. Only this man, I recognize. Toby! My boss.

Toby is in his mid-twenties and drop-dead gorgeous. I've always secretly had a crush on him, not that I ever let that be known or would

Lycan King's Captives 5

dare to. He glares at me with his pale blue eyes lined with thick, long lashes, his blond hair falling into his eyes. Then he jabs me in the chest with his finger.

"Sienna, what the fuck are you doing here?" he growls at me. He is a Lycan, which is vastly different from a werewolf. They're stronger, faster, and deadlier; nevertheless, Toby is actually a decent guy.

"I was trying to get to Tasha's," I tell him as he moves to pull me inside the club.

"You shouldn't be out after dark!" he growls at me angrily when the werewolf man grabs my arm.

"Where do you think you're going?" he purrs, and Toby spins around. A threatening growl leaves him, and the man backs up with his hands raised.

"Touch one of my employees again, and I will fucking skin you alive," Toby tells him.

"Woah, sorry, bro. Didn't realize," the man stammers. Toby drapes his arm across my shoulders, tugging me inside. Many eyes are cast our way as he leads me inside the club and toward his office. They drop their gazes quickly after one growl from Toby. When we reach the back of the club, the music slowly begins to drown out, and I glance over my shoulder when we stop. He stuffs me inside his office, and I back up when he growls menacingly. The door slams loudly behind us, and he twists the lock into place.

"Are you suicidal? You know better than to be on the main drag, Sienna!" he booms loudly. I cringe; I've never been in trouble with my boss, but I've definitely found his angry side tonight.

"Stay here, don't leave this fucking room. I'll try to find a cab to send you home in that doesn't have someone who will try to God damn eat you! What were you thinking? You know better, especially with who your parents were!" he snarls angrily, shaking his head.

I flinch at the reminder. My family is famous for being traitors to the king, and I was lucky to find this place to hire me. As soon as anyone saw my ID, it was a no! No one wants to hire the child of the man and woman responsible for killing the queen's sister. If it weren't for my uncle, I'd be dead along with them. Luckily enough for me, he was babysitting at the time. What they did has permanently damaged my reputation, and this is precisely why I must leave this city. Toby growls when I don't answer and snatches his cell phone off his desk. He points to the sofa, and I chew my lip.

"Can you call Tasha, please? I can't go home."

He eyes me for a few seconds, then tilts his head to the side. "Why not?" he demands, but I shake my head.

"Fine, I'm sending you home, then," he tells me, and I lean back on the sofa and groan. His eyes flick to me briefly before he starts dialing the number for a cab when a knock sounds on the door.

"Crap, he's early!"

"Who is?" I sit up in alarm, my eyes staring at the door.

"Just Mal. He owns the blood bar across the road. He's meant to be dropping supplies off and picking up the invoice. I hate dealing with him, but my supplier is out," he says, stalking toward the door. My eyes widen, and I remember what my uncle said earlier. Racing toward him, I grip his arm, and he looks down at me, giving me a questioning look.

"I need to hide," I whisper, and he seems taken aback by my words. He points to the door, and I nod.

"How much does your uncle owe him now?" Toby growls angrily. I shrug, not knowing. I just know he owes him. Toby grits his teeth, and the muscle in his jaw twitches.

"Sofa now! I'll handle it!" he snaps at me, and I stare at the heavy wooden door nervously when Toby gives me a shove toward the sofa and then points at it. I drop my gaze and wander back over to sit, wondering how much trouble I'll be in.

He mutters something under his breath and opens the door. "Mal, you're early," Toby tells him, motioning for him to enter. I peer up, taking in Mal. He's scarily handsome, and his cheekbones are so high any model would envy them. The light beard shadowing his face does little to take away from how clean-cut he looks in his immaculately tailored suit. His dark hair curls softly around the collar of his shirt as he drags his fingers through the strands. Immediately, he sniffs the air, and his dark eyes move to me, widening a bit as he takes me in.

"New toy, Toby?" he questions.

"Employee, I was about to send her home,"

"Won't find a taxi driver this late who won't dine on her; I can take her if you want. I recognize her scent. She is Sven's niece. I need to speak with him about settling his debt, and I was about to head over there to pick her up, anyway." Mal shrugs, and my heart rate picks up.

"How much does he owe this time?" Toby asks while Mal wanders around his office, gazing at the pictures on the wall.

"About eight hundred," Mal states like it's no big deal.

"Eight hundred? That's it. I'll cover it then and drop her home," Toby tells him.

"Thousand!" Mal says, and Toby stops.

"What?" Toby and I say at the same time.

Mal shrugs, "He placed her down to cover it, so I will drop her home to collect what belongings she needs. We will need to stop at my home first to collect the trade papers. I only have the buyout contract on me."

I jump to my feet. "Trade papers?" I shriek, and he turns to me with a sly smile.

"Yes, love, you belong to me now," Mal states, and my gaze snaps to Toby, who is staring at me in horror.

"Wait, Mal. She's barely nineteen,"

"She'll fetch a higher price then!" he shrugs, clearly uncaring. My heart beats like a drum in my chest, and my breathing becomes harsher. My uncle placed me down as collateral! He sold me!

Toby steps forward and shouts, "This is wrong! She's not a slave!"

Mal turns to him, his face twisted in anger. "She is now. I have the contract. You can do nothing about it, Toby. I don't know why you're getting so upset over this human. She is easily replaceable." Mal pulls out a wrinkled piece of paper from his pocket.

Toby snatches the paper and then glances down at it for a moment before he crumples it up in his fist and tosses it to the ground. "No! I won't let this happen! You can't do this, Mal!" His voice is strong and filled with conviction as he steps forward and places himself between Mal and me.

Mal's eyes widen, and his mouth forms an 'o' of surprise. Then he regains his composure. He laughs loudly, a cruel sound that echoes in the small room. "You think you can stop me? I have all the power here. I think you forget how much you owe me too, Toby. The girl is mine now.

If you have problems with that, you can shake her uncle down for what he owes; however, she is leaving with me."

Toby stands tall and meets Mal's gaze without flinching. "I will not let her be sold and turned into a fucking bloodwhore, or prostitute!"

Mal tilts his head to the side and clicks his tongue in annoyance. "You like her," Mal accuses. Toby quickly shakes his head while I chew my lip nervously, my heart racing.

"No, she is an employee," Toby quickly defends.

Mal laughs sinisterly. "So you keep saying, yet you're willing to cut all deals off with me and start a war; I would say otherwise," Mal chuckles. His dark, eerie eyes flick to me.

"If you can pay the debt she owes me, you can have her back. Until then, she is mine," Mal snarls, stalking over to me and ripping me off the sofa by my arm.

I cry out in pain, and Toby moves toward me, but Mal shoves him away.

"Remember your place, Toby. Fight me on this, and it will be your last fight," Mal reminds him before he pulls me out of the door.

My heart races as I'm dragged to the corridor, and I glance back to see Toby watching from the doorway, with an indecipherable expression on his face before he turns and slams his office. Mal hauls me outside into the street before shoving me toward one of his men, who seizes my arm and leads me across the road to another club. He pushes me through the blacked-out doors and into the club.

I scan the smoke-filled room, my heart racing. The place is dimly lit, and the air is filled with the sickly scent of blood. I have never been to this club before, although I heard the stories. It's a blood bar where the vamps come to feast on their prey. Glancing around, eyes watch me. People are dancing on the dancefloor under the strobing lights, and girls with chains around their ankles dance on poles attached to tables. At the same time, vamps look up at them as if they're the tastiest treat they've come across, and the half-naked girls are covered in bite marks, their eyes vacant as they sway their hips to the beat, their skin pale and clammy.

Suddenly, a hand grabs my arm and drags me forward into the main club area. I wince as the cold grip tightens around my arm, and I stumble forward as I am led out the back of the club to an office before being pushed hard onto a chair at a table in the center of the room.

Mal talks with one of his men about organizing his driver to wait at the side alley to pick us up while I stare vacantly at the wall, shocked at what has become of me. Only mere hours ago, I was excited because I was finally escaping the city, and now I've been sold off to cover my uncle's debt.

"What about Prince Xandros? He's been waiting in the VIP section for you. He doesn't look happy."

"He was supposed to stop by tomorrow, not tonight," Mal states, and the man who dragged me into the room shrugs.

"I guess he must have plans. I can tell him you're not here."

"No, it's fine. Grab the money from the safe and tell Sally to send him down to my office. I'll deal with the prince first and then deal with this mess," Mal tells the vampire man, whose gaze goes to me before he smirks.

"Very well," he states, striding out and leaving me with Mal, who exhales loudly as he turns to me.

"You better make me my money back, or your uncle is a dead man," he tells me.

"Can I trade him for me?" I ask.

Mal chuckles. "I'd have to pay someone to feed off that piece of garbage, so no!" He laughs when the door opens.

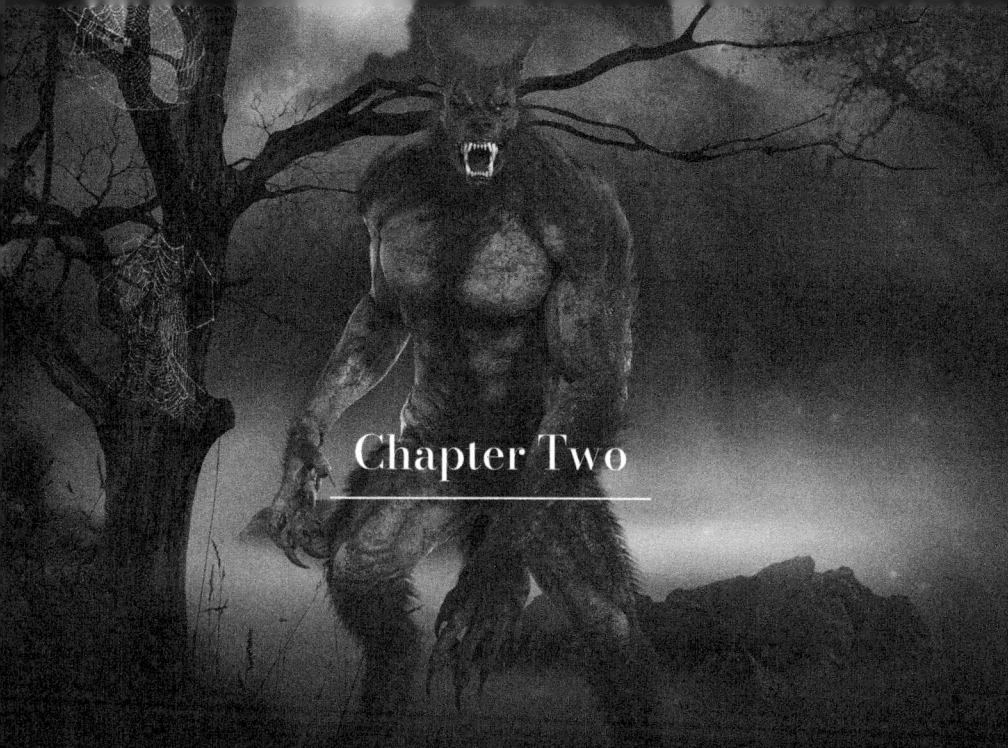

Chapter Two

I shrink back in my chair, my heart racing as the man steps into the room. He is tall and broad-shouldered, with an air of authority that seems to hang around him. His eyes are like deep ice-blue diamonds, glinting in a way that suggests he can see right through me, and they glow with intensity as they scan the room. His large frame fills the space, and I've never encountered an aura so menacingly strong.

He moves gracefully across the room, and I can smell a unique scent emanating from him, almost musky, with hints of smoke and something wild. His movements are precise and predatory, each one calculated and purposeful. I'm fixated, unable to tear my eyes away from him.

"Prince Xandros, what a pleasant surprise," Mal exclaims.

"Mal," the man nods as he wanders over to the desk. Only then does his gaze shift in my direction, and I suck in a sharp intake of breath.

As he comes closer to me, my fear rises. I notice his tan skin stretched tight over prominent cheekbones and a strong jawline. His dark hair swept back off his face in a way that suits him well. It is then I realize what and who he is—the Lycan Prince, next in line to become King. The man sniffs at the surrounding air, his eyes tracking my every movement even though I dare not move an inch.

His eyes finally settle on me again, and a chill runs down my spine; despite knowing nothing about him or why he's here, I know this man would be a force to be reckoned with if crossed. I brace myself for whatever will happen next.

"Who's she?" Prince Xandros questions as he peers over at me.

"Working girl, I recently obtained to cover a debt."

"How much?" the prince questions, and my stomach drops.

"800k," Mal answers and my eyes go to him to see him chewing his lip.

"I sent Andrew for your money, but I don't have all of it today. I was expecting you tomorrow," Mal states.

Prince Xandros's lips pressed together in a tight line, forming an expression that promises danger should I dare provoke it. "I'm sure we can work something out," Prince Xandros says, his lips tugging up as he looks me over from head to toe.

The prince slowly advances forward until he is standing a short distance from my chair. He brushes a single finger along my cheekbone; I flinch at its warmth but cannot bring myself to look away from him. With a slight smirk on his face, he talks in a low voice that resonates deeply within my chest as fear envelops me. My stomach sinks like I swallowed a lead weight.

"I think I found a way to settle the rest of your debt Mal," the prince murmurs. An ice-cold chill runs up my spine at his words, and my gaze frantically darts to Mal's as panic sets in. This man will kill me when he realizes who I am and what my parents did to his aunt.

I close my eyes and take a deep breath. I have to find a way out of this situation. "What do you want from me?" I ask in a voice only slightly wavering with fear.

The prince smirks again and steps back, taking his hand away from my face. He gazes at me thoughtfully then says, "I think you already know the answer to that." Deep down, I know whatever this man wants is beyond my power to stop, and he'll take it and kill me when he is done... unless I find another way out.

"You want her?" The question slightly shocks him and me as well.

"Is that an issue?" The prince asks, raising an eyebrow at Mal. Mal quickly shakes his head and drops his gaze to the floor. "No, Your

Majesty. If you want her, she's yours," he concedes. The man reaches for me; I stand before he can grab me. This seems to amuse him as he motions toward the door.

I have to find a way out of this situation, or else I will never see the light of day again. With that thought in mind, I start going toward the door—my only chance at freedom.

The prince's eyes narrow as they follow my movements. No doubt he knows I was planning something; the question is, what? He steps aside, allowing me to pass him by without any further confrontation. As I reach for the doorknob, I sense his gaze on my back – it is like an invisible force propelling me forward as adrenaline courses through me.

I hold my breath and open the door, taking one last look at the prince before stepping into the corridor and running. I know the danger remains, but at least I've given myself a fighting chance.

With newfound determination, I run, shoving between people aiming for the front doors. Only they are cut off at the last second, and I am forced to detour through the kitchens, where the sound of clanking pans and hushed conversation reaches me.

Without losing a beat, I keep running. Noticing a door, my hands hit it, and it bursts open, and I am met with the cold night air.

I step outside into the freezing winter air and a flurry of snowflakes drift down from the sky. I shiver in my thin jacket that offers little warmth as the bitter cold envelops my body. The stars twinkle and taunt me as I glance around to find I'm in an alleyway. With a deep breath, I take off running down the street, desperately trying to put some distance between me and Prince Xandros, who is chasing me. I can hear shouting from the bar, and I don't waste my time sitting around idle. Instead, I keep running, praying I can outrun them, despite knowing it is futile to try.

The cold winter air stings my face as I race down the snow-dusted streets. With a look over my shoulder, I notice the prince in pursuit, his long strides diminishing the space between us. Fear courses through my veins, and desperately I veer down another dark alleyway only to stop dead in my tracks when I see about a dozen figures lurking in the shadows ahead. They are vampires, and they're blocking my path. With their eyes glowing blood-red and fangs bared, they advance toward me.

Fuck. I peer around, searching for another escape; however, I find none when a growl fills the air, causing the vampires to freeze in place.

I see the prince and numerous guards entering the alleyway from my side. It's clear they are not here to play games.

The vampires react quickly and charge toward the guards, not recognizing the prince for who he is. The prince lunges forward at full speed, tackling two vampires at once before they can reach me. His powerful claws rip through their clothing and skin while his razor-sharp teeth tear into their throats. Though outnumbered, he manages to fend them off until I can make a break for it once again; I don't get far as I am cut off by the feral fighting. Fingers wrap around my arm, and I am jerked out of the chaos by the prince. His excitement at catching me is short-lived when he is tackled and his sharp claws slice through my arm like a hot knife through butter as momentum throws me from his grip. Stumbling, I barely catch myself before I faceplant the ground. My arm burns violently, as I clutch it trying to stem the bleeding. The sight of my arm is horrific, and I can clearly see the deep claw marks tearing their way across my skin. Blood is pouring out of the wounds, and stinging pain slivers up my arm. The pain and shock overwhelm me, and I scream.

After what feels like hours of chaos and confusion, I catch an opportunity to escape and seize it without hesitation. Quietly leaving the chaos and bloody fray, I sprint off into the darkness while they're distracted and spot the forest at the end of the street. With a final look back toward the alleyway, the guards and prince are still battling. Adrenaline pumps through my veins; my mind is racing a mile a minute.

I race through the dense forest. As I run through the trees and underbrush, branches whipping my face as if urging me faster. Ultimately, all sounds of pursuit fade away into nothingness around me. For a while, I keep running out of fear until I'm deep in the forest, my heart pounds loudly in my ears, making me stagger. I try to catch my breath as the eerie quietness of the forest sets me on edge. At first, the pain in my arm was a slight discomfort; the pain progresses to an unbearable level, and my skin becomes red and hot.

My head is spinning, and despite the freezing cold weather, I am drenched in sweat. Moving slower, vertigo rushes over me, and I stop trying to catch my breath. I grip my bleeding arm as I assess the damage. I've heard Lycans are creatures that can transform humans into Lycans. Their bites contain powerful venom that causes transformation, effectively marking the person they change and making them their mate. Despite this, their scratches can be lethal because it's toxic to their prey, which is supposed to stop them from getting far if they manage to escape.

While peeling the torn layers of my jacket, I gasp at the wound, which in such a short amount of time, has turned black and appears severely infected. The wounds are still fresh, oozing with a blackish-red liquid I know is filled with toxins from the prince. The cold sting of the prince's claws that ripped through my flesh, left behind a sharp reminder of just how close I'd come to death. Death appears to be not off the table as I eye the claw marks, feeling sick to my stomach.

I stumble forward, vomiting in the snow, emptying my stomach. Once I finish throwing up what little was in my stomach, I wipe my forehead, and notice how hot it is. My skin is clammy, and it takes every bit of willpower for me to rise to my feet and force myself to keep moving.

Continuing to push forward, the claw marks on my arm burn fiercely as they sear with the toxins from the Lycan Prince.

The further I walk, the more nauseous I feel as the toxins start to course through my veins and take hold. A violent wave of heat passes through me, my skin becomes clammy and tight until sweat starts to pour from me, while my heart races faster. Eventually, it seems every step is a mammoth task.

The surrounding trees seem to blur together in a never-ending wall of green, and yet I keep pushing forward. Each breath I take is labored, and every step causes intense pain. I still manage to make it back home as the trees begin to clear and spread out around me.

It feels like hours or even days have passed by the time I finally reach the end of my street. My vision is blurry, and I can feel myself burning up as I stagger and stumble toward my house. I blink back the specks, trying to steal my vision as I clutch the hand railing on the steps, steps that seem far steeper than normal. Forcing my body up the first step, I wobble on my feet.

Blinking, I try to clear my vision, which is tunneling fast. A second passes and the next thing I see is the steps rushing toward my face. The impact of my body hitting the stairs is unfelt, but I hear the air leave me in a huff while my eyes roll into the back of my head, and I am swallowed by darkness.

Chapter Three

Each breath I take makes my lungs wheeze. My skin burns with a heat I can't explain, my muscles tense, and I can't seem to relax. I feel as if I'm suffocating, and I can't do anything to stop it. My heart is racing, and I'm struggling to keep calm as I urge my eyes to open.

The sound of running water reaches my ears. I blink, and my eyes flutter open to see the moldy roof of our bathroom.

My mind is too preoccupied with the thought of how much pain I'm in. The water is freezing cold, and I lurch upright, clutching the sides of the tub. The sound of chains clanking nearby makes me scan my surroundings; only then do I see my hands bound to large bolts my uncle has fixed to the bathroom wall. One bolt leads to the chains holding my hands together. I try to scream, but my voice is hoarse.

My uncle enters the room, and his face is stern and unreadable in the dim light. He takes a step toward me, and I flinch, my heart pounding loudly in my ears. He raises his hand and points a crooked finger at me. "Quiet, I have a headache!"

Time seems to meld into one long moment as I take in his expression, my heart racing. He crosses the room and stands above me. The tension between us is palpable, and I can feel it in the air, like a static charge, as I wait for him to make the next move. All my senses are heightened as I anticipate what is to happen next.

"What?" I ask, yanking on my hands, trying to free them.

"Fucking, finally!" My uncle sneers, dumping a bag of ice into the water. His voice seems so much louder and more nasal than I remember. Even my eyesight seems stronger as I take in the brush marks on the wall from painting the bathroom last year.

"What are you doing?" I whisper, my voice shaking with fear.

"Mal called. He said you ran from him. I found you outside, passed out. What Lycan scratched you, huh?"

"Mal?" I stammer.

"Don't worry. I told him you weren't here," my uncle informs me, and I stare at him. I don't answer, my gaze glued to his. He sighs and shakes his head, then turns around. When I try to break free, he turns back.

He grabs my arm, and I scream, trying to break free. He raises his hand, and I flinch, expecting a slap, then he digs his fingers into the flesh of my right arm, then feels my forehead, and curses, "You're still burning up!"

"You didn't tell him where I was?" I ask, thankful.

"Of course not. I'm not telling him his goods are ruined. Gotta fix you up before I hand you over," he tells me, then turns around and retrieves a paper bag. He opens it, dumping the contents into the water. My brows furrow in confusion as I look at the wolfsbane floating around. He grabs a giant mixing spoon, the one that hangs above the stove usually, and starts stirring the water, creating a murky, purple-colored concoction. He takes a small bottle from the side of the tub, pours some of the liquid in, and continues stirring. "This will fix you up," he says.

"Huh?" I whisper, trying to figure out what he's doing.

"The wolfsbane will help neutralize the toxins in the water and your blood," he tells me. I gape at him, wondering what the heck he is talking about.

"Why is it necessary? I am not a Lycan."

"It's for the infection, kid. I've seen grown men turn rabid with infection. Surprised you haven't fazed. Most people turn rabid before it kills them. "However, this will quickly fix it," my uncle calmly explains.

I try to remember what I know about Lycan infections; however, the buzzing from the light is extremely distracting. Lycan infections are caused by the toxin that attacks the body, causing severe pain and weakness, then usually kills the host. The virus is spread from the poison in the Lycan's claws, making it extremely difficult to fight off without help, but this is the first I've heard of it causing people to go rabid. It is sometimes possible to cure an infection with wolfsbane. Though infrequent, accounts exist detailing its success. It makes me wonder if there is any chance for me since an ordinary Lycan didn't scratch me; I was scratched by the prince.

"That'll rid you of the poison long enough for him to collect you. I don't give a fuck if you die or kill him once the trade papers are signed." My uncle tells me.

No sooner than that, my skin burns as he tells me, "I can't hand you over like this." I try to jump out of the water, wondering what is happening, only to find chains strapped to my ankles which are attached to the wall, preventing me.

My scream is deafening as my skin begins to sizzle and burn. He has doused me in a wolfsbane concoction that is designed to temporarily block the effects of any poison from entering my system. The pain is intense, as if I'm ablaze.

All this will do is give him a window of opportunity to make the trade and for Mal to collect me, ensuring I am not dead by the time he returns me to the prince.

My uncle grabs a face washer, jamming it in my mouth. I try to spit it out when he punches me, my head whipping to the side and smacking the tiles. I see darkness for a moment only for him to duct-tape the face washer in my mouth. I try to reach for it with my chained hand when he yanks on the chains held with a bolt to the wall.

I am forced back under the water, my feet being dragged higher and forced on my back. I scream as the wolfsbane burns me, and I thrash when he yanks on the other chains, suspending my hands in the air.

"Quiet, you'll ruin the game!" he spits at me while I try to breathe around the duct tape. He then walks out, leaving me in agony as I scream in pain. I'm not a Lycan. Why is this stuff burning me?

Time escapes me as minutes seem like hours as the poison in my system writhes through me. My skin is blistered and bleeding in places, and the wound on my arm seems to be slowly closing over. I don't know what that means, nor do I care. I long for death. It would be better than this pain. I sense my life ebbing, my vision blurring, senses dulling, and I can barely move. Then darkness descends, and I am no more.

I have no idea how long I have been in here when the door opens and my uncle enters. He presses a clammy hand on my head and curses. "Fuck, I can't hold him off any longer. He's been calling for three days! He stopped by and checked your room to ensure you weren't here," my uncle Sven informs me.

Three days? I've been submerged in this tub for three days. My heart races as my uncle hurriedly pulls my limp body out of the tub. He wraps me in a towel and leads me out of the room. As I am led away, I can still feel the cold lingering on my skin.

He tosses me into my room, shutting the door, and I fall onto my mattress. I glance around the room, my eyes adjusting to the dim light.

Everything seems to have stayed the way I left it. The same posters are on the wall. My clothes are strewn everywhere. The furniture is upturned still. I shiver as I drag the blanket over the top of me. Some part of me is urging myself to remember something crucial. My memory fails me; I only recall the bitter cold sinking into my bones until it turns into blistering heat.

My breathing becomes harsher, my vision blurs, and I can hear my uncle on the phone downstairs. The more I focus on his voice, the clearer it gets. "I got her, Mal, I put her in her room," I hear him tell him. His voice shouldn't reach me; he is too distant. How is that possible? My senses are heightened, which is when I taste the coppery scent of blood on my tongue. My teeth, cutting into my tongue and cheeks, are sharper than usual.

I need to get out of here!

No sooner than I think it, I am standing upright. Confused, I blink around my room, trying to figure out how I moved so quickly when the door opens.

"Mal's on his way. Get some dry clothes on," my uncle tells me. His voice sounds different, and I stare at him. He even looks different. I can see every pore on his face; his skin appears yellower than normal, thanks to jaundice from his drinking.

"Did you not hear me?" he bellows at me before stalking over. He raises his hand to backhand me. I watch it move toward my face like it's in slow motion when I grab it. I blink at his wrist clutched in my hand, seeing it shake as he tries to break out of my grasp.

His strength is no match for me when a strange sound tears out of me. His eyes widen in horror when suddenly I hear a snap, and he screams a blood-curdling scream. I let him go, wondering why he made such a noise, and he staggers back, clutching his wrist. I stare at my hands in confusion when the scent of blood reaches my nose. When I look at my uncle, I sniff the air.

His wrist is bleeding, with the bone jutting out of his arm he attacks me. Only when he does, it's like time slows. With every move he makes, I anticipate and see it coming. The next thing I see is his crumpled form on the ground, my hand inside his chest, my fingers wrapped around his heart when I jerk it, just as a loud bang follows. In shock, I blink at what I did and what I am holding.

I killed him.

I killed my uncle.

With his heart in my grasp, I release it, horrified and sickened. His heart hits the floorboard with a loud squelch sound. That's when I hear a deep, husky voice behind me, making me spin to see the intruder.

"She's magnificent," comes a voice from the door. I take in the stranger, realizing he is in fact Prince Xandros. I stare at him, absorbing his features to memory, his dark features, his strong jawline, and plump lips when my gaze is drawn to his golden eyes. He puts his hands up, and I watch him, wondering where he came from and how he got in my house.

"I'm not here to hurt you; I'm here to help," he tells me, and I get up, backing away from him, finally coming to my senses as I remember he is the reason I am sick, the reason I got infected. No, he wants to buy me. He's here to take me. A rumbling noise fills the air, and I jump at the sound while the prince smiles wickedly. Then I realize the growling sound is coming from me.

His eyes flash, and he smiles, showing his canines. "Well, looks like I'll be doing this the hard way, then," he purrs before lunging at me.

His movements are so fast they're a blur. Not like when my uncle moved. He is faster and quicker than my mind can possibly track, yet flight or fight kicks in regardless. Every move I make, he anticipates, moving with ease until he pins me. My vision tinges red, his claws digging into my wrists as he pins them above my head in one of his. Tears prick my eyes, and a sudden overwhelming claustrophobia grips me. He trails a hand down my body as I lift my hips, trying to throw him off. Instead, he rocks his hips against me.

"Keep fighting, love. You're only making me harder," he purrs, and I freeze. He laughs as he presses his erection between my legs. I gulp down the dread pooling in my stomach. His breath is hot on my skin as he leans in. I can feel my body trembling in anticipation of what he'll do next.

I grit my teeth and close my eyes, waiting for the inevitable.

He moves away, and I hear him laugh again. "It seems I'm going to have to break you, little mate," he says, and I open my eyes to see him smirk, his eyes sparking with amusement. He leans in closer, and I can feel his breath on my face. His eyes twinkle with amusement, and I know I'm in trouble. I'm not escaping this monster any time soon.

"My King?" comes a deep voice behind him, and I turn my head at the sound, looking for whoever else is with him.

"Leave us!" Xandros growls, and I hear the man's retreating footsteps. King? He isn't a king. His father hasn't relinquished the throne to my understanding.

"Will you come willingly, or do I need to force you?" he asks, lifting his hand. He runs a finger down my cheek and then down my neck. My breathing becomes harsher, and his heat seeping into me makes my fever burn even hotter. I know I should resist, yet his touch sends a shiver of pleasure through me, and my body betrays me.

His deep amber eyes are locked on mine, and my heart starts to race as I realize I can't look away. His lips tug in the corners, and I am stunned by his beauty. Sharp canines protrude from his lips, and his eyes flash black, taking on a demonic appearance, his skin clear and smooth beside the ghosting shadows of his stubble, full lips, and high cheekbones. This man is pure perfection, and his body seems as hard as the steely gaze watching me.

I feel a shiver go up my spine as I meet his gaze, and I know I'm in trouble. He presses closer, and I can feel the warmth radiating from his body. He buries his face in my neck and groans lewdly, snapping me out of my dazed thoughts. Once I'm pulled in by his magnetic presence, I realize there's no escape as his hand slips beneath the drenched shirt, clinging to me.

His lips softly brush against my ear, sending a shockwave of pleasure through me. I close my eyes, knowing I'm completely at his mercy. I surrender to the magnetic pull between us. His touch is electric, and I can feel the heat radiating off him. His hands wander slowly over my body, sending sparks of desire through me that I don't understand. My body is craving his touch, despite being petrified of him. My mind is going in two different directions when he climbs off me. The moment he does, the fog clouding my thoughts lifts, and I blink up at him to see him extend his hand to me. I stare at it for a second before placing my hand in his and allowing him to pull me to my feet.

His eyes watch me, the same way they did at Mal's, drinking in my every feature, calculating my every move. I frantically search around for an escape route. I don't find one. His intense gaze has me pinned in place, and I am unable to move. My heart races as I attempt to take a step back; his hand tightens around mine. "Whatever you're thinking, I advise against it. You won't escape me a second time," he growls in warning, his tone turning icy cold as his eyes flash at me with the challenge. I swallow and nod. Not knowing how to respond, he lets my hand go, motioning for me to pass him.

Hesitantly I step around him, his eyes following me, and I glance at the door when my toes brush something. Peering down, I see my uncle, and I gasp, taking a step back. My eyes go to my hands that are drenched in his blood, and I blink. I killed someone; I killed my uncle, my own flesh and blood.

Warmth seeps into my back, and I tense, as the king's chest presses against me. His breathing is hard when he dips his head next to my ear, his breath fanning my neck, and I fight back a shiver. His huge hands fall on my hips, his fingers digging into my soft flesh making me realize I'm only wearing a wet shirt and my underwear.

"Choice is yours, little mate. You can either come home with me or rot in a prison cell for the rest of your life. Which is it?" he purrs and tears brim in my eyes. I nod once, having no intention of picking either option. My heart beats like a drum in my chest. Knowing both my options end with the same conclusion: me dead.

He nudges me forward and I tear my gaze from my uncle, stepping over his body and creeping toward my bedroom door. The further away from the king I move, the dizzier I become and I sway slightly. His hand grips my arm to steady me and I shake my head.

"It's just the effects of—" I don't let him finish, seeing the floor below, I run, jumping over the top of the railing. I brace myself for the pain I expect to race up my legs when I land. I experience no sudden pain; nonetheless, it disappears upon hearing his laughter. The sound makes me peer up to see him peering over from the floor above.

"Don't do it!" He chuckles darkly, and I glare at him.

"I'm not going anywhere with you," I spit back at him. He smiles wickedly, showing his sharp teeth. I take a step back, and he takes a step forward. I know he's not going to give up easily.

The king sighs heavily and shakes his head, moseying down the stairs. "Go on, then," he waves dismissively, and my brows furrow. I needn't be told twice when I hear the creak of a floorboard, making me pivot to glance in the living room. I see the man who interrupted us before, and he watches me carefully.

"Leave her," the king orders, and the man folds his arms across his chest, nodding toward the door.

They're letting me go? I dart my eyes to it and back to the man when I hear the king's footsteps coming down behind me on the stairs.

So I run, grabbing the door handle, and bursting out into fresh air, the coldness of it blasting my face. I stagger forward, enjoying the cooling sensation, when I hear the king's voice.

"Find out everything you can about her," he tells the man. I peer over my shoulder, and he seems unfazed by me, trying to escape as he talks with ease. Something tells me that should worry me, but I have a one-track mind, and that is to get out of here.

Running down the steps, the fourth one is covered in snow, and by the time I reach the bottom, the snow is up to my knees. Ignoring the cold numbing feeling of it melting against my blistering hot skin, I make a run for the trees. I dive into the safety of the trees, my heart pounding, the snow crunching beneath my feet. I take a moment to catch my breath and glance back.

My footprints are the only thing that proves I was ever here. As I glance back toward my house, the king slowly creeps down the steps. He sniffs the air before turning in my direction, moseying along like he is merely enjoying a stroll through the park. Not waiting around, I disappear into the dense forest.

The farther I go, the weaker I become, the blistering heat of the fever returning with a vengeance. My vision blurs, and I clutch a nearby tree, trying to catch my breath. As I make my way through the forest, vertigo washes through me, the snow making my toes numb.

Nausea kicks in, and I retch; an empty stomach results in dry heaves. The urge is so much more excruciating than the action itself as my body heats up overwhelmingly. My eyes roll into the back of my head, and the next minute I am falling. I welcome the ice-cold snow as it seeps into my skin, cooling the raging inferno bubbling inside me and threatening to boil me from the inside out.

The crunch of shoes makes me twist and peer between the trees to see a dark figure. The figure steps closer. His face is shrouded in darkness when his aura rushes over me.

He pauses, smirking down at me.

"What's happening to me," I mumble.

"Well, if you hadn't run, I would have explained. You are quite intent on escaping me."

I peer up at him, waiting for the effects to wear off. "You poisoned me," I mutter as I blink, trying to clear my vision. He nods and purses his lips.

"That wasn't intentional; considering your condition, your time is limited," he says.

"I'm dying?" I murmur.

Now completely immobile, my body paralyzed, he nods, confirming my suspicions. I take a deep breath and close my eyes, accepting my fate. As I come to terms with my impending death, I can feel my body slowly shutting down, unable to move or respond to my commands. I know this is it, and I can only accept the inevitable.

"Not that I will allow that to happen," comes the king's voice.

"You didn't notice how the effects of my venom coursing through you eased in my presence? There is no doubt you will die if I leave you here. Your body is calling for me. Now, my venom is in your system; the only one who can save you is me. It is a safety mechanism to prevent our prey from escaping and to prevent our mates, who will eventually be forced back to us. It eases off in my presence because your DNA has changed. You can sense me," he explains. I try to understand what he's telling me, but my mind is drifting.

"My body senses you?" I mutter as his arms scoop me up, and he cradles me to his chest.

"Hmm," he hums. "Yes, the farther you get away from me, the sicker you'll get. The closer you are, the more you'll crave me, and the more your discomfort will ease until I mark you."

I try to ask what he means; my words make no sense to my own ears, and my tongue feels thick in my mouth. He laughs softly.

"Yes, I'll mark you, make you mine. Then you'll crave me; additionally, you'll never want to leave me, and I can never let you go," he chuckles darkly, and the next second I feel his teeth pierce my neck. Pain sears through my skin, his teeth tearing through and sinking in deeply. My scream is ear-piercing, and black dots steal my vision as I thrash in his arms. When he pulls his teeth from my skin, a hot trickle of blood runs down my collarbone and chest. His tongue runs over the mark, and I fight to remain conscious.

"Shh, the worst part is over until you shift. You're mine now," he whispers before the darkness that stole my vision steals my thoughts, too. His voice is somewhere far in the background, soothing, and I feel the hot waves that have been tormenting me abate, and I lose consciousness.

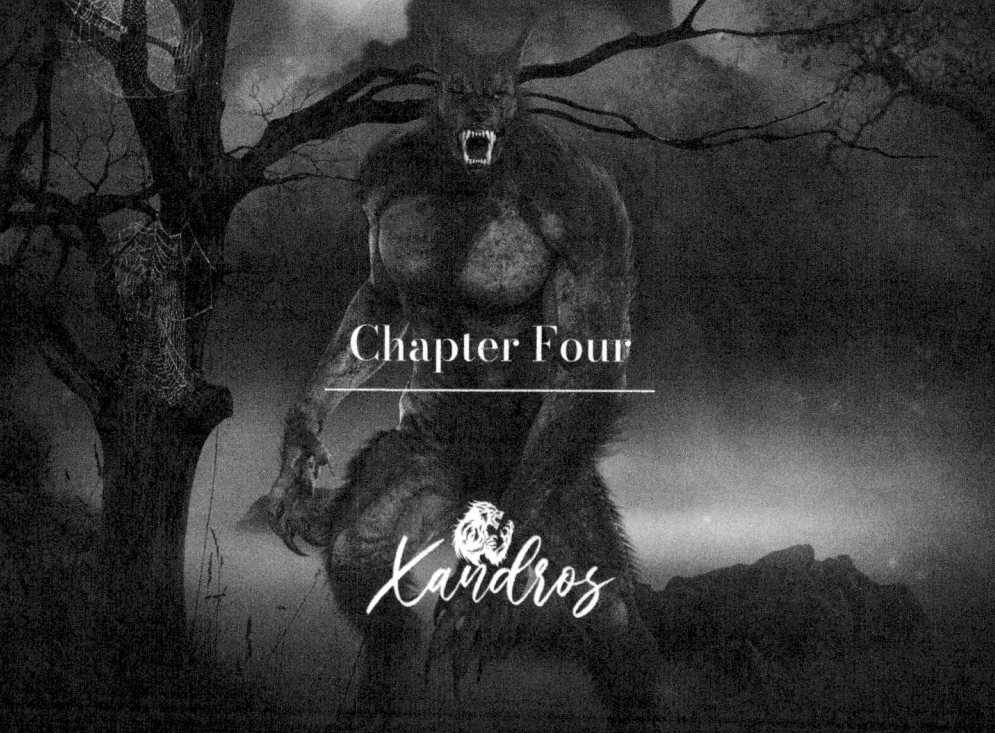

Chapter Four

Xandros

I didn't even know who the girl was, but for some reason, she believed she could escape me. Not in my city. Had Mal searched the house properly when I ordered him to, he might still be alive.

Well, he won't make the same mistake twice, or any mistake for that matter. Making my way back to the house, my Beta Javier is waiting in front of the run-down building where she probably spent her childhood. For some reason, this house feels familiar. I can't explain the déjà vu I have when I peer up at it.

"My king, what do you want me to do with the body?" he asks as he walks down the stairs and to the car. Javier opens the passenger door while I glance back up at the decrepit old house, the paint flaking from the harsh elements of this city. If it isn't one extreme, it is another with the weather here. Yet this house is so unkept it looks like a strong gust of wind could knock it over at any given second. Sighing, I peer down at my mate in my arms.

"Find out who she is and bring anything she might want to keep back to the castle. Then burn it." I order before ducking down and sliding across the seat. Javier peers inside at me.

"Burn it, sir?"

"She won't be coming back here. I will send the car back for you," I tell him, and he nods, shutting the door while my driver, Enzo, peers in the back. I nod to him, and he starts the car while I maneuver my mate on my lap to a more comfortable position.

"Is there anywhere you wish to go before home?" Enzo asks, glancing at me in the rearview mirror.

"No, home is all," I tell him, leaning my head back. Fuck, how do I explain finding her to my mother? She'll be furious because now she'll have to turn down King Dresden's arrangement. Not that I wanted to marry his daughter Carina anyway, but she will still be upset. I'll have to find a way to explain to her the wedding will be off. I take a deep breath and prepare myself to face her and my mother. Queen Anita Dresden and my mother are quite close. The Dresdens aided her when she required assistance; therefore, I expect her anger, though I believe she will understand the significance of destined connections.

My father couldn't care less who I marry; he hates King Dresden because the man has no limits. I don't know what his arrangement with his wife is; he openly hits on my mother and can become a bit too hands-on with her. My mother is oblivious to his advances, and his wife does not appear to mind his wandering hands.

Now my father will finally hand over the crown to me. I've been ruling as king anyway; nevertheless, until I married or found a mate, I couldn't officially take the title.

Lycan law states any future king must have a queen before taking the throne. It was a rule enforced after too many lone kings became cruel dictators. I hold one of the highest rankings, meaning the world and the seven kingdoms constantly watch my family. Two hundred and two years old, I know I'm under the most scrutiny of all. A king can only rule for two hundred years and then must hand the title down; unmated means the kingdom would be at risk in my hands because I am one of the oldest unmated Lycans in the world. Most don't remain sane past one hundred and fifty years of age without their mate.

The Dresden family offered their daughter to secure a permanent treaty between the kingdoms; I just hope my mate doesn't ruin the alliances because I can't marry Princess Carina now. She'll understand,

and my father will be delighted knowing I won't be marrying a vamp. So our usual agreements will hopefully stay strong. Carina will make a fine queen, and she isn't required to marry to hold her title; this was only a favor to my mother to strengthen the relations between our two kingdoms.

True mates strengthen us, and once she turns and awakens, my feisty little mate will make one hell of a queen.

My only hope is that we don't trigger any conflict between our kingdom and the vampire kingdom by turning down the marriage. The newest treaty depended on our marriage. Although even Carina is aware of the importance of mates; she searched for hers for decades before agreeing to this marriage, just as I have. And to think my mate was here all this time.

I haven't been home for days; I've ignored my fiancé and parents while searching for my mate. I was sure she would try to flee the city. We've had every seeker out looking for her.

With the sun setting, a deep orange and red light bathes the city's high buildings, throwing shadows on the walkways and plunging the lanes into a dusky glow.

Along the streets are stores and restaurants, with people strolling and talking or racing to get home. The human store owners barricade and bar their stores, preparing to lock down before our clientele changes. The smell of street food wafts in the air, and there is a sense of energy, excitement, and the potent stench of fear.

This time of day is the most dangerous, and most of the supernatural's are primarily night creatures. We are stronger at night, almost supercharged, Lycan aren't restricted to night like the vampires, they can't handle daylight for too long. We aren't sure why.

It didn't harm them; however, I believe that living in the shadows for centuries, evading humans, evolution adapted, thus making them also stronger at night. Lycans can go days without sleeping.

Enzo navigates the windy road leading toward the castle. By the time we reach the tall iron gates, the sun has fallen behind the trees and mountains calling on the night. The lanterns running on either side of the driveway along the hedges illuminate the road.

The castle coming into view makes me antsy despite its beauty. It is made of beautifully patterned sandstone, with tall towers and spires reaching toward the sky. Dark window frames with colored stained glass create an otherworldly feel.

Most humans stare in awe at this place. It is like stepping out of reality and into a picture book. Roses of every color fill the garden beds despite it being winter here. The weather is bizarre, one minute, snow. The next, it's blistering heat.

Earth truly is a marvelous place, mysterious. I've always found humans fascinating. I can only imagine how good it must feel to have such easily influenced minds, never having to decide for themselves when their governments decide for them. Now we do. Now supernaturals run the world, no longer hiding and starving in the shadows.

How good it must feel not to be driven by instincts that will never make sense to you, driven by hunger and desire so strong you can't refuse it. Pulling into the circular driveway, fountains sit in the middle, filled with orchids and lilies. This place could take your breath away, especially at night, with the fairy lights in the trees turning on, lighting the place up like some winter wonderland. As the car stops, Enzo jumps out, opening the door for me as servants come out to greet me.

I can't wait for her to see this place. I hope she loves it as much as I do, for this is now her home, too. Peering around, I suck in a deep breath. Finally, I can sleep, then wake up next to my mate. Something I have longed to do, and a true mate, not a chosen or forged mate, instead someone who is truly created for me by the divine.

Taking in my surroundings, knowing I won't be leaving my room until she shifts. It is evident the groundskeeper did the lawns yesterday because the grounds are well-maintained despite the thin blanket of snow, which gives the appearance the lawns are decorated with glistening diamonds.

Turning, the entrance is grand, with two towering stone pillars and an ornate wooden door. Servants glance between each other and step aside as I move toward the open doors. I nearly turn around and walk out when I spot Carina sauntering down the grand staircase toward me. Fuck! She is back already. My impression was that she wouldn't be back until tomorrow. No doubt my mother called her to let her know I hadn't been home.

"Xandros, my love." she beams happily, her paleness showing she is in need of blood. She smiles and rushes down the steps. Her smile slips off her face, and she halts in her tracks. Her blood-red eyes peer at the woman in my arms.

"And who is that?" she questions.

"My mate," I answer with a growl, not liking the way she is eyeing her.

Carina tilts her head, eyes trained on my little mate. I cautiously watch my fiancé for a second, gauging her reaction. Her long, dark hair hangs down to her waist, and her blood-red eyes seemed to pierce through her prey. I clutch Sienna closer as if to shield her. Lifting my gaze back to Carina, she clicks her tongue, stepping down a step. Carina always had an air of confidence and power, and her movements are graceful and elegant. But right now, she is furious. I can tell by the way she grasps the handrail, her knuckles white, and her sharp nails scratching into it.

"Excuse me?" she scoffs, placing a hand on her hip. Her tone is mocking, as if she doesn't believe what she's just heard. When I don't repeat myself, she tilts her head to the side and fixes her eyes on me. A challenging glint makes them sparkle as she slowly walks down the stairs toward me.

"I'll give you a chance to fix that statement, Xandros. We are due to marry next month, and you suddenly decide to bring home a stray?" she snaps at me. I bite back the urge to growl at her tone. Her shock and anger, I expected, but I won't be challenged, not in my kingdom.

"Who is she?" Carina demands, and I press my lips together.

"My mate, it doesn't matter who she is. You know the importance of mates," I tell her, peering down at mine knocked out in my arms, her face relaxed in her sleep.

"I know the importance of this marriage. Treaties depend on us. Kingdoms! And you suddenly claim another!" she yells at me. Clenching my teeth, I peer up at Carina.

"I understand how significant this union is," I reply firmly, "but I can't go through with it. Not now that I have my mate!" Hearing rushing footsteps, I curse under my breath. My mother's voice can be heard as her heels click on the marble floor.

"What in the world is going on out here?" she demands, and I take a deep breath and stand tall, preparing to face her wrath. She enters the room, and her expression says it all—anger which quickly changes to shock when she realizes I have another woman in my arms. Her lips part slightly as she looks at me, and her eyes move from my mate to me, then Carina, who now stands on the second step.

"What is the meaning of this?" my mother demands.

"Ask your son. He's the one claiming to have found his mate!" Carina sneers, casting a glare at me. She then bunches up her white floor-length gown at the hip before stalking off back up the steps. I feel somewhat guilty, but I'm not about to throw my mate away for a sham of a wedding.

"Is this true?" my mother asks, turning her attention back to me. Her eyes dart down at my mate in my arms. My mother's expression is one of disbelief. Her eyebrows furrow, and her lips purse as she stares at me. She begins to speak, then stops, her shoulders slumping as if in defeat. "You know what this means, right?" she questions.

I stare at my mother, confused. She has dark black hair curled and pulled into an elegant bun as the crown rests on her head slightly crooked. Her eyes, a deep brown, hold more wisdom than I could ever comprehend.

My mother wipes her hands on her dress, flattening it down as if she spotted a wrinkle. It was something she always did when nervous. She clasps her hands together, peering toward the stairs where Carina ran off. She wears a deep burgundy dress— her favorite color. Her presence fills the space in a way that is both comforting and intimidating.

"Carina has every right to challenge her. Your marriage has already been announced to the kingdoms. Either Carina chooses to step down, or you're—" My mother's eyes drop to Sienna in my arms.

"My mate's name is Sienna," I say to her, and she nods once before lifting her chin.

"Well, your mate will have to challenge her for her place at your side or become your concubine."

I growl at her words. "That law is outdated," I snarl. "I will not marry another when I have my mate right here!" My mother flinches at my anger, then her eyes soften.

"I know, I know the importance of mates; therefore, we must keep up with traditions. It would be the same if Carina found her mate. You would have to challenge him for her hand. You need to get Carina to agree, or we run the risk of starting a war between kingdoms. The marriage is already complete, Xandros. Carina carries our name already."

"Excuse me?" My mother looks away from me.

"Your father wanted to announce his retirement at the wedding. Hand the kingdom down. We sent the marriage paperwork off already, and it was returned today," she speaks softly.

"That wasn't to be done until next week!"

"I'm sorry, son. We didn't expect you to find your mate. The paperwork is done. The only thing left is the ceremony to make it official in the kingdom."

"Are you telling me I am already fucking married?"

"It's why you need Carina to agree so it can be annulled, or your mate is going to have to fight for your hand." I take a step back, horrified.

"You can't seriously expect me to be with another woman and keep my mate on the side. What woman would accept that?" I snarl.

"I know; I will speak with your father later about it. See what we can come up with. Right now, you need to focus on getting Carina to agree. For your mate's sake and this kingdom's," my mother says as her eyes dart down at Sienna. She sighs heavily as if the weight of the world is carried on her shoulders before my mother looks at me sadly.

I have to find a way to get Carina to agree, or else this would become a huge mess. I have to act fast. Still, it makes me wonder what will happen when my mate wakes up to learn I am married to another.

"I'll have the servants set up your old quarters while Carina keeps the main quarters. I take it you'll be wanting to remain with your mate?" my mother asks. I clench my jaw as if I am about to climb into bed with another when my mate is right here. I shake my head and give her a stern look. "We'll be staying together." She nods, understanding the unspoken message.

"Of course, I'll make sure to give you both the privacy you need. Until then, Xandros, keep your mate close. Until she shifts, she is still human," my mother tells me, and I don't miss the hidden meaning within her words. She is worried Carina will do something to my mate, which after earlier, I'm confident she'll try.

I nod, not trusting my voice. She pats my arm with a gentle smile trotting away. My mind is already spinning with plans for how to keep Carina away from my mate. Adjusting her sleeping body in my arms, I climb the stairs, heading to the east wing. The east wing of the castle is part of the old building, which has undergone renovations. Its stone walls in the halls made it seem darker until it opens up into an area that is more spacious and airier. Half the place has been renovated, once I moved into the king's quarters, I had no use for this side of the castle, so it has just remained closed off.

Stepping into the small foyer area, it opens up, large windows letting in plenty of light, which is a very different feel from the cold stone corridors, which offered minimal light.

Pushing the heavy double doors open, the sound of running has me turning back toward the hall to find six servants hurrying toward me. They all stop the moment they notice me, bowing low and apologizing.

"Your mother sent us to tidy up, My King," the head servant girl states, and I nod, motioning toward the doors, for them to enter. They hurry past with their cleaning supplies and immediately start opening the heavy drapes to let light in and crack the windows to rid the room of the stagnant air. Dust covers most of the furniture despite it being covered with white sheets.

The stone walls in my quarters have been rendered since I last stayed here. The bedroom is luxuriously decorated, with a large four-poster bed that has silk curtains hanging down either side. The walls are adorned with paintings, and there is a fireplace in the corner for extra warmth. One servant instantly gets to work lighting it while another two girls strip the bed of linen. I wait, staring at them while they rush around, preparing everything. It takes the two girls fixing the bed mere minutes to have it covered in fresh white sheets.

I lay my mate down, taking a seat beside her. Peering down at her, a presence behind me makes me glance over my shoulder. One of the servant girls is staring at her with a curious expression. She quickly averts her gaze, muttering a quick apology and telling me my mate is pretty. Returning my attention to my sleeping mate, I sweep her long violet hair behind her ear so I can check her. My gaze roams over her; she is beautiful. No one could deny that. I've never paid much attention to humans, and I can't usually stand being near them. However, my little mate is different. I do not want to be away from her. Just the thought makes a growl escape me as I watch her.

My mate's beauty is captivating, and her porcelain skin is flawless. Except for the scar I notice hidden along her hairline, it doesn't take away from her beauty. I can tell it's an old scar, but it makes me curious about how she got it.

I brush my hand over her cheek, which is quite warm. She shudders, and sparks I've never felt before rush across my fingers. Her soft pink lips are slightly parted as she squirms, reacting to a bond I never dreamed was possible.

Her cheeks are flushed, and her eyelashes are long and dark, framing her wide eyes. My gaze travels lower, taking in the rest of her. Her curves are delicate yet sinfully tempting, her body begging to be touched and explored. I want to feel her body pressed against mine, and I want to explore every part of her with my hands and my mouth.

I feel an overwhelming sense of protectiveness toward her. This strange urge to keep her close and make sure no harm ever comes to her sweeps over me. I never thought I'd feel this way about a woman, let alone a human, but here I am, ready to protect her with my life.

Had I not found her, I would never have imagined a bond to feel like this. Carina and I had been dating for just over a year before we got engaged.

However, she never induced even a hint of the desire I feel for my mate. It's impossible to explain. It seems irrational to feel so emotionally attached to a stranger, and a human one at that. It is almost impossible to explain or comprehend how powerful mate bonds can be. It's a connection that often transcends logic.

Hearing the door close, I take a look around to find the room immaculate, the fire blazing in the hearth, and we are alone. Returning my gaze back to my mate, her breathing is smooth and even, and her temperature has subsided, yet my mark on her neck is raised and angry.

Sighing, unsure how long it will take for her to wake, I tuck the blanket around her and pull my phone out of my pocket. I quickly message Javier to see if he has found out exactly who she is besides her first name. I shouldn't have killed Mal so quickly. Although, he did seem hesitant to tell me anything about who she is or anything about her uncle. All I got was her first name.

It makes me question who the other man was to her. He had shown up with a bag full of cash, wanting to buy her from him.

Javier investigated, and I learned he owned the club across from Mal's and that she worked cash in hand for him. It was obvious they were both hiding something, but in a panic about her whereabouts, I acted irrationally. The moment Mal called to say he was checking her house, I rushed to his club; I killed him when he came back empty-handed with less information than we began with.

I'm pulled from my thoughts when I feel the bed move slightly. I expected her to be unconscious for a while, so I am pleased to see her blue-gray eyes open. She appears confused, and I can't wait until she shifts and marks me so I can feel her more completely. She blinks up at me, her heart rate quickening as her memories slowly return. The next second she sits upright. I lean back, giving her space. The moment I do, she tosses the blanket back and runs for the door.

Sighing, I get up just as she yanks it open. Before she has a chance to run from me once again, I move, my arm wraps firmly around her waist, and I pull her against me. She starts thrashing and shouting at me immediately.

"Let me go, you fucking monster!" she screeches while she thrashes. I kick the door shut, dragging her back toward the bed. For someone so beautiful, her language is appalling, and the longer she fights against my grip, the more she annoys me.

When she bites me, however, I lose my patience and give her a hard shove, sending her sprawling onto the bed.

She crawls over it, trying to get away from me, and I grip her ankles, yanking her back to me before pinning her to the bed. I glare at her, and she returns my glare. Her hatred for me is palpable and burning brightly back at me, and my anger boils over. "You'd do well to watch your mouth," I snarl at her. She stares back at me defiantly, and I can tell she's not willing to back down.

My grip on her arms tightens, and she winces in pain. I lean closer, and I don't miss the sound of her gasp. "This is your last warning," I tell her. She may be my mate, but I am a king, and she'll learn fast that she won't get away with challenging me.

However, not fast enough when she headbutts me. A furious growl rips out of me as her head connects with my face, splitting my lip open. She tries in vain to escape me, however, my grip on her doesn't waiver, only growing tighter as my blood drips onto her chest.

Gripping her arms, I slam her back on the bed, then press my weight between her legs; she struggles against me. I grip both her wrists in one hand, which causes her to buck beneath me as she tries to throw me off.

My hand caresses her side, stopping at her breast, and she screams in frustration. I press my sharp teeth against the hollow of her neck. Her breath is hot against my skin, and I feel her body tremble with what I'll do next. I slide my hand down her body and back up, palming her breast. Pulling away, she goes to say something, but one growl silences her until I pinch her nipple, making her cry out in pain. I press my face close to hers.

"You try that again, and you won't like the consequences," I warn her. When she says nothing, I twist harder, and her lips open with a silent scream. Tears spring in her eyes, and she whimpers.

"Do you understand?" I snarl at her, and she quickly nods, so I let her go. She sucks in a shaky breath, her entire body trembling beneath me when she turns her face away from me. Guilt for hurting her nags at me when I see a mask of pain and humiliation clearly written on her face. I push off her and turn away, knowing I've made my point.

Sienna quickly moves away from me. She doesn't attempt to make another run for the door though. "You can be scared, Sienna. I would be the same in your position. I don't want to hurt you, but if you run from me again, I will have no choice." When she says nothing, I peer over at her. Her knees are pressed to her chest while she glares at me, and I grit my teeth.

"For now, you can't leave this room without me. It is not safe until you shift on the full moon. Until then, you remain by my side."

"Please, just let me go," she whispers.

"I can't do that. And you don't truly want that. You're just scared. Once the mate bond kicks in, you'll see. If you try to run before you shift and mark me, the bond will force you back or kill you!" I warn her. "Trust me, it's better to accept the mate bond than to fight it. You don't have to like me, but you will obey me—"

"And if I don't?" she sneers defiantly.

"Test me and find out," I growl angrily.

As she jerks her gaze away from me, I clench my teeth. "It's for your own safety. So get used to it, Sienna; mates are for life. You are mine now."

I can see the struggle on her face, just as I know she will have no choice and be forced to accept it eventually. I can only hope she will come to accept me as well. I won't force the issue yet, but I have to make sure she understands that it is for her own good.

This is not how I imagined things going when she woke up. I thought the bond would be in full swing now that I've marked her. However, nothing has changed, she still hates me and wants to escape me. I'm about to ask for her last name when I feel my phone vibrate. Digging it out of my pocket, I see it's Javier and quickly answer it.

"What is it?" I ask, and I can feel her gaze on me when suddenly the bed dips. I instantly get to my feet and turn my attention to her. She only looks around the room before looking behind me at the bathroom. She moves toward it, and as she passes me, I grab her arm.

"The door stays open!" I tell her, and she jerks her arm from my grip. My eyes flicker, and she glares at me continuing to the bathroom.

"We think we have found something," Javier explains.

"And?" I ask when he falls silent.

"For now, I need to look into a few things. I'm requesting leave until after the full moon."

"The full moon?"

"As I said, I want to verify rather than give you false information. I need to be sure."

"Javier!" I snarl.

"Xandros, please. Trust me on this. You want this verified before acting on it."

"Act on what? Speak now," I snap at him, angry by his refusal. When he refuses once again, I growl. I would have ordered him if he were in front of me. I sigh, knowing I can't over the phone.

"One week, not a day later!" I tell him, hanging up the phone when the shower starts. My eyes lift to see her step into the shower. Tossing my phone on the bed, I move toward the bathroom.

Chapter Five

Sienna

I can hear King Xandros arguing on the phone. It is nerve-racking trying to pee when the door is wide open, even though he is standing side-on and not even looking in my direction. After finally relieving myself, I desperately want to shower. Peering out the door, he is still on the phone. I want to close the door. Instead, I hide around the corner, ripping the last remnants of clothes off my body, which is just a shirt. My hands are covered in blood, and so am I. It smells sickly sweet and bitter at the same time. My skin feels sticky and gross.

My skin itches and crawls. One thing I've always hated about being scared is how itchy I become. And a shower seems a good enough reason to get away from him. So I turn the shower on, checking the temperature with my hand before stepping in.

Hopefully, he leaves, so I can try to find a way out of here. Maybe I can shimmy down a drainpipe. I conjure up multiple ways to escape when the shower screen door opens.

The draft is cold against my back, and I instantly jump, twisting as I do and moving away to see his intimidating form step into the shower. I glance up at him with wide eyes as he towers over me.

His eyes run the length of me, and I take another step back.

Becoming drenched in the scalding hot water when my back hits the tiles. His gaze is intense, scrutinizing me from head to toe with a piercing stare that makes me feel exposed and vulnerable.

I cover my chest by folding my arms. His eyes flicker at the movement, and he steps closer, caging me in against the wall as he puts his face under the water. I stare at the hard plains of his chest as the water cascades down his sun-kissed skin.

The hot steam fills the small bathroom as I admire his body. His strong, toned muscles look like they have been crafted from marble, each line and ripple perfectly placed. The more I take him in, the more I become aware of my heart racing. I look him over, feeling an unfamiliar yearning to touch him writhing through me.

His scent is tantalizing and thick in the air of musk and earth, with a hint of sandalwood; he doesn't just look manly and intimidating, he smells it. His scent is intoxicating as it overwhelms my senses. I want to move closer to him, thankfully the rational part of my brain holds me back. The foreign instincts scare me, making it difficult to comprehend what is happening.

He takes a step closer toward me, his deep dark eyes staring into mine, framed with thick lashes I am jealous of. His hand reaches out to cup my cheek. Instead of pain and anger, he is quite gentle, and I gasp, feeling slight tingles prickling my skin with heat.

"It's the mate bond," he tells me softly. "The closer you get to shifting, the stronger it will become." The thought frightens and excites me simultaneously, leaving me confused about what lay ahead. I don't want to be with this man. I don't even know him, but with his scent clouding my mind in this closed-in space, all I want to do is give in to the foreign urge to touch him.

The steam-filled shower seems to amplify the scent of his body. As I look him over, my gaze travels across every hard-cut muscle, I feel desire so strong stirring within me it makes me hold my breath.

He must sense the tension between us because he steps closer, leaning in until our faces are only inches apart. "You don't know if you want to run to me or from me," he murmurs in a low voice that sends a shiver down my spine. His hand on my face moves as he runs his thumb along my lower lip before tracing his fingertips lightly down the line of my jaw.

The air seems to spark and zap around us as we stand there, locked in each other's gaze. The energy between us slowly builds until it feels like it will consume me. His hand then moves slowly down my arm until it finds its place on my waist, where it begins to trace circles around my hip bone in an almost hypnotic rhythm that has my senses on full alert.

His voice then drops another octave as he steps closer, and his breath sweeps over my neck. My heart races erratically at his closeness, my mind foggy as my senses become overloaded by his mere presence.

Instinct wins over me as I blink rapidly, trying to fight the urge to move closer, to touch him. He seems to be enjoying watching me struggle by the smirk on his lips. The next second I slam against his hard chest, and tears prick my eyes as my lips crash against his chest.

His hand slips into my hair while my brain fights with my body, which suddenly feels alien to me. My nails rake down his flesh like I'm trying to carve my way inside him. It didn't feel like this when I woke up. Only fear enveloped me then. Now burning lust has taken over.

A strangled noise leaves my lips, caught between a moan and a whimper of frustration.

"It is natural for you to feel this way. My scent is strong in here from the steam. You'll learn to fight the urges. By then, you won't want to fight them, though." He chuckles.

My heart races as he pulls away slightly. He leans down so our faces are still close together as I peer into his eyes, searching for answers I can't find within myself. He gently caresses my cheek with the pad of his thumb before speaking again.

"It's normal, Sienna. If you want to touch me, you can," he whispers softly before leaning closer and pressing his lips to my forehead. The action sends shivers down my spine without warning. "Don't worry; I feel the same. It's distracting and antagonizing. I want you more than anything. I can barely control myself around you."

His words are both darkly seductive and frightening at the same time. This causes a rush of emotions I don't know how to process or express except through the intense heat pooling in the pit of my stomach. When he steps away, I step closer, and he chuckles, reaching for the soap beside me.

The smell of the soap replaces his scent, and the effects of his addictive scent fade away like background noise. My mind's fog lifts instantly, and my eyes go to his. He watches me for a second. His eyes scrutinizing.

"You'll get used to it. Get used to me," he tells me. Now, with some distance between us, I see him for what he is, the monster that kidnapped me—poisoned me, turning me into a monster like him.

I step away from him slowly, my back hitting the wall as I stare at him. He gazes at me with something akin to disappointment and understanding; it quickly passes, leaving only the monster in his place once again. He offers me a small smile before turning around and stepping out of the shower without another word. Xandros snatches a towel off the rack on the wall, tying it around his waist

While I'm left feeling confused and scared of the intense emotions coursing through me. It feels like something inside me has changed or is missing. My eyes dart to his back. No, whatever that missing piece is, he took it.

Something twisted and dark has awakened within me, something unfamiliar, almost seductive. All I can do is stand here as my mind reels from it all.

"I'll send for someone to get clothes for you. Don't leave the bedroom, or there will be consequences," he says, his voice returning to cold and authoritative.

He leaves without another word, and I'm left struggling to wrap my head around what just happened. I had been so close to succumbing. Had he not stepped away from me, I'm sure I would have done anything he requested, drunk on his presence.

The memory of his touch still sends shivers down my spine, like a reminder that something inside me has changed irrevocably, awoken by some carnal desire I'm not sure would save me or end me.

The shower runs cold by the time I finally emerge from its depths, more determined than ever to fight against these newfound urges. I just need to survive long enough to escape.

I step out of the shower. The bathroom is bright and airy, with white

Lycan King's Captives

tiles on the walls and floor. I wrap a fluffy white towel around myself, and I can feel the fabric's softness against my skin. The room is filled with steam from my shower, and the air is heavy with the scent of my body wash.

A large mirror hangs over the sink. I wipe my hand across it, removing the steam, and peering into the mirror at myself. Only the moment I do, I take a step back. My eyes burn brightly back at me, almost glowing.

"Where is Xandros?" comes a feminine yet harsh voice that has me jumping to look at the door. I find a woman in a flowing white gown that hugs her curves. She is tall and beautiful, and I suddenly feel like a gutter rat in her presence. "Are you mute?" she snaps, her face twisting in disgust.

I shake my head, and her lips pull into a snarl, revealing sharp, pointed fangs. Vampire! I stagger back away from her, and her eyes sparkle evilly. She laughs, a sound that sends a chill down my spine. The vampire steps closer, and I can feel her cold presence. She stopped a few feet away from me, her eyes still sparkling with amusement. "Well then, since my fiancé isn't here, I suppose you'll have to do." She smiles, revealing her sharp fangs again.

"Fiancé?" I gasp. "So, you're engaged?" I ask, appalled he could claim me while having a fiancé. My curiosity is piqued as to who she is because I swear she looks familiar. She continues to smile, her sharp fangs gleaming in the dim light. She laughs, the sound sinister despite how beautiful she is.

"Princess Carina Dresden, or I suppose it's now Zeppelin. Legally, we are married already," the woman taunts before stepping closer. I suck in a breath, tripping over the shower mat when she reaches for me. She clicks her tongue and grabs my hair.

"I'm being considerate enough to allow him to keep his side whore. The least you can do is offer a fucking vein slut!" she snarls as she drags me toward the bedroom. She shoves me, and I hit the ground hard.

She stalks me, and I crawl back on my hands and feet to escape her. She grabs my hair and pulls me closer to her. I can feel her cold breath on my face as she hisses, "You better keep quiet, or I'll make sure you regret it." I'm terrified, my heart pounding in my chest. Her fangs elongate, and I try to get away from her. My hand moves quickly, and I slap her. Her face twists to the side, however, her grip on my hair doesn't waiver. She growls. The sound is a low ticking in her throat.

The next minute she rips me to my feet, and my body is sailing through the air; I crash against something, pain slivering through my body, and I cry out then hit the floor. Before I have a chance to sit up, she has my hair in her hand again, jerking my head back.

"You dare hit your future queen?" she snarls, then yanks my head to the side, and I clench my eyes closed. I struggle to regain my composure, my hands shaking. I can feel her breath on my face as she leans in, her voice low and menacing. "You will never hit me again." A whimper escapes me, and I feel the points of her teeth graze my neck. The next second, I hear a whimper.

My eyes fly open to find Xandros has the woman's throat, his face a mask of rage. He looks at me with concern before turning back to her. He tightens his grip, and she gasps in pain.

"You will not touch her," he growls through gritted teeth. He releases her throat, and she backs away, her eyes wide with fear.

"You would pick some fucking random bitch over the future of your kingdom!" she yells, and I flinch.

"She is my mate!" he yells at her.

"And you're my husband!" she sneers.

"I didn't ask for this!" he yells back at her, and his words pain me more than they should. Like I am a second choice to her, and why wouldn't I be? He didn't want me, and I don't want him either, so why did those words carve through my chest like a hot knife? I clutch my towel closer, shrinking in on myself.

Suddenly, I feel dirty, like an intruder, a homewrecker, when I have done nothing wrong. I didn't ask for this. I try not to listen to them argue. That's his wife, I am… I am… what was I to him, then? Why bring me here claiming I am his mate when he is married? He has a wife, so what use is a mate?

"Exactly where do you expect me to fucking go?" she snaps at him, making me look up at them from my spot on the floor.

"Home, go home, Carina!"

She scoffs. "And humiliate myself even more? Should I tell my father my husband chose some slut he stumbled across in the city?" She shakes her head.

Xandros growls and presses his lips together. "I need blood. Either let me feed on your whore or give me yours!"

The feral growl that leaves him at her words gives me goosebumps.

"Fine, just leave. I will return to the room in a minute," he tells her, and I blink up at him. He will let her feed off him?

She looks at me one last time with an expression that says I am trash before turning and fleeing. She leaves and my heart's still pounding in my chest. When I turn to Xandros, I cringe as he glares at me.

His face is filled with anger and disgust, and I can feel the tension radiating off him. He takes a step forward, looming over me, and I am frozen in place, unable to move or speak.

"Did you hit her?" he snarls at me. I stare at him in disbelief before glancing at the door she just left through. He growls and grabs my face, forcing my gaze back to his.

"I asked you a question. Yes or No! Did you hit Princess Dresden?" His tone is menacing, and his grip on my face is tight. His eyes are burning into mine, searching for an answer.

"Yes... she attacked--" my words were cut off when his grip grows impossibly tight, my cheeks pressing into my teeth like they may snap under the pressure of his grip at any moment.

"Do you know what you've done? I leave for ten minutes, and you fucking provoke her. What you've done is punishable by death. Until you mark me, you're nothing just a fucking commoner, a..." he screams in my face while his twists into that of a Lycan. Sharp canines protrude, and his claws stab into my cheeks.

"A side whore," I barely manage to answer for him. A whimper escapes me, my lips trembling when he gasps, letting me go. He sucks in a deep breath while I stare at the floor. How is it possible that I actually want to go home back to my uncle? I never thought I would see the day when I would welcome his fists.

"Sienna, I didn't mean it like that." He exhales loudly, and I wipe my cheek, my blood smearing over the back of my hand when he moves with those inhuman movements and jerks my face up. Only this time, his grip is gentler. He curses, licking the pad of his thumb and moving it toward my face. I jerk my face out of his grip.

"I'm trying to heal you," he snaps at me, reaching for my face again, only I pull away. His hand falls away, and he stares at me, his face a mask of frustration. He takes a deep breath and steps back, turning away from me. I watch him silently.

"Go feed your wife," I tell him. Those words pierce my soul as I speak them. How is it possible to feel so strongly about someone I hate?

He turns to me, his eyes full of pain and anger. He stares at me for what feels like an eternity, then he turns and leaves without a word. My chest tightens, and he slams the door behind him. I stare at the door before hearing it lock. Forcing myself to my feet, I quietly approach the door, only to discover he has locked me in like a prisoner.

Turning back to the room, I move toward the large mahogany dresser with a huge mirror attached to it. Peering into the mirror, I can see her finger marks etched into my neck. I touch the bruising indents before my gaze moves to my face, four puncture marks on one side. However, the one where his thumb was, is the deepest, blood oozing and trickling down my cheek and neck.

Seeing those gashes reminds me of the monster that has me in his grasp. I look down at my hands, like I can still see my uncle's blood coating them. My hands are now clean since I showered. I can't help but think I will become the same monster Xandros is. What I did to him was no better. I killed someone, and I killed my family. I'm no better than my parents.

I rummage for some clothes, anything besides the wet towel making me cold. Digging through a drawer, I find an old shirt. I slide it over my head. Then I remove the towel and wander back into the bathroom to hang it up.

Chapter Six

Sienna

Hours pass, and Xandros does not return. After a while, I don't think he will, at least not tonight.

He's probably with his wife. He has a wife...

I am still trying to figure out how I fit into this situation. Why torture someone and expect them to watch you be with another?

I am about to recheck the windows and see if I can get one to open; I've been trying in vain for hours, each one has some key lock on them. And I can't find a key anywhere. The glass also isn't glass, it seems to be hard Perspex. Rechecking the largest window, I hear the door handle rattle. My breath lodges in my throat as I peer over at the door. Racing back to the bed, I quickly sit.

My heart beats like a drum as the doors slowly open. Some part of me is stupidly excited, hoping it is Xandros. However, it seems to be one of the castle servants. The young female servant is about my age, with long dark hair and deep brown eyes. She is wearing a navy dress with a white apron, and she has a warm, friendly demeanor.

"King Xandros said he couldn't return for dinner. So he asked me to bring some food for you." She uses her hips to hold the door open before grabbing a tray off the trolley. She comes in carrying a tray of food and drinks and smiles at me as she places it on the table and returns to her trolley.

"I've also come with some clothes; the king said you had nothing to wear," she tells me, grabbing a few black bags from a boutique store I've seen in the city. She sets the bags at the end of the bed.

"Where is the king?" I ask her, and she pauses.

"With Princess Dresden," the woman remarks. Her tone of voice is sour, which gives me the impression the princess isn't liked by her.

"Did the king say when he would return?" I ask her, moving to the table where she set the tray of food. Glancing down at the silver tray, there is an array of food, including an exquisite salad, a bowl of steamed vegetables, a small plate of roasted potatoes, a chicken dish, and a freshly baked mini-loaf of bread. For dessert, there was a selection of fruits, a bowl of custard, and a chocolate mousse. The drinks accompanying the meal included a bottle of red wine and a pitcher of sparkling water.

"The king wasn't sure what you would like, so we brought a bit of everything for you. I will set some drinks in the fridge for you and also a platter full of cheeses and meats." She grabs another tray off the trolley and a small bucket with ice in it before moving toward a wall by the closet. I never saw a fridge here. She then presses on the panel by the walk-in closet, and the wall presses in. She then slides a door open, and I find a small bar area. I blink at her, having not noticed the fake wall panel. She puts everything away and then closes the sliding door and wanders into the bathroom to collect the wet towels and dirty laundry.

My eyes go to the open door. Before I can even think of making a move for it, she returns, dropping the dirty laundry into a basket beneath the trolley. She then grabs some extra towels and toiletries and restocks the bathroom.

"What is your name?" I ask her as she comes out again. "Darcy, ma'am," she tells me with a warm smile.

"No need to call me ma'am; I'm Sienna," I tell her. She smiles and nods.

"Well, if you need anything else, you can call down on the phone that's in the bar area. The numbers are listed on the small panel on the wall for the kitchen and staff. If you need anything, don't hesitate to

Lycan King's Captives 49

ask." She then walks back toward the door, retrieving her keys, and I know she is about to lock me back in.

"Actually..." Darcy stops and looks back at me.

"I don't suppose you could help me with the windows. I have been trying to let some air in. The room is pretty stagnant—dusty from being locked up."

"Certainly," she smiles, wandering over to the large windows. She uses her keys to unlock the window and pushes it open. She then turns and smiles.

"Call down if you need anything else," she tells me before making her way back to the door. She then shuts the door and locks it.

Darcy unlocked the window. I blink at it. She just unlocked the window but locked the door. Did she not see an error in her actions, or did she think it wouldn't matter since I am human and the drop below would be instant death?

She clearly misjudged my determination to get out of here. I am willing to risk death if it means not being subjected to spending the rest of my life with King Xandros and his bitch of a wife. Fuck his mate bond. Ever since he marked me, I have felt fine, with no signs of a fever.

Moving to the bags of clothes, I dig through them, finding some dark blue jeans, a shirt, and a hoodie. There are also pajamas and undergarments; I grab the undergarments and blanch at the tiny pieces of sheer fabric.

Exactly what is this supposed to cover?

I hold up the sheer fabric that resembles string for how tiny the underwear is. Shaking my head, I pick up the see-through bra. At least I can wear this, and no one would see it. Digging through the last bag, I find a pair of flats and some socks, and also a pair of slippers. Snatching up the socks and flats, I groan, grabbing the small lace wedgie maker, too, deciding to put it on, anyway.

I slip them on and sigh in relief. They were snug but comfortable. I grab my shirt and jeans then head over to the window with my shoes. Sitting on the window ledge, I slip my shoes on and look out the window—big mistake. Never look down. Now I have; I feel nauseous. The fall isn't a mere two-story drop, it's more like four. Peering around, I look for a way down, spotting some vines that sliver and creep along the stone walls. I tug on one, and it breaks away easily.

Well, I won't be Tarzaning it out of here. I'm glad I tested it before I just climbed out and grabbed one. I look for another way to climb down when I come across the trellis, a deciduous climbing vine creeping along it with white and pink blooming buds.

I smile; that's my way out. There is just one problem. It's out of reach, and still the best chance I have. Climbing onto the ledge, I step out, balancing on my toes as I creep along the ledge, ensuring I keep a grip on the window. I stretch my fingertips grazing the trellis. I step a little closer, one foot dangling off the ledge as I stretch my arm.

My heart beats erratically as I wrap my fingers around the trellis, and I let out a breath. However, just as I let go of the window, a hand wraps around my wrist. I am ripped back inside the window and tossed to the ground. A squeak leaves my lips, and my hip aches from landing on it. Turning around, I find it's Xandros. He slams the window shut while panic grips me, and I back away from him when he turns to face me. He growls, and the sound makes goosebumps rise on my arms.

"I said test me. I didn't think you'd be stupid enough to," he snarls, stalking toward me.

I scurry away, but his hand latches onto my arm. He pulls me up and slams me against the wall.

"What do you think you're doing? Where do you think you were going to go, Sienna?" he growls.

Anywhere if it means away from him.

He grabs me. I shriek, and he lets me go instantly. His hot breath fans over my face, and I shrink back under his deadly gaze, too scared to answer him.

"Answer me!" he screams, shaking me.

"Why does it matter? You're fucking married!" I scream back at him.

"I will not be some side whore. Fuck your stupid mate bond. I never asked for this! I never asked for you!" I yell at him before shoving him. Unsurprisingly, he doesn't budge a step, and it's like pushing on a brick wall. Xandros growls, his eyes blazing furiously.

"And you think I did?" he snarls, his grip on my arms tightening as he pulls me from the wall and walks me backward. The backs of my knees hit the bed, and I topple backward. He climbs on top of me, pinning me to the bed.

"You think I wanted to be fated to a fucking human? To terminate my kingdom's alliance for a mate bond!" he sneers. "I'm risking everything to be with you, and you've done nothing but fight me!" Does he not remember the part where he kidnapped me? Took me against my will.

I try to speak; however, my throat is too dry. I only manage a croak as tears begin streaming down my cheeks.

"I never asked for you either, Sienna, still I accepted you despite being engaged! You don't get to run away from the mate bond when I can't."

"Then you should have let me die!" I spit at him.

He snarls and grips my neck firmly, his fingers pressing into my skin, and I can feel the heat emanating from his fingers as they tighten around my throat. His eyes blaze with fury as he speaks. His words drip with anger and something else.

"You think I want to feel this way? To want and need you? It wasn't my intention to have you as a mate, but don't believe for a second I will let you go." He growls, moving so he is positioned between my legs, and he presses his weight down on me.

"Whether you like it or not, you're stuck with me," he purrs, and his grip on my neck loosens, his hand moving down my chest to my breast.

"You can hate me all you want, but you won't deny me. You were made for me," he whispers, his eyes trailing down my body, his gaze hungry while mine is defiant.

"You are mine, Sienna," he purrs. His hand squeezes my breast while his words send a shiver down my spine. He tears my top, ripping the fabric, and I gasp as realization dawns on me. I struggle against him, swinging at him. He catches my wrist, so I use the other hand, clawing at his face. However, he doesn't budge or even make a noise as I scratch his face, drawing blood. Instead, he pins me to the bed, pressing his weight against me.

"Hate me all you want, Sienna."

His breathing is heavy, and his grip on my arms tightens as he forces me to stay still. He leans closer, his lips grazing mine as he speaks.

"But every inch of you is mine," he growls, and I feel the heat of his chest against my skin, and my stomach turns when he grabs my wrists and pins them above my head, trapping them in one of his.

His other hand moves down my body, and he palms my breast when I feel his claws slip out, shredding my bra to pieces. The next second, his teeth sink into the soft skin of my breast, making me cry out at the pain. I thrash when he sucks on the spot, soothing it with his tongue.

"These are mine," he snarls, his voice full of possessive hunger when his hand forces its way into my pants, and I buck beneath him, trying to toss him. His hand cups my pussy and sparks rush everywhere, like an electric current buzzing beneath my skin. He squeezes me, strengthening the tingling sensation. "And this?" He groans. When his fingers gently caress my slit, I shiver as he whispers, "Also mine." I gasp, my head spinning with the sensation that explodes over every inch of me.

His touch is electric, and I can feel the mate bond that binds us together. His words no longer hold any sense of mystery, instead a truth I can feel deep in my bones. I finally understand what he means about mate bond and realize I am connected to him in a way I never imagined possible. Despite knowing it's wrong, I suddenly crave his touch.

His fingers slide up and down my folds, making me moan. He teases my clit, tracing circles around it, and my body trembles with anticipation. "Do you still want to deny me?" he purrs.

His finger dips inside me, and I moan louder, my body quivering as my muscles clench around his finger. My back arches off the bed. His thumb rubs my clit, and I gasp as a wave of pleasure washes over me, his lips crash down on mine. His finger moves in and out of me faster as he increases pressure on my clit, then growls when my pants restrict him.

His lips pull away from mine as he stands suddenly, gripping the waistband of my pants. The warped fuzziness of the bond lifts like someone tossed icy water over me, making me come back to my senses when he rips my pants off, tossing them aside. My heart beats faster at what I was about to allow him to do when he unbuttons his shirt. With the haze lifted, I shiver, shuffling further onto the bed to get away from him. His command rolls over me, stealing the air from my lungs and paralyzing me.

"Remain where you are," he commands, his voice turning into a purr as he rids his shirt.

My heart sputters frantically in my chest when I see him unzip his pants, only to kneel on the bed before me.

"Spread your legs." I grit my teeth against his command. My hands fist the sheets as I fight it in vain. His hands grip my ankles, and sparks rush everywhere. The bond igniting from his touch burns as it sets me on fire.

"Open your legs," he purrs, sliding his hands from my legs to my knees. His touch is featherlight and gives me goosebumps. When his warm tongue glides over my skin from my knee to my thigh, my legs fall open.

After a second, I no longer want to fight his touch. Instead, I crave it.

His hands travel back up my legs as his tongue continues to explore my body. A soft moan escapes my lips as pleasure rushes through me. My body trembles in anticipation as his hands grip my hips. He plunges his tongue inside me, and I gasp, my back arching as I revel in the sensation. My body quivers as the pleasure builds until I'm on the brink of bliss. His lips curl into a satisfied smile, and he suddenly pulls away, leaving me trembling and wanting more.

I reach for his pants, and he smirks, watching me struggle with the bond and pulling his pants down since I have no idea what I am doing. I just know I want him, need him. Some baser instinct I know isn't human taking over me, and suddenly the tips of my fingers burn violently, making me cry out. Blood stains them when suddenly I feel my fingers cut through his flesh. He hisses, pushing them down for me, when I realize why my fingers burn, my blood staining his abs and pubic line.

I blink at my fingertips, seeing sharp claws have pushed out of my nail beds. That fascinates me for half a second when he releases himself. His cock is huge. Then again, I haven't seen one hard before.

Some thought slivers through my head, telling me I should ask him to go slow. My body has other ideas and is acting on its own because I'm reaching for him, despite not knowing what to do with him. Xandros is quick to grip my wrists, shoving me back on the bed before crawling between my legs, my hands trapped in one of his.

"I would like my cock to remain attached to me, at least until you learn to control that," he purrs against my lips before kissing me.

His body presses me further into the mattress with his weight. His hands roam my body, exploring and teasing me with every touch. I can feel my desire building, growing intensely until it threatens to consume me. My desire to touch him back also makes me whine in frustration. However, he holds me in place before moving a hand between our bodies and positioning himself at my entrance.

I gasp at the sensation when he suddenly thrusts himself inside me in one hard motion. My mouth opens in a silent scream as I forget how to breathe. Pain, as I've never felt before, slivers through me as warmth coats my thighs. It hurts... it hurts is all my brain can conjure. I can't see past the blinding pain tearing through me as he continues to move. He thrusts inside me harshly with no reprieve, not allowing me to get used to the feeling, to allow me to stretch around him. No amount of tingles or bond can mask the pain I feel.

"Fuck, you're tight," he groans against my shoulder while tears slide down my face. I want to tell him to stop, that I am choking on air. "And wet..." he murmurs when he pulls back slightly to kiss me, only he jerks away instantly. "Sienna?" he questions while I blink back tears. He peers down at me for a second and then suddenly rips himself out of me.

"You're a fucking virgin?" he snarls, his words sounding shocked and angry. Sitting up slightly, I see my thighs and the bed drenched in blood, and so is he. I briefly wonder if I got my period spontaneously because the bed is soaked; there is so much. The pain as I move is proof that he just tore me. "Shh, it's fine. I... I will fix it. I can make the pain go away. My blood and saliva can heal you," Xandros murmurs, crawling back onto the bed.

My virginity? He can't fix that now that he's taken it. "Shh, why didn't you tell me you were a virgin? Fuck!" he curses, sucking on his fingers.

"You never asked." I whimper when his fingers skim across my core. I cringe at the pain, but the tingles return, lessening until the pain fades completely. I blink at him.

Lycan King's Captives 55

"Yeah, since you worked for Mal. I just assumed you were one of his whores."

Did he just call me... His words burn me.

My stomach sinks at his words. He basically called me a slut. He seems to realize what he said because he tries to correct his choice of words. However, now it is too late because I slap him.

I gasp at what I did. My newly found claws, which I hadn't realized weren't retracted, slash down his face. Blood sprays across mine. The noise that leaves him makes my eyes widen, and I freeze beneath it.

His growl is threatening and predatory. It sends ice-cold chills down my spine when his face twists in his rage, his hand finds my hair, and I cry out when he rips my hair out jerking my head to the side. His canines extend, and he looks savage as he partially shifts.

"You were warned about pushing me," he snarls, then sinks his teeth into my neck. My voice becomes hoarse as I scream. The sound tearing out of me burns my throat violently until the noise is barely a rasp. His teeth sink so deeply into my neck they carve into my bones, drilling into me, while black flecks flit through my vision until eventually stealing it completely when I pass out.

Chapter Seven

Sienna

I awaken to a world of pain, my body aching as if I've been put through a grinder. Every muscle protests as I try to move, and I remember the events of the night before, the way Xandros' face loomed above me when I slapped him. The fear I felt in that moment when his face twisted in anger.

As I try to move, I realize something has changed. The pain is bearable, almost dull in comparison to what it was before. He must have healed me somewhat because the throbbing between my legs and burning pain is no longer there. He also put a shirt on me, covering my naked body. Pinching the neck of the shirt, it is saturated with his manly addictive scent.

As I lay there, my mind races. Where has my mate gone? How will I survive this man as my mate? My world feels like it has spiraled out of control overnight, and now I have awoken into an alternative narrative, an alternate version of my life.

These questions are quickly pushed aside as the bathroom door opens. Xandros steps out, making me sit up abruptly, not wanting to be caught off guard around this man, this predator, and that is exactly what he is.

As I take him in, I find myself caught between captivated and petrified.

His body glistens from the shower, his muscles rippling with every movement. This man is all muscle, hard, and perfectly sculpted; it just adds to the allure of him and the primal instinct that screams at me to run, warning me he could so easily end me.

I find myself unable to tear my gaze from him, like a moth to a flame as his presence consumes me. Despite knowing I'll be burned, I know I would still walk into the flame just to be near him. It's an instinct that washes through me, which I relish and loathe. How one person can hold so much power over another should be illegal; the mate bond growing stronger the more I am around him makes me nervous.

One part of me knows he'll be my undoing. That my blood will stain his hands like ink by the time he's done with me. Another voice screams out for him, telling me that death would be a small price to pay for feeling those hands wrap around me like a warm embrace.

He leans against the door frame, watching me, and I can feel his presence. The intensity of his gaze, as he studies me while using another towel to dry himself.

"You're awake, finally," he states, his voice low and laced with a dominance that intimidates me to no end. I nod my head once, tearing my gaze away from him.

He steps toward me, and my breathing becomes harsher as he stops in front of me. His fingers brushing against the bite mark on my neck, and I can feel my heart racing as he continues to speak. Using his finger to tilt my chin up, he forces me to meet his cold hard gaze.

"This will not happen again, Sienna. You must learn to obey if you ever want out of this room. Do you understand?" I nod hesitantly, my mind racing with a mix of fear and excitement. Xandros is a dangerous man, and I know I need to be careful around him. Another part of me is equally defiant to him. Refusing to bow down to him, another war I can't seem to win. Logic says shut your mouth, unfortunately that isn't what happens.

"You can't keep me locked in this room forever!" I snarl. His grip on my face turns painful, and his gaze flickers, eyes turning black, he laughs, a deep rumbling laugh that sends shivers down my spine.

"Oh, but I can, Sienna," he says, his voice dripping with an underlying warning, daring me to disobey him. "You're mine now, and you will obey me. It's safer for you if you do." His words linger in my mind as he lets me go and walks to the closet, tossing some clothes on the bed. I can only stare at them, my mind racing with confusion and anticipation.

"Last chance, Sienna. You disobey me, and you will never leave this room again. Now get dressed. I have to head to the city," Xandros says firmly, his tone leaving no room for argument. I nod slowly, knowing I'm now trapped in a world of his making, a world full of both pleasure and pain. Once I'm dressed, Xandros seizes my arm, his grip is unrelenting, like he thinks I will dare try to outrun him.

As we make our way toward the sleek, black car waiting outside, I can feel the tension between us growing, electric and palpable. Xandros opens the door, gesturing for me to enter first, I hesitantly slide in, feeling the rich leather beneath me. He follows, and I move as far to the other side as the car will allow. Xandros growls, making me glance at him nervously.

He points to the seat beside him, wanting me closer; I stare at the middle seat, not really wanting to be closer to him. His mood sets me on edge, knowing I stand no chance with his proximity so close and his scent muddling my thoughts. My refusal annoys him because he pulls me onto his lap, his arm wrapping around my waist, holding me firmly against his chest.

"Drive," he orders the driver, his voice dark and commanding. Xandros sweeps my hair over one shoulder, leaning so close his breath on my neck makes me shiver.

"Listen closely, Sienna," he warns, his hand beginning to roam over my body before it grabs my hip in a punishing grip. "In the city, if you try to run, I'll hunt you down and make you regret it." I swallow at his words.

"And if you embarrass me by causing a scene, I'll put you on display over my knee and spank you for the entire world to see." I shiver, knowing they aren't idle threats. Would it kill him not to threaten me for once? Not show me how powerless I am against him?

"Am I clear, Sienna?" he asks.

"Crystal," I breathe when his tone shifts, promising dark things. "Good girl," he purrs, his grip on my hip loosening when he presses his lips against my shoulder.

"However, if you behave and abide by my rules, you'll be rewarded," he adds.

"What do you mean?" I ask, my voice trembling with a mix of fear and anticipation.

His hand roams over my body, making me gasp as he takes his time exploring every curve and contour. His breath is hot on my neck as he purrs, "You'll find out soon enough." His fingertips ghost over the skin beneath my shirt, making me gasp before he slips his hand into my pants and cups my pussy. My eyes instantly dart to the driver, yet his eyes are focused on the road.

"Will you behave for me, Sienna,"

I chew my lip, refusing to answer.

My heart pounds against my chest when he squeezes me, earning a startled noise from me as sparks flood me. His fingers tease my slit when his fingertips circle my clit. I slam my legs shut on his hand, only to feel the vibration of his purr against my back. His nose trails along my shoulder and neck to the back of my ear. "Open your legs for me." I shake my head. Does he not see the driver sitting right there?

"Don't make me tell you again, Sienna." I turn my face toward his, his gaze dark, promising me I won't like the consequences if he has to repeat himself. So reluctantly, I do, which he takes advantage of straight away by shoving his finger inside.

Before the shocked noise of his actions can escape me, his lips cover mine, his tongue tasting every inch of my mouth and stealing my breath. At the same time, his fingers continue to tease and torment me, dragging me closer to the edge. My hips move against his hand, unable to control the urge, my surroundings disappearing as my mind is consumed with the sensation he is building.

"See, being mine isn't so bad after all, is it?" he purrs against my lips. I nod hesitantly. My mind is a whirlwind of conflicting emotions and sensations. He chuckles darkly as he brings me closer and closer to the edge of ecstasy.

Just as I reach the brink, he withdraws, leaving me desperate and wanting.

"Now behave," he orders. "And when we leave, I may just finish what I started."

The door opens, and Xandros helps me out of the car, his arm still around my waist. As we walk into the city together, I feel I'm being led into the unknown, with Xandros controlling my every move. I can feel the weight of his possessiveness, and I know I'm in danger.

In spite of the danger and fear surrounding him, my body craves his touch, despite the consequences. It's a terrifying and intoxicating realization, and as we navigate the bustling streets, I'm left to ponder my fate. My body aches from the pleasure he's shown me.

As we make our way through the bustling streets, I am completely overwhelmed by the sensory overload surrounding me. Everything feels foreign and unfamiliar, a stark contrast to the life I once knew. Xandros leads me into a grandiose restaurant. The atmosphere is opulent and sophisticated, a world away from the pub where I used to work.

A poised and elegant waitress approaches us, her eyes lighting up with recognition when she sees Xandros. "Good afternoon, Your Highness," she greets him with a graceful bow, and then, turning her attention to me, she asks, "How is Queen Carina?"

I stiffen at the mention of his wife, feeling small and insignificant, like nothing more than a dirty mistress. Xandros, however, snatches the menu from the waitress's hand and replies in a cold, uninterested tone, "I don't know, and I don't care."

The waitress chuckles nervously, her gaze finally landing on me. "Oh, I'm sorry. I didn't see you with the king," she says, her eyes lingering on my neck for a moment too long. I can sense she is a vampire, and it sends shivers down my spine.

"Apologies, King Xandros, I didn't mean to be rude to your... friend," the waitress stammers, her gaze shifting between Xandros and me. Xandros's eyes snap to mine, and I try to shrink myself in my seat. I am embarrassed and hurt by his apparent reluctance to acknowledge our bond.

"She's not my friend," he says slowly, his eyes piercing me instantly when my gaze snaps back to his. His expression is arrogant as he adds, "She's my mate."

The waitress nods, a hint of fear in her eyes before dropping her gaze.

Xandros orders, "Two of my usuals, Mara." The waitress hurries away, and Xandros turns to me, his eyes filled with amusement. "Did you really think I would deny who you are like I'm embarrassed by you?" he asks, a smirk playing at the corners of his lips.

"Are you?" I question, my voice wavering. "You seem to give me a lot of rules, like you're worried I'll embarrass you."

"The rules are for your safety," he replies, his voice serious. "Speaking of rules, I have some more for you."

He begins listing more rules designed to protect me from Carina, who he fears may try to harm me. I am to remain in my room unless he says otherwise, and I am not to speak to, or react to, Carina if we cross paths. I glance out the window.

It's then that I spot Toby, my former boss, watching me from across the street. My breath catches, and I quickly look away, feeling even more trapped than before.

Thankfully, Mara returns with our food, giving me a reason not to sit there awkwardly, trying to avoid Xandros's observant gaze. As she sets the plate in front of me, I thank her quickly before staring down at the plate. I'm amazed at the presentation. The dish is beautifully arranged with vegetables, some I can't even name, having never seen them before. It also has succulent meat and a delicate sauce I've never tasted before. It's exquisite, but my anxiety prevents me from fully enjoying it.

As we eat, Xandros questions me. "Tell me about yourself. I know nothing about you."

I nearly choke on my mouthful of food. I know if he discovers who my parents are, he will kill me. So instead, I lie. "Ah, I'm nobody. I lived with my uncle and worked at a pub," I answer vaguely. Xandros watches me intently, and I know he senses my deception.

"If you weren't one of Mal's working girls, does that mean that other man... what's his name?" he asks.

"Toby," I reply, feeling a cold shiver down my spine.

"Is he who you worked for?" Xandros growls, and I nod, glancing out the window again. Toby is gone.

"What else should I know about you?" he asks, his eyes boring into me. I shrug, trying to appear nonchalant. "There's nothing else to know," I lie.

"Now that is a lie," he says quietly, his voice laced with a dangerous edge. "You know I can hear it when you lie, right? Your heart flutters oddly. I can also feel it through the bond, your deception. The bond isn't in full swing for you. However, I've felt it since the moment I laid eyes on you. You might want to keep that in mind next time you try to lie to me."

I stare down at my plate, feeling cornered. He continues. "It's fine. I'll let it slide this once. You will tell me eventually. If not, I have other ways of finding out."

My stomach churns, and I try to focus on finishing my meal. "Now hurry up and eat," he says, his tone lighter. "I want to take you shopping."

With each step we take together, the line between captivity and desire grows more and more blurred. Just like a switch is flicked, he changes from cruel and threatening to sweet and pleasant. Being around Xandros is like dealing with someone who has multiple personalities. It sets me on edge, waiting for the next one to come forward.

After the meal, he takes me shopping, guiding me through a maze of luxurious boutiques filled with silk and velvet. Despite my discomfort, he insists on buying me clothes, even though the price tags make me feel even more out of place. I've only shopped at thrift stores. The thought of spending so much on a single pair of jeans, when it could pay the electric bill for six months, is incomprehensible to me.

He drags me from store to store, the price tags making me feel like I'm losing touch with the world I once knew. Each store we visit is more luxurious than the last; it makes me feel worse because I know I look out of place beside him.

"Try this on," Xandros demands, holding up a delicate lace dress that costs more than my entire wardrobe combined. I hesitantly take it from him, wishing we could just go back to my cage, at least locked in the room, people don't gawk and stare. In the dressing room, I slip into the dress, surprised at how well it fits, and how soft it feels against my skin, despite the lace. I step out to show Xandros, and his eyes widen in appreciation.

"You look stunning," he murmurs, reaching out to brush his fingers against the fabric. His touch sends a shiver down my spine. I can feel the darkness within him as his eyes flicker – the seductive pull I'm powerless to resist.

As we continue, Xandros selects more for me to try on. It makes me feel as if he is dressing up a doll for his own amusement. As we float through the stores, I notice Xandros is also buying clothes for himself – dark, expensive suits that make him look even more powerful and dangerous, not that he needs the help. Regardless, it makes me feel better knowing he didn't just bring me to buy clothes.

As we leave the store, I finally think we are returning home when he drags me into another. I fight the urge to groan. My feet hurt, I'm tired, and sick of playing dress up. He selects a stunning gown for me, the deep red fabric shimmering in the dim light. He insists I try it on, and when I emerge from the dressing room, his eyes darken with desire.

"You look like a queen," he whispers, leaning in to kiss my neck. I shudder at his touch, my body betraying my fear as my pulse races beneath his lips. I know I should be repulsed by him, by his darkness and his control over me, but I can't deny the strange allure he holds.

As we exit the store, I catch sight of Toby again, his eyes filled with concern as he watches me from a distance. I drop my gaze quickly. Before I can react, Xandros's hand pulls me toward the car.

As we walk, relief fills me when I notice Toby has disappeared.

However, that relief is short-lived when Toby suddenly appears beside me, grabbing my arm. "I thought it was you," he says, pulling me into a hug. My entire body tenses and I freeze when Xandros growls behind me. He's so close that I can feel the heat of Xandros's body and the sharp sting of his claws as they slice into my arm.

"When are you returning to the pub?" Toby asks, his voice desperate. Xandros answers for me, his voice cold and dismissive. "She's not. Now, if you'll excuse us."

Toby steps in front of me, blocking my path. "I wasn't asking you," he challenges the king. Toby obviously doesn't understand the danger he's in. I quickly intervene, trying to defuse the situation. "The king is right, Toby. I have to go."

I give him a pleading look, hoping he'll understand just how precarious our situation is. He seems to catch on, his eyes flicking between Xandros and me. "I guess I'll see you around," he says, pulling me into a quick hug. As he does, I feel him slip something into the side of my pants – a small piece of paper. "You know where I am if you need me," he whispers into my ear, just loud enough for Xandros to hear.

"She won't," Xandros snarls, his grip on my arm tightening. I watch as Toby reluctantly releases me and creeps away, my heart aching at the thought of leaving him behind.

Xandros roughly pulls me toward the car, the driver already waiting with the door open. He shoves me inside, causing me to smack my head on the edge of the door. I quickly scramble across the seat, feeling the blood trickle down from my hairline as Xandros climbs in beside me, his anger palpable.

As the car pulls away, he begins to scold me, his voice furious. "How dare you hug another man. I should have killed him." Tears fill my eyes as I realize just how volatile my new life will be—constantly walking on eggshells around Xandros.

"Do you like him? Is that it?" he demands, his voice cold. I remain silent, knowing admitting any feelings, platonic or otherwise, for Toby would only put him in more danger.

"Answer me!" he screams, his fist slamming into the back of the passenger seat.

I jump, my eyes meeting the driver's in the rearview mirror. The man offers me a look of pity before averting his gaze. Xandros seems to calm after his outburst, his attention turning to the window as he mutters under his breath.

When we arrive back at the castle, Xandros storms out of the car and circles around to my side. I try to slide across the seat and escape through the other door. However, he grabs me around the waist, yanking me out of the car. When he notices the blood on my forehead, he pauses and moves to touch me, his voice filled with remorse. "I'm sorry," he murmurs. I brush his hand away.

The action seems to anger him even more, and he roughly tosses me

Lycan King's Captives

over his shoulder, carrying me into the castle and back to our room. He throws me onto the bed, and I brace myself for what's to come. The darkness in his eyes warns me the worst is far from over.

I quickly drop the piece of paper down the gap of the headboard on the bounce. Rolling over, I stare into the eyes of the man who has claimed me as his own.

Xandros is still raging as he glares at me, lying on the bed. He opens his mouth to say something when servants burst into the room carrying bags from our shopping trip. Xandros holds his tongue, but I can see the fury simmering beneath the surface.

I try to take advantage of the brief reprieve and climb off the bed, wanting to escape him, even if it's just to the bathroom. Xandros growls, his gaze pinning me in place. The sound draws the attention of the servants, and realizing this, Xandros snaps at them to leave. They rush out of the room, closing the door behind them, and I'm left alone to face my mate's wrath.

Xandros's eyes narrow as he stares at me, his voice low and dangerous. "Tell me, Sienna, do you like him? Is that why he felt so fucking comfortable approaching you in public?"

"No, it's not like that. He was only my boss," I quickly reply, my voice trembling.

"Liar," he hisses, grabbing my throat and pressing me into the bed. Fear courses through me, and I don't even try to fight back. No, it will only worsen things. "How can you say that when I'm your mate? You said it yourself. The mate bond would prevent me from wanting to be with anyone else..." I blurt out when his grip tightens, threatening to cut off my air.

"Prove it... Prove you only want me."

The pressure on my windpipe causes me to gasp for air. "Prove it!" he screams in my face.

His threat hangs in the air like a suffocating fog, making it impossible for me to think straight. As his grip tightens, I panic. Desperate, my hand reaches for his cock, grabbing him through his pants. Xandros freezes, his gaze dropping to my hand on him. My heart races, remembering how painful it was the last time he touched me, but I don't know how to calm him down.

A twisted smile crosses Xandros's lips as he seems to approve of my touch. Realizing this, I hesitantly lift my head to kiss him, trying to hide the terror coursing through my veins.

The moment our lips meet, his anger seems to lessen. His hand gripping my throat remains firm, growing tighter and more possessive with each passing second. I inhale deeply as he moves his lips to my neck, releasing my throat and biting me softly, sending a shiver of pleasure through my body. My nervousness grows when his hands start to roam, exploring my body with a hunger that intensifies with each passing second. His touch is no longer gentle, but rather strong and demanding. His bites become harder, and I feel myself responding to his aggression despite the pain they cause.

As I gasp for air, my head spins from the intensity of his touch, my body instinctively arches into him. He tightens his grip on me, and I can feel the anger and jealousy in his touch, a primal desire that both terrifies and excites me. Our eyes meet, as he lifts his gaze, teeth sinking into the soft tissue of my breast. His eyes flicker dangerously, and the darkness swirling within them sends a shiver down my spine.

"You won't talk to him again; you won't look at him. If he ever crosses our path again and you respond or acknowledge him. I will kill him," he warns, and I squeeze my eyes shut, unable to handle the intensity of his searing gaze. Only when I do he bites the side of my breast hard.

My eyes open and I cry out, yet he doesn't seem to care he is hurting me, even as I feel my blood trickle down my ribs. "You belong to me," he growls, his voice tinged with fury.

"Do you understand?" I nod, not wanting to anger him. However, instead of my answer pleasing him, it seems to have the opposite effect as he pulls back a little, fingers biting into the soft skin on my arms.

"I don't think you do," he growls, as tears flood my eyes.

"Maybe I should show you who you truly belong to." He pushes me harder into the bed, his hand pinning my wrists above my head in one of his, my trapped wrists grating together painfully in his tight grip.

"Who do you belong to, Sienna?" he snarls. The rough fabric of the bed sheets scratches against my skin as he leans down, his breath hot against my ear.

"Answer me! Do you understand? You're mine, now and forever." When I don't answer, he grips my throat and growls, "You belong to me. Say it! Say you're mine." I'm terrified and aroused all at the same time, my heart racing as I feel the intensity of his gaze. His anger and possessiveness send a thrill through me, and I can feel myself wanting to give in to him, but also not, knowing by doing so I am giving him the control and fear he craves. I'm also terrified of what will happen if I don't.

Tears prick my eyes, and his grip on my throat loosens, allowing me to speak. "I'm yours," I assure him, my lips quivering. He watches me for a few tense seconds, eyes wild while I breathe harshly.

His lips find mine again, and this time the kiss is wild, a fiery storm of passion and anger. The bond instantly reacts to his touch. Painful or not, it doesn't seem to care. I struggle against his grip, yearning to touch him, to feel his body against mine. He doesn't relent, keeping my wrists firmly in place as he devours me with his mouth, tongue, and teeth. His mouth moves to my neck, leaving a trail of fiery bites in his wake. I cry out, pain and pleasure erupting deep within me.

He smirks at my reaction, an edge of darkness in his eyes that sends a thrill of fear through me. Still I don't want him to stop; I crave the intoxicating mix of pleasure and pain only he can give me. His free hand moves to my breast, gripping it roughly, making me gasp as my body betrays me, responding to his harsh touch.

His thumb flicks across my nipple, eliciting a moan that echoes through the room. With each passing second, his touch grows rougher and more demanding, and I can feel my resolve crumbling beneath the weight of his desire. As he trails kisses down my body, I feel a new sensation building within me.

A primal need I have never experienced before, raw and untamed, threatens to consume me. I can feel the hunger and anger inside him, a force that calls to my soul on a level I can't explain, and I know I am powerless to resist. He moves between my legs.

His eyes lock onto mine as he positions himself at my entrance, and I try to move up the bed away from him. His hands grip my hips dragging me back to him.

My breathing grows harsher. The memory of the pain he caused me last time springs to the forefront of my mind. "Who do you belong to?"

he purrs, his fingers digging painfully into my hips. I shake my head, unable to give him the answer he wants, knowing what he is about to do.

His grip tightens, and I bite my lip to keep from crying out. He leans forward and whispers in my ear, "You belong to me." He runs his cock between my folds, making me cry out, and squirm to get away from him when his eyes dart to mine.

"Shh, breathe, Sienna..." he growls softly, leaning forward as he strokes my hair and presses a gentle kiss to my forehead. I close my eyes and I take deep breaths, attempting to regain control of my body when he pulls away.

"Look at me!" I open my eyes to find him watching me. He stares at me and there is something in his gaze that calms me, something that makes me feel like I'm exactly where I belong.

He holds my gaze as he repositions himself, and I can see the raw desire and intensity in his eyes. I swallow hard, as I brace myself for what is coming. He slowly eases his grip, running his hands up my body in a soothing motion. "Breathe, Sienna. Just take a deep breath," he says softly. His voice is gentle, and I can feel my panic start to ease. I focus on his eyes and take a deep breath, feeling my heart rate start to slow. He smiles, a hint of relief in his eyes.

"Good. But this will hurt," he warns.

In a sudden, forceful thrust, he enters me. I gasp, and he stills, his hands holding me in place when he leans down, lips hungrily devouring mine. Eventually, he pulls back, his eyes dark and smoldering.

"Shh, you're fine," he murmurs while my body trembles beneath him, trying to get used to the intrusion.

After a few moments, my body relaxes. He pulls away, studies my face, and then pulls out before pushing back in slowly, his dark eyes watching me, testing me. He begins to move slowly and steadily at first. As my body adapts to him, he moves quicker, picking up speed.

His thrusts become harder and more forceful, and I can feel him pushing me to my limits. I respond eagerly, my body arching to meet his with each thrust. He grabs my hips, gripping them tight and slamming himself into me. I moan against him as his lips find mine, his tongue aggressively exploring my mouth, lips bruising and punishing.

I cry out, both in pain and ecstasy, as he begins to move within me, each thrust harder and more powerful than the last. The room fades away, and all that exists are the two of us, locked in this dance of messy desire. His hands roam my body, leaving bruises and marks. I lose myself in the sensations, my body shuddering with each thrust, each bruising grip, each biting kiss.

The pleasure builds, growing in intensity until I feel as if I might shatter into a million pieces. And just as I am about to break, he flips me onto my stomach, pulling me up onto my hands and knees. My face heats at the position he has placed me in, his hands smoothing over my ass when he suddenly slaps me. My back arches at the burning pain.

"Grip the headboard," he orders, his voice rough with desire. I obey, my fingers clutching the wooden frame for support as he enters me from behind, his hands gripping my hips with bruising force. The new angle sends waves of pleasure through me, and I know I am close to the edge.

He reaches forward, his fingers entwining in my hair, as he pulls my head back. His lips meet mine in a brutal, awkward kiss, a fierce reminder of how easily he can break me. With a final, brutal thrust, he sends me spiraling over the edge, my body convulsing from the climax, leaving me breathless.

He slows for a second, letting me ride out the waves when his hand moves from my hip and across my stomach, then it glides down between my legs, his fingers teasing my clit.

I gasp and open my eyes, my hair still clutched tightly in his fist. "No more, please. I can't take anymore," I beg.

His eyes flicker oddly and he smiles and replies, "You can. I'm not done with you yet." He lets go of my hair and palms my breast while he continues to rub my clit. The other hand drifts down my body, teasing and caressing my sensitive skin. When he rolls my clit between his fingers, my head rolls back on his shoulder, his nose grazing across my cheek when he pulls away slightly to look at me. His eyes are dark and intense, and I push back against him.

"See? You can take more. Now ride me." He pulls out of me and sits on the bed beside me, leaning against the headboard.

Gripping my hips, he drags me on top of him, pushing me onto him. I gasp, the sensation of him inside me again making my head spin.

He looks up at me, his eyes burning with desire. He guides me with his hands, pushing my hips up and down and guiding my movements. "Fuck. you're tight," he groans, his grip tightening on me, fingers biting into soft flesh.

His lips press against my ear, and he growls, "Faster." His words send a thrill through me, and I obey, pushing myself faster and harder against him. I can feel his breath quicken against my skin, his grip tightening on my hips. He groans, watching me ride him. "So beautiful." His words make me blush, my body heating up with pleasure when he leans forward, his lips latching onto my nipple.

I move faster, gripping his shoulders as I ride him, my body trembling with pleasure.

"Come for me. I want to feel you squeeze my cock." His words make my skin tingle with desire and my body responds to his command, almost as if it was waiting for it. My walls squeeze him, my pussy pulsating as my orgasm ripples through me, making me still and tense. His grip on me tightens, moving me, forcing me to ride the intense waves washing through me. I'm exhausted and want to sleep, yet his grip on my hips grows harsher.

His hands move to my ass as he rocks me against him when it comes down on my right cheek. I cry out at the pain, only for him to grip my ass in a punishing grip. "Next time, I gonna fuck this ass," he promises darkly before slamming me down on his cock, making me gasp.

"Faster!" His voice is dark and intense, and I can feel his desire radiating off him. I move faster, my body trembling with exhaustion and pleasure. He groans.

"Show me how much you love my cock." His words make my body heat up, and without thinking, I obey, pushing myself harder against him.

Xandros grips my hips tighter, thrusting up to meet me. With one last thrust, he groans, his body filling me with his warmth. I collapse onto his chest, my body trembling with pleasure and exhaustion, trying to catch my breath. His fingers skim up my spine gently before moving into my hair, massaging my scalp. He presses his lips to my cheek before sliding me off him and tugging my body against his as he pulls the blanket up over me.

"Rest," he purrs, the sound vibrating against my back. My eyes are already closing as I drift off, content for once in the arms of my monstrous mate.

∼

I awake with a moan. The sheets move against my skin as Xandros moves, sending goosebumps across my body. My senses suddenly sharpen and amplify in a way I've never experienced before. I can tell it's dark, even with my eyes closed, however, the darkness enveloping us doesn't feel oppressive. Rather, it's comforting, like a soft blanket wrapping around me. The air smells musky, the scent of our lovemaking still lingering in the room. I roll over, inhaling deeply as I move, and I'm instantly flooded with Xandros's masculine scent. It's intoxicating and overwhelming, and it makes me want to touch him. My entire body yearns for his touch, craving his embrace.

As if drawn by a magnetic force, I roll into him, burying my face in his neck. His hand sweeps across my side, and sparks ignite under his touch. "Go back to sleep, love," he groans. Sleep is far from my mind.

"Hmm, you're not going to go back to sleep, are you?" he purrs when my lips touch his chest, my hands claw at his skin, and he hisses when his arm wraps around my waist, tugging me closer.

"Ah, my little monster has sharp claws," he groans, helping me crawl on top of him. I know his words should worry me, yet my sole focus is on the feel of his warm skin beneath my fingertips. His eyes glow in the darkness back at me, fluorescent, and mesmerizing.

"You woke me, so help yourself," he purrs, positioning me above his hard cock.

"You know what to do," he growls when an embarrassing whine leaves my lips. I wiggle lower and lift my hips, sinking down on his cock with a groan.

My teeth feel sharper, my sense of smell is heightened, and all my senses seem to be solely focused on him. My entire body buzzes with a tingling vibration that creates friction, I feel drunk on his presence. I rock my hips against him. As I move, I bite him, my nails digging into his chest. I lose myself to senses I can't understand, nor do I care to understand them.

The taste of his skin floods my mouth, salty and addictive, making me crave more. The smoothness of his chest contrasts with the subtle roughness of his stubble when I press my lips against his jawline. The sound of our bodies moving together, the rhythmic thud of his heart, makes mine race even faster.

The bed beneath us creaks softly, the room filled with the scents of sweat and sex, and it only intensifies the desire coursing through me. The coolness of the room, the softness of the sheets, every sensation only seems to amplify the pleasure coursing through me.

Somewhere in the back of my mind, I know something isn't right, that my bizarre actions should scare me. I should be worried about these changes, but I'm too overwhelmed by the sensations flooding my body to care. Xandros seems to be all my mind can focus on, him and him alone, nothing else matters. And once again, my surroundings blur into one, and so does the night.

The room is silent except for our heavy breathing, the glow of the moonlight casting soft shadows on the walls. I trace the contours of Xandros's face, feeling the heat of his skin beneath my fingertips. His eyes, like two black pools, hold a depth of emotion that both frightens and intrigues me. I want to know every thought, every secret hidden behind those eyes.

My body trembles with fear and desire, the raw intensity of the strange sensations both threatening to consume me. I can feel the beating of his heart beneath my palm, the rhythm syncing with mine. Our breaths mingle, each exhale warm against the cool night air.

As I continue to move against him, I notice the way the moonlight dances across his face, highlighting the sharp angles of his cheekbones and the curve of his lips. His eyes seem to shine with an otherworldly glow, as if they are filled with the secrets of the universe. One I have found myself a part of without realizing what that fully means.

The heat of his body envelops me, and I lose myself in the sensations of our connection. I am drowning in the intensity of his touch, the way his fingers trace patterns on my skin, the warmth of his breath against my neck. The world beyond the confines of our room ceases to exist, and all that matters is the feel of him against me, the depth of our passion.

A spark that ignites with every touch, every caress.

And as the night gives way to the first light of dawn, I know everything has changed. The world as I once knew it has been shattered, replaced by a reality filled with him, desire, and an all-consuming obsession that knows no bounds, that isn't rational.

"Sienna?" Xandros' husky voice next to my ear makes me shiver. I groan, not wanting to wake up. His hands tug at me, and I know he is trying to pick me up, but I feel sore all over and swat his hands away, which earns me a growl. I'm disoriented and confused, and when I look at his chest, I gasp. Xandros's chest is covered in small, red marks from sharp claws. They are deep enough to be visible and clear enough to show they were made by claws. His skin is slightly raised, the evidence of my earlier actions: deep, red scratch marks marring his skin. He doesn't seem bothered by them. I closed my eyes, only to open them when I feel something cold press against my lips. "Drink," he growls at me, and I shake my head, trying to curl back up to sleep.

He won't let me, though, pulling me against him and propping my naked body up. "So disobedient," he purrs, nipping at my shoulder.

"Drink, and then eat," he says, pressing a glass of water to my lips. I take a sip, not realizing how thirsty I am until the cool liquid hits my tongue. I snatch the glass from him, gulping it down greedily. "Good girl," he purrs, his hand skimming over my stomach as I drain the glass in seconds.

"I'm not hungry" I ask. My voice is hoarse and weak, even to my own ears.

Xandros grips my chin, tilting my head back as he looks at me, his eyes serious and concerned. "Your body is changing, Sienna. The mate bond seems stronger than I initially thought. I believe you may shift earlier than anticipated." he tells me, his eyes darting to my lips, his thumb brushing over them. "You need to eat," he states.

I ponder his words as he gets up and struts away, leaving me to process what that means; the idea of shifting petrifies me. I try to lay back down and go back to sleep.

The bed dips when he returns. "Sienna, up. You need to eat," he snarls at me, and I groan, curling into a ball under the sheets. He rips the blanket off me, making me shudder at the cool crisp air in the room.

Ignoring my refusal to eat, he sets a tray down on the bed and grabs me, pulling me around to face the food and leaning me against the headboard like a propped-up doll.

"Stay, if you move, you'll go over my knee," he warns, and I puff out a breath. Like a child, much to my embarrassment, he begins to feed me, not allowing me to protest. He forces food to my lips the moment I finish chewing, preventing me from refusing. He gives me pieces of grilled chicken, steamed vegetables, and warm, crusty bread dipped in warm broth. Even when I complain I'm full, he insists I continue.

He presses another piece of chicken to my lips, and I press my lips together, feeling on the verge of exploding. I shake my head when he speaks. "One more mouthful," he tells me, and I open my mouth reflexively, which makes him chuckle.

Relieved when he finally sets the tray aside, I try to roll away from him, he tugs me back so I'm straddling him. "Ah, transitioning Lycans are so grumpy. You're not sleeping, not yet," he growls, wrapping my legs around his waist. He carries me into the bathroom, exhausted, I let him do as he pleases with me. Instead, I opt to turn my face into his neck, inhaling his comforting scent.

He sits on the edge of the bathtub and fiddles with the taps, filling the tub with warm water. He adds herbs and soap to the water, making it smell strongly of lavender, rosemary, and eucalyptus. The soothing scents permeate the air, filling my senses and calming my racing thoughts as I melt into him.

Once the bath is ready, Xandros stands and steps into the water, still holding me in his arms. He maneuvers me around so I'm sitting between his legs, my back resting against his chest. As the warm water envelops us, I feel some of the tension in my muscles begin to ease.

With slow, gentle movements, he washes me, using a soft sponge to scrub my skin gently. He takes his time, paying attention to every inch of my body, massaging my aching muscles as he cleans away the remnants of the night before.

As his hands move over me, I moan, my senses coming alive and overwhelming me, making me ache for him. When his hand moves over my stomach, I grip his wrist, needing him to touch me to stop the ache.

Lycan King's Captives

He chuckles when I guide his hand between my legs. I should be embarrassed by my actions, so demanding and whiny.

"Oh, Sienna, you insatiable little thing," he purrs, his fingers teasing me but not entering.

"I never thought I'd see the day when I'd have to keep up with you." His voice is seductive and teasing, making me want him even more.

"Haven't you turned out to be quite the nymph?" he laughs, and his breath is warm against my ear. Finally, he slips his fingers inside me, and I moan at the friction he creates. It's not enough; I crave more, his fingers unable to satisfy the aching need within me. "More," he purrs, then nips my shoulder. "Such a greedy little monster," he purrs.

"Please, Xandros," I beg, my voice trembling and desperate as my hips move in time with his hand.

"I need more. So much more."

He seems to consider my request for a moment, his fingers continuing to stroke me, driving me to the edge of madness, but still not enough.

"You're insatiable, but so am I," he murmurs, gripping my chin and turning my face up to look at him. He wears a wicked grin as he leans closer, his breath sweeping across my lips.

"Let's see if we can wear each other out," he purrs.

I moan in pleasure, his fingertips pressing on my clit as he speaks, my body already aching for his touch. He lifts me out of the bath, water dripping from our bodies, and carries me to the bed. He tosses me onto the sheets, making me bounce on the soft mattress.

"The sheets," I say, worried about ruining them. He just smirks at me, crawling onto the bed as water drips from his body.

"They'll be ruined either way," he purrs, positioning himself between my legs and gripping my knees.

"Open your legs for me. Show me that beautiful pussy," he growls, and his eyes flash wickedly. His canines protrude from between his lips. I comply, opening my legs to him invitingly, and he doesn't hesitate to accept the invitation. His hands grip my hips, holding me steady as he buries his face between my thighs. His tongue slides over me, sending intense pleasure through my body.

He flicks his tongue over my clit, and I can feel the warming sensation building inside me. His hot mouth leaves no part of me untouched as he devours me. I cry out, rocking my hips against his mouth as I come, my body trembling, my back arching as the pleasurable ecstasy ebbs and flows through me. I collapse against the bed, Xandros crawls up my body and wraps his arms around me, pressing his lips gently to my shoulder. He drags me up the bed further. I feel my cheeks flush with heat and embarrassment. I press my face into his neck, breathing in his heady scent.

He gently strokes my hair, his hands still gently caressing my body as his lips move against my skin, nipping and sucking on the mark on my neck. I feel his lips curve into a smile against my skin before he pulls away, and I reluctantly open my eyes. He looks down at me, his eyes filled with the same burning desire I felt moments ago. I know no matter how much time passes, I'll never be able to get used to the bizarre feelings this man induces.

Chapter Eight

Sienna

I wake up to the dimly lit room as the morning light tries to peek through the curtains. The warmth of the fireplace casts flickering shadows on the walls, creating a cozy atmosphere. I stretch, feeling the soft sheets against my skin, trying to recall the events of the night. They flash by in a blur of passion and sleep, leaving me with a hazy memory.

As I sit up, I notice the door to the room is slightly ajar, and I catch a glimpse of a maid slipping out, carrying a bundle of dirty laundry. The faint fragrance of fresh laundry drifts my way, and I take a deep breath, feeling the comforting scent engulfing me. I scan the room, finding the maid has set fresh linen on the arm of the couch, and I also spot a tray of food positioned on the coffee table by the fireplace. My stomach growls, demanding attention, and I can't resist the temptation.

I slip out of bed, my bare feet touching the cold floor, making me shiver. I tiptoe over to the tray. Gripping the silver lid, I lift it off and reveal our breakfast, which consists of scrambled eggs, crispy bacon, and a small pile of buttered toast. My mouth waters, and I pick up a fork, ready to dig in. Just as I'm about to take my first bite, strong arms wrap around my waist, startling me and making me jump.

"How do you feel?" Xandros's husky voice asks next to my ear, his breath warm on my neck, and I lean back against him.

"Hungry," I murmur, still eyeing the food. He chuckles, pressing a soft kiss to my temple, before releasing me to wander off to the bathroom. I watch him for a second, mesmerized by the sight of his plump ass. Stealing a piece of bacon off the tray, I take the opportunity to slip into his closet, grabbing one of his shirts to cover my naked body and finding some underwear. I slip them on, the soft fabric caressing my skin as I return to the tray of food. I sit on the plush carpet, my back against the couch, and begin eating while enjoying the warmth offered from the fireplace.

Each bite is an explosion of flavors, the salty bacon contrasting with the creamy fluffy eggs, and the toast providing a crunch I didn't realize I was craving. The savory taste of the meal lingers in my mouth, and I relish every morsel, then pouting when I finish mine. The warmth of the fire on my skin adds to the cozy feeling, making me content and relaxed. Xandros emerges from the bathroom, dressed in a pair of loose gray sweatpants, his chest is smooth and bare, dark hair dusting across his chest and down his abs, escaping into his pants.

I watch him move around the room, looking for something, his abs round and tight. The muscles in his chest are well defined but not overly so, and his golden skin catches the light, reflecting it as he moves. Though for some odd reason my marks no longer mar his skin, which upsets me a little, his skin completely blemish free and untainted.

Finally, he finds what he is looking for, which turns out to be his phone. He joins me by the fire, sitting beside me as he slides his plate between us. "Eat, I can feel you're still hungry," he orders, and I am like a bottomless pit, starving, so I don't bother to argue. We eat together.

There's a comfortable silence between us, but I can't help noticing how he keeps checking his phone, his brow furrowed. He shakes his head.

"What's wrong?" I ask, my curiosity getting the better of me.

He exhales, the noise sounding frustrated. "Javier, my Beta, should have been back last night, I think he's avoiding me for some reason," he says, his voice tinged with concern.

"Where did he go?" I ask him. Xandros watches me for a second.

Lycan King's Captives

"To get information for me on someone," he purses his lips, biting down on his bottom. I can sense the worry in his tone.

"As I said, I have ways to find out information on people, Javier is one of those sources, he's well connected," I feel a pang of worry from the way Xandros watches me, telling me the person Javier is looking into is me which makes me nervous. It makes me wonder what will happen when he learns who I am. Although I am shocked he hasn't ordered that information from me. Maybe he is hoping I will tell him more.

"I might have to leave you here tomorrow night while I attend to some business in the city and hunt down Javier, I'm positive he's back by now, he's just avoiding me," he says with a growl.

"Can I come with you?" I ask, hoping to escape the confinement of this room. I look at him, my eyes pleading.

He shakes his head, and I feel the weight of his refusal like a stone in my stomach. "Definitely not. Not until I know I can trust you," he growls, his tone firm and final. I never ran off last time, I've done everything he's asked of me.

I swallow hard, my appetite suddenly gone. I watch Xandros for a few minutes as he returns to fiddling with his phone, texting someone. The more I sit, the more my situation weighs on me. A wave of sadness washes over me, I say nothing as I peer around the room. Despite the little luxuries it offers—luxuries I never had at home, like good heating, a soft bed, and my own bathroom—it is still a prison—a fancier one, but a prison no less.

When we finish eating, Xandros places the tray on the coffee table, and I use that as my escape. I get up and make my way back to the bed, feeling the softness of the mattress beneath me as I lie down wondering if it is truly possible to sleep your life away; if my life will always be confined to this room I might as well try. As I snuggle beneath the blankets, the bed dips as Xandros follows, tugging me against him. His touch no longer excites me and I squirm, wanting to be left alone, but his hand slips into my underwear. However, this time, I pull it out, causing him to growl.

"Sienna?" he growls.

"I want to sleep," I tell him, my voice toneless, defeated.

"Are you seriously chucking a tantrum about me not taking you with me?" he snarls. I don't answer; his question doesn't warrant an answer when he believes it to be a mere tantrum. It isn't. It's about feeling like a prisoner. How would he like it if he was confined to four walls and told to be happy about it? When I don't answer, he shoves me away. He stomps into the closet, retrieving clothes and then leaves the room, slamming and locking the door behind him.

In that moment, I realize I've become nothing more than a sex toy to him, and a tear slides down my cheek. The room suddenly feels suffocating, like the walls are closing in and I need some fresh air.

I get up and head toward the window, drawing the curtains aside. Stupidly, I can't resist the temptation, and I try to open the window, but as expected it is locked tight and I sigh, pressing my head against the glass.

The view outside is breathtaking, with the sun slowly rising over the horizon, casting a warm glow on the landscape. The sight is so peaceful, and I take a deep breath, pretending I can feel the fresh air fill my lungs.

The vibrant colors of the flowers in the garden, glistening under the dusting of melting snow, the fluttering of the leaves in the gentle breeze I may never feel again, and the sound of chirping birds that have more freedom than me. I sit on the windowsill until my butt aches before dragging myself back to bed.

Chapter Nine

Sienna

The sound of the door opening makes me sit up. Despite being angry with him, excitement bubbles up thinking it is him. Disappointment floods me when I notice it is just a servant. After a few moments, and tidying up on her way, she moves to the door.

The faint sound of her footsteps echoes in the silence, and I feel a sudden ache in my chest. She slips out, turning at the last second and noticing me watching her. She bows her head, giving me a sad smile before slipping out the door and locking it. I peer around. Xandros is nowhere to be found, and I wonder if he's coming back.

My gaze scans the room, and I spot a tray of food positioned on the coffee table by the fireplace. My stomach growls, despite this the thought of food makes me nauseous. What I really need is him, but he's not here. The mate bond aches with his absence, and I feel empty and lost.

I get out of bed, my bare feet touching the cold floor, and make my way back to the window. The curtains are still drawn, and I hesitate to take my seat on it. The view outside is no longer breathtaking, but a reminder of my captivity.

The vibrant colors of the flowers in the garden, the fluttering of the leaves in the gentle breeze, and the chirping of the birds only serve to taunt me. I miss my old life, even though it was far from what I would have chosen for myself. At least it was mundane and predictable back then, at least I was free and not confined.

I slump against the windowpane. The room feels suffocating, and I need out of it, my panic growing more the longer I am trapped here without any distractions. I get up and head toward the door, hoping to find a way out. It's locked, and I'm trapped. The realization hits me harder despite knowing this already, and I feel a lump forming in my throat as I yank on the handle, twisting it and shaking it, trying to break the lock.

I sit on the bed, my back against the headboard, and wrap my arms around my knees.

The silence is deafening, and my thoughts are consuming me. I miss my uncle, which is ridiculous, at least he was someone to talk to—well to yell at me— right now I would take that familiarity over this silence; my friends, the few I had, and I miss my old job, the routine of my mundane old life. I miss the freedom to make my own choices, to live my life the way I want. Now, I'm nothing more than a prisoner, a possession of a man who only wants me for his pleasure.

The tears start to flow down my cheeks, and I can't hold them back. The sobs wrack my body, and I feel like I'm falling apart. The pain in my chest intensifies, and I clutch at it, hoping to ease the ache. It only gets worse with each passing moment.

Hours go by, and I'm still sitting there, lost in my thoughts. The sun has shifted, casting a different light in the room. The door creaks open, and I peer up, hoping to see Xandros. It's once again one of the maids, carrying a tray of food.

"Are you hungry, miss?" she asks, her voice gentle as she notices the full tray still sitting where she left it at lunch.

I shake my head, feeling sick to my stomach. She places the tray on the nightstand and retrieves the old one, then leaves without another word. The smell of the food makes me nauseous, and I turn away from it.

The room is still silent, and I'm alone with my thoughts again. The ache in my chest has subsided a little. I wonder where Xandros is, what he's doing, and if he even cares I'm here. Or, perhaps he has simply forgotten me?

My thoughts go to Carina. Is that where he is? With his wife? While I rot here. I shouldn't be jealous, but I am. He is hers and I want him too, even though I shouldn't. She is more suited to him, and it's clear she hates me, and why wouldn't she? She should hate my guts! I am her husband's dirty little mistress, and nothing more.

As the night falls, I crawl back into bed, feeling the emptiness of the room; it makes the room colder, hollow, every movement, twitch, or sound echoing in the darkness. I close my eyes, trying to shut out the thoughts. They keep coming. The memories of my old life, the pain of my captivity, and the ache of the mate bond. It's all too much, and I wish I could escape it all. Wish I could escape this life.

Chapter Ten

Sienna

An entire night passed, and half of today is already gone since Xandros left. I can't shake the feeling of emptiness that's settled within me. The mate bond has me craving his presence, my body aching without him. I hate how dependent I've become of him. He has become an addiction, and despite trying not to think about him, my mind always wanders back to what he could be doing. My thoughts are obsessive and possessive of him. I hate it but can't help it.

I sit on the windowsill, resting my head against the cold glass of my prison, watching the gardener tend to the gardens outside. The door to my room opens, and I glance over to see the maid entering. She moves around the room, and I pay her no mind until she calls out to me.

"Ma'am, your lunch order?" I turn to look at her briefly, she stands with her hands clasped in front of her, her blue blouse buttoned up to her throat, with black slacks on, she appears to be my age and stares at me like a deer in headlights. Returning my gaze to the window, I ignore her.

"Ma'am, the king sent me to ask what you want for lunch, you never called down?" she insists, her voice wavering slightly.

"Nothing," I mutter, my attention now focused on a bird that perches on the window beside me. I watch it enviously, longing for the freedom it seems to have while I'm the one trapped in a cage.

"I have a cheese platter?" the woman suggests, once again, I ignore her. She leaves the room and returns a moment later. I hear a crash, followed by the woman's shriek. Glass shatters, and I jump, turning to see her on the floor, having tripped over the rug and broken a vase that sat on the lamp table next to the armchair. Blood streams down her arm where she landed on a shard of glass, and I rush over to help her. She pulls the large shard out of her forearm, blood spurts out, and I panic while she stares at her arm in shock for a second and then sighs.

The woman assures me she's fine, when I notice the cart outside the door and dash out to grab a hand towel. As I step into the dimly lit corridor, it dawns on me that this could be my chance to escape. I glance down the hallway, toward the bright airy foyer at the end, then back at the open door where the woman is still cleaning up the mess.

With a heavy sigh, I snatch a tea towel, knowing the woman will probably get in trouble if I try to escape. Just as I turn back toward the door, I hear hurried footsteps. My heart races as I turn to see Xandros approaching. He stops in his tracks, and looks at me in shock for a second. That shock wears off quickly and turns to anger, his eyes blazing.

"How did you get out?" he snarls, marching toward me. I back up at the feral sound of his voice, bumping into the maid's cart. Xandros seizes my arm tightly, his claws piercing my delicate flesh as he drags me toward the bedroom door. He shoves me back into the room, and I stumble to catch myself on the dresser. He slams the door shut, prowling toward me.

"You know you don't leave this room!" he yells, pointing a finger in my face, I feel the blood drain from my face.

"I was just getting a hand towel," I try to explain, pointing to the injured maid, his gaze follows my finger then his eyes dart to the maid, his expression darkening.

"You left the fucking door open!" he snaps at her, taking a step toward her. My heart races at his fury as he turns it on her.

He stalks toward her and seeing her bewildered look, I rush in front of him, my hands shaking as I press them flat against his chest. "Xandros," I murmur and he snarls at me.

The woman freezes, her eyes wide with fear. "She did nothing wrong," I plead, my voice stuttering as he tries to push past me, he grabs my arm and his grip is punishing.

"Xandros, please. She hurt herself, and I was just trying to help, she did nothing wrong." Xandros looks down at me, he is livid and over something so stupid.

"You don't leave the room!" he bellows at me, his face inches from mine. I drop my gaze, but he grabs my face, forcing my gaze to his.

"I'm sorry, she was bleeding, and I—"

"You don't leave the room! She would have healed! She isn't human! Furthermore, she knows better!" he interrupts, his anger palpable as he turns his anger back on the woman.

"I didn't notice she left... I'm sorry," the woman apologizes.

Xandros growls.

"I'm sorry I didn't know, I am new here. I only started yesterday to replace—" she pauses, her eyes flitting to me momentarily. She drops her gaze to the floor. "I'm sorry, My King," she murmurs softly.

His eyes dart to me, and she stops talking briefly. "There are no excuses. I'm sorry, My King," she finishes, her voice trembling.

Yet I was still stuck on her saying she was replacing someone. Who? Did she mean Darcy? What happened to Darcy? Did they fire her or worse? My heart beats faster at the thought.

"Just get out, and don't let it happen again," he snarls at her, and she jumps at the tone he uses and so do I. She doesn't hesitate in rushing out of the room and the door softly clicking shut before I hear the jiggle of keys as she locks it then twists the handle to ensure I am trapped inside.

The woman exits the room, leaving me frozen in place with Xandros. Turning to my mate, my stomach churns violently for a few seconds while he paces the room, growling, as if he is trying to contain his anger. Eventually, he stops, rubbing his temples, and exhales loudly. Xandros makes his way to the closet. He tosses clothes onto the bed and begins to undress, toeing his shoes off and unbuttoning his shirt. He pulls his shirt off, tossing it aside.

My gaze scans him lingering on the fang marks on his neck, and my stomach drops, knowing he was with Carina. It's the only explanation. I assumed he was, yet seeing the proof of it lacing his skin makes me feel sick. While I was here suffering and craving him, he was with another woman, his wife. It's stupid that I am jealous of her. Xandros catches me staring and looks down, cursing under his breath." Wait... Sienna, it's not—"

He reaches for me, I slap his hands away, causing him to growl. "You know she is my wife!" he snarls.

"And I am your dirty mistress, your little secret locked in this godforsaken cage!" I scream back at him, my voice cracking. He seems taken aback by my outburst, and my throat aches from the force of my yelling.

"Sienna..." He reaches for me again. I lash out, hitting and punching him wherever I can.

"I hate you. I fucking hate you!" I scream as he tries to deflect my blows. He growls, grabbing me and pinning me against the bed.

"Enough!" he screams in my face, and I stop fighting, realizing it's useless. And there is no point giving him more "so-called" reasons to punish me.

"Are you done?" he asks, his voice icy. I press my lips in a line, my eyes stinging with the tears I am trying to hold back. Since yesterday, I have craved his presence, yet he never showed up, then when he does it turns into this mess.

"You knew I was married. I have obligations to my kingdom and my *wife*. You will learn to deal with it or—" he stops. "It's only temporary. I need her to sign the divorce papers, so for now, I need to give her what she wants."

"What if she wants you?" I ask.

His jaw clenches. "As I said, it's only temporary to keep the peace between kingdoms."

My eyes burn with tears. "Were you with her last night?" I ask him, my voice coming off angrier than intended.

"Yes, I had to attend a dinner with her parents. I didn't fuck her, if that is what you're wondering. I slept in her quarters on the couch!" he says.

I say nothing, staring off toward the window. He releases me, muttering under his breath. "I have to leave in an hour. I have an important meeting in the city."

"Good for you," I tell him bitterly, climbing off the bed and retaking my place on the windowsill. He curses, storming into the bathroom and slamming the door shut. I hear the shower turn on.

I don't know how much time passes, but I hear him trying to talk to me as he gets dressed. When silence falls, I realize I've zoned out and let out a sigh. "Sienna!" he commands, and I roll my eyes, turning to look at him as he stands by the bed, doing up his suit jacket. When he is done, he points to the bed where I see a dress laid out. "Get dressed. We leave in ten minutes." he snaps at me before doing up his other cuff link.

My emotions are a whirlwind of fear, anger, and confusion. Why would he want me to go with him now, after all that's happened? Despite my feelings, I comply, hastily getting dressed in the clothes he left on the bed. I can feel his eyes on me as I move to strip my clothes off, but I refuse to look at him.

The scent of his cologne hangs heavily in the air, and it churns my stomach.

I pull on a dark blue dress, trying to ignore the way the fabric clings to my body, making me feel exposed under his gaze. Xandros says nothing when he passes me a pair of black glittery flats. I sit on the edge of the bed and slip them on, feeling nervous with him standing over me.

The room is dimly lit, shadows casting eerie patterns on the walls now that the sun has gone down, and the atmosphere feels heavy with tension.

We leave the room, the anger and hurt still simmer beneath the surface, but for now, I push them aside and focus on the opportunity before me.

I'm leaving the room, *finally* leaving the room. As we step outside the door, I see three maids waiting in the hall, one of which is the girl he yelled at earlier, making my thoughts go back to Darcy. I want to ask but am afraid of the answer.

"Your mother sent us to clean the room while you're gone." Xandros nods but says nothing in answer to them. He points down the hall. "Go on," he growls.

The hallway outside is cold and uninviting, the stone floor sending chills up my spine as we walk. I can feel the weight of Xandros's presence behind me, oppressive and suffocating, as he tells me the directions to go in. My heart races in my chest, a mix of excitement and fear—excitement that I was leaving, fear of wondering where we were going.

As we descend the staircase, the lights lining the walls cast flickering shadows, making the descent feel like a journey into the depths of hell. When I reach the bottom, he grabs my arm.

I glance at him, he says nothing instead, leading me outside to the waiting car. He opens my door, not letting me go until I am stuffed inside. Xandros slides across the seat, forcing me over and a nervousness creeps in. Humans rarely go out at night, so I'm feeling uneasy now. I wanted nothing more than to leave that room. However, now, faced without the nightlife of the city, I realize how foolish that is to have wanted such a thing.

"Where are we going?" I ask, nervous now.

"Mal's club."

I gulp down the dread that lodges in my throat.

"You wanted to come with me so desperately, you got what you wanted," he snarls at me.

The drive to the city is filled with anxiety, my heart pounding as we venture further into the city. The night sky is a deep, velvety black, lit up with stars that seem to taunt me with their distant beauty. As we draw nearer to our destination, my fear grows with each passing mile, the cityscape looming larger with every turn.

Xandros pulls out his phone and dials a number, his eyes fixed on the scenery outside his window. I overhear the conversation as he leaves a voicemail, his voice tense and impatient.

"Javier, I know you're avoiding me. I don't know why, but I am headed to Mal's. Either meet me there, or I will send people out looking for you. You have two hours! Don't make me send people out looking for you!" With that, Xandros stabs his phone screen with his finger before pocketing it, muttering to himself.

As we arrive at the nightclub, the chaotic scene before us is almost overwhelming. The streets are filled with vampires, Lycans, and werewolves, all reveling in the night. The air is thick with the scent of blood, danger, and excitement, causing my heart to race even faster as I realize exactly how out of my element I am.

Xandros leans over, his voice a low growl as he lays out his rules. "You stay by my side, you don't wander! You don't talk to anyone or look at anyone! Am I clear?" I nod, trying to swallow the lump in my throat. "You're to be seen, not heard," he adds harshly, grabbing my arm as the driver opens the door.

Stepping into the club, the bouncer immediately recognizes Xandros and allows us to bypass the queue. The atmosphere inside is sinister and blood-curdling. Women with chains around their ankles are tied to poles, dancing naked on tables and little podiums, their bodies covered in bite marks. The music is pounding, sending tremors through the floor and up into my body. The dim lighting casts eerie shadows, the air heavy with a mix of sweat, alcohol, and something darker, more sinister. Blood.

Xandros leads me to a table where three men in suits are sitting. Their eyes flicker over me, appraising and possessive, and I shrink back against Xandros, trying to make myself as small as possible. He pulls out a chair for me, and grips my shoulder, pushing me down into it. I sit, my legs trembling beneath me. My eyes take in the men at the table. They appear to be in their thirties, and their menacing red eyes watch me. I avert my gaze when a waitress wanders over offering drinks. When she sets an amber liquid in front of me, Xandros takes it.

"Maybe wine?" the waitress suggests. "No, water. She won't be drinking," Xandros states, not paying her the slightest piece of attention, making me wonder if that is because I am sitting beside him, because the other three men gaze at her like she would be a tasty snack. She leaves, returning with some water, and I sip it, glancing around the place.

The conversation at the table is a low hum in the background with my racing thoughts. I try to focus on their conversations, but the pulsating beat of the music makes it difficult to concentrate. Instead, I watch the people around us, the different creatures all united in their pursuit of pleasure and blood.

As the night wears on, I feel like a pawn in some twisted game, my presence a symbol of Xandros's control over me. I glance at him, his face a mask of cool indifference as he engages in conversation with the men around us. Beneath the surface, I can sense the tension. His grip on my knee tightens when I wiggle or move, a firm reminder not to draw attention to myself.

I watch in horror as the women are fed on and pulled around, the rowdiness of the place escalating. The atmosphere grows darker and more sinister, and I know I shouldn't be here. I regret wanting to leave my prison. I'm cold, need to pee, and struggling to keep my eyes open.

However, peering around, I look for a bathroom when I notice him. Amidst the chaos, I see a figure appear from the mass of gyrating bodies. Toby. I immediately drop my gaze, not wanting to draw attention to him. The swift movement causes Xandros to glance at me. I try to sneak another look for Toby, when I do, he is gone, much to my relief.

The night drags on, and the vampire men appear to be amused by my presence. One of them smirks as I set my glass on the table, "She's a pretty one, Xandros." Xandros's grip on my knee tightens painfully, causing me to cry out. The man chuckles, "What a pretty voice. I bet she moans beautifully."

Xandros's voice turns cold and dangerous as he replies, "Keep your eyes off my mate, or you'll find out just how sharp my claws are."

The man quickly apologizes. "I didn't realize she was your mate. I thought Carina was to marry you." Xandros nods, acknowledging the strange situation and my cheeks heat with embarrassment.

"So, she's allowing you to keep her as a concubine of sorts?" one of the men asks. Xandros replies with a dismissive shrug, "Something like that." The man laughs, while I feel like a toy, something he keeps on the side. "Well, we all need a plaything, though first I've seen a mate be the toy. I can't bear being away from mine, or do you prefer her close. How does Carina get on with her?"

"She doesn't," Xandros answers, glancing at me.

"And that doesn't bother you? How does that work?" the man asks, looking genuinely intrigued by this rather strange choice of conversation.

"It just does. Carina knows she is my mate, they both accept it whether they like it or not, right, Sienna?" Xandros asks, turning his head to look at me.

"Like I have a choice," I mutter before I can stop myself, his grip on my thigh turns bone breaking.

One of the men laughs, while the one who asked the question stares at me with pity, which I find rather odd.

"Seems not all are happy with the situation," the man with a beard, laughs.

"She'll get over it," Xandros states and I press my lips in a line, averting my gaze away from them, trying my best to ignore them.

"So you plan on keeping both?" he asks.

Xandros says nothing else, though his silence speaks volumes and that makes my stomach turn.

As the night wears on, my need to use the bathroom becomes unbearable. I feebly grip Xandros's leg under the table, causing him to look at me. His gaze is piercing, and I shrink under it as he grips my hand, squeezing my fingers in warning, to not embarrass him.

I blink back tears, feeling my fingers crack, in his crushing grip. The other men at the table are watching me, their expressions a mix of curiosity and amusement.

Finally, I can't hold it any longer, and I pull my hand out of Xandros, my fingers finally regaining feeling. I tug on his jacket, only for him to snap at me. "What?" His tone makes me jump and my knee hits the bottom of the table making everyone's drinks rattle.

"Calm down, My King, you're scaring your mate," the man across from me says.

If looks could kill I'm afraid that man would be dead. Xandros sits back in his chair while I glance nervously around the table, everyone falling silent. I watch as his phone rings and he snatches it off the table.

"Fucking finally, Javier," he snarls. My eyes go to the bathroom again.

"Xandros?" The same man from before says pointing to me. Xandros growls and looks at me.

"I need to pee," I whisper, and he looks at the bathrooms across the room. His tone is cold.

"Then go." My heart races at the thought of walking through the club alone. "No one will touch you, not with me here. They all saw you walk in with me," he assures me.

"Hang on, Javier," he answers.

As I push my chair out, he grabs my arm. "Remember, I'm watching. Don't try anything," he warns, finally releasing me. I nod and rush to the bathroom, feeling everyone's eyes on me.

The moment I burst into the bathroom, I take a deep breath, only to gasp when I spot Toby leaning against the sink basin, his arms folded across his chest.

The shock of seeing him sends a shiver down my spine, and I glance at the door. I wonder what he's doing here, and what it might mean for me if Xandros catches me with him.

Toby quickly walks over, locking the door. "You didn't call me?" he snaps. I shake my head.

"How did you know I was here?"

"Ashley, the waitress, she called the moment she spotted a woman with Xandros," he tells me. I sigh, shaking my head moving off toward the toilet cubicle when he grabs me, tugging me back to him.

"Toby, you shouldn't be here. He'll kill you if he finds out you're in here," I tell him, but he grabs my face in his hands.

"I know you don't want him, Sienna." I shake my head. It doesn't matter what I want, the mate bond will always draw me back to Xandros.

"I know a witch. She can break your bond. I will get you out..." Toby tells me, and I blink at him.

"What?" I ask, a little dumbfounded.

"A witch, then we run. I can get us out of the city. We can start off fresh somewhere else. Somewhere away from that monster," he growls, cupping my face in his hands.

"You're being ridiculous, Toby. You'll get us both killed and why do you even care? I am just an old employee," I tell him, pulling away and rushing into a cubicle. I lift my dress and quickly pee.

"You don't believe that. I know you don't. Don't pretend you don't feel the same way about me as I do you," he tells me. I furrow my brows. I shake my head and finish peeing. Leaving the cubicle, I move to the sink basin and wash my hands.

"You are insane," I tell him when he grips my face, forcing me to look at him. I stare at his handsome face.

"Tell me you feel nothing for me?" he says, and I chew my lip. I thought I did, but do I still? The bond makes things complicated. I don't know what I feel that is real and the bond.

"Toby, what you're asking—"

"Is for you to be with me. Run with me. I love you. Unfortunately, it took that asshole stealing you from me to realize that," he exhales, pressing his forehead against mine.

"Just think about it and call me when you get a chance. I will find a way to get you out of the city," he tells me, pressing his lips to my forehead before slipping out of the bathroom before I can protest.

Chapter Eleven

Sienna

The air feels suffocating as I leave the bathroom, my heart pounding erratically in my chest. Toby's words echo in my ears, a tempting offer of escape from Xandros that seems too good to be true, yet one I am not sure I can take. The bond we share aches just with him gone momentarily and that is not something I am sure I can live with for eternity.

As I step out into the club, I instantly notice a change in the atmosphere. Everyone has stopped what they're doing, and their eyes are locked on me; it is like I've stepped into some alternate reality, everyone watching me with scrutinizing eyes. It makes me wonder what has happened in the brief moments I have been gone. The music continues to blare, only it's drowned out by the palpable tension that fills the room.

I walk slowly back to Xandros, doing my best to ignore the stares that burn into me. As I approach the table, I see Javier, the king's Beta. It makes me pause, recognizing the man from my uncle's house. He is engaged in a heated discussion with Xandros; he seems to be trying to reason with Xandros over something. I strain to hear their words over the thumping music, their tense expressions tell me something is very wrong and whatever Javier is speaking with him over is the cause of conflict in the air.

My heart skips a beat when I see a file in Javier's hand with a picture of me on it. My heart palpitates, and my breath comes out in short raps as it dawns on me. Xandros lifts his head and locks eyes with me, and a guttural growl rips through him. His lips curl back revealing sharp canines, and his eyes become dark and demonic. His jaw is clenched and his nostrils flare, and a feral energy radiates from him. He looks like a wild animal, ready to attack. His entire body is tense, and his muscles spasm with barely contained rage. The air around him is charged with hostility and danger chilling me to the bone, a palpable reminder of the beast he can become.

In this moment, I know he knows who I am – not just as his mate, but as the daughter of traitors, traitors who betrayed his family.

As panic sets in, I glance at the exit, thinking of Toby's words and the possibility of freedom. Wishing I ran when I had the chance, that I escaped with Toby. Now I'll be lucky to escape with my life. Xandros's voice slices through the air, filled with rage. "Don't you fucking dare think about it!"

My instincts kick in. Fight or flight has already taken over, and my body moves on its own. I turn and sprint for the fire exit, my legs carrying me faster than I've ever run before. The sound of Xandros's growl and the chaos in the club fade as I burst through the door and into the cool night air.

As I push my way through the bustling people, I can feel their sneers and glares. The streetlights seem too bright and they overwhelm my senses. My fear only rises as I make my way through the streets running as fast as I can, running off pure adrenaline. The smell of garbage and exhaust fumes linger in the air, along with blood and the sickening scents of too many colognes. I can hear the distant sound of a train, and cars honking their horns as I dart across the alleyway, a cab narrowly missing me. Glancing over my shoulder I see the crowds of people parting as Xandros chases after me.

I run through the streets, my heart hammering in my chest, knowing Xandros is not far behind me. My lungs are burning, still fear keeps propelling me forward. I take turn after turn, trying to lose him. I know it's only a matter of time before he catches up.

Taking a sharp turn, I find myself cornered in a dark alleyway. "No!" I gasp, staring up at the tall apartment building encasing me, and dumpsters blocking off the alleyway at the end I took the wrong one. The smell of damp trash and my desperation fill the air with each ragged breath I take. I glance around. There's nowhere left to run—no way to escape the fate that's been chasing me since I left the club. I turn, seeing Xandros rush past the end of the alleyway, only to stop. I press my back against the cold brick wall, my breath coming in ragged gasps, as I wait for Xandros to find me which is mere seconds when his fluorescent eyes glow back at me as they lock on mine.

A growl tears out of him that raises goosebumps on my arms as he stands there, at the entrance to the alley, his eyes burning with fury. I know I can't escape him now, and I brace myself for whatever comes next. He stalks toward me, his steps calculated and menacing. Within the blink of an eye, he stands beside me, moving with a speed that is impossible to track.

"You thought you could just run away, Sienna?" he snarls, his face inches from mine. I feel his breath, hot and heavy, on my skin. "You really thought you could escape me?"

I tremble, fear and desperation coursing through me. "I-I'm not my parents, Xandros. Please, you have to believe me."

His expression darkens further, and he grabs my arm, his grip like iron. "You think I care about that? You think that changes anything?"

I let out a whimper, feeling the tears well up in my eyes. "Please, Xandros, I was a baby. What they did had nothing to do with me."

He laughs bitterly, the sound cold and unforgiving. "It's too late for that, Sienna. You should have told me the moment I met you, instead you tried to hide it."

My heart aches at his words, and I know any hope of convincing him otherwise is slipping away. "Xandros, I wanted none of this. I didn't choose who my parents were. Can't you see that?"

He steps closer, his eyes searching mine, as my back digs painfully into the brick and for a moment, I think I see a flicker of doubt in his gaze. Just as quickly, it vanishes, replaced by the steely cold eyes of a man I know who wants nothing more than to kill me.

The alleyway feels even colder, and I can't stop the shivers that wrack my body. "Did you think I wouldn't find out? I bet you thought it was hilarious keeping that from me. You're a traitor to the kingdom, my kingdom! I fucking marked you!" Xandros roars, his face twisting with rage, the veins in his neck bulging with his fury. I cringe at his anger. My heart skips frantically, erratically, palpating harder with each passing second.

"I'm not my parents, Xandros," I plead, my voice shaking, tears streaming down my face. "I never killed your aunt. I'm not responsible for their actions." His fist connects with the brickwork next to my head, a chunk breaking off, and I flinch.

"This is why Mal wouldn't tell me who you are! You all lied to me!" he screams in my face, his voice echoing off the walls of the alley, filling the air with palpable tension. He grabs my arm with crushing force and starts dragging me back down the street. The people in the street watch in horror and fascination as I stumble and try to keep up with his furious pace.

"I won't have a traitor for a mate," he spits, shoving me forward and pointing to the limo at the end of the street, where I can see the driver opening the back door. "Walk. I can barely look at you, let alone touch you."

I glance around nervously, desperately looking for a way out; the path is lined with people, all staring at me with disgust and hatred, having overheard his yelling and accusations. "Try it. Run and I'll break your legs!" Xandros snarls, shoving me again when I hesitate.

As I make my way back to the limo, people sneer and call me a traitor. Someone even spits on me, and a few others throw things, hitting me with painful accuracy. I shriek when a lit cigarette hits my cheek, slapping frantically as it rolls between my cleavage and burns me. I gasp through the pain but am shoved abruptly from behind by Xandros forcing me to keep moving. My cheeks burn with shame. As I reach the car, I look over at Toby's club across the road and see him standing there, watching the scene unfold, his eyes filled with some indecipherable expression, arms folded across his broad chest.

"Get in the car," Xandros snarls, gripping my hair and yanking me toward the open door. I cry out, hands gripping as strands of my hair pull painfully from my scalp. Tears sting my eyes. Toby clenches his jaw and disappears back inside his club; he's powerless to help me or maybe is not wanting to, I'm unable to tell. Xandros shoves me into the back of the limo harshly, my head bouncing off the corner of the door with a loud thud, causing me to hit my head on the door frame. Pain explodes through my skull.

"Be gentle, Xandros. You're hurting her," Javier says, his voice filled with concern, trying to reason with my volatile mate.

"You lied to me, kept this hidden. You should have told me the moment you suspected anything! Don't tell me what to do with her!" Xandros snaps his anger a living, breathing thing, consuming anything that can be considered a redeemable quality, leaving nothing but the monster, the ruthless cruel Lycan King.

I wipe the blood from my forehead that is trickling warmly down my face where the door cut me open. Then Xandros slides into the back of the limo with me, slamming the door shut.

Fear sits in the pit of my stomach, a heavyweight that threatens to crush and suffocate me. Xandros's rage is a dark storm cloud that fills the small space of the limo. He clutches his hair and punches the seat, over and over, his breaths coming in ragged gasps, his knuckles turning white. I tuck my knees to my chest, my hand gripping the door handle as the limo navigates the windy streets and abrupt traffic that keeps stopping and going. The leather chairs, slashed to pieces where his claws have torn through them, the stuffing spilling onto the floor, covering the floor with white tufts of cushioning.

"What have I done?" he repeats, his voice barely a whisper now, cracking under the weight of his emotions. "What have I fucking done?"

As the limo starts to move, I stare at the floor, my vision blurred by tears, while feeling my blood trickle down from my hairline, the wound throbbing with its own pulse. I try to make sense of the chaos and heartbreak that has become my life. Just when I think I'm managing to survive this nightmare everyone calls life, I am thrown another curve ball. I wonder what the future will hold for me, or if I am doomed to suffer for the sins of my parents.

The car ride is torturous, each passing minute stretching into eternity as I feel the pressure of Xandros's anger bearing down on me. His ragged breathing is the only sound in the limo, making the silence even more oppressive. I flinch every time he punches the seat, or growls, fearing his anger might redirect toward me at any moment as I press closer to the door as if I can mold or blend into it.

The tension is thick, suffocating me, and I feel like I can't breathe. I wrap my arms around myself.

Chapter Twelve

Sienna

The drive home is an unending torment, my heart pounding in my chest as my thoughts spiral into the darkest recesses of my mind. I wonder what will happen next. I wonder if Xandros will kill me or cast me aside like a worthless object. I can only pray for the latter. The tension in the limo is suffocating, and I feel as if I'm trapped in a nightmare I can't escape, no matter how hard I try. The castle lights come into view as the driver turns on the never-ending driveway, trees lining each side as the pebbles crackle under the car's weight as we pass through the tall iron gates.

When we finally arrive at the castle, Xandros hops out of the car, leaving me to sit there, trembling uncontrollably. He leans back in and growls, his voice dripping with venom, "Get out of the car, Sienna." I whimper and flinch at the sound of his voice, my entire body trembling with fear.

"Get out!" he screams, his fury echoing through the air like a thunderclap as his fist comes down on the roof of the limo, denting the steel. Guards rush out of the doors, followed by his mother, Queen Adina, and father, King Rehan. As if this night couldn't get any worse, now I will be forced to face the woman whose sister was brutally murdered by my parents.

"Xandros, what is going on?" his mother asks, panic tainting her voice. His mother stands near the car door wearing a pair of silky pajamas and her hair is in curlers. She looks like a normal woman and not the regal queen she is used to being seen as. Despite the panic in her voice, her posture is still tall and proud, and her eyes are still sharp, taking in what's going on.

"Nothing, Mother. Go inside," he tells her. His mother glances into the car and sees me bleeding, her lips parting in shock at my face which I know must be a mess of tears and blood.

"Xandros!" she scolds, moving toward the door. He grabs her arm with a snarl. "I said to go inside," he growls, his aura crackling around him like a storm.

His father gets in his face, his voice raised in anger. "You dare speak to your mother like that!" Xandros growls right back at him, his eyes blazing with fury. It is impossible to deny the uncanny resemblance he shares with his father, though his father is far older, despite still looking only in his forties. Lycans age far slower, and I know the man is at least from the medieval days, though his age I can't be sure of. His father, however, resembles a Viking king, his face angry, tough, his demeanor much the same as he challenges his son.

"Then get your wife inside because speaking is far from what I feel like doing right now, Father," he warns. King Rehan wears blue plaid pajamas. His red robe falls to the ground behind him when Carina saunters out, a smug smile on her face. Her slim figure accentuated by her short, silky slip pajamas. The thin fabric clings to her body, her nipples hard beneath it, giving her a seductive aura. Her dark hair cascading down her back, her smokey eye, and her full lips make her look dangerously gorgeous despite the bed clothes she is wearing.

"Looks to me like Xandros just found out about his little mate's true identity. Bet you're glad I didn't sign those divorce papers now, right, Xandros?" she mocks, her voice a seductive purr.

"What is going on?" his mother demands, her eyes darting between Xandros and Carina.

"Nothing! Inside. I will come to see you in a minute," he snarls at her before turning his gaze to Carina.

"You knew?" he accuses, his voice filled with betrayal.

"Of course I knew who she was. You forget whose family executed them! She smells exactly like her mother! I should know; I've tasted her, though I wonder if her daughter tastes as bitter as that bitch did!" Carina sneers, her words cutting through me like a knife.

"Sienna, out now!" Xandros commands, and I obey, my legs trembling as I step out of the car. He seizes my arm, and his mother asks, "Wait, who's her mother?" she asks, looking at her son, but it is Carina who is all too eager to tell her.

"Rosaline Draven," Carina tells her, her voice dripping with disdain. My blood runs cold as the weight of her words settles over me. I swallow hard as Queen Adina turns slowly to look at me with shock. "Draven?" she stutters, her eyes wide with disbelief. She looks to her son, searching for confirmation.

Xandros clenches his teeth, his jaw tight with anger. Adina's gaze turns murderous as it settles on me. Her hand whips out faster than I can track, her claws raking down my face. Her claws slice through my flesh like razors. Blood spurts everywhere, coating me in the warm, coppery liquid.

I cry out, my face burning as I clutch it, while Xandros just stands there, his expression unreadable. Javier looks away, his face a mask of something I can't decipher, and King Rehan looks on in shock. Carina's smug smile widens as she folds her arms across her chest, pushing her breasts up.

"Put her in the fucking dungeons," Queen Adina snarls before storming off into the castle. Instantly, guards step forward and grab me, their grips like iron bands wrapping around my arms. I struggle in their hold, their grips are like shackles, tight and unrelenting, only growing stronger the more I struggle. "No, please! I didn't do anything," I beg. My cries fall on deaf ears and Carina smiles smugly like she just won some prize I wasn't aware we were competing for. I cry out at their bone crushing grips, my vision tainted by the blood getting in my eyes as I panic.

More guards race forward to seize me, their grip like iron on my battered body as they grab my legs. I stare at Xandros. Desperation etched on my face and is audible in my voice. "Xandros, please, I am your mate," I beg, my voice trembling.

"I can't have a traitor as a mate," he says. His voice is cold and detached as if our bond means nothing to him. He looks away, his expression unreadable. My heart shatters into a thousand pieces at his dismissal and I stop fighting, knowing it's pointless.

My eyes dart to Carina, who saunters over to Xandros, looping her arm through his. I take one last look at Xandros before turning away. Tears sting my eyes, but I refuse to let them fall. I take a deep breath. "Come, love, let's clean you up," she purrs at him, her voice dripping with satisfaction.

Xandros shrugs Carina off and storms off inside, abandoning me at the mercy of the guards.

They drag me around the side of the castle to a massive concrete building hidden among the dark, foreboding forest. The forest is dark and oppressive, with thick trees that block out most of the moonlight. The guards are gruff and unsympathetic, their grips bruising my arms as they drag me along. My feet can barely keep up, and my shoes are lost in the process. I can feel my toes scraping against the rough ground when I trip, landing on my hip, yet they don't stop, not even giving me a chance to get back to my feet, instead dragging me harshly across the landscape. Each movement sends a sharp pain through my body. Despite my struggles, the guards hold me firmly, not allowing me to escape.

As I approach the dungeons, I am filled with a sense of dread. The air is heavy and still, the trees looming over me like silent sentinels. The entrance to the dungeons is a heavy, iron door, and the windows are barred. The walls are thick and made of cold, gray stone, and the only light comes from a few torches flickering in the darkness. It is a haunting and domineering sight, and my heart sinks at the thought of being trapped within its walls.

They open a huge metal door that leads to a set of stairs. I see nothing, only darkness as we descend the stairs, my feet aching from the cold, which only gets worse the deeper we get. The place is freezing, like I've been chucked inside a freezer.

The dungeons are filthy, the air damp and heavy with the scent of mold and whatever other excrement; a sewer would smell more appealing than this place. They drag me down the stairs, their grip unyielding, and chuck me into a cell with a small window. This is the only source of light in this bleak, lonely place. The window is so high I can only see outside if I stand on my tiptoes, straining my neck to catch a glimpse of the world outside, not that the world out there offers anything to me—it never has.

The guards lock me in, their laughter echoing off the walls as they leave. I realize with a pang of despair there isn't even a bed in the cell—nothing but a cold, grime-covered concrete floor and a filthy toilet in the corner. There are cobwebs and spiders in every corner, and the sound of rats scurrying around is ever-present. The walls are stained with blood, the shackles and chains hanging in the cell across from me are a reminder of the horrors that await me if I dare to attempt to escape. I huddle against the damp stone wall, trying to warm myself. However, the dungeon chill seeps into my bones, and I can't stop shivering.

As I sit there in the darkness, my thoughts race with fear and despair. I can't believe Xandros, my mate, abandoned me so easily. Was our bond truly worth nothing to him? I wonder what will happen to me now, locked away in this cold, dark cell. Will I be left here to rot, forgotten and alone? Or will they decide I am too dangerous to be left alive? Tears stream down my face as I contemplate my fate. All I can do is wait and hope for the best while knowing there will be no best outcome. I close my eyes, taking in a shaky breath.

Tears fill my eyes, and I can't hold them back any longer. As they stream down my face, I realize I am truly on my own, left to face the consequences of a past I was never a part of. The pain in my chest is a constant ache, a reminder of Xandros's careless dismissal.

The darkness of the cell presses in on me, suffocating me with its oppressive weight—the cold seeps into my very soul, chilling me to the core. I hear the howls of wild wolves in the forest, and the taunting laughter of the guards who stand outside the small barred window serving as a haunting reminder of the fate that could await me.

I clench my fists, and the pain grounds me as I try to regather myself, knowing my crying is only bringing the guards outside something to mock me further for. My heart races, and I feel my face flush as I try to regain my composure and focus on the present. I take a deep breath and open my eyes. For a moment, I'm able to forget the pain as I focus on my breathing and the smoke clouds that fill the air with each breath.

Chapter Thirteen

Xandros

The guilt of abandoning Sienna is like a crushing weight on my chest, suffocating me, threatening to consume and destroy me. The look on her face when I didn't defend her will forever haunt me, along with the scars I know she now bears from my mother's hand.

The mate bond between us screams out in agony, causing me pain I can't ignore. Frustration courses through me like a raging river, threatening to sweep me away and drown me in its rapids.

I wander into the billiard room, my footsteps heavy and echoing in the silence as I pace the floor trying to make sense of the events that took place. The more it nags at me the more enraged and betrayed I feel.

I make a beeline for the bar, desperately hoping the amber liquid within the bottles can drown out the torment that consumes me. I pour myself a drink. The clink of the ice against the glass is a stark reminder of the coldness I showed Sienna. I take a sip, and the burn of the alcohol is nothing compared to the pain in my heart. I take another sip, and the tears that have been threatening to fall burn my eyes. I know I'll never be able to forgive myself for what I did.

As I take another sip, my mother storms into the room, her anger palpable, her dressing gown billowing behind her as she storms into the room like a raging storm.

"Xandros, you cannot keep her here. She's a traitor, the daughter of the woman who killed my sister! I want her gone!" she exclaims, her voice shrill and laced with venom. Her eyes blaze with her need for revenge, and her need to hurt my mate.

"And you know it's not that simple. She's my mate!" I snap back, my voice strained and filled with anguish.

"She doesn't deserve to be your mate, Xandros. She should be executed for her family's crimes!" she argues, her eyes filled with fire and fury. My father moves to try to calm her down. She shrugs him off, stepping away, her gaze cutting through him.

"Adina, you know Xandros can't kill her now that he's marked her. It would destroy him," my father interjects, attempting to diffuse the volatile situation. My mother is beyond listening to reason.

"I don't care! I won't have that woman as my daughter-in-law!" my mother yells, her face flushed with her burning anger.

"This isn't about what you want! I have to figure out what to do with her. I can't break the fucking bond you're asking for the impossible!" I reply, my voice rising in frustration at the situation I've found myself trapped in.

"Figure something out? You should have never let it get this far, Xandros!" she accuses, her eyes blazing with disappointment and rage.

"I didn't know, Mother! None of us knew!" I shout back, feeling my control slip away like sand through my fingers.

"You should have looked into her before marking her," my mother persists, her voice dripping with contempt.

"She was fucking dying. There wasn't time for me to look into her background!" I scream back at her. She goes to speak again, and I lose my temper, my fist coming down on the bar, the bottles on the shelf rattling loudly.

"Enough!" I roar, my patience finally snapping like a brittle branch in a hurricane. In a fit of fury, I hurl my whiskey glass at the fireplace, causing it to explode in a shower of glass and flames. The sound echoes throughout the room like the shattering of my resolve.

My chest is filled with a swirling mix of emotions: anger, frustration and fear. My parents are frozen in fear, taken aback by the sheer force of my outburst. The billiard room is eerily silent, the only sound being the crackling of the fireplace from the broken glass that now lies scattered across the floor. My anger and frustration swirl within me like a tornado, threatening to consume me.

I glance around the billiard room, my parents' fear of me palpable in the air. I can feel their judgment and disapproval pressing down on me like a heavy weight. I want to scream, to lash out and break something, anything, to make the feelings go away. Instead, I just stand there, silent and livid, as the fire from the fireplace crackles and burns. After a while, the silence in the room becomes deafening and unbearable.

I storm out of the room, leaving my mother and father behind, their voices fading into the distance like the ghosts of my past. As I stalk through the empty corridors, the weight of the situation bears down on me, my chest tight and my breath shallow. No matter what I do, someone will be hurt, and I can't shake the feeling it's all my fault.

My heart aches for Sienna, the woman I've marked as my own, now locked away in the depths of the dungeons, her pain echoing through me, her fear evident in the sinking hole in my stomach. The darkness that surrounds her seeps into me, clawing at my very soul. And yet, my mother's words ring in my ears, the haunting memory of a past impossible to escape.

I find myself torn between loyalty to my family and the bond I share with Sienna, a connection that defies logic and reason. The storm within me rages, threatening to tear me apart as I struggle to find a way through this impossible maze of emotions and consequences. It takes me ages to come back to my surroundings, not realizing in my anger I have gone back to my old quarters, a room I shared with her and I can still feel her presence in the room, as if she is still here with me.

Chapter Fourteen

Sienna

Days in the dungeon meld together into an endless, torturous nightmare, punctuated only by the gnawing hunger that twists my insides into knots, the thirst that burns my dry throat. By the third day, my body screams for sustenance, my throat parched, and my lips cracked and bleeding. I'm filthy and freezing. While the pain from the mate bond is like a thousand knives stabbing into my heart, only adding to the agony I am already in.

My thoughts swirl around me like a tornado, a storm of fear and confusion. Is Xandros truly going to let me waste a way down here? Has he forgotten me already? Does his bond not scream out in agony, as mine does? Each moment stretches into an eternity, despair wrapping its icy fingers around my soul, choking me with its suffocating grip.

Suddenly, the sound of the door creaking open shatters the silence I've been trapped in for days and I scramble to the far corner of the cell, trembling with fear, wondering if this is when I die. Panic grips me like a vice, and I brace myself for whatever fresh horror awaits. Then, Xandros's scent reaches me, and my heart lurches in my chest. My bond crying out in relief. He's come to release me; he's finally seen reason.

He steps into the dungeon, carrying a tray laden with food and a jug of water. His eyes once filled with warmth, now look upon me with disbelief and horror at my pitiful state as I stare up at him. His gaze sweeps around the cell, taking in the squalor, and he turns to the guard who accompanied him.

"No blankets?" he asks, his voice tight with anger. The guard takes a hesitant step away from him, Xandros's deadly aura filling the cold space, making the air chillier than it was a second ago.

"Your mother said no one was allowed in or out," the guard explains, his voice quivering.

"What about feeding her?" Xandros questions, his frustration boiling over, and the veins in his neck press under his skin as his eyes blaze.

The guard shakes his head, unable to meet his gaze. "You mean she hasn't eaten?" Xandros's eyes narrow, and the guard shakes his head once more. Xandros growls, snatching the keys from the guard and passing him the tray.

As Xandros steps into the cell, I rush toward him, desperate for the comfort of his touch, his scent, anything to stop the burning cold ache of the bond. Like frostbite, it burns my soul.

Xandros remains frozen and stiff, only growling at me as I bury my face in his chest. He pries my arms off him and a whimper escapes me when he shoves me away so hard I hit the wall, the air escaping me at the force he used. My body crumples on the floor.

"Don't touch me!" he snaps, and my stomach sinks in response to his cold words. He's not here for me, he's not releasing me from this torturous nightmare.

The guard walks in and sets the tray on the ground. My gaze darts to the jug of water, and I reach for it with trembling hands. All the while Xandros watches me like I'm trash he found in a gutter. Clutching the jug, I retreat to the corner I was huddled in, gulping down the water as if it were the elixir of life.

Xandros uses his foot to slide the food tray toward me. I snatch a bread roll and look up at him, pleading with my eyes for some shred of compassion or mercy.

He turns and walks out, leaving me alone in this cold, bitter place. Desperation claws at me, and I call out to him, racing toward the bars and clutching them. "Please, please don't leave me here." He pauses for a second, then growls and continues walking, abandoning me once more. The sound of the dungeon door closing echoes loudly, making me realize how truly alone I am here. I stagger back to my corner, the only one that isn't wet from the dewy air and leaking pipes.

Ravenous, I devour half the food on the tray before stopping, realizing I must ration it, not knowing when my next meal will come. My stomach rumbles with hunger, and I'm already out of water because I stupidly drank every drop, leaving me feeling weak and even more helpless.

As the day turns to night, sleep eludes me once again, my body aching from the cold unforgiving floor, and sores taint my skin from the abrasiveness of the rough ground. My face, though thankfully no longer burning from the slashes, is still marred and rough around the edges. Staring at the barred window, I can tell it's snowing outside because a small pile of snow has gathered on the floor under the window. Desperate for water, I grab my jug and crawl to it. I scoop some of the snow into my jug, praying it will melt and provide me with a few sips.

I huddle in the corner, my teeth chattering, and I'm shivering uncontrollably from the freezing cold. My heart aches with the pain of betrayal, and the overwhelming feeling of helplessness washes over me like a tidal wave. The abandonment of my mate, the harsh treatment from his family, and the uncertainty of my future all weigh heavily on my mind, crushing me painfully.

My thoughts drift to Xandros, and I wonder if he feels any guilt about leaving me like this. Does the bond between him and me not cause him pain, as it does me? The unanswered questions and the lack of connection to him leave me feeling even more lost and alone.

As I curl up tighter, trying to preserve any remaining warmth, the cold seeps into my bones, leaving me shivering and weak. My soul feels shattered, and the depressing darkness of the dungeon only heightens the misery that has settled over me like a blanket.

Chapter Fifteen

Xandros

The hollow look in Sienna's eyes haunts me, the smell of her fear mocks me, and the state I found her in taunts and nags at me.

The weight of my impatience bears down on me as I pace the billiard room, awaiting my mother's return. With each passing second, the walls close in around me, suffocating me with their extravagance, as my anger simmers just beneath the surface, a volcano ready to erupt.

The ticking of the grandfather clock in the corner grates against my nerves. Each tick is a reminder of Sienna's suffering. The gilded furniture, the velvet curtains, and the expensive artwork all serve to remind me of my family's wealth and power and the fact that with all that power, I've failed to help my mate, failed to help Sienna.

The sound of laughter from the other room serves as a reminder of how carefree the rest of the castle is while Sienna is enduring pain and suffering. The smell of cigars and brandy in the air further reinforces the disconnect between my life and the reality of Sienna's condition.

Finally, the door swings open, and my mother and Carina stride in, their arms laden with shopping bags and chattering excitedly about the upcoming wedding. My nostrils flare as the scent of their perfume fills the room, a sickly-sweet reminder of the life I'm expected to live with that woman on my arm, a woman I do not desire to be with. Rage boils within me, and I storm forward, seizing my mother's arm.

"Xandros?" my mother startles and drops her bags on the giant billiard table. My father walks in behind them and immediately moves to get between us.

"You've been starving her!" I snarl at my mother, my voice shaking with fury. My father steps back; shock etched across his face. "Adina, is this true?"

My mother's eyes flash with anger as she defends her actions. "She should be grateful she's still breathing! She'd be dead if I had my way!"

"How can you be so heartless? She's not responsible for what her parents did!" I shout, the anguish in my voice palpable as those words settle around me.

"And yet, she is of their blood! Their sins are a part of her!" my mother retorted, her voice cold and venomous.

"I can't leave her down there. It's killing me! If she dies, I'll die!" I plead, desperation clawing at my throat.

"Why should I care for her? She deserves nothing!" she snaps, her eyes blazing with a fire that matches my own.

"Enough!" my father interjects, his voice weary. "We cannot let our emotions dictate our actions."

My mother pulls out of my grip.

Carina steps forward, drawing our attention to her. For a split second, I forgot she was even in the room.

"May I suggest something?" she asks, her voice dripping with what I can only call false sweetness. Everyone turns to look at her.

"Xandros needs his mate since he has marked her already. Maybe we should let her back into the castle. She can stay in Xandros's old quarters."

My mother shakes her head, her anger still simmering. "So, we just let her get away with what her parents did? Treat her like a queen! Let her carry on and be at his side?" I remain quiet. Part of me wants her—Sienna—closer, so I want to hear this so-called idea of Carina's. That sweetness to her tone wears off a little when I see her lips quirk in the corners.

Carina shakes her head, feigning innocence. "No, put her to work.

Make her earn her luxuries like food and a warm bed. Make her a servant. Better yet, let me have her as my handmaiden," Carina suggests, and I scoff; I don't want her near Sienna.

"No!" I snarl, my protective instincts flaring.

I turn to Carina, suspicion gnawing at me. "Why would you suggest that, Carina? What's your angle here?" I narrow my eyes at her— scrutinize her— searching for hidden motives.

Carina's face remains a mask of innocence. "I simply want to help, Xandros. It's clear you need her close. I only thought this would be a suitable compromise for everyone," she states, and I raise my eyebrows. I've known this woman for far too long and can tell when she is lying.

My mother cuts me off before I can argue further, her voice cold and unyielding. "No, I will accept this. You want her close? Fine, but on my terms. You can keep your mate, Xandros. She is Carina's handmaiden, a servant, and nothing more!". My mother snatches her bags from the billiard table quickly and storms out of the room. My father sighs heavily, following her which leaves me with Carina. I instantly turn on her gripping her neck. "What are you playing at?" I demand.

"You want your mate, and I want the marriage to go ahead. It's a win-win for both of us. Your mother would not have let you keep her as your maid. However, she knows I hate her just as much, and therefore, you keep your mate, and the treaties between our kingdoms remain strong," Carina tells me. "Now, love, I would appreciate it if you would unhand me before this turns into our first lover's quarrel."

I let her go, watching her for a second, she turns to the bags she brought in as if nothing at all just happened. She pulls out two pieces of silk cloth. "Which one? Cream or white?"

"Excuse me?"

"I don't like the tablecloths, and I am changing them from royal blue. Which ones, you can choose?" she tells me, and I point to one randomly, not caring for tablecloths. Carina smiles and pecks my cheek before sauntering out. All the while, I think it should be Sienna choosing, she is the woman I should be meeting at the end of the aisle, not a woman I feel nothing for.

Chapter Sixteen

Sienna

The night I hoped would be uneventful turns into one of my biggest nightmares as pain erupts suddenly, tearing through my body with a ferocity that leaves me gasping for breath, every nerve ending ablaze. Helplessness crashes over me like a tidal wave, and terror clutches at my heart as I struggle to understand what's happening to me, feeling so utterly alone as the pain intensifies and grows worse, every bone aching like they are thickening and stretching, pulling from the sockets. The coldness of this place only adds to the aching of my bones.

As my body begins to contort and change, I focus on the sensations, trying to make sense of the incomprehensible. My bones crack and shift, and my muscles twist and reform beneath my skin with agonizing slowness that has me passing out only to come to with the next enduring crack. The pain is indescribable, like being ripped apart and stitched back together all at once. My vision blurs then sharpens, colors and shapes appearing more vividly than ever before, as though the world has come alive in ways I never thought possible. With new clarity, that is both mesmerizing and terrifying.

My hearing becomes more sensitive, and I can now pick up on the faintest of sounds echoing through the dungeons—the distant dripping of water, the scurrying of unseen rodents in the shadows. The scent of damp and decay is overwhelming, making me want to throw up, the stench invades my senses like a suffocating potent cloud. The stench burns my nose and throat. I can taste it.

My body grows larger, and more powerful. The horrifying realization dawns on me that I'm shifting into a Lycan. Into a monster. A monster he made me into. Panic surges through my veins, the fear of the unknown gnawing at my sanity while ripping apart my insides.

As my transformation completes, I take a shaky moment to explore my new form. My senses are heightened beyond anything I've ever experienced, the world around me seems both familiar and entirely alien. I have an undeniable strength coursing through me, a power I've never known before and it terrifies me, because I do not know what it means or what it might bring let alone how to use these new senses without hurting myself.

However, with this newfound power comes an increased sensitivity to the bond between Xandros and me; it's like a dam wall has burst open, tidal waves of emotion so strong it steals the breath from my lungs and nearly brings me to my knees.

The pain of our separation is unbearable, a constant ache that threatens to consume me entirely. I have an urgent need to be near him, to seek comfort and security in his arms. However, I know I am trapped in this cold, dark cell, a prisoner of fate. A prisoner of his. I'm no one. Only an unwanted bond.

Fear and pain continue to course through me. However, I can't ignore the feeling that this transformation has unlocked a part of myself that was always hidden away, waiting to be discovered. I am both fascinated and repulsed by the creature I have become, torn between the power and the darkness that now resides within me.

The walls of the dungeon seem to close in around me, suffocating any hope of escape. The torment of my isolation is amplified by the maddening knowledge that Xandros is somewhere above me, beyond my reach, with his wife. Desperation claws at my soul, and I struggle to adapt to my new reality. My heart is heavy with the weight of my uncertainty. There's a new thing to contend with: trying to decipher the emotions I can feel emanating through the bond, the touch that belongs to Princess Carina, her caresses, though unwanted, I can feel like she is pawing at my body, my soul tugging painfully. I know I will have to eventually accept her presence.

I can't bring myself to do it. I can feel the pain emanating from my soul, a pain that only I can understand. I must find a way to cope with my reality, yet it is cruel that he expects me to live with her like this, living with knowing it's her on his arm, while I rot in this cell.

As I wrestle with the depression that threatens to engulf me, I can only hope one day Xandros and I will find a way to heal the rift between us and embrace the bond that fate has forged between us. Until then, I remain a prisoner—not only of these cold, unforgiving walls but of the bond we share together. I haven't even marked him yet. My teeth ache to do so, and my bond tugs at me, too.

My fingertips graze over my teeth, razor sharp and deadly. Then my clawed hands linger on the mark on my neck, the one he gave me, a mark I'll never be able to give him. I can feel his presence, his scent, his soul. I can practically feel the warmth of his touch, even if he's not here with me. I can almost hear his voice, whispering in my ear, telling me everything will be alright when I know it won't be. It is hard to fathom that without having marked him the bond could be so violently strong already.

I wipe my eyes as tears spill, the saltiness I can smell in the air, the slashes marring my face from his mother feel rough, crinkled in this form, some part of me hoped they would heal, but feeling them beneath my furry fingertips I feel the scars with so much more definition.

Chapter Seventeen

Xandros

I pace the floor in my room, my heart pounding in my chest as Carina and I argue about her suggestion to have Sienna as her handmaiden. I still can't wrap my head around it.

"How could you even suggest such a thing?" I demand, my voice shaking with fury.

Carina stares at me, her eyes filled with judgment, and for a second, I actually thought she truly did have feelings for me.

"Xandros, I'm trying to be understanding and be merciful. Allowing her to be my handmaiden will let you keep your mate close while we maintain the alliances between our families."

I grit my teeth, torn between my love for Sienna and the hatred I feel for her parents. She's the daughter of monsters, and yet, the bond between us is undeniable.

"I can't believe she's the daughter of the people who destroyed my mother, destroyed me," I argue, my voice heavy with emotion.

Carina sighs, placing a hand on my arm. "I know, Xandros. But doing this will allow you to remain strong and our marriage to go ahead. Only a few people will know of her existence."

I stare at her.

"Those who know we can force quiet."

I shake my head, struggling with the conflicting emotions swirling inside me. "How can I accept that, knowing the truth about her family? How can I deny her when she is in front of me?"

Carina's eyes fill with tears as she pleads, "Please, Xandros, we can find a way to make this work." I stare at her. This woman never shows emotion, yet the idea of me canceling the wedding seems to petrify her.

As I'm about to respond, a crippling pain tears through me, stemming from the mate bond. The bond strengthens beyond comprehension, and the pain is so intense it brings me to my knees.

Carina rushes to my side, her eyes filled with concern. "Xandros, are you okay? What's happening?"

I gasp for breath, struggling to speak. "The mate bond... Something's wrong."

Carina's eyes widen when she looks out the window. "The full moon is tonight, Xandros. She must be shifting for the first time."

My heart races with panic at the thought of Sienna going through such a transformation alone. Carina bites her lip, then speaks softly, "Go... go be with her."

I stare at her in shock, noticing a single tear rolling down her cheek. "Carina?"

"I get it, Xandros," she says, her voice trembling. "I understand, and I may not like it, but it can't be helped. It's fine. Just go. I'm going to take a shower, anyway."

Torn by her strange actions and the need to be with my mate, I hesitate for a moment before making my decision. I rush to the dungeons, finding Sienna shifting back into her human form, naked and covered in blood from her painful transformation.

Her head snaps up as I enter, her eyes glowing a fluorescent green. She looks desperate, longing to touch me, yet all I can see when I look at her is the face of the woman who destroyed my mother. The memory of that betrayal cuts through me like a knife, and I struggle to contain the anger bubbling inside me.

I speak coldly, trying to ignore my heartache.

"You'll be brought back to the castle tomorrow, and there will be rules." My voice is harsher than intended.

"Please, Xandros, please don't leave me," Sienna begs as I turn to leave. Turning back to look at her, the desperation on her face... I can't stand the sight of her broken form, so I open her cell door. She flinches, moving away from me despite the desire to touch me that I can feel emanating from her.

"Get up," I order, stepping back out of the cell. She hesitates for a moment before finally standing and moving toward the door.

"Now! Before I change my mind," I snap, and she moves faster than I've ever seen her move before.

As she rushes toward me, she wraps her arms around me, and I can't deny the feeling of comfort and warmth her embrace brings. The warmth of her body against mine is both soothing and electrifying, but the ghost of her family's actions haunts me. I start to wrap my arms around her in return, but the memory of her family's betrayal stops me. Gripping her hair, I shove her away.

"I didn't say you could touch me," I growl, turning away and walking up the stairs.

"I'm naked," she protests, her voice trembling.

I pause for a moment, my heart aching at the sight of her vulnerable state. Then, the anger and hurt resurface, fueling my resolve. "Not my problem," I tell her coldly, and I keep walking. If I give in to her, my mother will see it as special treatment and punish her worse than I am right now.

Sienna hesitates, then follows me with tears streaming down her face. As we climb the stairs, the weight of my decision weighs heavily on my chest, my heart a tangled mess of emotions. I know I'm hurting her, but my own pain and fear of what my mother will do have me conflicted. I'm trapped in a storm of conflicting feelings—love and hate, desire and fear, longing and anger.

When we reach the top of the stairs, I glance back at her, taking in the sight of her tear-streaked, filthy face, her eyes pleading for understanding and mercy. I want to reach out and comfort her, to tell her everything will be alright. The face of her mother, the woman responsible for my family's suffering, flashes in my mind, along with the tortured look on my mother's face when we found my aunt also does, and I can't bring myself to do it.

"You'll have a room in the castle," I say, my voice strained.

Sienna's eyes fill with tears, and she nods in acceptance. I watch her for a moment, my heart breaking with every tear that falls, knowing I am the one causing her pain. The scars of the past run too deep, and my loving her would put her at risk.

Chapter Eighteen

Sienna

Each agonizing step through the forest feels like I'm living a nightmare, my heart pounding wildly with fear. My newly heightened senses pick up every rustle and whisper, making the shadows dance menacingly around me, even the trees as their branches whip my skin. The darkness even more so; it's frightening with heightens senses, appearing to have no end as if threatening to swallow me whole. The further I walk, the more the darkness of the forest seems to close in, suffocating me as I follow Xandros, feeling like helpless prey led by a ruthless predator to its death.

Despite the terror clawing at me, I marvel at the haunting beauty of the castle grounds and gardens at night as we break out of the trees. Twinkling fairy lights are strung through the trees, casting a magical glow on the snow-covered ground, creating an eerie contrast to the sinister atmosphere that encases it. It is deathly beautiful.

The cold seeps through my bare feet right into my bones, and I shiver violently, my arms wrapped around myself in a futile attempt to ward off the freezing air that pierces my skin like a thousand icy needles, my toes numb from the snow and the cuts and grazes sting from the ice-cold air adding to my torture.

Xandros remains silent and unfeeling as we walk; his demeanor is as cold as the snow under my feet. His footsteps are resolute and unwavering, his callousness more chilling than the frigid air. He doesn't pause or glance back at me as I stumble over loose debris, and I know trying to run would be pointless. I feel a growing sense of dread as we approach the castle, as if he is walking me to the gallows, leading me to my demise.

My feet slow as we get closer, and I can see through the windows. Servants tending to their chores and people rushing around. When I spot the guards walking around the perimeter though, my heart sinks even further, weighed down by despair. My naked, filthy state is unbearable, and I pause, not wanting to go any closer, not wanting them to see me like this.

"Sienna!" Xandros calls out, his voice harsh and unforgiving, like the crack of a whip against my already battered soul. I wrap my arms tighter around myself as if they alone can cover me.

"Can I have your jacket?" I plead with him, my voice barely a whisper. I am desperate for even the smallest bit of coverage to shield me from the gazes that will inevitably follow. My vulnerability is tangible, and I can hardly bear it. I've never felt so exposed before in my life. He glances at me, his eyes running the length of me and he clenches his jaw then looks away as if disgusted by the sight of me.

He only snarls in response, "Hurry up," and continues walking, completely ignoring my request. His cruelty stings like a slap to the face, leaving me feeling more exposed and vulnerable than ever. This walk of shame is a torment beyond anything I have ever known as we near the path. The moment his feet crunch on the gravel all eyes turn our way.

With no other choice, I force myself to follow him, keeping my gaze fixed on the ground as I feel everyone's eyes on me. The burning shame within me intensifies. This walk of shame is a torturous trip that seems to stretch on forever.

When we finally reach my room, Xandros unlocks the door and steps aside, motioning for me to enter. I look at him. "Inside before I change my mind and make you walk back to the dungeons."

I hastily step over the threshold, wondering now if I was safer there. I walk in, my body trembling from the cold and humiliation. As I turn back to speak, he slams the door in my face and locks it, leaving me alone once again.

The sound of the lock clicking into place echoes through the room like a death bell calling for me, and I sink to the floor, my heart aching from the pain of Xandros's rejection and the crushing weight of my own shame. My loneliness feels like a living thing, wrapping its icy fingers around my heart and squeezing until I can hardly breathe.

The bond calls for its mate. How is one expected to live like this? It's vile and degrading, heartbreaking. Never in my life have I felt so weak, so small and it's not even my fault. The stupid bond beating inside me calling for that monster.

My soul dependent on him, it's truly sickening. I'd rather hate him then long for him; the bond could at least offer that small reprieve.

Unable to handle the empty, noiseless room, I decide to shower, yearning for the sensation of warm water to envelop my skin like a comforting embrace. A whimper escapes my lips as I place my hand under the water and find the water is hot. A small luxury, one I won't take for granted ever again.

Stepping under the water, it cascades down my body, washing away the dirt, the grime, and some of the humiliation I've been through.

If only it would wash away the bond and snuff it out of existence.

Cupping my hands under the water, I gulp it down greedily, letting the warmth seep into my bones and thaw my chilled insides. The scent of soap fills the room, along with my blood as it cascades from my hairline and from my face.

I scrub my blood-caked nails; it becomes an obsession as I try to remove the dirt and blood under them. I scrub myself raw, my skin burning with ferocity. Then I just stand there, staring at the tiled walls as if they alone will crack open and give me the answers I am so desperately wishing I had. Like how I can be blamed for my parents' actions. That makes no sense to me.

As the water runs over me, it feels like a baptism, a desperate attempt to cleanse myself of the unbearable pain I've endured. When I step out of the shower, I wrap a towel around myself and wander into the walk-in closet. I find some clothes and discover a shirt belonging to Xandros. It smells like him. One part of me wants to shred it because it reminds me of him. Another part of me wonders if it will help soothe the ache of the bond, so I slip it on, his scent does seem to help some, but not much. However, right now, any victory shall be celebrated no matter how small; even if it is only a shirt that stops the niggling longing even briefly.

Wrapped in the remnants of his scent, I feel both comforted and tormented by his absence. I venture out of the bathroom, searching for a way to warm the frigid room.

I find a small box of matches and huddle around the fireplace, desperately trying to ignite the wood. It's futile. The fire keeps going out, and I feel a surge of frustration, my desperation mirroring the dying embers. Striking the match once again, I hear the door handle twist, making me freeze as I turn my head.

Suddenly, the door opens. Xandros returns, and I freeze as I watch him pace, his every movement exuding anger and tension when my fingers suddenly burn, making me shake the match and drop it when it burns my fingers.

His presence is like a storm cloud, heavy and oppressive. I can feel the bond more intensely now, and it's as if it's tearing me apart from the inside wanting to get to him.

He starts rambling, his voice strained with the weight of his emotions. "This bond... It's unbearable." He grits his teeth, clenching his fists.

"I hate you, and still, I'm cursed to crave you." He grasps his hair and crouches on the spot, his breathing heavy. "How is that even possible?" he murmurs, then growls furiously.

"How can you have such a hold on me?" he snarls, lifting his head to glare at me. I remain silent, watching him as he struggles with his conflicting emotions. His anguish is a reflection of my own.

He then gets up, walking to his bar area, which I forgot about in my desperation to start the fire. He snatches a half-drunk liquor bottle, twists the cap off, and drinks from it, his eyes trained on me as he does. I stare at him like a deer in headlights.

He drains the bottle, and I sigh. *I could have made better use of it by setting this fire,* I think dryly.

"I can't sleep. I haven't slept in days. All I can think about is how you betrayed me. How you're the daughter of monsters!" I flinch at his anger as it spews out of him and he tosses the liquor bottle, it smashes against the walls, the sound hurting my ears as it shatters, making me clutch them.

"All I can fucking think about is how much I want you." He smashes the room up in a fit of rage, tossing the furniture as if it weighs nothing as he stalks toward me. His fury is a whirlwind of destruction that leaves me trembling with fear. I whimper, and he turns his attention to me. My eyes widen at my mistake, and I jump to my feet.

The storm in his eyes suddenly becomes more intense and frightening. When he grabs me, "This is your fucking fault!" He shakes me then he kisses me, pawing at my shirt, his touch rough and demanding. "Xandros!" I shriek when he rips my shirt.

"You're hurting me," I tell him. My voice is barely a whisper, but it's as if he doesn't hear me. "I want to sleep; I need sleep," he tells me, his voice desperate and raw.

"I need you." He kisses me again, and as much as I want to hurt him, I can't seem to deny the bond when instinct takes over, and I kiss him back, hoping he'll see I'm not my parents, hoping he'll soothe my aching bond.

He clutches me to him, kissing and licking me as he walks me backward. The back of my knees hit the bed, and I fall back onto it. Xandros stares at me hungrily, and I reach for him, seeking some semblance of comfort in the storm of his emotions.

Instead, he grips my ankles and flips me onto my stomach, dragging me to the edge of the bed. I push up off the bed, my toes digging into the carpet when he shoves me back down before undoing his pants and entering me from behind roughly.

Sparks rush over my skin, at his touch despite it being harsh, and I try to pull away and turn, wanting to touch him, to feel the warmth of his skin against mine, but he won't let me.

His thrusts are rough and unyielding. Once he's done, he leaves me there, exposed and used, like a discarded toy. "This changes nothing. You're still a traitor, and I will never forgive you." The words are like shards of glass, cutting deep into my already wounded heart.

He then leaves before I can even turn around to face him. The door clicks shut, and I sink to my knees, realizing I've been reduced to a bed toy.

I drag the blanket off the bed, wrapping it around myself and moving back to the fireplace, and picking up the box of matches to find only one left. I wish he could have at least started the fireplace for me or offered a kind word, some insignificant gesture to ease the unbearable pain that consumes me.

Instead, I lay there by the cold fireplace, cold and alone.

The bond is somewhat sated for now, but the painful reality remains—I am unwanted, unloved, and utterly broken. The once beautiful room is now a battlefield ravaged by our mutual torment and his destruction.

After a while, I find the energy to move, and I curl up on the bed, pulling the covers around me in a desperate attempt to find warmth in the icy void that has become my life.

The lingering scent of Xandros on the ripped shirt I wear is both a comfort and a curse. It is a constant reminder of the man who has become both my salvation and damnation.

As I lie in bed, the weight of the night presses down on me, suffocating me with the knowledge I am utterly alone in this world.

My thoughts are a whirlwind of pain and despair. Each memory of Xandros is a bitter reminder of the life we might have had if not for the sins of my family.

The ghosts of my past haunt me, whispering I am unworthy of love and that I will forever be tainted by the blood running through my veins.

As I lay there, shivering and broken, I wonder if I am doomed to remain locked in this endless cycle of pain and heartache, the weight of my parents' past sins forever dragging me down into the abyss.

I laugh at the next thought that flits through my mind. Only time will tell, and now I have all the time in the world, eternity. Fucking death would have been kinder than immortality living like this.

Chapter Nineteen

Xandros

I can feel the tension in the room rise as my parents begin to chat over dinner. Carina's gaze burns into me as I sit in awkward silence. However, my mind is solely focused on Sienna and how I treated her. I used her. There is no other word for it, and it sickens me. At the same time I shouldn't care for her. I hate her, I try to remind myself, yet that anger for her is blurred with my need for her.

Finally, my mother speaks up, breaking the tension.

"Are you alright, son?" she asks softly.

"I'm fine," I answer curtly.

Carina, however, has other ideas as she adds in her own commentary.

"Xandros brought Sienna back to the castle," she says, her eyes darting between me and my parents. "She'll start as my maid in the morning."

Anger rises within me as Carina looks in my direction, almost as if daring me to deny her words.

My mother nods as she takes a sip of her wine.

"Good, I'm being very tolerant, allowing her back in my castle," my mother says, her voice barely containing the contempt that is evident in her words.

"My castle," I snarl.

"Not until after the wedding. You may technically hold the title of king, but nothing formal has been announced yet, son."

My father's words do nothing to quell the emotions that are raging within me. I feel them boiling over as I glare at the table, thinking of my mate and the feeling of her in my arms.

I barely notice my parents engaging in conversation as I contemplate my situation. The night drags on, and the meal we are having consists of roasted duck, glazed carrots, and a side of creamy mashed potatoes.

My mother, an elegant woman with a regal manner, takes dainty bites while my father, a sturdy man with a stern face, digs in heartily. Carina, her hair cascading down her back and her green eyes gleaming, only picks at her food. Mostly because I know she already had blood, which suppresses a normal appetite.

Eventually, the meal is finished. Once I find enough reason to abandon the small talk, I excuse myself and quickly storm out of the dining hall, heading back to my room.

When Carina arrives soon after, I immediately lunge forward and grab her throat.

"What the fuck are you playing at?" I snarl.

"Next time you visit your whore, try not to come to dinner smelling of her. I may accept you need her, but there's no need to rub it in my face!" Carina snarls back. "You reeked of her! Your mother asked me earlier where you were. I know exactly what you were doing with her. Do you think your parents can't smell her?" she asks.

I suck in a breath and let go of Carina. I can still feel the anger boiling inside me. Furthermore, I want answers, and I want them now.

"What are your intentions? Why are you stirring all of this up right now?" I ask her.

Carina's expression softens as she reaches up to rub her throat. "Xandros, I know this is all difficult for you," she says. "You're betrothed to me. It's not fair for you to be carrying on with Sienna behind my back. At least not publicly."

I let out a bitter laugh. "Is that what you think this is about? Me cheating on you?"

Carina hesitates before nodding slowly. "I mean...yes. Isn't it? I don't care that you are fucking her, Xandros, but don't make it so fucking obvious. I don't need my father asking questions, sham marriage or not!"

I shake my head and take a step closer to her. "No, Carina. This isn't about cheating, or anything like that. It's about me wanting someone who isn't you." As soon as the words leave my mouth, I know they are the truth. This marriage will be the death of me. Despite hating Sienna, I love her. This is torture of the worst kind. She is the forbidden fruit.

Carina looks taken aback for a moment before recovering herself. "And what about our engagement? What about your duty to our kingdom?"

"To hell with duty, Carina! I can't spend the rest of my life with someone who makes me feel so suffocated and unhappy."

Carina snarls, baring her fangs. "And I am not going back to my father. Keep your mate. This wedding is going ahead!" she spits at me.

"You really still want to parade around like some... loving married couple! I don't want you!"

"But I want you!" Carina screams at me.

I scoff. "Really? Because you weren't so sure when I first met you!"

"Things change," Carina states, not elaborating. I rub my temples in frustration. This entire thing is a mess.

"Your mother will never approve of her. Think about this, Xandros. It is a win-win situation for both of us and her. You get to keep your mate. I am not stopping you from being with her, just don't flaunt her where people can see!"

"You think it's that easy?" I ask her.

"You have no choice!"

"You're up to something. I fucking know you, Carina. What is it you want from me?"

Carina grins, a wicked glint in her eyes. "Don't act so innocent, Xandros. You know exactly what I'm doing."

I frown, unsure of what she means.

"I'm manipulating this situation to my advantage," she continues. "I want you to remember you belong to me. We are already legally married! Sienna is just a plaything, nothing more. She will never replace me."

I grit my teeth, feeling the fury building inside me once again. I've had enough of Carina's games.

"You dare speak of Sienna like that? She's my mate," I growl.

Carina scoffs. "Your mate? Don't be ridiculous. You think I would let some commoner come in and take my place as queen?"

I step forward menacingly, but Carina doesn't flinch.

"I'll do whatever it takes to keep my place as queen," she says coldly.

My heart sinks as I realize the depth of Carina's goals. I know then that it won't be easy to break free of her grasp.

"Just remember, Xandros, unless I sign those papers, Sienna has to challenge me for your hand. You and I both know that is not a fight she'll win," Carina snarls. I clench my fists in frustration.

Carina is right.

Sienna would never win a fight against her, especially if it comes to the throne. And Carina will go to any length to make sure she stays in power. But I won't let her hurt Sienna, either. Carina wanders off to the bathroom, stopping at the door.

"Don't risk your mate, Xandros. Most women would have told you to get rid of her. I haven't asked that. But don't push me to do something we'll both regret."

"I won't let you hurt her!"

"I never said I would, but for her sake, and mine, you can't be cuddling your mistress, especially in front of your mother or father, she is to be my maid, and I will treat her as such, just ensure she crosses no boundaries."

"You and I both know now she has shifted; it is going to be almost impossible for her to resist the bond."

"Then command her. Her life is not the only one on the line here!" she snaps at me.

"What is that supposed to mean?"

She pinches the bridge of her nose. "It doesn't matter. I'm not the person you have to worry about. I am okay with this. It's your mother who wants her dead, not me. I have no vendetta against her, unless she comes for my throne. Are we clear?" Carina asks me.

Lycan King's Captives 133

"For now..." I growl.

Carina raises an eyebrow at me.

"I'll have the maids send for her tomorrow," I tell her, and Carina nods once stepping into the bathroom, and shutting the door.

I curse, falling onto the end of the bed and placing my head in my hands. Her parents caused my family so much anguish, and I'm not sure if I will ever be able to see past that. But I fucking want to at the same time.

I need Sienna, but having her means putting her life at risk. I have to eventually come to terms with the monsters who brought her into this world and also get my mother to see reason, which won't be easy.

Maybe it is best to keep my distance, not just for me, but Sienna? Maybe it will be easier if I pretend she is nothing more than a bed toy. Though the thought sickens me.

How fucked up does one have to be to love and hate their fucking soulmate? Never in my life would I have conjured up such a scenario where I want to love my mate as much as I want to kill her.

Chapter Twenty

Sienna

I stare at the flickering flames in the fireplace, hoping they will stay lit for once, when Xandros's voice interrupts my thoughts, and I feel his hands on my shoulders at the same time the fire dies.

"Can you start the fire first?" I ask.

"I'm not here to start the fire," he responds.

"It's freezing in here. If you want something, then so do I. Start the fire!" I snap, my patience wearing thin. Xandros growls in response.

He pulls me up from my spot on the floor and closer; I push him away, tears burning in my eyes. I'm nothing but a toy to him. He has made that abundantly clear.

"What do you want, Xandros?" I ask sternly; my voice filled with defiance.

"You know what I want," he responds coldly

His words feel like a slap in the face, bringing me back to reality. I have nothing to give him, no love, no affection, nothing.

"I don't have anything for you, Xandros," I say, my voice trembling with anger. "So, just leave."

He steps closer, his eyes dark and intense. I feel his breath on my face and his heat radiating from his body. I tense, preparing for a fight.

"You think you can defy me?" he questions, his eyes narrowing.

I roll my eyes, knowing deep down I can't defy him if he orders me. "Then you're wasting your time. I'm not giving you what you want until you start the fire," I say firmly. "If you don't, I have nothing to give you."

Xandros's jaw clenches, and I can see the rage burning in his eyes. He grabs my wrist, his fingers digging into my skin.

"You will give me what I want," he says menacingly.

I yank my arm away and step back, my heart pounding with fear. Still I refuse to back down.

"No, Xandros," I say, my voice quivering with what is left of the tiny spark of courage. "I won't."

He grabs me again, pulling me close with anger etched on his face, his hands on my waist. I try to break free, it's futile, he's too strong.

"You will give me what I want; you don't get to say no to me," he growls.

He rips my clothes off, forcing me onto the bed, and I fight him, trying to push him away when suddenly he slaps me hard across the face. My cheek burns furiously, and I stop struggling, go limp, and stare blankly at the ceiling. Xandros kisses me, his lips hard against mine. I don't kiss him back. He pulls away and stares down at me, his eyes burning with anger.

"What are you doing?" he snarls at me. I say nothing, just stare off blankly. Xandros growls and punches the bed beside my head. I flinch, fear coursing through my veins. He grabs my arms and pins me to the mattress, his lips crashing against mine. I try to growl at him, but no sound comes out. He pulls away, his eyes filled with rage. So I close my eyes, and remain limp.

I shake my head and feel tears stinging my eyes. I can't do it anymore, fighting him every night with no result. "Sienna?"

"Just get it over with," my voice is robotic, defeated. He pulls the rest of my clothes off and pushes between my legs. He growls menacingly. "Why are you lying like that? Do something!" I turn my face away from him, refusing to look at him. He growls again and punches the bed once and then twice.

"I'll start the fire," he snaps.

I don't respond. Why is it so difficult for him to just do one small thing? It's not like I asked for much. This room is like a freezer. He growls when I don't respond, pushing off the bed and climbing off me. He stares at me for a long moment, his jaw clenched and his eyes unreadable.

"If you want sex," I say firmly, pointing to the fireplace behind me. "Start the fire first." He growls, then turns and stalks over to the fireplace, striking a match as he kneels. I take in a deep breath of relief as the flames catch life around us, filling the room with warmth. Hoping tonight, I might actually get some proper sleep without being awoken by the cold.

For a short second, I felt triumphant, a small victory. Until he turns around, his aura is menacing, angry that I dared demand anything from him. As I attempt to get up to give him what he came here for, he shoves me back onto the bed with so much force it nearly knocks the air out of my lungs. He grips my hips and flips me onto my stomach. My bond screams to touch him, and is only amplified when he grabs my hips, yanking me to the end of the bed.

"Xandros?"

"No, I did what you asked!" he snarls, shoving inside me.

His grip is like a vice, his hands bruising my hips as he thrusts harder and harder.

His breathing is shallow, and his eyes I can feel boring into the back of my head. I try to close my eyes and block out the pain. It is impossible. His body is like a machine, mercilessly pounding against me. Tears streak down my face, if he notices he doesn't seem to care. He just keeps going, faster and faster, until he finally reaches his climax and then pulls away without another word.

For a few seconds, I lay there, my body trembling from exhaustion and relief that it's over. He has gotten what he wanted, to him, it is nothing more than a physical release, a transaction of sorts. He is angry and rough, punishing me for not giving him the affection he craved. When he's done, he turns to leave.

"I want to watch TV," I blurt. "This room is too quiet. And I would like to be allowed out of here."

Xandros growls, stopping at the door, his entire body tense

"You start work tomorrow as Carina's maid," he says, his voice cold and cruel. He slams the door shut and leaves me alone in the room, once again feeling used and worthless.

I stare at the door, unsure of what to do next. Xandros had left me here, in this cold, dark room. The walls seem to be closing in on me, suffocating me with their emptiness. I shiver, pulling the thin blanket tighter around me. The only source of light is a small flickering fireplace, casting eerie shadows across the room.

I try to push away the memories of Xandros's touch, his vice-like hands on my body. I try to forget how cold and rough he was. My mind wants to forget, my body can still feel his touch, his scent lingering in the room, and now he's gone. My stupid bond—the one I detest so much—cries for the monster. Death would have been kinder than putting up with this misery daily. Used as he seeks, and left broken a little more each time he visits.

Chapter Twenty-One

Sienna

I don't know how much time passes when the door creaks open, and I freeze in terror, my whole body shaking—Xandros strides in, his expression a mask of cruelty.

"Get dressed," he barks, throwing a bundle of clothes at me.

I scramble to my feet.

"Where are you taking me?" I whisper, my voice shaking.

Xandros doesn't answer, only giving me a cold, hard stare. "I said get dressed," he growls, his voice low and menacing.

I quickly obey, my fingers trembling as I pull on the uniform he gave me. I can feel his dark presence hovering over me, and I can only imagine what he has in store. I try to steel my nerves and comply.

Once I'm dressed, Xandros grabs my arm, his grip like iron, and pulls me along behind him. I stumble to keep up with his long, purposeful strides, my heart racing with fear and anticipation.

We walk down a long hallway, past countless doors and chambers. The castle is silent, save for the sound of our footsteps echoing against the stone walls. The castle is eerily silent, the darkness seeming to press in around us like a physical presence. I can feel the almost tangible weight of Xandros's presence and his cruel intentions. I know his gaze is on me, and I'm filled with a sense of dread and unease. The hallway stretches on, the echoing of our footsteps growing ever louder as we pass door after door.

Finally, we reach a large one made of wood, and Xandros pushes it open. We step into a grand hall filled with opulent furniture and gilded decor. The room is filled with a mix of luxurious furniture. Persian rugs adorn the marble floors, while velvet curtains hang from the tall windows. The walls are filled with fine art and intricately carved woodwork. In the center of the room is a large fireplace, its flames casting a warm glow over the whole room. The air is thick with the smell of incense and the faint sound of music playing in the background. Overall, it is a room of grandeur and opulence. The room is empty, save for a lone figure sitting at the far end of the room.

It's Carina.

My stomach drops as I realize what's happening. Xandros is parading me in front of his betrothed, as if I'm nothing more than a possession, a toy to be shown off. I glance at Xandros anxiously.

Carina looks up as we approach, a cruel smile curling her lips. "Well, well, well," she purrs. "Look what the cat dragged in."

Xandros doesn't respond, merely pushing me forward and making me stumble until I'm standing in front of Carina.

"Good morning, Sienna," Carina says. "I trust you slept well?"

I don't respond, merely staring at her, not wanting to provoke her. This is the woman he lies beside every night while I toss and turn, my bond screaming and aching for his presence while all I get is his cold demeanor, this woman gets his love.

Carina stands, circling me like a predator sizing up its prey. "You know, Xandros told me you weren't very obedient last night," she says, her eyes flickering with amusement. He tells her what he does with me. Hearing this makes me uncomfortable. Do they sit down after he uses me, discuss it over tea about how much he crushed me, and laugh about it?

I feel my face flush with shame and rage. How dare she talk to me like this.

Xandros clears his throat, and Carina turns her attention to him. "Enough, Carina." he states, his tone icy and detached.

Carina steps forward, her eyes never leaving Xandros's face. "I just want to remind you, my love, of your place. You may have your little plaything here, but let's not forget who you're betrothed to. Who owns her?"

Xandros snarls, his grip on my arm tightening until it feels like my bones will snap. "I haven't forgotten anything," he growls.

Carina smiles as if she's won something. My heart sinks as I realize I can do nothing to escape this nightmare. He is giving me to her? I can't believe what I'm hearing; Xandros is using me. He has no love for me, only hate and a need he can't control.

"Very well, leave us. She can start in the bathroom." I peek at Xandros, hoping he won't leave me with this woman who so obviously hates me. My stomach sinks when he nods and stalks off, leaving me with Carina. "Go wait in the hall; one of the maids will show you what to do," she dismisses me with a wave of her hand.

Despite how vast the castle is, I feel claustrophobic within its walls. My new quarters are cramped, and I can hear the muffled sounds of the royal family arguing in the distance. I try to ignore it and focus on my tasks as a maid, even with the added distraction of my chores, my mind keeps wandering back to Xandros. It's like a physical pull I can't resist, even though I know I should.

As I clean the room, I hear footsteps approaching and tense. It's Carina, and I can feel her eyes boring into me as she surveys the room. "You'll be taking care of our bedroom quarters as well. You'll do that once you're finished here," she says, her voice cold and commanding. "And don't be snooping through our stuff."

I bite back a retort, knowing it won't help me.

Carina is just as dangerous as Xandros, and I need to tread carefully around her. As the day wears on, I find myself caught up in a whirlwind of tasks and duties. I serve meals, clean rooms, and do laundry, trying to stay invisible as I move about the castle. Still I can feel the eyes of the other staff members on me, and I know they're gossiping about me behind my back. I try to keep my head down and ignore them, I feel like a pawn in a game I don't fully understand. Finally, as the day comes to an end, I'm exhausted and can't wait to go to bed, which is what I do the moment I step into the room; I don't bother getting out of my clothes, I fall face first on the bed.

As I lay in my bedroom, tears stream down my face. Being forced to spend the majority of the day in his chambers, the one he shares with her has played havoc with my bond, hurting it.

I try to push him out of my mind, forgetting how his touch makes me feel, even that is impossible. My body yearns for him, even as my mind screams for me to run.

As I lay here, lost in my thoughts, I hear a knock at the door. It is one of the maids coming to tell me I'm needed in the king's chambers.

I know what that means. Xandros is calling for me, and I can't refuse him. I drag myself out of bed, wiping away my tears as I make my way to the king's chambers.

As I enter the room, Xandros is waiting for me. His eyes bore into me, cold and unfeeling. He doesn't say a word as he grabs me by the arm and pulls me toward him.

I try to pull away, and he holds me tighter, his grip bruising my skin. Xandros drags me to another room, the spare beside the one he shares with Carina, and pushes me down onto the bed, his eyes dark with lust. I know what he wants from me, and I give it to him, even though it feels like a betrayal to myself.

As he takes what he wants from me, I'm filled with an emptiness. This isn't love. This is just a twisted game of power and control.

When it is over, Xandros gets up and leaves without a word. I lay there, feeling broken and used, knowing tomorrow will be the same.

I can't escape him, no matter how hard I try. He is a part of me now, a part I hate and love in equal measure.

After a while, I find the courage to pull my clothes back on and step back out into the hall. When Carina rounds the corner, she stops, looks at me up and down, then sneers; I drop my gaze, knowing she can smell him on me. She then storms into the room they share while I sneak back into mine as if I'm the one who did something wrong. He is my mate, yet I am made to feel like the whore, the homewrecker.

Chapter Twenty-Two

Sienna

The next morning, a maid comes to fetch me. She leads me to Carina's chambers, where I spend the day following her around, serving her meals, and attending to her needs. Carina is polite enough, that doesn't change the fact that I'm still a prisoner—nothing more than a possession to Xandros and a slave to his family, and they treat me accordingly.

In the evening, we gather for dinner. As usual, Xandros sits at the head of the table, and I am relegated to standing at the side. I try to ignore the hunger gnawing at my stomach as the rich aroma of food fills the room.

Midway through the meal, I overhear a conversation between Xandros and Carina's father. "Why does the girl bear your mark, Xandros?" he demands.

"She is my concubine," Xandros replies without hesitation. "So, yes, she bears my mark."

Carina's father looks at me, his eyes dark with anger. "You have marked another while married to my daughter?" he demands.

Xandros just shrugs. "She belongs to me. As I said, she is my concubine."

Carina's father looks at her. "And you're okay with this?" he demands.

"Yes, Father. You know, Lycans turn crazed without their mates."

Carina's father shakes his head.

Carina leans in and whispers something in Xandros's ear. I can't make out what she is saying, though it can't be anything good because Xandros's face turns red with anger.

"Fine," he says, taking a sip from his glass. "Do what you want with her," he says, and Carina waves me over. I don't move, not liking the crazed look on her face.

"Now, Sienna, you're Carina's maid. You'll do as she asks," Xandros warns. When I still don't move, his fist slams down on the table making me jump. "Now!" Hesitantly, I move closer, my heart racing.

Carina grabs my wrist and yanks me toward her. She sinks her fangs into my neck, and I cry out in pain. I can feel the blood draining out of me, and the room begins to spin.

Xandros's jaw clenches, but he doesn't move to help me off the floor. Instead, I clutch my neck, feeling woozy as I make my way back to the spot where I had been standing. I lean heavily against the wall, feeling dizzy, and betrayed by Xandros for what he allowed Carina to do.

When dinner is over, Xandros remains, drinking his whiskey while everyone moves to the billiard room. I try to fight back tears as I clean up the table, disgusted by what I've become. Xandros walks over to me, his face hard and unyielding.

"I have no choice," he tells me. "You know that," he whispers. I ignore him. It's too late for his apologies.

"I am not just your sex slave; I am her blood bag now," I whisper bitterly. He takes a step back, staring down at the ground. There's a moment of silence between us before he speaks again, this time his voice soft.

"It is what it is," he tells me, and then he stalks out, leaving me alone with my thoughts.

As I finish cleaning, I can feel the wound on my neck healing. It does nothing for the emotional pain which remains at seeing my mate so easily give me to her to snack on.

I make my way back to my room, and as I lay on the bed, I feel the loneliness and despair wash over me. How did my life come to this?

Chapter Twenty-Three

Sienna

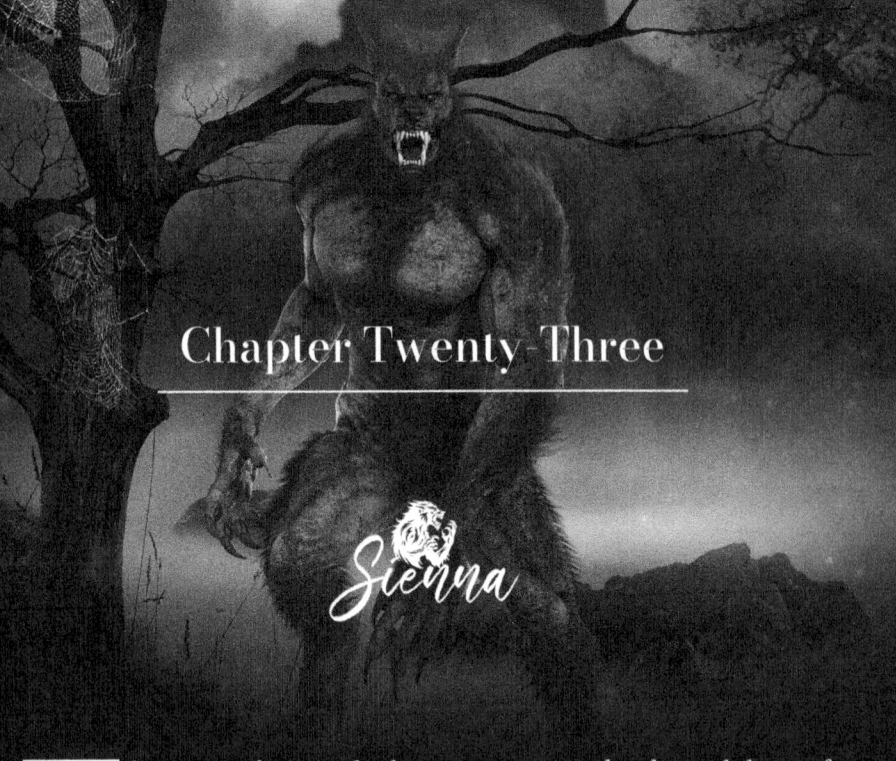

The sun peeks over the horizon, painting the sky with hues of orange and gold as I wake. My body aches from the previous night's events, my neck throbbing where Carina bit me. The prospect of facing another day in this castle, serving Carina, is daunting. Still, I push myself out of bed and start my day.

As Carina's handmaiden, my duties are endless. I serve her breakfast, lay out her clothes, and tidy her chambers. While I work, I observe her with Xandros. They sit close, their hands often touching, their laughter echoing around the room. It's a scene of domestic bliss, and it shreds my heart every time I see it.

The day wears on, and I'm summoned to the luncheon held for Carina's parents. The air buzzes with conversation, and laughter rings out. And all I can focus on is the gnawing emptiness in my stomach, and the heaviness in my heart. When Carina's father brings up grandchildren, my heart stutters.

"I expect to hear the pitter-patter of little feet soon after the wedding, Xandros," he says, clapping Xandros on the shoulder.

Xandros nods, his face impassive. "In good time, let's get through the wedding first." His eyes flicker to mine for a brief moment before returning to his father-in-law.

My heart sinks. I can't bear the thought of Xandros and Carina having children, though now it's been mentioned, it seems inevitable, so instead, I remain in the shadows trying to go unnoticed when the head maid points to her tray, wanting me to fetch another from the kitchen. I wander off, taking some dirty dishes with me, thankful to escape the dining room.

However, as I'm bustling around in the kitchen, a cold shadow falls over me. I turn around to find Carina's father towering above me. I freeze, the blood in my veins turning to ice.

He's an intimidating figure. His eyes, a chilling ice blue, regard me coldly. He's the embodiment of every vampire tale I've ever heard, and I find myself trembling in his presence as he cages me against the counter. My hand clutching the tray that holds full wine glasses, trembles, the glasses chinking loudly as they rattle.

"My daughter may have agreed for you to remain with Xandros, since Lycans are pitiful creatures who can't survive without their mates," he begins, his voice cold and calculating. "But mark my words, girl. You get in the way of our kingdom's treaty, and the future you meet will be worse than the one bestowed on your parents."

His words hit me like a punch, and I recoil in fear. His threat hangs in the air like a chilling promise, and I can't shake off the feeling of dread that washes over me.

Xandros walks into the kitchen, Carina in tow. My gaze shifts to him in panic, and he seems to pick up on my distress, yet his face remains neutral.

"Everything alright, Father?" Carina asks, her eyes scanning the room.

"Yes, of course. I was asking the help for a fresh glass of wine," he says, his eyes cutting to me. I quickly nod, holding out a tray of wine glasses. Carina chuckles lightly, "Exactly why we came in, too," she chuckles. "Thank you, dear," he tells me, snatching an extra glass off the tray and passing it to his daughter. He leaves with Carina, and I let out a breath I didn't know I was holding.

However, Xandros remains and when I try to leave, he blocks my exit, his eyes narrowing. "What happened?" he demands.

Lycan King's Captives

"Like you care. Go play house with your wife," I sneer, shoving past him.

Back in the dining room, the conversation has shifted to babies once again, and I try my best to ignore the conversation until I hear his mother speak up. "We're actually going next week to look at baby stuff and set up a nursery." Xandros's mother's eyes sparkle with excitement. I notice Xandros's startled expression when I shift my eyes to him.

"Really, Mother?" he asks, and she giggles.

"Of course, the vampire king is not the only one looking forward to grandchildren," she says, her eyes twinkling. I feel a lump forming in my throat, and I turn away to hide my tears as I wonder how badly that will hurt to see him father her children.

"As long as he doesn't knock up his mate, things should be fine. You are using protection, right, Xandros?"

"Father," Carina objects.

"Nonsense, Carina, don't lie to me and tell me he is allowed to keep his mate, and hasn't touched her?"

"That is none of your business," Xandros snarls.

"You're marrying my daughter, Xandros. The last thing we need is a scandal because you fathered a mutt to the treasonous whore," he sneers, and I suddenly feel the gaze of everyone on me.

"She's on birth control," Xandros states. That's a lie. Still, his words make me wonder if he will force me on it.

"That won't be an issue," Xandros states, glancing at me. However, I can tell the change in topic to her husband's mistress has made Carina extremely uncomfortable as she glares at me.

"Make sure it isn't," her father states.

I turn my gaze away, focusing on my task. I'm so lost in my thoughts I almost don't hear Carina calling me over. Then I feel her sharp fangs sinking into my neck, and reality comes crashing back. I whimper, the pain and humiliation unbearable as she feeds on me, while everyone chats like it is no big deal. Yet to me, it is. My gaze meets Xandros's. He clenches his teeth and looks away, as if he can pretend it isn't happening, as long as he doesn't watch. Once she is done, she discards me like I'm garbage.

When the luncheon is over, I bolt back to my room, my heart

hammering against my rib cage. My tears fall as I start to clean my room, desperately trying to occupy my mind with something other than the throbbing pain in my neck, and my shattered heart.

It's then that I spot it. A small scrap of paper tucked under the bed. It's the phone number Toby gave me. A lifeline. Glancing around, I wonder how I will be able to call him without a phone, when I remember the phone used to call down to the staff in the hidden bar area. Moving toward the panel, I push on it and the wall opens up to the hidden area.

It takes me two seconds to find the handset attached to the wall. I snatch it, wiping my tears and unfolding the piece of paper. Nervously, I wonder if the phone can call out of the castle or if it is only a line to the servant area. Dialing in the numbers, I glance at the door nervously when it rings, and my heart skips a beat.

"Please pick up," I whisper to myself, my hands shaking when the ringing stops.

"Toby," I whisper when he picks up. I nearly burst into tears when I hear his familiar voice.

"Sienna?" he breathes out in relief.

"I need to get out of here." I choke on my sob.

"I was worried Xandros had killed you."

"I need a way out, Toby," I whisper.

"Shh, shh, don't cry. Leave it with me," he reassures. "I will speak with the seekers, and we will find a way out of the city together. I'm so glad you're okay. You have no idea how worried I've been." Tears brim in my eyes, knowing he was worried about me. At least someone missed me. But, how can I have a future with Toby when I belong to Xandros?

"Xandros has marked me," I confess.

"Then I will mark you, and once you mark me back, it will solidify our bond and destroy his," Toby says.

I fall silent. Could it really work? Would that be enough to protect us from Xandros? "Please tell me you haven't marked him, Sienna?" Toby asks, worry lacing his voice.

"No, I haven't, and I don't think he would allow that," I reply.

"Thank the goddess. It's nearly impossible to break a full bond,"

Lycan King's Captives

Toby sighs in relief. His words offer me a glimmer of hope in this sea of despair.

We plot my escape, Toby's reassuring voice promising help from within the castle. As I hang up, a knock echoes through the room.

It's Xandros. He strides into the room, his eyes burning with a familiar desire. He advances, and I step back.

"No," I say firmly, my voice shaking.

"Please, Xandros, not tonight!" I plead with him.

He doesn't stop. Instead, he uses the mate bond, his calling so strong I can't resist him as he slides his hands up my arms.

"Why do you pretend you can fight our bond?" he purrs, his hands moving to the buttons of my blouse. Sometimes I wonder the same thing; it's clear I have no say or control here.

I fight it as much as I can, despite it being pointless when eventually, I succumb, my body betraying me as I give in to his touch.

My body betrays me as his lips caress my neck. I try to turn away, but it feels like my feet are stuck to the carpet. All the doubts and fears just seem so far away at this moment.

The heat between us is unbearable, as Xandros slides his hands over every inch of my skin with passionate intensity until all fight leaves me entirely—my body craving his touch, whether I want it or not.

Xandros trails kisses down my throat before finally pressing his soft lips against mine. His mouth moves with determination, making sure there will be no chance of escape this time around.

His lips brush against my neck, sending shivers down my spine. My mind screams no, but he wraps his arms around me, and I find myself molding into him, considering giving in to the feelings of pleasure that swirl throughout me. He moves us toward the bed without breaking contact with me and we fall onto it together in a tangled mess of arms and legs. His hungry kisses get more passionate as he takes control completely, leaving little room for resistance—yet I still try to pull away when his hands move up toward my chest. My hands move to his chest in an attempt to shove him off.

Xandros pins both hands above head as if reading my thoughts, stopping any movement on my part, apart from feeling every sensation he induces.

"I'm being gentle. Don't make me become forceful, Sienna." His words seem to whisper more than just a warning. They hold pure desire.

I close my eyes in surrender. "Good girl," he whispers, and I feel him smiling against me as he increases the pace of his kisses, exploring every single inch of my skin with gentle caresses which is vastly different from the last few times when I felt used, like a toy. My body trembles under his touch as if eager for more pleasure that it can barely handle—my core pulsing with an overwhelming energy I never knew was possible before this moment.

As Xandros slides deep inside me, it's like all time stops around us; each sensation is enhanced by the euphoria only a mate bond can bring forth, causing fireworks of ecstasy between us, until we tremble together.

With trembling fingers, I pull him closer to me, my eyes closed in bliss. Just when I'm about to reach the peak, Xandros pulls out of me, leaving me aching for more. I gasp in surprise and open my eyes.

My body is still trembling, and my heart is racing. I take a deep breath and open my eyes, only to be met with a sudden chill as ribbons of his semen coat my stomach. He stares down at me, his face serious and his voice firm.

It's like he threw a bucket of ice over me. "Tomorrow, I will have a doctor send for you. You need birth control," he tells me, leaving no room for argument.

"Sienna? Did you hear me? I can't risk you getting pregnant. Hopefully, you're not already. If you are, we'll have to take care of it." I stare blankly at the ceiling, his words sinking in. Does he truly feel none of the pain he causes me? The swift change in his demeanor gives me whiplash.

"Sienna?" he growls when I still don't answer.

"I heard," I answer, my voice sounding robotic.

I can feel the tears stinging my eyes, and I quickly blink them away, feeling used. I am nothing just some fuck toy to him. I nod in agreement, not trusting myself to speak. He leans down and kisses me softly, and then pulls away. He gets dressed in silence and exits the room without another word, leaving me alone in the aftermath. My body aches, and my heart feels heavier than ever. I feel used, discarded. As I lay there, my thoughts drift to Toby.

I will escape. For my sake, for my freedom, I have to.

My resolve hardens, as I drift off to sleep, I dream of a future outside these castle walls, a future where I'm free. Free to be with Toby. I just hope he can find us a way out.

My heartbeat is frantic against my ribs as I lift the phone to my ear. Every ring is a sharp stab of fear that someone will catch me. The door suddenly swings open, and I nearly drop the phone in alarm. My breath hitches as another maid steps into the room.

My heart is pounding as I turn to face the maid. I search her expression for anything untoward. All I see is sympathy as she quickly glances at the door.

"I was just calling down to service," I lie.

"Any other maid, you better lie better than that," she tells me, and I chew my lip wondering if she'll snitch. She appears to be about my age.

"Calm down, I won't tell. We maids gotta stick together," she whispers.

"Besides, you're friends with Toby, aren't you?" she asks, her eyes gentle. The relief is so immense I can hardly speak, knowing this must be one of the maids Toby told me about. I nod, a lump forming in my throat. She nods back at me, a shared understanding passing between us. "I won't tell anyone. I'll even help you, if I can. But Carina has called for you, you need to meet her in ten minutes."

My shoulders slump with relief and gratitude at her kindness. Tears prick my eyes as she steps closer and takes the phone out of my hand. She begins dialing a number before handing it back to me with a reassuring smile on her face.

"I will wait for you and keep an eye out, be quick," she says softly before leaving the room.

I stare at the handset in shock for a few seconds before finally gathering up enough courage to place it to my ear. The line crackles before someone picks up on the other end, their voice timid and unsure: "Hello?"

"Toby?" I whisper, my voice shaking slightly. The relief I feel upon hearing his voice is huge.

"Sienna? Is that you?" comes his reply.

I can hear the surprise and relief in his voice, and it makes me smile.

"Yes, sorry, I haven't had a chance to call; Carina has been working me like a workhorse," I tell him.

"It's fine as long as you're okay,"

"I'm fine, though one of the maid's caught me on the phone, she said she won't tell."

"Tall, red hair and green eyes, smells like lavender?" he asks, and I furrow my brows.

"Ah, yes," I answer.

"Tyra, the girl I was telling you about. I was wondering when she would find a way to you," he tells me, and I let out a breath, knowing I can trust the girl if Toby does.

The day passes in a blur, the world beyond the castle walls seeming more and more like a distant dream. However, as I am cleaning the sitting quarters near Xandros room, I overhear Carina fighting with her father before he departs, their heated words echoing through the empty hallways.

"Ensure he stays away from the mutt he calls his mate. If this treaty is ruined, Carina, you'll be the one punished," he warns her, his voice laced with venom.

I quickly hide out of view, my heart pounding as he leaves. As I turn to walk away, a soft sound stops me in my tracks. It's a quiet sobbing, coming from the room Carina's father just left. I edge closer to the door, peering inside to find Carina, her face buried in her hands as she cries. It's a sight I never expected to see, and it leaves me feeling strangely unsettled.

I hesitate for a moment, before finally gathering up enough courage to enter the room. She looks up at me in surprise before wiping away her tears and sitting up straight again.

"What are you doing here?" she asks, her voice still shaky from crying.

"I... heard you talking," I stammer out nervously. "Are you alright?"

She takes a deep breath before responding. "It doesn't matter," she says softly before finally meeting my gaze again with teary eyes. "My father wants you gone because he thinks Xandros is going against the treaty between our two families."

My heart aches at her words and I take a few steps toward her, not sure of what else to do or say.

"He seemed pretty mad?" I ask her.

"You have no idea. Xandros wasn't the only one forced into this sham of a wedding, only I didn't expect to fall in love with him," she admits, plucking a tissue from the tissue box. "Not that it matters, he'll never love me, not when he has you."

Does she truly believe that? Because if only she saw how he treated me when she isn't around, she would find it worse than when she is.

"So you love Xandros?" I ask. This is by far the strangest conversation, talking to the wife while I am merely his mated mistress.

"I think so, or maybe it's just the freedom he brings, away from my father," she whispers, then shakes her head.

"Why am I telling you this?" she mutters more to herself than me.

We sit there together for a few moments in silence until she takes another deep breath and stands up slowly. "Thank you for checking on me," she tells me with a faint smile before excusing herself from the room, leaving me alone with my thoughts. A few seconds later she returns, and it is like the woman who sat crying next to me was merely a figment of my imagination.

"When you're done cleaning here, you can start the bathrooms," she tells me, wandering off.

I shake off the bizarre feeling, reminding myself her problems are not mine to worry about and I never should have involved myself.

As night falls, an unfamiliar emptiness engulfs the castle. Xandros doesn't come to me like he usually does, nor does the doctor he said that he would organize. It makes me wonder if it has anything to do with the argument I overheard, did Carina ban him from seeing me? And what about the doctor supposed to put me on birth control? Did he forget or perhaps Carina has banned him from seeing me so it's no longer needed now.

The mate bond is a relentless torment, a gnawing pain that flares to life with every passing moment. I thought it was painful seeing him with Carina, yet it's even more excruciating not seeing him at all.

Chapter Twenty-Four

Sienna

The days pass slowly, each one more painful than the last. Xandros is absent from my life, and it feels like I'm living in a nightmare. After the second night he doesn't visit me I know something is going on. No amount of distraction can make me forget the emptiness that has taken root in the castle. Even when I am in his presence, all I feel is an unsettling unease because he does not acknowledge me, like he has decided to distance himself as well. Though he does not speak to me, our bond is still screaming for attention.

Carina returns back to her cold self, and I am positive now that I imagined the entire scene of her crying in my head. Every day, Carina passes by and gives me a cold smile that speaks volumes about her opinion of me. She knows exactly what I am, and still she shows me no mercy. It's clear she blames me for her suffering, so why do I feel sorry for her as well. She is stuck in a loveless marriage and must endure humiliation from her husband's mistress every day. It is odd feeling sorry for his wife when I am his mistress.

I keep to myself as much as possible, and focus on my duties as a maid. I spend my days cleaning and polishing the floors of the castle until they shine like never before, while enjoying my private phone calls with Toby each night. Yet even those are becoming shorter, his temper growing more each day since we have still found no way out for me. The castle is heavily guarded, and even Tyra hasn't been able to sneak back to see me.

One night, while taking out the trash, I hear faint music coming from inside Xandros's library room that makes my heart skip a beat. As I move closer to the door, I realize he is talking to someone.

"My father will be furious if we push the wedding back another month, are you insane?" Carina snaps at him. I peek through the door, seeing her pacing with her flowing white dress, cascading to the ground.

"Is this about her?"

"Of course it is!" Xandros bellows.

"Calm down, both of you. Can we find a way around this?" I hear another voice, peering in a little more, I find it is Xandros's mother who is sitting in an armchair by the fire.

"Well, any suggestions, I am all ears," Xandros grumbles at her.

"We push the wedding back like he wants."

Carina tosses her hands up in the air.

"Wait, I have an idea," Carina glares at Xandros, and I notice he leans forward a little more.

"We find a way to safely break the mate bond."

Xandros scoffs. "You want me to give up my mate?'

"That is exactly what I expect."

"You think you can change fate, do the impossible?" he laughs.

"What if she can?" Carina whispers so low I barely miss it, yet her words make my heart falter.

"You're seriously entertaining this?" he asks her.

"You can't even touch me because of her, don't think you are the only one suffering here," she snaps at him.

"It's the right thing, Xandros."

"And what of Sienna?" he snarls, and my heart flutters at his words.

"What of her, your mother is right. I've seen it before, a bond can be broken."

"I'm not giving up my mate."

"Then you give up the kingdom!" his mother snaps.

Silence falls for a second. "You have a month. Either you find a way to be with Carina and give her father what he wants, or we break the bond, and Sienna dies when we do. The choice is yours, Xandros, because Carina is right. We back out of this marriage, it will start a war!"

"I have kept my distance from her like you both fucking asked."

"Yet it has only caused a bigger rift between you two. Do you think no one has noticed? The whispers around the castle, this gets back to her father, and it will cause more issues," his mother states.

Forcing myself not to think further on it, I quickly discard the trash, then hurry back to my room, hoping none of them noticed me eavesdropping outside his door.

However, later that night. My bond aches even more. I don't know if it is the bond or overhearing them talk so candidly about breaking the bond I share with Xandros and letting me die that hurts the most. Either way, my bond screams for my mate.

The night is quiet and still as I make my way outside Xandros's quarters, the pull of the mate bond is too strong to resist. I can't stay away from him any longer, it aches too much. It seems like every time we are in the same room, it intensifies painfully and I need some relief. Yet his mother's words play on my mind.

I stop in front of his door, unable to go any further, hesitation rushes through me, wondering what I am planning to do. It's not like I can barge in when his wife lies beside him. His scent lingers here, mixed with the faint smell of incense and Carina's perfume. I want to go inside and lie down next to him. I know that would be a bad idea, so instead, I curl up near the door where his scent is slowly drifting under the crack in the door, hoping it will offer me comfort, or at least some rest. I have barely slept in days, and each night gets worse.

It offers a small measure of comfort, a balm to the raw pain of the bond. The ground is cold in the open area. My entire body aches from the icy air. As I close my eyes, slowly, I drift off into an uneasy sleep.

As morning dawns, I open my eyes reluctantly with dread filling my heart as reality sinks in once again - nothing has changed, and I am still bound to Xandros against my will. A noise sounding from inside the room makes me jump to my feet. With a heavy heart, I stand, flattening my clothes, before hastily making my way back to my room, hoping I go unnoticed.

Chapter Twenty-Five

Xandros

I can feel the mounting pressure closing in on me, suffocating me from all sides. Carina's father calls, his voice a sharp icy demand that sends a shiver down my spine.

"I want this treaty backed up with my grandchild, Xandros. And unless you give Carina one, you are to stay away from Sienna," he commands.

The tension in the castle is palpable, a heavy weight that threatens to crush us all. I know I should comply, do what is expected of me, still I can't bring myself to do it. I can't sleep with Carina, can't even bring myself to get aroused in her presence. It feels like a betrayal, a violation of the bond I share with Sienna.

I stand in my grand office, the walls seeming to close in on me as I hold the phone to my ear. The chilling voice of Carina's father echoes in my head, his demand for a grandchild piercing me like a dagger.

"We're postponing the wedding," I find myself saying. The words hang heavy in the air, a declaration of defiance. It's a risky move, one that could easily backfire. I need time – time to figure out what I truly want, and how to protect Sienna.

There's silence on the other end of the line, and I can almost hear the gears turning in his mind. "Postponing?" he repeats, his voice dripping with venom.

"Yes," I reply firmly. "We... we are trying to find a way to break the bond. It's causing complications."

The lie slides off my tongue smoothly, though it leaves a bitter taste in my mouth. I have no intention of breaking the bond with Sienna. It's the one thing that's real, the one thing that's mine in this twisted game of power and politics.

My words seem to appease Carina's father, at least for now. "You better fix this, Xandros," he warns. "This treaty is crucial for our kingdoms. Do not let your personal feelings interfere with our plans."

His words hit me hard, a stark reminder of the tightrope I'm walking on. I'm torn between my duty to my kingdom and the mate bond, the invisible tether that ties me to Sienna. Every day, the conflict within me grows, the two sides pulling me in opposite directions.

As I hang up the phone, a sense of dread settles in my chest. I'm caught in a web of lies and deceit, and with each passing day, I'm sinking deeper. I can only hope I find a way out of this mess before it's too late, before I lose not only Sienna forever, but our kingdom.

The treaty. It's been the backbone of my reign, the only barrier keeping my kingdom from crumbling into chaos. When my mother went on a rampage after the death of my aunt, slaughtering thousands of humans while hunting Sienna's parents, it was Carina's father who saved us. He stepped in and threatened the Elder Council with war if they dared to tear down the Lycan Kingdom.

In the world of supernatural politics, collateral damage is an accepted part of the game, and those residing in my city would have been exterminated without a second thought. It's happened to kingdoms before, when their rulers lost control, and I couldn't let it happen to mine.

So, I made a deal with the devil—Carina's father. In exchange for his protection, I promised to marry his daughter. That was before I found my mate. Before Sienna walked into my life and turned it upside down.

I've heard the stories, of course. Lycans driven to the brink of insanity because they couldn't find their mates. No one ever warned me that finding my mate could be just as devastating. The mate bond is a force of nature, powerful and unyielding, and it's pulling me in two directions.

On one hand, there's Sienna - my mate, my other half, the one who makes me feel complete. On the other hand, there's my kingdom, my people, who rely on me for their safety and survival. There is also the betrayal of my mother; she hates Sienna, and she has reason to. However, Sienna is my mate.

Caught between the rock and the hard place, I find myself struggling to keep my head above water. Every day is a battle—a fight to keep my kingdom safe, while protecting the bond with my mate.

As I sit in the silence of my office, the weight of my responsibilities pressing down on me, And the worst part? I have no idea how to fix it.

The only thing I know for sure is I can't lose Sienna. She's become my beacon in this storm, the one thing who keeps me sane amidst the chaos.

For her safety, I have stayed away. I don't visit her at night, haven't in days, though I can feel my absence tearing her apart, even though every fiber of my being yearns to be near her. I can't risk giving my mother, or Carina, a reason to hurt her, to lock her away in the cells again. The thought of her suffering because of me is unbearable—a constant, throbbing ache in my chest.

The distance between us only serves to amplify the pain of the bond, and I know I can't keep this up forever. Sooner or later, something will have to give. The weight of the world is bearing down on me, and I'm not sure how much longer I can hold on.

With each passing day, as the pressure mounts and the stakes get higher, I wonder *how much longer can I keep this up?* How much longer until I'm forced to make an impossible choice? And when that day comes, who will I choose? My mate, or my kingdom?

And in the end, will it even matter?

I push the heavy, mahogany door of our master bedroom open, stepping into the softly lit room. An unexpected sight freezes me mid-stride. Carina, once a symbol of immaculate perfection, now sits on the edge of our oversized bed, a picture of ruin. The traces of her expensive mascara are smeared across her cheeks, and her usually impeccable hair is disheveled, her skin blotchy. She looks far from the composed, impeccable woman I am used to. The phone in her hands feels like an ominous sign of what's to come, knowing whoever she just spoke to has upset her. That person probably being her father.

The entire room, usually reflecting our immense wealth and power, is tainted with an uneasy, chilling tension. It is so thick I can almost taste the salt of her tears in the air. The bedposts carved from ebony stand tall, the gilded mirror reflects the flickering flames from the fireplace. The room, as decadent as it is, screams death, and the flames emanating from the fireplace resemble my life burning around me with no way to extinguish their existence; even the plush carpet feels unnaturally cold under my bare feet.

Carina's blood-red eyes lock onto mine, their depths swirling with a storm of emotions that unsettle me. Betrayal. Hurt. Anger. Fear. They all claw at me as she meets my gaze, leaving invisible scratches on her hardened exterior. If fire had a face, it would be hers at this moment, her eyes matching the burning embers of the fireplace.

"I just got off the phone with my father, Xandros," she hisses, her voice a grating whisper against the pressing silence. "You've postponed our wedding!" she clenches her teeth.

I divert my gaze, the guilt coiling like a venomous snake inside me. I've always been able to face consequences head-on, this time, the confrontation is unwelcome. I know she is hurting, so am I. So is my mate.

My throat tightens, but I manage to maintain a calm façade. "I thought we needed more time to sort things out," I respond, trying to keep my voice steady, not wanting to fight with her, not tonight.

"More time?" she laughs, the sound sending a chill up my spine.

"I thought it was for the best...for us until we figure things out," I retort defensively, the words scraping my throat raw.

Carina erupts into a cold, haunting laugh, the sound echoing in the room like an icy death. Her phone lands with a thud on the silk duvet. "This isn't about 'us', Xandros. It's about that damned girl. That little mutt you're so fond of."

"Carina," I warn, a cutting edge to my voice.

"No," she cuts me off, rising from the bed. "That bitch is ruining everything. Everything was fine until you found her!"

My heart pounds against my chest like a drum, matching the tempo of my mounting anger. "Her name is Sienna," I snarl, my canines baring instinctively.

Her burning eyes turn deadly, frosty even. "I agreed to let you keep her, Xandros. But I won't let her steal you from me. Marry me, or I promise, I will remove her from the picture myself. I won't lose to that little whore!" she screams angrily.

Her words ignite a rage within me, hotter than the roaring fireplace nearby. "You lost to her the day I laid my eyes on her, Carina!" I snarl, her face twisting at the betrayal of my words, clearly stinging more than any physical blow. She slaps me, her hand striking my cheek with a force that sends my head reeling sideways. I press my lips in a line, my hands fisting at my sides, anger coursing through me. Yet her hand wasn't totally undeserved.

With that, she storms out of the room, slamming the door so hard it rattles the paintings on the wall, making one fall to the floor. A heavy silence fills the room. Alone and furious, I make my way to my office, the scent of rich mahogany and old books comforting me as I step inside the huge room. The floor to ceiling bookcases take up most of the space; this place has always been a sanctuary to me, just like my library. I sit down at my desk, the cool leather of the chair a stark contrast to the burning anger within me. I need to figure out what to do. I try to untangle the web of problems, spinning in my mind when a knock on the door intrudes my solitude.

Lifting my head, I glance up to see my father stepping into the room. Despite the situation, a sense of warmth washes over me. No matter how tough the circumstances, he's always been a rock for me, at least when my mother isn't watching.

My father steps in, his presence a beacon of stability amidst the chaos. "Heard you've postponed the wedding?" he asks, the corners of his mouth twitching upward.

"News travels fast," I reply, a hint of a smile playing on my lips despite my turmoil. "Did mother send you to berate me?"

"Quite the situation you've found yourself in, my boy. Your mother is fuming, so I thought you could use some company. Misery loves company, doesn't it?" He pours himself a glass of whiskey, the amber liquid swirling in the crystal tumbler.

"Bring another bottle then, Father. This one," I gesture to the half-empty bottle in front of me, "is reserved for my sorrow."

He lets out a hearty laugh, reaching behind him to grab another bottle from the bar. "That sounds like a plan, son." We sit here, in the quiet, nursing our drinks and unspoken thoughts. Despite everything, I can always find reason from my father, even if it is only behind my mother's back.

～

As we enjoy our drinks, the comforting silence between my father and me gives way to a heavy atmosphere after a while; he's holding back. "You're doing it again, old man. Holding out on me," I prod. "Just spit it out. Unless it's about mother withholding...well, you know. That's a mental image I'm still trying to erase after your last over-sharing of your bedroom horrors."

His low chuckle reverberates around the room. "She does hold quite the grudge," he quips, sipping his drink. I agree, knowing my mother all too well.

"Look, if you're here to talk me into marrying Carina, save your breath." He shakes his head, making me sit back, confused.

"No, son. I'm here to tell you not to discard the mate bond. It's killing you, and I can see it." I instantly stiffen, ready to argue about the necessity of the treaty, when he interrupts me. "The treaty has loopholes, son. Mates are one of them. The marriage to Carina isn't public yet. We can still fix this mess."

I raise my eyebrows, taken aback. "You want me to call off the wedding?" I ask incredulously, his words in front of my mother say the opposite. His soft sigh brings a wave of defeat through me.

"I just want my son to be happy. As for your mother, she won't accept Sienna... not yet. Give her time. She needs to see past Sienna's parents' sins. I know it's hard, and your mother has a knack for making things more complicated than they need to be."

"And this loophole?" I ask, still unsure of his proposal. His eyes glint, a sly smirk pulling at his lips. "If the mate is found before or after the marriage, she can still fight for you. It won't breach the contract or the treaty if she fights for your hand."

The notion is preposterous. "Carina will kill her."

"Then train her," he retorts simply with a shrug.

"How can I train her if I'm not even allowed to be near her until after the wedding?"

"Find a way, Xandros. Or get Carina to accept the divorce. Just... figure it out." He rises, placing a comforting hand on my shoulder before heading to the door. "And mom?" I call out, my heart sinking at the thought of confronting her again to tell her I won't go through with marrying Carina. He pauses, turning to me with a knowing smile. "I'll handle your mother," he says, turning and pauses again.

"Xandros," my eyes meet his, "your mother isn't the only one who needs to see past Sienna's parents. She may be their daughter, but in my observations of the girl, she is not them. You were never asked to forgive her parents, so maybe you can forgive yourself; their deaths weren't your fault, just like they weren't Sienna's, so blaming her won't ease your guilt. Just like you, she is a victim in all this," he adds. I swallow guiltily and nod once.

As the door shuts behind him, a whirlwind of thoughts start spinning in my head. Yet a glimmer of hope flickers amidst the chaos. The fear of the unknown is far too crippling, if only Carina would accept the divorce, this would be so much easier on everyone. I also know that will never happen.

Chugging the rest of my drink, I get up and leave my office. Returning to my room, I find it empty. Carina is nowhere in sight. With a sigh, I throw myself onto the bed, my thoughts wandering toward Sienna. The bond buzzing between us, alerting me she's awake. A pull I can't resist tugs me toward her, leading me to the other side of the castle, right outside her door.

I knock lightly, but when there's no answer, I go to unlock the door only for it to push open. It's always locked. Opening the door, I find the room empty. A surge of panic courses through me. My heart beats a frenzied rhythm in my chest as I take in the empty room, the untouched bed. "Sienna!" I call out. No answer. I rush into the bathroom, calling her name, yet she is also not in there.

"Sienna!" The silence that follows is a haunting echo of my worst fears when I catch a hint of familiar perfume. Carina's perfume. Pulling my phone from my pocket, I dial her number. The phone rings out, so I try again while walking out of the room as I hunt for them. Once again, I get her voicemail and a snarl leaves my lips.

Chapter Twenty-Six

Sienna

Buttoning up my pajamas, I step out of the bathroom and turn to the fireplace that has become my personal nemesis. I prod the dying fire with the poker.

I'm about to pick up another log, hoping it catches alight, when my room is suddenly invaded by a person I least suspect. "Get dressed!" Carina's command slices through the tranquil silence, her voice as cold as the icy draft that seeps into this room each night. Her entrance is abrupt and uninvited, unsettling the peace I've cocooned myself in for the night.

Her appearance is unlike anything I've seen before. Not only that, but her mascara is smeared, giving her an almost spectral look. Her usually well-contained hair is a disordered mess, and her eyes... her eyes are the personification of torment. I can see unshed tears glistening, making them seem more glassy than usual. This isn't the composed Carina I'm accustomed to, and it fills me with a chilling dread. She wanders over to my dresser, plucking some tissues from the box and cleaning up the mess of her mascara.

A question forms on my lips, and I swallow it down as I catch the dangerous glint in her eyes as she peers back at me in the mirror. The tension in the room is electric, charged with Carina's unpredictable wrath. My fingers fumble with the buttons of my pajamas, my heart pounding wildly against my rib cage.

"Why? What's—?" I stutter. She cuts me off.

"Did you hear me? I said get dressed. We're going out!" I scramble to my closet, pulling on the clothes closest to me, my hands trembling.

Once dressed, I turn to find Carina hunched over the minibar. She uncorks a bottle of Xandros's whiskey, pours herself a glass, then another, which she shoves into my hands. I instinctively pull back, and her icy glare has me swallowing hard, taking the glass from her.

I balk at the offering, but her cold, hard gaze leaves me no room for refusal, as I down the glass choking on its harshness.

"Are you... alright, ma'am?" I dare to ask, my voice wavering slightly from the burn of the alcohol.

Her answer is a scornful laugh, one that leaves an icy trail down my spine. "Ma'am? Makes me sound so old and worn out. Well I guess I am old, that's beside the point, I am nobody's ma'am," Her voice fades into a bitter whisper as she takes a hefty swig straight from the liquor bottle. "We're leaving."

The words leave me stunned, and I barely have a moment to process before her hand clamps around my wrist. Her grip is ironclad, dragging me along as she strides with purpose through the castle's grand hallways and out into the open air. Her impatience manifests in the form of her foot, tapping rhythmically against the cobblestone floor.

Her demands for a car echo around us, making the guard nearby jump into action. I feel like a lamb being led to slaughter.

"But...where are we going?" I ask, my words getting swallowed by the night.

Carina doesn't answer, her stony silence causing the icy tendrils of fear to weave their way around my heart and twists knots in my stomach.

Carina impatiently taps her foot, scanning the area for something.

"My Queen?" the guard asks hesitantly.

"Where's a fucking car when you need one?" she grumbles, rounding on the guard standing nearby, "You, fetch me a driver, now!" The poor man scurries off, leaving me standing there with Carina under the dim moonlight that is being obscured by the clouds.

Lycan King's Captives

"Where are we going?" My question falls on deaf ears once again as Carina continues to ignore me, pulling me further away from the castle toward the fountains, her grip never loosening. Panic rises in my chest as we move further from the castle. I've yearned to escape this place, although right now, I feel far from safe with Carina.

A few heartbeats later, a sleek black car pulls up beside us, and without releasing her death-grip on my wrist, Carina yanks open the back door and pushes me inside. She slides in after me, her harsh breaths filling the air in the confined space.

The driver takes off, and I gaze out the window, the castle's imposing structure growing smaller in the distance. My throat is dry, my heart pounding with fear. My chest tightens at the sight of the castle, which had been both my cage and my sanctuary. Now, it's just a distant silhouette against the night while Carina fixes her makeup, using a small compact from her clutch.

The city lights begin to blur as we race through the silent streets. The tension inside the car is palpable, a volatile mix of fear, uncertainty, and the stench of Carina's alcohol-tinged breath. I can barely focus on anything else, the overwhelming sense of impending doom wrapping around me like a cloak.

"Where are we going, Carina?" I manage to ask again, my voice barely more than a whisper. The words hang heavy in the silence of the car. Carina seems lost in her own world of thoughts.

She leans back in the plush leather seat, her eyes closing as she takes a deep, shuddering breath. The veneer of strength she usually wears has all but shattered, revealing a woman on the brink. For a moment, I forget she's the one who's been tormenting me.

"The city," she whispers after an agonizing silence, her voice so soft I almost miss it. "We're going to the city."

As her words sink in, a cold shudder ripples through me. The single word resonates in the tense silence. The city. With Carina... at night. A place I spent my human years fearing. Night is when the monsters come out to play, yet now I am one of them. However, that doesn't make me feel any better, since Xandros has ordered me never to shift. I might as well be human still, just with heightened senses.

The moonlight casts an eerie glow on Carina's face, revealing the lines of worry and the sheen of tears her foundation couldn't quite cover. A newfound fear grips me. If this woman, who prides herself on her strength and ruthlessness, is this broken, just what kind of terror awaits me at our destination? The car pulls up in a part of the city I am not familiar with, though it doesn't hold the same seedy edge that Mal's or Toby's held at night. We stop outside a nightclub.

Stepping into the club is like entering a world I never knew existed. Neon lights flash across the darkened space, casting a surreal glow on the patrons. The bass from the music is a tangible entity on its own. Jazz music playing from speakers drowns out every sound except the beating of my heart. It seeps through my body and syncs with the pulse of fear that's beating within me. Carina's hold on my arm is firm, leading me further into the depths of the club.

An aura of power radiates off Carina, causing patrons to part and give way. Their eyes linger on us, a mix of curiosity and wariness. I can't shake off the feeling of being blind to the danger as we navigate through the crowd. I glance at Carina, her icy exterior seeming to take pleasure in the control she commands.

Carina is a force, captivating and terrifying, while I stand beside her like a shadow, her presence eclipsing mine, which I am perfectly okay with; I don't want the attention she is getting, I can practically feel their eyes boring into us. It's clear she's respected; out of awe or fear, I am unsure.

The thought does little to alleviate my worry. I'm the outsider, the unwanted tag along on a night that feels like a twisted version of a girls' night out as she downs so many drinks at the bar that it would leave me on the floor. I sip mine, but as soon as I finish one, she is pushing another in front of me.

Her phone continuously rings in her bag, each time earning a growl from her that has the barmaid jumping.

After a few hours, Carina suddenly halts her drinking and her gaze meets mine, a predatory glint in her eyes. "You remind me so much of your mother," she says, the words slurred with the alcohol she's been consuming.

I can't hide the surprise that washes over me at the abrupt conversation; for the most part we have sat in stony silence. I never knew my mother, though her ghost seems to haunt my every step, tarnishing the ground I walk on with her ghostly shadowed footsteps. Cursing me to a fate that was destined for her, punishing me every time I try to step out of the image of who she was. "I suppose you hated her as much as everyone else?" I ask, the bitterness evident in my tone. I brace myself for her response, expecting the same scorn and distaste I've become accustomed to hearing.

She surprises me when she answers. "No, actually, I find it oddly comforting, though I must admit, I do hate you. Your presence is set to ruin everything, just like my father claims. Still, you remind me of her," Carina rambles, her words slurred and eyes glassy from the copious amounts of consumed alcohol.

My heart pounds in my chest. "You knew my mother?" I manage to ask, my voice barely above a whisper.

Carina laughs, the sound off-kilter and out of place in the tense atmosphere. She stumbles off her stool, and I am quick to reach out and steady her. Her skirt has ridden up during her stumble, and I quickly adjust it for her, when I notice a table of nearby men watching her with their leering gazes. The gazes of the men are like hungry wolves, watching their prey, it unsettles me.

"I'll tell you a secret," Carina whispers into my ear, her breath carrying the sweet, intoxicating scent of the margarita she has been drinking. "I loved her," she confesses, her words sending a jolt through me. "Which is making it extremely difficult to hate you."

Then, without another word, she grabs my arm. "Where are we going now?"

"To find something stronger, unless you're offering a vein?" she tells me, and I shake my head. She snorts. "Didn't think so, come on." We're off again, this time in search of something 'stronger'. She doesn't have to clarify what she means, I already know. As we leave this club, I hear the scrape of chairs. Glancing over my shoulder, I see the six men who were watching her move to leave as well.

The next stop is a blood bar. The sight of humans willingly offering their veins to the vampires is unsettling, to say the least, though not as unsettling as those forced against their will. I watch as Carina selects a woman, pulling her into a booth and out of sight. I turn away, trying to ignore the reality of this world I've been thrust into.

However, it's short-lived as Carina tugs my arm and pulls me into the booth as well, closing the curtain. I freeze, as Carina lowers her lips to the woman's neck. Her eyes flutter closed, and a soft moan escapes her lips as Carina begins to feed on her. It's revolting, my stomach roiling with nausea and fear. I want to scream and run away from this place, but my feet are rooted firmly in place.

The girl starts to turn limp in her arms. "Carina... You're killing her," I whisper, pulling on the girl's arm. She pulls her fangs from the girl's neck, gripping the girl's chin; the girl has a goofy smile on her face when Carina shocks me when she kisses her.

"So pretty, you best leave before I gobble you up," Carina whispers. I help the girl stand, and a nearby worker helps her by taking her away from the other patrons toward the back near the staff entrance, yet as I move to close the curtain of the booth. I notice the men from the previous club; I make eye contact with one, the sparkle in his gaze and the way he smirks makes me shut the curtain quickly.

The danger of this situation presses down on me like a heavy weight. Carina, even in her drunk state, is clearly a well-known figure, though I'm realizing not in a good way. The men outside our curtained sanctuary clearly have scores to settle with her. However, the danger doesn't stop there because I am no fighter and can't shift and as I peer down at Carina slumped in her chair, it's clear she is not only intoxicated but blood drunk.

I am grappling with panic and confusion when a foreign sound resonates through the cramped booth. It's a ringing phone, and I search for the sound, before realizing it's coming from Carina's clutch. She smacks her clutch haphazardly as if that alone will make it quiet, and it falls off the chair beside her. I scoop it up, unzipping it and looking at the screen. The caller ID displays a name that sends a new wave of fear coursing through me yet also relief. He's going to kill me. Although, he may have to get in line if my thoughts of the men outside are correct.

Lycan King's Captives

Xandros. The ringing slices through the drunken haze enveloping Carina, she is far beyond answering it as she giggles to herself.

I swipe to answer the call, my pulse echoing loudly in my ears.

"Where is my mate, Carina!" The voice on the other end is frantic and seething. "I swear, if you've hurt her—"

"It's me, Xandros," I interrupt him. There's a heartbeat of silence, then he breathes out. "You're alive," he breathes out. I'm certain he would know if I were dead, it's not like either of us can escape the buzz of the bond.

"You're okay." His words are not a question, but a sigh of relief. I shake off the thought of him caring for me. I can't afford to dwell on that now because I know it's only a façade.

"Where are you?" he demands, and his tone brings me back to reality.

"Some blood bank bar, Carina is drunk as shit and..." I glance back at Carina, and my heart sinks as I see her passed out against the wall of the booth.

"What's wrong?" Xandros asks, picking up on the anxiety in my voice.

"She's passed out," I whisper, scanning the increasingly hostile crowd around us as I stick my head out the curtain.

"Where is her guard?"

"She didn't bring one, we are alone... ah, Xandros?" I tell him, my voice barely above a whisper. "I think we were followed by a group of men; they were watching Carina and I at the other club," I admit. His growl resonates through the phone, making me flinch.

"I'm on my way, and don't you dare think about running, Sienna." Xandros's icy tone sends chills down my spine as he ends the call. I'm left staring at the phone in my hand, then at Carina, who is slumped in her seat.

Then whispers creep through the heavy curtain separating us from the bar. The men outside are becoming increasingly agitated, their comments growing more venomous.

"Isn't that the vampire bitch, our future queen," one sneers.

Another adds, "It's unlike the future king to leave his betrothed unguarded." Another man from the other club laughs.

"Easy pickings, I've always hated that bitch." The hostility in his voice makes my skin crawl.

"I owe that king a bit of vengeance, took my fucking eye when he killed Mal," one growls. The atmosphere outside the booth is a boiling pot of resentment and hostility.

With rising dread, I realize we are sitting ducks. Against all logic, I try to rouse Carina again. I could abandon her to whatever fate they have in store for her, but I would never be able to live with myself if they hurt her when I could have helped her. "We can't stay here, Carina. We aren't safe here," I whisper, pulling on her arm. Carina is dead weight. As if on cue, the curtain is ripped open, three men crowding the entrance of the booth, their menacing expressions promising nothing good.

I'm caught off guard and stumble back and nearly fall on Carina's lap. The men eye Carina behind me with undisguised malice. One reaches for her, grabbing her wrist. Summoning the last shred of courage, I force myself between them. "Back off, the king is on his way." I warn the man. He smirks. "Is that right?" he laughs. I slap his wrist when he reaches for her again. "I said leave her, if you touch her the king will kill you," I sputter.

One man sneers—the man missing an eye. The only thing left is just a hollow socket on one side. "We best be quick, then." His words echo in the space, and they send my heart hammering against my ribs. My words of warning have fallen on deaf ears, and I can only hope Xandros arrives soon.

As much as Xandros is feared, it's clear he's also hated.

I lean down to Carina, whispering, "Carina, you need to get up." Before the words have fully left my mouth, the man snarls. The sudden glare of the bar lights is blinding. The three burly men cram themselves into the booth, their ravenous eyes falling on Carina.

Though they clearly recognize Carina, they don't seem to know of Xandros's mate. Their attention is solely on Carina, who has become an easier target in her current state.

"Back off!" I warn them. Their reaction is far from what I had hoped for. Their smirks turn crueler.

Another scrutinizes me and recognition flits across his face. "I recognize you, you're Sienna... whatsy's face's niece," he smirks. "Your uncle owes me $1500! Best settle that debt while here." With that, he grabs my wrist with a grip that could crush bones.

My struggle proves futile as they haul me out of the booth and toss me onto a nearby pool table. I instantly thrash as they jerk me around like a rag doll. My legs kicking frantically while they try to pin me.

In the midst of the chaos, I catch sight of Carina being dragged away. She comes to just in time, awareness flooding her face as she is bent over a pool table nearby. "Sienna?" she mumbles, panic lacing her voice as she pushes off the table, only to have her head slammed against the wood. It's too late; they've begun tearing at her clothes, their cruel laughter mingling with the deafening beat of the music I know will forever haunt me.

"Do you have any idea who I am? Get your fucking hands off me!" Carina snarls, her voice echoing through the now nearly empty club. Peering around, I see most patrons have left, even the staff have abandoned us as I kick and thrash in panic. One of the men responds, "Oh, we know exactly who you are, love. Now you're going to know who we are," the man answers her.

My foot connects with one man's face. On the pool table, I scramble to my knees, and my eyes land on a pool cue, I crawl to it. Grasping it, just as fingers lock around my ankle. I swing blindly with all my might; the cue connecting with one of the men's groin. He doubles over, letting me go. I bolt off the table, heading for Carina. She's managed to fight one off, when another—a vampire—has sunk his teeth into her neck. Her scream is cut off abruptly, replaced by a gurgling sound that has my stomach churning when I am cut off by another man.

"Stay back!" I snap at him, trying to keep my eyes on both men.

Suddenly, the screech of tires outside steals my attention, my heart hammering even louder. As I turn back to Carina, I see her ripping a man's heart from his chest.

"Oh, you've fucked up," she taunts, albeit shakily. Her victory is short-lived, as another man shoves her back over a pool table after punching her. One man lay dead at her feet, leaving five to contend with.

"You think so?" the man laughs, while I am backed into a corner by three others, brandishing my broken pool stick while trying to keep track of the two men who have Carina. They are tall and muscular, with dark eyes full of malice boring into me, Their faces are twisted in menacing sneers, and one has a deep scar down his face. They move toward me with predatory grace. They wear dark clothing, ripped and stained with blood. One has a leather jacket on, the other a cloak that I can tell is expensive by how thick it is. Their hands are clenched into fists, and they have an air of danger about them. Two of which I swear I've seen in Toby's bar or Mal's, so I know they frequent the seedier areas of the city, which means it won't end well for us.

"I know so," Carina laughs. The man holding her wrists to the table glances at his friend. "I may be the king's wife, but she is his mate and that?" Carina laughs, nodding toward the door. The sound of car doors opening and closing outside sends a wave of silence through the room. Everyone freezes, our ears straining over the music. "Is the sound of your death." Her words hang heavily in the air. The men glance at each other nervously.

It seems as if the door has opened on cue, and Xandros steps inside, accompanied by his guards. All eyes turn to Xandros as he strides into the club, his eyes scanning the room. Xandros is an imposing figure, standing tall, leaving no questioning of his authority. His features are sharp, and his gaze is intense. He is dressed in a black suit, and it is crinkled, which I find odd; he always looks impeccable. As he moves further into the room, his presence commands everyone's attention, the men watching him fearfully, and his presence alone is enough to fill the room with tension. His gaze sweeps over the scene—Carina bent over a pool table, a man cowering away from her the moment he steps into the room, and me, petrified, brandishing a pool cue.

His eyes burn with a fury that could ignite the air itself. He's a tempest made of flesh, and I am caught in the eye of his storm.

His gaze lands on me, and the room shrinks until it is only us. The dim light paints shadows on his face, turning him into a terrifying apparition of his usual self. When eyes find mine, for a moment, time is suspended in the space between our locked gazes. There is an entire conversation at that moment, a silent promise of wrath and retribution.

"What do we have here?" Xandros growls, the deadly timbre of his voice sending chills down my spine. The men around me shrink back, their once bold stances now wilted in the presence of the king. One of them stammers, "We didn't know they were yours."

A low growl escapes his throat, rippling through the room like a menacing premonition. The men around me instinctively back away, their smirks faltering at the sight of the furious king.

"Carina, are you okay?" he calls over to her, not taking his eyes off the men who dared touch us. She pulls herself to a standing position, one hand clutching her torn clothes, a mad laugh escaping her lips. "Oh, they'll wish they never touched us, Xan."

"Sienna," he says, his voice barely audible over the pounding music. "Are you okay?"

I shake my head, unable to find my voice. The pool cue still feels heavy in my grip, my fingers numb from the strain.

"You knew exactly who they are," Xandros speaks menacingly.

"No, My King, we would never."

A humorless smile spreads across Xandros's face, a predatory gleam in his eyes. He saunters through the room, taking in the carnage with an air of detached calm.

"Grab my wife," he instructs his guards, never breaking his stride. They rush to obey, pulling Carina off the pool table.

Turning to me, Xandros picks up a pool stick, twirling it effortlessly between his fingers. The question he poses is deceptively gentle. "Did they hurt you, Sienna?" I shake my head, my pulse still pounding in my ears. They hadn't hurt me—not yet—it's clear from their leering faces they had every intention to.

"We were just helping them get home, they freaked out," one man splutters, desperation tinging his voice. Carina laughs at this, a maniacal sound that bounces off the walls. "Liar, liar, pants on fire," she teases, her voice wavering as it slurs.

"No...she is drunk, my—" the man's voice dies in his throat as Xandros sends the pool stick flying. It finds its mark, spearing through the man's mouth and pinning him to the drywall. His eyes widen in shock as he convulses violently, choking on his own blood before going still.

The room erupts into chaos. Xandros moves with lethal precision, seizing two pool balls from the table. His eyes blaze with an intense fury as he launches himself at the remaining men. There's no hesitation, no mercy, only the brutal efficiency of a seasoned fighter.

His movements are a blur, a deadly dance of violence. The crunch of bones, the wet sounds of impact, and the screams of the men fill the room. Every swing, every hit lands with deadly accuracy, reducing the once arrogant men into whimpering heaps on the floor.

When the dust settles, Xandros stands in the middle of the carnage, his chest heaving. Blood splatters his face, and his hands are stained with it. Around him, the men lay sprawled on the ground, gasping before becoming lifeless corpses. The men's blood-soaked bodies crumpled against the floor and broken furniture, each face masks of pain and terror.

Blood is everywhere on the carpet, pooling, creating a lake of red. As Xandros moves, his boot splatters it, causing the crimson to spray and fleck.

The man's grizzled face is a mask of insanity, his eyes bulging and red, his mouth gaping.

Their faces contort as they choke and sputter, as if they will never willingly give in. This is a fight they can't possibly win.

I stand petrified. The guards clutching Carina and me are the only ones left standing. The sickening smell of blood fills the air.

"They touched what's mine, Sienna. Don't look so shocked. Dead men bleed red," Xandros states and my eyes flick to him. I listen to their last raspy breaths, watching their chests rise and fall in a desperate attempt to survive.

His gaze is cold, and his hands flex around the now bloody pool balls. The tang of copper in the air, the odor of blood and bile. The king is back in control, and there's nothing except death in his wake as he drops the bloody pool balls onto the table, one sinking into the pocket while the other leaves a bloody trail along the table as it rolls.

"You didn't run?" he questions, tilting his head to the side.

"I couldn't leave her with them."

His brows crease in the middle. "You could have. Why didn't you? You had a chance to escape," he asks, walking slowly toward me. My eyes go to Carina, who is now slumped passed out in one guard's arms. "They would have raped her," I stammer.

"So?" he asks, his eyes watching me, scrutinizing my every move. I can't tell if it is anger or admiration in his gaze as he steps closer to me and raises a hand to my chin. His fingers are cold against my skin, and I force myself not to flinch away.

"I couldn't leave her with them," I repeat steadily, forcing down the fear that is rising in me.

Xandros's expression softens ever so slightly as his hand drops away from my face. "You risked your life for her," he says quietly and nods toward Carina. "Why?"

I hesitate before answering, still unsure of why I had done it or of what this might mean for me. "Because no one should have to go through that," I finally answer truthfully, meeting his gaze without flinching.

"You are an odd woman. Carina has done nothing but keep us apart, and you would remain to protect her, when she doesn't deserve your protection?"

"I'm a woman," I growl like that should be explanation enough, and he raises an eyebrow at me.

"You are," he answers, stepping in front of me, his hands bloody when he cups my face in them.

"Something you'll never understand, my reasoning doesn't matter, not to a man," I tell him.

"You speak in riddles."

"No, I am pretty sure I spoke clearly, Xandros. I didn't abandon her because I know exactly what it's like to be forced against your will," I sneer, and his thumb stops brushing my cheek, stopping below my ear.

"I have never forced you."

"Using the bond against me is the same thing; you know I can't fight the bond, I am not used to my instincts to fight them, but you, you are."

"You're mine," he growls, becoming annoyed, still I refuse to release him from my angry gaze.

"That is exactly the problem, Xandros. I am yours, but you're never to be mine. I am property, one of your captives," I tell him, and he lifts his chin, his gaze turning unsettling.

"Put Carina in the car," he calls over his shoulder. The guards leave, leaving me with my angry mate.

"It appears you think you can talk back to me now," I hold my breath waiting for whatever punishment he decides to come.

I step back from him, and he pauses when my ass hits the pool table. He clenches his jaw, and my heart skips a beat in fear. "Come," he says, turning abruptly on his heel and walking toward the doors.

I can feel his anger radiating off him in waves, and I don't dare to speak or even look up at him. We make our way to the parking lot, and he stops abruptly. He turns to me and his gaze is menacing and full of rage.

"Now, Sienna! Don't make me chase you," he warns, and I swallow, knowing I have no choice. Reluctantly, I follow him outside to see the staff of the blood bar waiting outside along the sidewalk. Xandros waits by the open door of the car, his stony gaze glaring at the brickwork of the club he's parked in front of. As I near him, he does not meet my gaze. Ducking my head, I slide across the seat, and he climbs in after me.

The car immediately takes off and I move to fix Carina's skirt that once again has ridden up, before grabbing the throw blanket between the limousine seats and tossing it over her. Sitting back in my seat, I find Xandros watching me with an indecipherable look on his face.

I turn my attention to the window, watching the city lights pass me by. The silence in the limo is cold, deafening and no one speaks. I kinda wish for Carina to wake up, at least then the tension wouldn't be so thick with Xandros attention on his wife instead of me.

As we reach the iron gates of the castle, I sit up straighter, eager to go back to my prison of a room. Never have I wished for that cold ass room so much. I'm exhausted and want nothing more than to be in my own company. However, as the car pulls up, I find that won't be allowed. "Wait," Xandros calls, as the driver opens the door. My heart skips a beat in surprise. I thought we were already done with our silent journey back to the castle. The driver opens my door, and I wait for Xandros's command.

When he says nothing, I roll my eyes, and turn back to see him scoop up Carina, lifting her from the seat. "I need you to open the doors for me," he tells me. Of course, that is what he wants me for; an errand girl.

Shaking my head, I climb out of the limo as he slides out with her in his arms. I lead him through the castle back to his quarters, opening doors like he asks. Finally, opening the bedroom door, I leave him with his wife and make my way back to the other side of the castle, to my gilded prison. The door is open, and I step inside, only to hear footsteps come up behind me. With a heavy sigh, I wait for the maid or whoever followed me to lock me inside.

However, I'm surprised to see Xandros step into the room, closing the door behind him. He moves to the fireplace to get it going, while I choose to ignore his presence by wandering into the bathroom. If he is starting the fire means he wants one thing, and one thing only. He can at least let me shower first. Stripping my clothes off, I turn the taps on, and I am about to step in when I feel his presence behind me. The air is suddenly pungent with his scent.

"Can I at least shower first?" I ask him, gritting my teeth. He runs his fingertips down my arm, sending shivers through my body despite my best efforts to remain still. When he doesn't answer right away, I glance over my shoulder to see him watching me intently. His gaze is so intense it feels like a thousand needles pressing into my skin.

He slowly comes closer and wraps his arms around me from behind, resting his chin on the top of my head and sighing.

"Can I join you?" he whispers in a soft, broken voice that makes me shiver even more than before.

Like I have any choice, ignoring his words I step in, and he removes his shirt, then his pants, letting them slip to the floor. As I said, I don't have a choice. He invades my space as I shower, bumping into me as he washes himself. I shower quickly, choosing not to linger and get this over with, so I can hopefully sleep. Stepping into the bedroom, I ponder whether to actually bother getting dressed. I just got my new pajamas and these ones are actually warm, I don't want him ripping them like he usually does.

Xandros steps out a few moments after me and wanders to the walk-in closet. He disappears for a few seconds while I dry myself, then crawl into bed, waiting for his calling to slip out and subdue me as he likes to do.

I am surprised when Xandros crawls in beside me, tugging back the covers and tugging my back against his chest. I tense, expecting him to do something. Instead he just sighs and wraps his arm around me securely. Confused, I glance over my shoulder to find him wearing shorts. His usually pale skin now shows shades of pink on his cheeks as he has a peaceful expression on his face.

"You don't like your new pajamas?" he asks softly. I furrow my brows, yet before I can question his odd behavior, I hear his breathing even out, his breath warm against my neck. Glancing over my shoulder again, I find him asleep with a look of contentment on his face. Did he just want some warmth tonight?

Unable to wrap my mind around it all, I make myself comfortable and drift off into a deep sleep, too.

Chapter Twenty-Seven

Sienna

The next morning when I wake, Xandros is gone, his side of the bed cold, like he has been gone for a while, only his faint lingering scent remains, reminding me last night was not some nightmare my mind conjured up. Getting up, I get dressed, getting ready for another repetitive day.

As the maid unlocks my door, the other servants give me strange looks. I navigate my way through the castle to the kitchens for breakfast, which consists of burned toast because I forgot to turn the toaster down. As the day goes on, I don't see Xandros, and I find Carina's absence bizarre; she usually has a never-ending list of things for me to do, ensuring I don't get a chance to rest while with her.

The castle is abuzz with whispers and murmurs. The wedding has been postponed. I overhear one of the maids gossiping about it, and my heart skips a beat. A flicker of hope ignites within me, only it's quickly extinguished by the weight of reality. I'm still trapped here, still bound by the mate bond to a man who is supposed to marry another woman. So where does that leave me now? He clearly doesn't want me and even if he did, I don't want to be a prisoner, plus his mother hates me, that is a disaster waiting to happen.

As I'm dusting off a tall bookshelf in the library, I hear voices coming from the adjacent room. Curiosity piques, so I quietly creep closer, pressing my ear against the heavy oak door.

The voices grow louder, and for a heartbeat I catch a glimpse of a familiar figure through the keyhole. Carina. My heart jumps into my throat as she talks to someone else, her voice low and urgent. The other person's voice is not hearable, so I figure she must be on the phone, since I can make out parts of their conversation.

"Father, please, I will convince him. You don't need to send for me." Carina's voice echoes through the door, laced with desperation.

A cold, harsh voice responds, though it is crackly, so I definitely know it's the loudspeaker on her phone. His voice sends shivers down my spine. "You should've thought about that before you jeopardized the treaty, Carina. If Xandros doesn't marry you, or you haven't fallen pregnant by next month, you'll have to face the consequences."

My heart pounds against my chest as I listen in, fear coiling in my stomach like a venomous snake. I've never heard Carina sound so vulnerable, so scared. I quickly retreat, not wanting to be caught eavesdropping.

Later that day, I find Carina in the garden, her face pale and eyes red-rimmed from crying. As much as I despise her, we're both pawns in this game, trapped in a life neither of us chose.

"What's going to happen to you if you go back home?" I find myself asking. She doesn't answer for a long time, her gaze lost in the blooming roses. She lifts her head and raises an eyebrow at me. "I overheard you, speaking on the phone this morning," I admit, and she sighs heavily, returning to staring at the gardens.

"I can't go home, Sienna," she finally says, her voice barely a whisper. "If Xandros doesn't marry me or give me a child, I might not have a choice."

For the first time, I see a glimpse of the woman beneath the façade, a woman trapped and scared, much like me. I don't ask any more questions, and we spend the rest of the day in silence, each lost in our own thoughts, each grappling with our own fears.

When she heads back inside, I follow beside her when we spot Xandros. He pauses and so does his mother as they walk down the stairs toward us. "Did you just come from the gardens, dear?"

Lycan King's Captives

Carina nods. Queen Adina eyes me, her lips pursing before she turns her attention back to Carina. "Well, the weather is lovely today," she says, the tension in the room becoming suffocating.

"Tea, Adina?" Carina asks her and Queen Adina smiles. "Sounds lovely," she answers, and Carina turns to me. "You are finished for the day," she dismisses me, and I watch her leave with Queen Adina; however, Xandros remains. I glance at him.

"Did you really postpone the wedding?" I ask and he watches me for a second.

"Yes, I pushed it back a month," he answers. I clench my teeth, and swallow down the strange lump that forms in my throat. My bond aches for the man, and I despise it just as much as I despise him.

"Sienna?" he murmurs, stepping closer to me, and I take a step back. "I have chores," I whisper, stepping around him when he grabs my arm. He pulls me back in front of him, dropping his head to lean closer. "I... everything will work out, I'll keep you safe," he whispers.

"From whom?" I ask. Does he not realize the pain he causes me by forcing me to watch him play house with another woman.

"From my mother, Carina. Who else?" he whispers.

"And who will keep me safe from you?" I ask him, and he stands straighter, staring down at me. His lips part and I hate how my eyes instantly go to them.

"I won't hurt you, Sienna."

"You already have, you do, by forcing me to remain here when clearly you don't want me."

"That's for your own safety, I have to keep my distance. Do you think the bond doesn't affect me?" he growls.

"You're not the one who sleeps alone every night, you're not the one forced to watch me be with another," I whisper, my eyes stinging at how much those words hurt leaving my lips.

Hearing footsteps, Xandros lets me go, and I make haste to get away from him, climbing the steps and rushing to my room.

Chapter Twenty-Eight

Sienna

I spent the rest of the day in my room, only leaving when it was time to help with dinner. As usual, I lean against the wall waiting to be called on by Carina. Xandros doesn't touch his food, instead stares vacantly at the wall, as if deep in thought. His parents try to rouse conversation out of him, it only gets them short answers.

"Do you have any plans tomorrow, Carina? I am planning to go into the city to find my dress for the wedding." Queen Adina states, taking a bite of her dessert.

"Actually, tomorrow I am leaving. My father wants me to go home for my mother's birthday. I'll be gone a week," she answers, which grabs Xandros attention.

"You didn't tell me you were leaving."

"My father called this morning. I'll only be gone a week," she shrugs.

"Well, you should take Xandros with you, it would be good to get away from all the drama here," his mother says, her eyes flicking to me. Carina's face lights up as she looks at Xandros like a deer caught in the headlights. I swallow at the thought, it is painful enough with Xandros being across the other side of the castle, let alone gone an entire week.

"Hm, Father would like that?" Carina answers, staring at Xandros who clenches his jaw.

"I can watch your maid, no need for her to tarnish your time away," Adina states, and his father clears his throat awkwardly, earning a glare from his wife. "Well, then glad that is sorted, you can both go away for the week, tell your mother I said happy birthday."

"I never said I was going, Mother," Xandros growls.

"Nonsense, it would be rude not to," his mother snaps, shooting him a glare. A small, hollow laugh escapes Adina's lips. Xandros bites back a growl.

Carina's breathing increases, her eyes dart from face to face around the table as his mother stares at Xandros expectantly.

"No," Xandros states without looking away from his plate, his face expressionless and unreadable.

"Come on, it would be such a nice trip for you both," she pleads with him. He finally looks up at her, and I can feel my heart thumping faster in my chest as our eyes meet. His gaze is intense as he turns his attention to his mother. He stares at her for a few seconds before sighing heavily and agreeing to go along with it.

The rest of dinner goes by slowly as I think about what this means for me and Xandros. I wonder how painful it will be with him gone. When it is time for us to retire, I race back to my room.

Once back in my room, I call Toby. My fingers are still shaking as I punch in his number, the fresh memory of the night's events playing out like a horror film in my mind. It's late, and the fear that's humming in my veins has effectively stripped away any desire to sleep.

The line connects, and Toby picks up on the third ring. His voice is thick with sleep, "Sienna, what's wrong?"

"We need to move our plans forward," I say, trying to keep my voice steady.

Silence from the other end, then a low curse, "Shit, what happened?" Toby asks, worry lacing his voice.

"Later," I say, glancing nervously at the door. "Did you speak with the seekers?"

Toby lets out a soft sigh, "One of them has agreed to help us get out of the city next week. I've been thinking about how to get you out, and I think the best option would be to hide you in the laundry run. Tyra has been placed on that detail, and she can smuggle you out in the crates," he tells me and I lean against the mini bar.

"When?" I ask.

"I was going to call you tomorrow; the seeker I spoke with said another week before he is placed on the tunnel post." I curse under my breath, why couldn't it be this week, this week would be perfect since Xandros will be away.

"Can't do it any sooner?" I plead.

"Not until next week, why?"

My heart pounds in my chest at the thought of escaping, the raw fear consuming me.

"Okay, but we need to be careful, this week, I might not be able to call you. I'm being left with Adina, Xandros is leaving for a week with Carina..." I whisper.

"He's what? He's marked you, mates can't be separated, it could force you into heat, or worse make you ill. I can't believe he agreed to such a thing," Toby snarls.

"Well, it will be good practice when with you, I guess."

"You'll have me, a few hours won't hurt, however, a week, that is going to be hell for you, Sienna, maybe not him since you haven't marked him. I've heard being separated for long lengths causes pain that has driven Lycans insane." His words make bile rise in my throat.

"This is bad," Toby's voice is grim, the fear for me clear in his tone.

I'm about to respond, to assure him I'll try to remain in contact during the week, when the sound of my door handle twisting sends my heart into overdrive. In a panic, I hang up the phone quickly, shoving it back on the hook before jamming the phone number back in its hiding spot. I rush to close the bar doors, spinning around just in time to see Xandros walking into the room. His gaze is icy and hard as it locks onto me.

"Who were you talking to?" His question is cold and demanding, carrying an implicit threat. The familiar fear claws its way up my throat, and I wonder how much of our conversation he overheard. "No one," I answer cautiously as he steps into the room. His eyes track me as I make my way to the fireplace, and stoke the dying embers.

Chapter Twenty-Nine

Xandros

As I make my way down the dimly lit hallway, a knot of dread and anticipation builds in my stomach. The trip to visit King Vin and Queen Anita Dresdan isn't something I'm looking forward to. The thought of leaving Sienna, even for a week, gnaws at my insides. I worry about her safety in my absence. More than that, I dread the pain our bond would cause her once we're miles apart.

I contemplate the situation with a frown, my boots echoing hollowly on the marble floor. My mother would undoubtedly seize this opportunity to terrorize Sienna. To keep her safe, it was necessary for me to show I was willing to negotiate the treaty. In this twisted game of power, my presence at the Dresdan's court would keep my mother's claws at bay. At least, until I manage to convince Carina to sign the divorce papers.

Just as I'm about to reach Sienna's door, I pause, hearing the soft lilt of her voice. My fingers curl around the doorknob just as Sienna's voice drifts through the door. "Well, it will be good practice when with you, I guess." Who is she talking to?

I unlock her door and push it open. My heart skips a beat as I step into the room. Sienna is standing by the bar area, her eyes wide with surprise... and something else. Fear.

"Who were you talking to?" I ask her. Her face instantly drains of color, her eyes widening and her heart beats like a drum in her chest. She scrambles away from the concealed bar and moves toward the fireplace, she begins stoking and stammers, "Ah, no one." The elevated tempo of her heartbeat and the sharp tang of fear betray her words.

I survey the room, taking in its deserted state, then fix my gaze on her. "I heard you," I tell her, and her body tenses further. The fire crackles low in the grate and her eyes reflect the glow of the orange dying flames. Her hands twist in each other, the tension evident in the way she moves.

The room is empty. There is no one here, and yet I know she was speaking with someone. I still peer around. The light from the fireplace illuminates the room in a soft, warm light. It hides the secrets of the room, casting each piece of furniture in shadow. The room is strewn with both Sienna and my clothes from last night that I left here after I got changed; I can tell she hasn't bothered to tidy up.

"I was talking to myself, Xandros. As you can see, no one is here," she rushes out, moving away from me toward the dresser. I follow her, the scent of her fear, her nervousness, filling my senses. I corner her against the dresser, my chest pressed against her back. As I inhale her scent, desire coils within me. It is an intoxicating blend of her fear and my arousal, mingling together, becoming mouthwatering.

"You wouldn't be lying to me, now, would you, Sienna?" I purr into her ear.

She laughs nervously, a false brightness in her voice as she pushes me away. I don't budge. Her hands ball into fists, and she takes a step away from me, only to bump into the dresser, there is nowhere she can move from me, her eyes dart from my face to the windows and back again.

I step toward her, her body a magnet for my hands. I stroke her arms, gently coaxing her to relax. "Who were you speaking to?" I ask again, my eyes watching her face. "No one," she breathes, shoving and moving toward the bathroom. I watch her disappear, not liking her behavior; it seems off.

Alone, I pour myself a drink, my mind mulling over her odd behavior. My eyes catch the sight of a misplaced phone, a piece of paper peeking from beneath a mug. Glancing at the bathroom door, I hear the shower turn on before I retrieve it. It is a phone number, one I don't recognize. A twinge of anger hits me as I pull my phone from my pocket and snap a picture of it. My suspicions were clearly not misplaced.

Entering the bathroom, I am wanting to confront her when I'm immediately hit with the sight of Sienna's naked form in the shower, the steam from the hot water wrapping around her like a misty veil. Her scent grows stronger in the humid room, instantly making me forget my anger as my cock twitches in my pants at the sight of her.

"What time do you leave tomorrow?" she asks, her voice too casual. The steam from the hot water makes her skin glisten, the droplets sluicing down the slopes of her breasts and hips, her eyes closed as she runs her hands through her hair. Her legs spread just enough for my eyes to see her beautiful pussy.

I watch her as I undress, and she peers over at me when I don't answer, her eyes trailing over my body. "One of the maids will bring you a TV tomorrow. It will help keep you distracted until I return," I inform her as I unbutton my trousers. I let them fall to the floor, loving the way her gaze follows. Her tongue darts out, scraping the bottom of her pouty lips. She is sin—my sin. Opening the shower door, I step into the shower, and she quickly moves, allowing more room "I'm also having some of my clothes brought here. My scent will help lessen the pain of our separation."

"Will it hurt?" Her voice is barely a whisper.

"I'm trying to make sure it doesn't. Javier will stay here with you, and if it becomes too much, he'll call me, and I'll find an excuse to come back," I assure her. She just nods, still facing away from me.

"Does Carina know you're here?" Her question catches me off guard, but I regain my composure quickly. "Yes, she's aware, and she understands," I respond, leaving out the part about how reluctant Carina had been about me intending to spend the night with her.

Silence fills the room as I turn her to face me, pressing her against the shower wall.

The water running down her body and her hair make her glow before my eyes.

Her gaze is what I love most, though. It's on me, in me, a violent storm of whirling violent lust. Her pupils are blown, her body quivers and her lips part. She can hate me all she wants, she won't ever deny me, not because I won't let her, and I know she can't.

Despite the scar my mother gave her, the one I want to desperately heal her of, she is as beautiful as the night I first spotted her. Her small frame trapped by my larger one with her hair hanging in loose wet curls, her eyes the color of the stormiest night.

My hands trail up her side, barely touching and despite the heat in the room from the shower, goosebumps cover her skin at my touch, her nipples hardening as my hand cups it, my thumb brushing over its hardened peak.

"You have me now, Sienna, so take what you want. As much as you want. I'm spending the night here tonight," I tell her, my voice rough as I fight the urge to fuck her against the shower wall. I want her, crave her, and need her just like I need air. The things I want to do to her drive me crazy. Her scent engulfs me, rolling over my senses like viscous honey, coating my skin and warming it.

"I don't want anything from you, Xandros. I just want my freedom," she retorts.

I lock eyes with her, "Your freedom I also own, Sienna. Just as I own you. I'm here now, use me to stifle your bond, or don't. We both know you will. So stop fighting it."

Chapter Thirty

Sienna

Xandros's words ricochet through my mind, an unnerving echo of truth. The bond between us is like a twisting knife, cutting deeper with each passing day. I wish he would use his calling, use the bond to force my compliance—it would be easier to despise him that way. Instead, he is gentle, a stark contrast to the cruel man I know him to be.

His powerful gaze is locked onto mine as he says, "Your freedom I also own, Sienna. Just as I own you. I'm here now, use me to stifle your bond, or don't. We both know you will. So stop fighting it." The words wash over me, a torrent of dark promises and deep truths.

My gaze shifts down, tracing the contours of his chest. His dark hair, wet, clings to his muscular form. Each muscle ripples with power and strength, a testament to the true king he is. Using my eyes, I trail lower, taking in his taut abdomen and his cock standing hard between his thighs. Desire coils within me, tightening with each beat of my heart.

His hand finds my hair, threading through the damp strands. I stay still, conflicted. There's a part of me—the part connected by the bond—that yearns for him, for his touch. Yet my pride, my sense of self, refuses to succumb. His question lingers in the steam-filled air, "What do you want, Sienna?" I remain silent, reaching for the soap instead. My movement brings me closer to him, his hard cock brushing against my thigh. The contact sends a spark through me, a memory of his girth stretching me, so do the memories of his rushed climaxes, the unfulfilled need he leaves me with.

His hand leaves my hair, and his grip moves to my chin, forcing my head back. "I know you want me, yet you deny yourself," he murmurs. His words provoke a bitter laugh. "Better I deny myself, than have you deny me when you're done with me," I whisper, and for a moment, his eyes soften.

"I don't want to hurt you."

"Yet you keep doing it," I retort.

His thumb brushes across my lips, a gentle gesture that contradicts his intentions. I am just a toy to this man, nothing more, I won't let his gentle touches and teasing remove the image of the monster he can truly be.

"Would you rather me use my calling? You're being defiant, I can feel it. Just like I felt you lying to me earlier," he whispers, and my heartbeat quickens, his accusing tone sending a jolt of fear through me. "And you were lying, weren't you, Sienna?" He questions me again about my earlier conversation, and I falter, hands trembling as I deny his accusations. "You're mistaken," I whisper.

"Do you like being punished, Sienna? Is that it?" he asks, his voice deep and resonating. I shake my head. His words are a cruel taunt, a reminder of the unbridgeable gap between us. I am his mistress, he is a king, I am no one, and he is my master. Never to compare, never at his side, forever at his feet. My back is against the cold shower wall, trapped in his overpowering presence, yet still he finds room to close the impossible space between us more. His whisper filling my ear within a breath later, nibbling on my earlobe, sending shivers down my spine. "You can't escape me, just like you can't escape our bond. So, quit trying."

My hands tremble against his chest, unsure if they wish to push him away or pull him closer. "I'm feeling generous. Tell me what you want, Sienna, and I'll forget you lied to me. Just this once," he says. I'm overwhelmed, drowning in a sea of confusion and frustration. His question about the calling strikes a chord, I know if I deny him, I will also risk him questioning me more, so reluctantly, I nod.

A pleased purr escapes him, "Good girl." His calling washes over me like a tidal wave, breaking down my resistance. "What do you want, Sienna?" he purrs. I bite into his chest, the taste of his skin mixed with water intoxicating me. Tears prick my eyes as I fight the urge to answer, to yield. "I want..." My voice trails off, drowned by the sound of the shower. "I want to taste you. I want to fuck you."

"Now that you can do," he replies, with a smirk. He urges me onto my knees. His gaze is demanding, possessive. "Open your mouth," he orders. I comply, my hand already wrapped around his hard length, yearning to explore, to taste him when he grips my chin. His thumb brushes my tongue, and I nearly choke on a gasp. He removes his thumb, replacing it with the head of his cock.

His eyes flash as he thrusts deeper, the sensation making me gag.

"Relax your throat, breathe through your nose, and eyes on me," he purrs. The possessive glint in his eyes makes me shiver. I follow his instruction, knowing later I will hate myself for it, but right now I can't seem to bring myself to disobey him, wanting him just as much as he knows I do.

I suck in a breath as I look up at him, following his command to keep my eyes on him. His hand threads through my wet hair, gripping tightly as I take him deeper into my mouth. I let my tongue swirl around him, exploring, savoring. The sounds that escape him encourage me, driving me further. His hips jolt forward as his climax hits, and I swallow down his release, his taste mingling with the hot water.

Before I can fully process what happened, he is pulling me up, his mouth crashing onto mine in a searing kiss, his taste still lingering on my tongue.

He breaks away, guiding me under the shower once more. His touch is gentle yet teasing as he washes my body. Each stroke of his hand on my skin winds me up more, my body shuddering under his touch, anticipation causing my heart to race.

Dried and wrapped in a towel, he leads me back to the bedroom. The playful smile he throws my way doesn't help to ease the tension that is built within me. He continues his teasing torment, his fingers and lips skimming across my flesh as he dries me, a soft moan escaping my lips. If he walks out right now, it will be pure agony.

"You smell divine," he purrs, a husky note in his voice. His gaze is smoldering, drawing me in as he climbs onto the bed. "Come to me, Sienna," he commands. The intensity in his eyes makes my heart pound in my chest. Hesitant yet eager, I crawl onto the bed after him and straddle his waist, ready to take him. He stops me, his strong hands gripping my hips.

"What if I want to taste you?" he purrs, his fingers tracing patterns on my thighs. His proposition sends shivers up my spine. His dark gaze meets mine, the question hanging in the air. I bite my lip, an eager nod answering him.

Before I can process his next move, he shifts, lifting my body and positioning me over his face. A squeak leaves me at the position he has placed me in, and I try to climb off him. His commanding voice echoes in the room, "Grip the headboard." His hot breath sweeps across my core, causing me to shudder, followed a second later by his tongue as it sweeps across my folds, a gasp escapes my lips as he explores, teases. Each stroke sends waves of pleasure coursing through me, I grind down on him, riding his face until my climax washes over me.

With a rapid move, he flips me over, climbing out from under me. "Retake the same position," he orders, the authority in his voice undeniable. I comply, shivering with anticipation. His hands grip my hips, and I feel him take me from behind. His rhythm is relentless, driving into me over and over.

His hand comes down on my ass, the stinging sensation followed by the soothing caress of his palm. "You won't lie to me, Sienna, or next time it won't be my hand it will be my belt, understood?" he growls. Tears prick my eyes at his words. Each spank is a reprimand for my deceit, yet his teasing touch, his words of praise, only serve to fan my desire. It is a brutal line between pain and pleasure, and I am unsure of it.

"Such a good girl for me," he purrs, "You want this, don't you, Sienna?" His words are punctuated by another thrust, another spank, further adding to my frustration. I yearn for release, I yearn for him, yet every time I think I am close, his hand comes down on my ass, tainting it and stealing my breath. I beg for him, my words a desperate plea. He chuckles darkly, "That's it, beg for me, Sienna. Beg for my cock."

His rhythm grows erratic as I whimper beneath him, my body teetering on the edge of release. He pulls back, denying me my climax. "Not yet," he whispers, his tone one of mock sympathy. The frustration is overwhelming, each teasing stroke driving me closer to the edge, only to be denied once again. My ass feels welted as he strikes me again, and I have no doubt his handprint will be a branded bruise tomorrow.

"Please... Xandros," I whimper, my voice breaking. His reply is a dark sound echoing in the room, a cross between a purr and growl, it's predatory as he thrusts into me one more time, my climax shattering through me. He follows soon after, his hold on my hips tightening as he stills. The room falls silent, save for our panting breaths, our bodies a tangled mess of satisfaction and regret. And I know there will be regret; I gave in to him as I always do, yet this time is different, this time he let me finish and just the same as last night he pulls me against him cocooning me in his embrace, and an embrace I know I loathe and love in the same breath, as I feel his heart rate even out against my back.

I wonder what it will feel like when he leaves. Will he call when he is gone? Will he miss me? All these thoughts swirl around in my head until I finally drift off into a troubled sleep.

The next morning arrives too soon, and I am filled with dread as Xandros packs his things into a bag, yet he was right; two maids came in and set up a flat screen while Xandros packed his suits. These were far from holiday clothes. He barely acknowledges me as they move to set it up in the room, sending a cold chill down my spine that makes me long for his presence even more than before. A few moments later, another maid walks in with a trolley, followed by Javier.

"That's your entire wardrobe," Javier tells him as the maids, wearing gloves, start tossing them on the bed. "No one changes those sheets or steps foot in this room after I leave, no matter the reason, am I clear?" Xandros snaps at them and they all nod. The statement makes me question how painful his absence will be if he is going to the extremes of barring people from entering in case they tarnish his scent.

But I don't get to ask any of these questions because once everyone leaves, Xandros orders my silence, laying out the rules for his mother, not to back chat, not to get in her way, not to anger or upset her. Basically, I shouldn't breathe or look in her direction. When a knock sounds on the door, he kisses my head and climbs off the bed. When he opens the door, I see it's Carina; she doesn't enter, or say anything, instead, she stares down the corridor. As they leave the castle, I am filled with worry and fear of not knowing what will happen while he is gone.

Chapter Thirty-One

Xandros

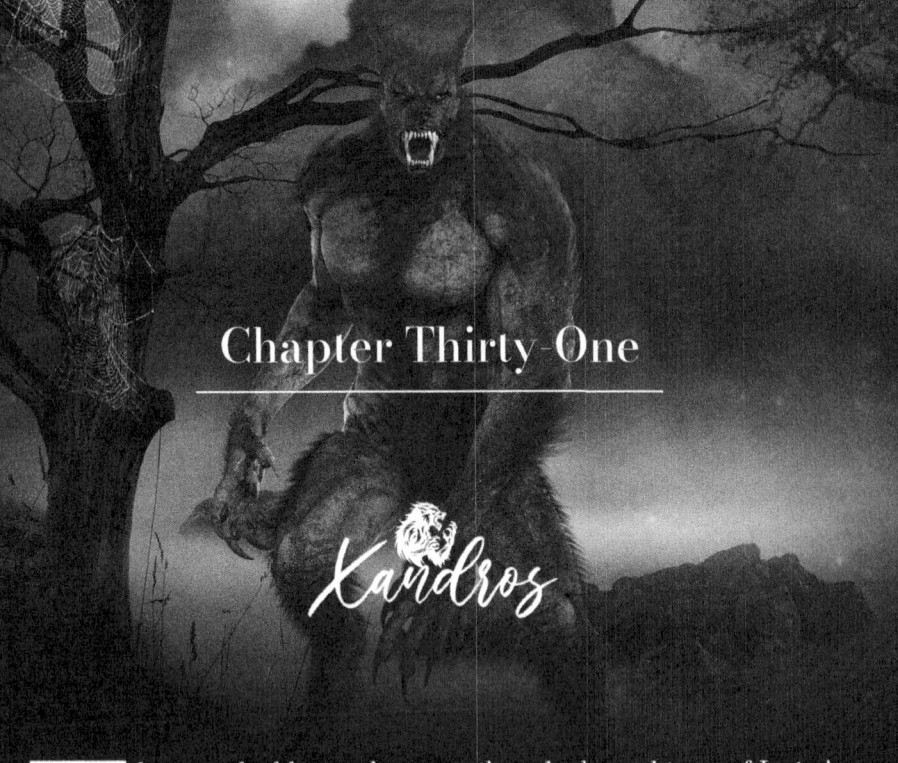

The room had been silent—so silent the low whisper of Javier's voice seemed to echo off the walls and fill the vast space.

"That's your entire wardrobe," he had said, gesturing to the bed, where I had the maids and him pile all my clothes. I hope it will be enough, yet her anxiety through the bond tells me already it won't be.

I watched silently as the maids—with their gloved hands moving swiftly and efficiently—had them go through my clothes in the master bedroom, also through the laundry for anything that smelled strongly of my scent. (Well, except for my underwear, I have limits.) They tossed them onto the bed without any regard for order or arrangement, quickly depositing them as they try to handle them as minimally as possible.

"No one changes those sheets or steps foot in this room after I leave, no matter the reason. Am I clear?" I say, my words carrying a sharp edge, a warning. The maids nod hastily, their eyes lowered before leaving the room.

Javier glances at me, a slight smirk on his face. I know now he had been testing me—determining whether I would leave Sienna to suffer. He does not agree with how myself or my parents have treated her and even now I am regretting my actions. "No one is to enter," I tell him. "I mean no one."

He simply nods and says, "Yes, ma'am." I growl at him, and he laughs, sauntering out of the room and leaving me with my mate. Her anxiety makes me more anxious.

And now, here we are, standing in my old bedroom—a small, sparsely furnished room that had once been a storeroom before I had moved back in here, and now it's Sienna's.

Sienna watches from the corner, her eyes wide, her face reflecting an array of questions I'm not willing to answer. Not now. Not when we are on the brink of something that could break us or bind us forever.

Once the room clears, I turn to Sienna. Her presence is a calming balm to my restless soul. I help Sienna with the TV, hooking it up to the Wi-Fi and handing her the remote. Once I see she has mastered it, I lay on the bed, pulling her with me. "You need to remember, Sienna, no back talk, no getting in her way, not a word to upset her. Just try to go unnoticed," I instruct, my tone clipped. The rules seem harsh, but I know my mother. And I know what Sienna must do to survive in my absence.

In the middle of our conversation, a knock interrupts us. My attention is drawn toward the door, which I open to find Carina standing on the other side. She says nothing, her gaze fixed on the corridor. As she and I leave the room and the castle, I'm filled with a sense of worry I try hard to suppress.

Reaching the stairs, I see Javier waiting at the top. I grab his arm, holding him back as Carina strides ahead, pulling my phone from my pocket. I send the photo of the phone number I took to his phone. His phone bings and he pulls it from his pocket. "Look into this number for me. And keep an eye on Sienna," I demand, holding up the spare key to her bedroom. His nod of understanding doesn't completely soothe my concerns. "My mother's promised to do the same." I add, my voice lower, grimmer. "Don't leave her alone with my mother; you are to remain with Sienna at all times well, except the bedroom, but—"

"I'll sleep in the hall, got it," Javier tells me, If I trusted anyone else, I wouldn't put this all on him, however, Javier is the only one I know who would keep her safe even against my mother. Nodding, I stride out to the car and climb in.

Carina's excited chatter is the soundtrack to the drive, her voice a relentless wave of words and mocking laughter. I tune her out as much as I can, my mind preoccupied with thoughts of Sienna. I grunt occasionally, nodding to show I'm listening. The truth is, I can't wait to get back to Sienna and away from her incessant voice. She is like an annoying chihuahua, constantly yapping with all her falseness; it is sickening.

We arrive at the castle as the sun begins to dip in the sky. It's an imposing structure, centuries old, complete with towering turrets and sprawling gardens.

The castle is decorated in rich, deep colors of reds and black. It looks exactly what one would picture from the outside, what a vampire's crypt is expected to look like. However, inside the place is vastly different. The floors are a polished honey oak, and nearly as old as the castle itself. Situated in a vast valley with mountains to surround it, the castle is both a fortress and a monument.

As we step inside Carina's parents' castle, Queen Anita's words echo in my ears. "Rehan tells me you two are trying for a baby," she coos. Anita leads us through the corridors. The long hall is lined with heavy oak doors and hung with drapes of red velvet. Her words replay in my mind until we are seated in the huge dining hall. The news throws me off, even more so when Carina eagerly pitches in, describing the nursery and her plans. My mind reels at the implication, the thought of touching Carina far from appealing.

Dinner is halfway through when Javier's call comes. Everyone at the table looks at me and Carina kicks me under the table. I glare at her and turn my head into her father. "If you'll excuse me," I say, not waiting for an answer, heading to a corner of the room for some privacy.

"Javier," I answer.

"The number belongs to Toby Donovan," Javier reports, his voice steady and neutral. A surge of fury rises within me, the name bringing a wave of anger rushing through me. I fucking knew it. "I'll handle it when I get back," I growl, before instructing Javier to ramp up Sienna's security in my absence.

As I end the call, I take a moment to glance back at the dinner table. Its lively atmosphere is a stark contrast to the turmoil brewing within me. Walking back to the table, I retake my seat.

I hardly hear any of the conversation. It feels like I've gone into autopilot mode. My mind is stuck on what her words mean. Is she going to try to run off with him?

"Xandros?" Carina's voice pulls me from my head, her hands trailing up my thighs. I glance around, finding I am in her room. I don't even remember walking here or remember her showering. I peer down at her where she kneels between my legs, her fingers pulling at my belt. I stand abruptly. "What are you doing?" I snap at her.

Her touch I find repulsive along with her scent.

Carina stands and steps closer to me, her hands coming up to rest on my chest.

She looks up at me from where she kneels before me, her lingerie obscenely see-through. Her nipples peeking out of the lace fabric. I avert my gaze; she is not Sienna.

"Xandros," she whispers, my name sounding like a purr on her lips.

I take a deep breath as I calmly take her wrists in my hands and push them away from me, stepping back from her advances. "No," I say firmly. "I cannot be with you." I urge her to understand. Carina is not a rational woman at the best of times.

"No, Carina," I say firmly, pushing at her shoulders.

"You haven't touched me since she came along, at least try to make this marriage work," she says pleadingly.

I shake my head, regretting the guilt that rises in me for hurting her as much as I do. "That's the thing, Carina, I don't want it to work, I don't want you. Still you keep trying to force my hand," I snap at her.

Carina takes a step back and looks away, her eyes brimming with tears. I realize how cold and callous my words sound and I sigh, taking a moment to regain control of my temper before sitting back down on the edge of the bed. The moment I do, she is crawling in my lap. Her bare skin against mine is like acid.

I try to push her off, when she entwines her arms around my neck. I can feel the discomfort in my chest and can't help feeling angry at myself for ever giving her a chance. It was never going to work.

She kisses me, her lips moving in desperation against mine. I try to pull away, and she deepens the kiss, her hands roaming my body. This is not what I want, not what I need. My mind is consumed with thoughts of Sienna and the safety she needs. I have to focus on her, keep my mind clear and sharp for the task at hand.

"Carina, please," I say softly, "I can't do this."

But then I think of Sienna, and my anger rises once more, pushing Carina away from me with a force that leaves her on the floor. She stares up at me with hurt in her eyes, and I know I've made things worse between us.

I can see the glint of anger behind her teary eyes. Likewise, she stands too, facing me.

"This isn't just about you," she says through gritted teeth. "This is about me, too."

"How?"

"I am your wife! And I deserve some attention."

"I know that, but she is my mate, so you'll have to find attention elsewhere," I reply.

She crosses her arms in front of her chest. "It's always Sienna. That's all it seems to be these days."

"We both know this cannot work between us any longer; it stopped working long ago." I peer around the room for a moment before saying anything else and then finally meet her gaze again with an unapologetic expression on my face.

"I know what I want, Carina," my voice is gentle yet firm as if speaking to a child who has yet to understand reality.

"And what you want isn't me." She finishes bitterly before rolling over in bed so that her back faces me.

"No, it's not. I've never wanted you; you were an arrangement, you don't want me either you just want freedom from your father, I am not blind," I reply. It took me a couple of days to figure it out, but it makes sense, she is almost rational when she is alone, yet the moment she hears from her father she becomes overbearingly cruel, and cunning.

"Am I right?"

"More than you know," she answers.

"So you'll sign the divorce papers?"

She laughs bitterly. "Not a chance. You may feel trapped with me, Xandros, what you don't realize is, I am also trapped with you. However, you are wrong about one thing, I have actually come to love you. Despite what you may think," she says softly, wrapping her arms around herself.

I sigh. "And for a time, I thought I could love you, Carina. Now I realize I was only fooling myself."

"Do you love Sienna? Or is it just the mate bond?" she asks.

I furrow my brows.

"I love everything about her, it's who her parents are that I have the issue with."

Carina laughs. "Yeah, well your mother is a handful. A loveable one, she is better than mine, anyway," she whispers the last part.

"So you're willing to break the treaty for her?"

"I'm trying to find a way I don't have to, yet you are making that impossible, Carina. We have a month to work things out, after that I will declare war on your father's kingdom, for her,"

"And your mother?" Carina asks.

"That I haven't figured out yet," I admit. "Sign the papers."

"I can't."

"Why?" she doesn't answer, instead moving to the bathroom. Why is she being so difficult? What does her father have against her or her mother?

My mind is a mess as I stroll the halls of the castle.

Chapter Thirty-Two

Sienna

As soon as Xandros departs, Queen Adina springs into action, putting me to work. And no matter where I go or what I do, his Beta follows. It's like having an additional shadow, one that refuses to detach even when the sun is gone. However, his presence I don't mind, it is a distraction. I feel it around lunchtime, a guttural gnawing, not only from my stomach but the bond as well. It's as if it senses Xandros's absence, causing an uncomfortable throbbing.

Just as I sit to devour my lunch, a simple egg sandwich, Queen Adina waltzes into the kitchen. "Did I say you could eat yet?" Her voice is venomous, dripping with scorn. Her eyes feel like they could burn holes in me.

"I always have lunch at this time. It's when it's scheduled," I protest, turning my gaze toward Javier, he remains motionless and impassive.

"You'll eat when I say you've earned the right. Now get up!" Queen Adina's words echo around the room. She leads me to the foyer, where a maid is waiting with a bucket of water and a toothbrush. She points to the driveway lined with a rock wall. "You are to scrub every rock and boulder. When you're done, you may have lunch," she dictates, leaving me outside, the enormity of the task sinking in. The driveway is over quarter mile long from the front door to the iron gates!

All day all I can hear is the metallic clank of my buckets hitting one another, the slosh of water from the scrubbing, the grating of the toothbrush against the rocks that is nearly down to its plastic base, its bristles nearly worn completely. Glancing around, I am barely halfway around the horseshoe that moves around the outside of the fountain. The sun is slowly disappearing behind the forest.

The wind whistles through the trees, carrying the sound of the forest. Like a horde of hungry animals, their hoots and growls sounding as if they are waiting for night to fall, so they can hunt, planning to gobble me up.

By the time I finish scrubbing the horseshoe part of the driveway, it's late into the night. My skin is blistered from the sun, and chapped from the wind. My fingers bleeding, my lips cracked, my hair matted with soap from my bucket, and knees aching. Queen Adina stands in the doorway of the castle, watching me. "Lazy girl. Well, no point cleaning in the dark. You can finish it at first light in the morning."

Reluctantly, I get up, each movement sending fresh waves of pain through my body. "I suppose I should let you eat," Queen Adina snaps, pointing toward the kitchen before sauntering off. The thought of walking the distance to the kitchen seems too much. I decide to forget food for the day and head back to my room, Javier steadying me a few times as I sway on my feet climbing the staircases. I make my way across to the other side of the castle.

"Ignore her. You really should have eaten. You'll feel worse tomorrow," Javier whispers, his voice low and concerned. I dismiss his advice, making my way to the room. The moment I step inside, I'm enveloped in Xandros's scent. It makes the bond ache more, if that's even possible. Staggering to the bed, I collapse onto it, the smell of him providing a guise of comfort. I pass out, exhaustion taking over me.

I barely feel like I've shut my eyes when a loud rap on the door startles me awake. "Slave, get up! You're late!" Queen Adina's voice booms from the other side. Javier unlocks the door, and Queen Adina barges in, halting abruptly as she takes in the state of the room and Javier's hand stopping her crossing the threshold. "Look at this mess. You live like a pig. You've destroyed his clothes," she snarls at me as I rub my eyes, trying to wake up.

Javier steps in. "Xandros had them sent here so she doesn't fret. I'm sorry, my Queen, but his orders rank above you. I can't let you enter this room," he tells Queen Adina. She looks like she might explode. Yet she doesn't enter, tapping her foot impatiently as I stumble around, changing into fresh clothes, gulping down water from the bathroom sink, and splashing some on my face.

Once again, my day is filled with laborious cleaning, working under the harsh sun, and the bitter cold. Snow fell last night, so it sinks into my flats making my toes numb. My every movement echoes the pain of his absence - along with the pain of working from sun up to sun down.

I can barely contain the searing pain in my body, a hundred needles piercing through my muscles with each movement. My stomach is so empty it feels like it'll eat itself alive, while the wound in my soul rips and tears deeper every second, its raw agony, too much for me to bear. Even with a deep exhaustion weighing heavy upon me, sleep refuses to come. Just when I think it can't get worse, Queen Adina pulls me out of bed for yet another day of tormenting labor. I drag myself through another nightmarish day under Queen Adina's care. Every breath I take is pure agony as I struggle just to keep going.

It's like the queen takes pride in punishing me further without Xandros here to protect me. However, my physical pain is nothing compared to the gaping wound in my soul—an agonizingly intense burn. The bond feels like a bleeding scar that won't ever heal.

I am at my breaking point, brought to it by the weight of exhaustion and hunger, coupled with the agony that comes from having one's freedom taken away. Javier's voice is like a lifeline, offering me strength in a moment when I feel none. He holds out his lunch to me, his insistence that I need it more than him overpowering my reluctance. Every bite feels like a laborious chore, as if the muscle fatigue in my body has now extended into my mouth. My stomach continues to growl angrily, yet hesitation lingers until finally I give in and eat. The small morsel does nothing for the emptiness inside me, but Javier's words fill its place, an assurance that Xandros will hear of his mother's dreadful treatment, imparting a tiny bit of solace into my overwhelming despair.

"How can she despise me so much? I didn't do this to her sister," I say out loud, silently hoping for a response.

Javier clears his throat and replies, "And the baby."

My heart drops as I struggle to comprehend what Javier has just said.

"Her sister was pregnant?" He nods in confirmation. Despite desperately wishing it wasn't true, all evidence points to Javier's words being true.

"Yes, her treatment of you is cruel; I do not agree with it just so you know. We aren't our parents, and she should know that better than anyone else; her father was a ripe bastard, yet she seems to forget that her father killed her father-in-law, yet King Rehan never blamed her. Despite what he did, he still loved her."

"So she is not only a bitch, she's a hypocrite." I sigh, then cover my mouth at my words, glancing at him worriedly. He snorts, tapping my shoulder.

"You can speak freely; you're safe with me," he tells me, and I smile thankfully.

"So, what else can you tell me?" I ask, wanting to know more.

"What do you want to know?" he grumbles bitterly, his angular face chiseled with sharp edges. His gaze is fixed on the castle walls, rising high in the sky. He kneels with surprising swiftness and grabs my bristle brush, thrusting it into the murky bucket of soapy water. My heart sinks as I realize he's taking over my task. I watch as he begins scouring the stone path that winds around the castle, quickly taking over my cleaning duties.

I move to set down my meager lunch when I feel his burning gaze upon me once again. "Eat. I'll finish your work here," he commands, his voice laced with a hint of exhaustion. I know he stands outside my door all night; I've heard him in the corridor. His dark brows are furrowed in resignation as he works, scrubbing the years-old stains from the pavement with a fast hand. "Hopefully we can be done before nightfall," he mutters.

A war wages within me between staying put and protesting his takeover of my work or accepting his help and having enough time for dinner. I resign myself to the latter.

I hesitantly take a bite of his sandwich, my mind racing with questions.

"How far along was her sister?" I ask apprehensively.

Javier's gaze falls and his shoulders sag. "Five months. They were expecting a little girl."

"I don't remember hearing about her husband. Did my parents kill him, too?" Juggling questions in my mind, I watch Javier's face tense with agitation.

"Princess Neve was single; she hadn't found her mate yet," he murmured, his voice barely above a whisper, as if he didn't want to hurt me further.

"You said she was—"

"Pregnant? Yes, she was a surrogate for Queen Adina." My world stops at his words. Time freezes. I now understood why she hates me.

The revelation hits like a cold wave crashing against me, drenching me from the inside out. The shock engulfs me as understanding dawns on me - why Adina hates me so viciously; the baby...

"Wait... the baby..."

"Was to be Xandros's sister. When Adina was pregnant with Xandros, the kingdom was attacked by humans, and Adina was injured badly. Xandros was cut from her prematurely, and somehow he survived, leaving her with a damaged womb; she tried for centuries to have another baby. Instead, her father had a daughter; when Neve was old enough and Adina managed to help her escape her father, Princess Neve agreed to be a surrogate for Adina and Rehan. That wasn't public knowledge, though."

His admission leaves me much to ponder. It explains her vile hatred toward my parents, to humans.

But I am not my parents.

"What do you know of Carina and my parents?" I ask him, remembering what Carina said the night she was drunk.

"What do you mean?" he asks, and I shrug, wanting to know what he knows.

"I know she helped kill them; she handed them over. They tried to flee to the Dresden Kingdom afterward, but Carina and her father brought them back. Your mother Rosaline was Carina's handmaiden," he tells me.

"And my father? Emil?" I ask.

He shakes his head. "I'm unsure, I always felt he was innocent; he begged they spare you; that is why you were given to your uncle," he tells me.

"If she was Carina's handmaiden, why were they here?" I ask, confused. The Dresden Kingdom is hours away from here.

"The Dresdans were visiting for Christmas; they came to discuss the treaty agreements."

"The arranged marriage?"

Javier shakes his head. "No, that came later when Xandros failed to find his mate."

"I don't understand," I admit, confused by all the council politics and royal rules they seem to follow.

Javier sighs heavily, pausing in his cleaning. "Lycan men turn mad without their mates; the original treaty, though, was put in place after King Rehan gambled the kingdom away; he failed to pay taxes to the council; King Vin Dresden is the one who bailed them out, and, in turn, Xandros was placed in charge of running the kingdom. His father was deemed unfit; he was a terrible gambler. Xandros has been running this place for over a century. It just wasn't known; he holds the title of king, yet legally, it couldn't officially be announced until after he found his mate or married; it would have caused panic to those living here. An unmated king is seen as a dictator, well that is what history books show for Lycan's, unmarked and unmated they can turn rabid, their souls untamed."

"So all Lycans?" I ask, my curiosity piqued. I had never thought about what kind of power a Lycan would have; it seemed like a fairy tale granted to only the most powerful rulers.

Javier let out a hushed chuckle. "No, not all Lycans. See, royal bloodlines stem from the gods, and once they get into power, it goes to their heads. It's why they need a mate around to share the burden with. That kind of power changes people."

"What kind of power?" I inquire further.

"The power of command," Javier replies darkly. "Lycan auras are stronger than even vampire compulsion, and with a mate, that command is shared between them both. Xandros has had the command for over two hundred years, yet despite being under constant oversight by the council, he's managed to remain mostly sane...so far. That's why you're so important; once you mark him, you'll be just as strong as him," Javier explains, his eyes boring into mine.

"So why doesn't he just command his parents to accept me?"

Javier shrugs. "Guilt, he has some stupid guilt over his aunt and sister. Xandros pretends he doesn't have a sister; most say it's easier. Not only that, his mother will pitch a fit if you're stronger than her. Carina and he are already legally married, there are rules around mates and wives, and divorces when it comes to treaties. I know Xandros is worried that if you challenge Carina for his hand, she'll kill you."

"What do you mean?"

"A challenge is to the death, Sienna. If she kills you. Xandros's hand will be forced, he'll have to mark her to keep his sanity and ensure the treaty." I chew my lip nervously. I am definitely no fighter, especially against a vampire. I might as well offer her a vein, she'll take it, anyway.

"So why does he feel guilty?"

"Because he gave your parents the key to Neve's quarters. Your mother said she was taking lunch up to her. He mistook her as one of his own servants. Neve was on bed rest, and paranoid; her quarters were always locked down. Anyway, Xandros gave your mother the key to her quarters, yet when she didn't return it, he went looking for her and found his aunt dead, and your parents had fled the castle grounds."

I swallow, sick to my stomach.

The questions die on my lips as I leap off the rock that had been my refuge for far too short a time. Gripping my toothbrush, I drop next to Javier and get back to the never-ending labor from which there is no escape.

Hours become an eternity of pain and suffering, and when the sun finally begins to set, marking the end of another agonizing day, I trudge back to my room desperate for Xandros's comforting scent. Instead of finding relief, all I find is bleach—an acrid smell that burns my nostrils and chokes me with anger.

I collapse onto the floor with a deafening thud, and Javier's horrified gasp resounds through the air behind me. Immediately he summons a maid who trembles as she speaks. "Queen Adina... she ordered us to clean it." Her words strike me like lightning bolts, hammering home the painful reality that my last source of comfort had been taken away. Xandros's scent—my only source of comfort—is gone.

Hot tears cascade down my cheeks, blurring the reality I'm now forced to endure. A deep void surges within me, aching with loneliness and sorrow. I curl up on the cold floor, feeling even colder as the sterile smell of bleach fills my nose and lungs. Javier crouches beside me.

"It's going to be alright; I can call him right now and he'll come back," he says in a gentle voice. My throat tightens as I attempt to swallow the lump that has formed inside it when he mentions Xandros. Rational thought clouds my mind as desperation fills my heart, yet I simply nod, unable to utter any words.

Chapter Thirty-Three

Xandros

I jerk awake, my senses assaulted by the blaring ring of my phone. Sienna's anguish ringing through the bond like a siren in my head. My eyes snap open and the cold air seizes my lungs, making me shudder. In a daze, I realize I've fallen asleep on the couch instead of in my own bed. The chill in the air wraps around me like an icy embrace, seeping deep into my bones and filling me with dread. Carina's sickly-sweet fragrance is heavy in the air, awakening something primal within me—something angry. Her scent brings me no solace or warmth, a stark reminder of her absence. Sienna's absence looms over me, tugging at my heartstrings like a cruel puppet master.

My entire body aches from the crushing weight of Sienna's pain that radiates through our bond. How could I have been so selfish as to leave her alone for three days? Paralyzing guilt and fear swell inside me, threatening to tear me apart. She must be suffering horribly without me by her side. Desperation and guilt pulse through me, squeezing my chest. I need to be with her.

The chill in my veins intensifies as a fog escapes my lips, the oppressive darkness swallowing me whole. I am desperate for warmth—for hers. The bond throbs incessantly, demanding my obedience, demanding I go to her. Desperately, I grab my phone and see a heap of neglected messages pouring in one after another. But before I can even check them, Javier's voice booms through the mind-link, his normally calm demeanor replaced by urgency.

"Why aren't you answering your phone, you sleep like the dead," he growls at me.

"What is it, why is she... Sienna." I struggle to keep my thoughts straight, my mind solely consumed with the bond I share with her.

"Xandros," he says urgently, "Your mother had your room stripped of your scent. You need to get home!"

"She what!" I snarl, my mother will pay for this. She knows how fragile mate bonds are, and what she has done is beyond cruel.

"Xandros, she's in distress," he exclaims desperately, worry lacing his voice as he speaks. "Your mother had your room cleaned, erasing your scent from it. Sienna is frantic, her temperature has plummeted dangerously low. You need to get here right away."

Tension courses through me, raging and unrelenting. It fills my muscles with intense energy that makes them burn, throb with uncontrollable pressure. Panic surges through me as I imagine Sienna shivering in the bathtub, cold and alone. Her delicate body is vulnerable to any threat, like a flower stripped of its petals by the harsh winter frost. The idea causes me pain, and an overwhelming sense of dread rushes from the top of my head to the tips of my toes. I can't bear the thought of her suffering without me there for comfort and warmth.

"Where is she?" I demand.

"In a blanket next to the fire. She won't let me near her."

"Get her to the bathhouse and saunas, turn the heat up as high as possible, I am on my way," I tell him, frantically searching around for my wallet and keys.

"Xandros, that means I have to touch her."

"Keep her alive, only you in the bathhouse!" I warn him. He is the only one I trust, clearly I can't trust my own family, but I know he'll obey any order I give him, even if I am being irrational.

"See you soon," I cut the mindlink, no doubt to handle Sienna. She'll reject any scent not belonging to me, so I know she'll fight him.

Anger courses through me at my mother for subjecting Sienna to such torment. She should never have been treated this cruelty.

Without a second thought, I turn to Carina, desperation clear in my expression. "Carina, I need to go home. I need to be with Sienna," I say, my voice tense with determination. Carina, still groggy from sleep, blinks at me in confusion.

"What should I tell my parents about your sudden disappearance?" she asks, concern etched on her face. I dismiss their worries with a wave of my hand. "Tell them whatever you need to. It doesn't matter." Panic swells inside me once more. All that matters is getting to Sienna.

I hastily gather my belongings, my mind focused solely on reaching my mate. Clothes are thrown into a bag, my wallet is retrieved, and in the blink of an eye, I am ready to leave. The urgency is unbearable, my need to be by Sienna's side overwhelming.

The drive back to the castle feels endless. Every second spent in the car feels like an eternity, the walls closing in on me. Impatience gnaws at my insides, urging the driver to go faster. I repeat the same words over and over, "Hurry up, we need to get there."

Nothing else matters except getting back to Sienna. The thought of her struggling through this pain alone is more than I can bear, and I'm filled with a sense of dread. I can't bear the thought of her suffering because of my stupidity.

Finally, we reach the castle, and I jump out of the car before it has even come to a stop. I hurry toward the bathhouses without hesitation or thought, my heart pounding in rhythm with each step I take.

I rush into the bathhouse, my heart still pounding in my chest. There, I find Javier, his eyes filled with worry as he watches over Sienna.

The bathhouse is dark, except for the golden glow of the fire's flames. The glow of the embers bathe the room in a golden light. Shadows are cast along the walls, flickering like flames.

The bond between us pulses with pain and fear. A symphony of emotions that mirrors the sound of a wounded animal, crying out in agony.

The rattle of her breath, it doesn't sound right. It sounds like she won't survive much longer. Moving toward the far corner, she is huddled in the shallows.

Sienna's form is small and shivering in the bath, her skin pale and her lips as blue as the veins underneath her skin.

Buttons pop and fly everywhere as I rip my shirt off before dropping into the water beside her. Her pale form lies limp in the bath, her skin icy to the touch. The sight tears at my soul, igniting a fire within me.

My hands are warm as I pull her into an embrace and lay her down on my chest, urging her to feel the bond, feel that I am here with her.

I hold her close to my chest, willing away the coldness that radiates from her body. Her skin is ice-cold, like I'm holding a corpse.

The cold cuts through my flesh and bones from Sienna, but I push past it, warming her body the best I can. The ice and stone of the bathhouse sucks the warmth from my body like a freezer, I push past that too, ignoring the biting chill her cold body causes.

Sienna's eyes flutter open as I hold her close, her voice barely a whisper. "Xandros," she murmurs, disbelief and relief evident in her tone. She didn't expect me to come back for her. I hold her tighter, my heart breaking at her words. "You did come home. Javier said you would..." she trails off, burying her face in my neck, her teeth chattering next to my ear.

"I would burn the world down around me to come back to you, if needed," I tell her, my voice filled with raw emotion.

"My world has been burning since you met me. I don't want to burn anymore. I want to extinguish the flames," she whispers, and tears prick my eyes.

"Don't say that, Sienna. Stay with me." The words escape me like hot embers from an inferno, burning through everything in their path and leaving nothing behind except scorched earth. Her words burn me, she'd rather die, than fight to remain here with me.

Sienna's smile flickers into existence, and she reaches up to touch my cheek. Her touch is like a sudden shock, jolting me with energy in the midst of chaos.

"For what?" she breathes out when her hand slips from my face, hits the water and splashes me. "Sienna?" I murmur.

As I hold her, her body grows increasingly limp, slipping further into unconsciousness. Terror grips me, and I shake her desperately, trying to rouse her, to keep her awake.

"Sienna, don't leave me," I beg, my voice laced with desperation.

"Take my strength...mark me." Her response is weak, her body unresponsive to my pleas.

I can feel the darkness closing in around us, and I know we're running out of time. Sweat drips down my face as I clutch Sienna tighter, willing all of my energy into her lifeless form. It's not enough, and I feel the panic rising within me.

"Stay with me, Sienna," I yell, my voice echoing off the walls of the empty room. There's no response from her, only silence.

I call out to Javier, his name a desperate plea. "Javier, where is a healer! We can't lose her," I demand, my voice cracking with fear.

"Should be here any minute, your father sent for one earlier," he answers just as my parents rush into the bathhouse, their faces wrought with worry and guilt. I recognize my mother's expression—she is fully aware of the gravity of her decisions that have led us here, the repercussions of which might cost Sienna her life, and in turn mine. I know if she passes away, a part of me will die too; she dies and so do I, maybe not physically, but I might as well be dead when the craze hits, and my mother knows this. She knows I won't be recognizable as her son when it does. A growl tears out of me at the sight of her.

I pull Sienna's limp body into my arms, and with a sense of determination I have never felt before, charge out of the bathhouse with my mother trailing behind me. She trails after me, crying apologies as if they will make up for what she has done. I barely hear her. All I can focus on is finding a healer and saving Sienna's life before it slips away.

My steps are hurried and purposeful. I try to ignore the fear that keeps slipping into my thoughts, keeping my grip on Sienna unwavering. With each moment that passes, I feel the weight of responsibility pushing down on me. Sienna helpless in my arms, so fragile and vulnerable. It fills me with terror and frustration. The castle seems endless as I desperately search for a healer, each second ticking past like centuries when my father sings out behind me.

"Javier mind-linked, the healer is setting up in her room," he calls out, and I turn for the stairs, taking them two at a time.

My mother stands nearby, her guilt clearly written in her eyes while I glare at her. The healer stabs the needle in my arm, and attaches the line to Sienna. Mate bond saliva and blood have healing properties for the mate, now I just have to pray our bond isn't irreparable because if she rejects it, she'll die. The healer looks upon Sienna with his gentle yet determined hands working with precision. My heart races with fear, an unyielding helplessness falls over me as he works tirelessly to revive her fragile form back to life. Everything depends on my blood healing her since she can't mark me—for Sienna's life, our bond, our future together.

Don't let her die, I plead silently. "Please don't let her die," I whisper. My mother's movement makes me growl as she moves to step closer to me.

I hiss through clenched teeth, "If she dies. You'll wish that death had taken you as well. Mark my words, Mother, not even Father will stop me from killing you." My eyes burn with the intensity of my warning, and I can practically see her body shudder in fear.

Yet I mean every word. My mate dies, so will she.

Chapter Thirty-Four

Sienna

My life ebbs away with every labored breath; I am dying. The throbbing beat of my own failing heart resonates in my ears, each pulse a painful reminder of my mortality. Relief washes over me, a strange sense of peace, knowing my suffering will finally come to an end. The agony of the mate bond has been a part of me for so long I welcome death with open arms, comforted by its sweet release. I bask in the bliss of finality, knowing I will no longer be held captive by the chains of his enslavement. I have longed for this release, to escape the torment of the mate bond that has kept me captive. In death, I will be free from the chains that bind me to him. Free of him.

Then, amid my surrender, a flicker of something. Despite my desire to succumb to the pain, something foreign sparks within me. Xandros, I can feel his presence calling out to me through our bond. His scent is strong and unmistakable, and he pleas for me to hang on louder than ever. Why? Why would he want me to stay in this wretched state of agony? How much more suffering could I possibly endure? My thoughts wage an internal war as my body remains immobilized, helplessly fighting its own battle. Our connection trembles like a single thread in the wind, yet it still holds.

A surge of energy courses through my veins like a roaring river, as if his love is an unstoppable force that has broken down the walls I have built up around me. Every ounce of pain returns. Breaking through the bliss that comes with death, forcing me back to him.

My heart races as the bonds of his control wrap around me once more. My chest clenches as I feel a flutter deep in my soul—the stirring of hope that I can break free. It's too late; the bond is already tightening its grasp around me. Waves of energy course through my veins, and I can almost feel his blood stirring within me like a ruthless master demanding absolute obedience. My entire body strains with the effort to break free, and yet I remain tethered by an iron-clad grip. It is a never-ending battle between my will for freedom and the unyielding force that binds us together.

When I regain consciousness, I find myself sprawled across Xandros's chest, his alluring aroma filling my lungs. His warm fingers delicately brush through my hair, a gesture that should evoke comfort instead haunts me with distrust. He stares at me with relief in his eyes, thankful for my return, while I am left confused and disappointed.

"Thank the Moon Goddess, I thought I lost you," Xandros whispers. "You're safe. I'm here, Anna," he whispers, fingers gently stroking my face. Anna, since when did we move to nicknames? It took death for endearment; no death taught me clarity. Words are merely what he speaks. How can I believe him? He is a walking contradiction, his actions proving time and time again that he does not truly love me.

Tears stream down my face, and he whispers soothing words, assuring me I am safe and that he will protect me. I shake my head, anger welling up inside me.

I become frantic, and he tries to calm me, but I refuse to be pacified. I push him away, the rage burning within me. "It's okay. I'm here, I'm right here," he tells me. Does he not see that this is the issue? "Mark me, you can mark me, she'll never hurt you again, you'll never be taken from me again." He offers his neck, urging me to mark him, to solidify our bond.

"And be tied to you forever?" I laugh bitterly. "No, Xandros, that is not why I'm upset. I'm angry because you forced me back to endure more of this torment."

The healer races to Xandros, desperately trying to explain away my reaction. She reassures him my response is perfectly normal. "She's fine; this sometimes happens, My King. Her senses may be thrown off balance due to her overwhelming proximity to death."

Overwhelmed? Off balance? I've never been clearer! Her words fall on deaf ears as I cackle in a manic state. A haunting laughter that chills the air and pervades every corner of the room. "What's wrong with her?" Xandros worries, trying to stop me from escaping his grip. Now he wants to pretend to care, to act like a worried mate? I laugh, a piercing sound that slices through the air like a blade.

"She's a little manic, a little jumbled," the woman says as I slap her hands away while Xandros's grip tightens.

"I've never felt clearer!" I scream, fighting off the hands that try to restrain me. Xandros orders the healer to leave, believing he can handle me on his own. But I refuse to be subdued. She doesn't hesitate to go, as if she is frightened of me.

"Calm down," he pleads. "You're fine. I'm right here."

I scoff at his words, the absurdity of his reassurances.

"That's the problem! I don't want you. I hate you!" I scream, my voice filled with the anguish of betrayal. How could fate be so cruel as to hand me back to the man who tortures me most?

In a moment of uncontrolled fury, I roll, only for him to roll with me, so I move quickly and kick him off the bed. Xandros crashes to the floor, and I immediately run for the door, only for him to catch me around the middle. Swiftly I drop my weight, twisting out his grip, and lash out at him, my hand sliding across his chest as I swing blindly at him.

Blood spills from the wound I inflict upon him, staining the floor. As I stare at what I did in stunned silence.

My eyes go to my trembling fingertips, and I realize I have partially shifted, my claws extending in the heat of the moment. The realization leaves me stunned, questioning how that is possible when he has ordered me to never shift.

Yet, just as quickly as the claws emerged, they retreat, leaving me defenseless and vulnerable. With a feral growl, Xandros bares his claws and advances toward me. In an instant, I am immobilized by fear, my body seemingly crafted from stone. Fear clamps its burning grip around my heart, knowing there will be no escape from his retribution for my disobedience.

I stumble back, cowering away from him, pleading desperately in a vain attempt to protect myself. "Wait, Xandros! Please, I'm sorry! It was an accident, I swear!" My words quiver with terror as I plead for mercy, yet his expression remains unforgiving. His lips curl into a cruel sneer as he looms nearer.

With every step he takes closer, my feet stumble backward. His strides grow longer as I try to retreat, desperate to create the space between us.. My back slams into the unforgiving wall. His hands crash down like thunder on both sides of my head, blotting out all escape. I close my eyes, then feel his breath sweep across my face; his growl makes goosebumps rise on my skin; my entire body feels electrified, charged with fear. "Just like I mean this," he growls, gripping me tightly. I struggle against his hold, my body writhing in his grasp.

In one swift motion, he grabs me in an iron grip, and I'm powerless against his strength as he tosses me onto the bed like a doll. I scramble to escape. He captures my ankles, yanking me back before pinning my wrists above my head. His grasp on my wrists is tight and unrelenting, his eyes blazing with a new kind of emotion. His body presses against mine, trapping me between his strength and the mattress.

I meet his gaze with defiance, determined to stand my ground, then I see a flicker in his eyes that undoes me. With one swift move, he captures my lips, searing them with fire and passion that melts away the confusion coursing through me. Love and hate intertwine until I can no longer tell which is more potent.

I struggle against him, still unable to let go of my anger and resentment. His kiss, like a tempestuous flame, ignites conflicting emotions within me. I am torn between the anger that simmers beneath the surface and the undeniable attraction that draws me to him. As his lips claim mine, I find myself succumbing to the whirlwind of sensations. His touch is both demanding and tender, his lips coaxing a response from me I'm unwilling to give.

Amidst the storm of desire and fury, a voice within me screams, demanding I resist, that I refuse to submit to him once again. I squirm, my muffled protests lost in the intensity of our kiss. It's as if we're caught in a dance of opposing forces, his dominance battling against my defiance.

Finally, he breaks the kiss, his breath ragged as he gazes into my eyes. The room is filled with charged silence, the weight of our desires hanging heavily in the air. I can see the conflict in his eyes, the struggle between his love for me and the darkness that has consumed him.

"I won't hurt you, Sienna," he whispers, his voice laced with desperation. "I never wanted to hurt you." His words echo through my mind, stirring memories of the pain and suffering I endured in his presence. There is also a flicker of vulnerability in his expression, a vulnerability that tugs at my heart until I remind myself of the monster he can be, truly. My monster.

As he continues, his hands traveling down my body, tracing every curve and dip, I find myself losing control. The way he touches me, the way his lips trail down my neck, as if all the pain and hurt disappear. His hands move faster, rougher. He seems desperate for my touch, as if he's been starved of it for months.

As he tears at the hospital-like gown I've been placed in and bares my body to his hungry gaze, I feel a tremble wrack my body. It's like dark energy coils within me and draws strength from my heartache. A part of me knows this is not how it should be; what he did to me was cruel and unforgivable. Yet here I am, giving in to him once again with unreserved passion.

My body responds to him despite the fear and mistrust that swirls within me. I'm helpless to resist the pull of his lips, the possessive nature of his kiss that speaks to a depth of passion I cannot deny. I find myself melting beneath his touch, my limbs surrendering to his every command.

Xandros breaks away from my lips and stares down at me with blazing eyes. "You hate me?" he growls, his voice low and dangerous. "I'll make you love me," he says with a fierce intensity that sends shivers down my spine.

"You can't force love," I say, my voice breathless.

"Can't I?" he challenges, and then he kisses me again, more demanding and deeper this time, leaving me gasping for breath and craving more of him.

"I hate you," I murmur against his lips even as I arch my body against his, lost in the passion he ignites within me.

"I'll make you love me," he repeats, his voice rough with desire, before he takes me again and again into a world of ecstasy where nothing else matters, only the fierce possession he claims over my trembling body.

"And I'll make you regret it," I promise him.

Chapter Thirty-Five

Xandros

I groan as I feel the heaviness of my body, aching from the strain of the previous night. My mind is clouded with thoughts of how to mend the shattered pieces of our relationship and how to get Sienna to forgive me. My mind reels with possibilities of how to repair the damages done and gain Sienna's trust. Yet her rage has put a barrier between us, I must break it if I want to keep her safe. However, the treaty looms like a storm cloud, threatening to rip apart everything, taunting me with its promises of destruction and chaos.

Sienna stirs beside me, and I brush a kiss on her forehead. As she sits up to face me, I'm met with the gaze of a total stranger. The bond between us is still strong, yet something has fractured deep within her; a chasm of hatred I can't comprehend or bridge. Every fiber of my being screams for her as our eyes lock, instead of passion and love, all I see is a seething hatred. Something has shifted within her, something I can feel through the bond yet cannot fully understand. It's as if an abyss has opened up between us, a gaping wound that will no longer heal. Her repulsion for me is unmistakable, yet still the bond persists, an invisible shackle that keeps her chained to me.

She springs from the bed with haste, almost as if propelled by an unseen force. Her feet move soundlessly across the floor, and I watch her with a dread that stretches out like a noose around my neck.

"Where are you going?" I murmur, my voice laced with concern.

"To shower... alone!" she retorts with finality.

"No, I need to speak with my parents. Before that, I need you to mark me. Come here," I tell her, my voice filled with a mix of urgency and desperation.

"I'll pass, thanks," she replies coldly, her words like icicles, cold and unforgiving.

My voice thunders with the power of a Lycan King. "Anna! Come to me now!" My words seem to cut through her, freezing her body in place and I feel the battle between us in every moment as rivulets of sweat form across her skin. Though I can sense the anguish my command causes her, she holds firm before me, unwilling to break under my command. I can sense the pain my command inflicts upon her, yet she resists, forcing me to release the command before I cause her further harm or our bond.

"You will mark me!" I tell her, determination coursing through my veins. I rise from the bed and move behind her, gently gripping her shoulders to make her face me.

"And what of Carina?" she utters through gritted teeth, covered in a veil of hate-filled despair.

I clinch my jaw and ball up my fists, barely containing the anger that threatens to burst forth. "What about her? I don't care for her; all I want is you," I snarl, my confusion quickly turning into frustration.

"Do you intend to still marry her?" she demands, her eyes boring into mine looking for any deceit.

"It doesn't matter; the marriage is merely a contract, nothing more," I admit, my words heavy with regret and sadness. All while hoping she will understand the complexity of our situation.

She scoffs at my words, the sound cutting through the air. "So, you expect me to accept marking you while you're bound to another woman?"

My heart clenches at her words, the pain of her rejection coursing through me. "Sienna, please," I plead, my voice filled with my desperation and frustration. "I don't want her. I want you."

Lycan King's Captives

Her eyes blaze with anger as she walks away, shutting the bathroom door and locking it. "Sienna!" I call out, my voice filled with a mix of frustration and longing.

She ignores me at first, but my persistent knocking and pleading eventually sway her decision. Reluctantly, she opens the door and steps out, a towel wrapped around her body.

"I don't want to talk to you," she says coldly, her words like shards of ice.

"Sienna, please listen to me," I demand, taking a step closer to her. "I know I messed up, but I need you to mark me. It's for your safety."

"I can fend for myself," she snarls, her ferocity palpable in her voice.

"My mother—" I begin, only to be cut off by her harsh words.

"To hell with your mother! I don't need you looking out for me. Don't you get it, Xandros? I wanted to die!" she screams, her voice shaking with boiling rage.

Her words pierce me like a thousand knives. The hurt in her voice slices through me, reminding me of the depths of her torment. Instinctively, I reach out to her.

"I won't let you die," I tell her firmly.

"That wasn't your choice to make, you shouldn't have forced me back here," she whispers. The agony in her voice rips through me, reminding me of the despair she has been feeling. I inch toward her, raising my hand to her face. She flinches away, and I continue moving forward.

"I know I caused you pain," I murmur, my voice filled with grief. "And I'm so sorry for that. You have to accept that I need you to mark me."

"Why?" Sienna asks contemptuously, her eyes shimmering with unshed tears. "So that you can own me as your property?" Sienna utters bitterly, tears starting to trickle down her cheeks. "For you to keep me as your plaything? So you can have your way with me whenever you damn please?"

I throw my head back in desperation, frustration causing me to clutch my hair. What doesn't she get? "No, Sienna. Don't turn away! You have to mark me; it's the only way I can protect you. Just give me five minutes!"

Her gaze softens, a flicker of vulnerability shining through her anger. She crosses her arms over her chest, a defensive gesture that doesn't hide the pain etched on her face.

I take another step toward her, my hand still raised. "Sienna, I love you," I admit, my voice filled with raw emotion. "You are my mate, and nothing will ever change that. I will do whatever it takes to make this right, to mend what I have broken."

"But not enough to fight for me," she whispers, her voice barely above a breath.

A pang of guilt courses through me as I realize the truth of her words. I failed her, failed to protect her, and fight for her when she needed me most. "Sienna, I am fighting for you," I protest, my voice filled with determination. "I am risking everything, even the stability of my kingdom, to ensure your safety. I need you to meet me halfway."

Her eyes bore into mine, searching for something. I reach out to touch her cheek, my thumb caressing her skin gently. "Please," I beg, "just hear me out."

Her gaze is wary yet receptive. "What is it?" she asks, her voice tinged with a mix of skepticism and longing.

I take a step closer to her, closing the physical and emotional distance between us. "I know I can't undo the past."

"No, you can't. Just get out! I won't listen anymore to your fake promises and false words," she says pushing off my chest. I go to argue with her but then there is a knock on the door that startles us both. Moments later, Javier walks into the room and Sienna moves to the shower, hopping in and closing the screen.

"Xandros?" Javier calls out. I growl and wander out to the main room. "Your mother wishes to speak to you." Just hearing the mention of her angers me, she nearly killed my mate. The hatred I feel for that woman right now... there are no words to describe it. "Your father has requested your presence, too." I grit my teeth. No doubt he is there to play referee to our fight.

I nod stiffly at Javier, still lost in my own thoughts. "I'll be there shortly," I mutter, my voice laced with bitterness.

Javier hesitates, his eyes scanning me cautiously. "Is everything alright?"

"No," I snap, my anger and frustration coming out in a harsh outburst. "My mate doesn't want to mark me, my mother tried to kill her, and now my father wants to play the middleman."

Javier's expression turns grave. He places a hand on my shoulder, offering a small gesture of comfort. "You'll figure it out," he tells me confidently.

I snort derisively at his words, feeling hopeless and lost. "I don't know how," I admit, the weight of my responsibilities and mistakes crushing me like a boulder. "I've never been in a situation like this before."

"What situation, the treaty?" Javier asks curiously.

I shake my head in frustration. "This... this conflict between Sienna and me. Usually I can make her comply with the bond but not this time," I say, struggling to find the right words to express myself. "I'm torn between my duty to my kingdom and my need to protect her. She won't fucking see reason."

"Well, one issue at a time. Whatever your parents wanted to see you about seems urgent." I sigh looking back at the bathroom door. Shaking my head, I follow Javier choosing to deal with Sienna when I return.

As I walk toward the throne room, all I can think of is Sienna. I know I'm failing her, failing to be the mate she needs and deserves. My thoughts are interrupted as I enter the throne room and see my parents waiting for me. I instantly growl when I lay eyes on my mother, and she hangs her head. My father's hand reaches out to grab hers.

"Xandros, we need to talk," my father says, his tone serious and stern.

I scoff. "If it's coming from her, I don't want to hear it, Father, she nearly killed my mate!" I yell at him. He looks at my mother, his eyes full of disappointment.

"I have already spoken with your mother," he says, keeping his eyes trained on her.

"Spoken to her?" I laugh, what did he do? Scold her like a disobedient child.

"Please, Xandros, I didn't think she would deteriorate so... qui—"

"You didn't think? Exactly what was your intention?" I snarl, taking a step toward her. Javier grabs my arm, and I growl at the action, he simply shakes his head.

"My mate hates me because of you, because of the distance you forced between us."

"And I'm sorry, I truly am, I... I know I made a mistake," she pleads, tears streaming down my face.

"And Sienna?" I ask her and she swallows, glancing away toward the wall.

"You're not sorry at all, you're just sorry you nearly killed me, aren't you?" I tell her. She says nothing, and I know I am right. I turn to leave when my father speaks again. "Vin Dresdan called moments ago."

I growl, not wanting to deal with my father-in-law right now.

I take a deep breath and brace myself for whatever news they have for me. "What is it?" I ask, trying to keep my voice steady.

"Your mother has received a message from him," my father begins, his eyes locking onto mine. "They want to discuss the treaty. He wasn't too happy when he learned of your departure in the middle of the night,"

My heart sinks at the mention of the treaty. The thought of being forced into a loveless marriage to strengthen ties between kingdoms makes me sick to my stomach. "What did he say?" I ask, already dreading the answer.

"They want us to send a representative to discuss terms," my mother answers, her voice clipped and businesslike.

I nod slowly, trying to think.

"You want to break the treaty," my father says abruptly and my mother gasps.

"That will start a war," my mother exclaims knowing exactly the consequences of the council coming down on us. Her father after all was the reason these laws were put in place, yet Vin backed us with the council, and if he revokes his favor, not only is my kingdom in debt to him but also at war with him and the council.

"No, we'll find another way, you can't just breach the treaty, you're already married, we would risk—"

"Losing the kingdom," I finish for her.

"You'd really risk your throne for her, wouldn't you?" my mother says like she is just figuring that out.

"I'd kill for her," I warn her.

My father growls. "Enough, we already have a fight on our hands, we can't be fighting amongst ourselves, not if we are truly going to war with the Dresdans," my father states. Yet I can see the guilt on his face, he is the reason we are in this mess.

"The council we can handle, that won't be an issue now that you've found your mate. They don't have to worry about your sanity once Sienna marks you, but Vin— he will declare war." He curses under his breath.

"Carina won't agree to the divorce?" my mother asks. I shake my head, and she runs her fingers through her hair. "So that leaves Sienna to challenge her which will force an annulment, or—"

"War," my father breathes, and I nod, chewing my lip.

"Sienna doesn't stand a chance against her, she will struggle to shift,"

I admit, I never should have suppressed her Lycan side.

"So where does that leave us, leave the kingdom?" my mother asks, staring at my father. He thinks for a second and I pray he has an answer because right now I have none.

"Keep up the arrangement."

I go to protest, when he holds up a hand.

"For now, we don't need a war. You've held the wedding off an extra month; that gives us a month to speak with the council, clear this debt with Vin and also to get Carina to agree to the divorce, we have time,"

"Then what? Carina won't go along with it."

"We ask to renegotiate the treaty, come up with something else perhaps, or seek permission from the council to break it."

"And what do we offer the council, Father? We have nothing to offer. Legally, right now, Vin owns us!"

"We'll think of something. Have Javier start looking into the Dresdans, I will send word to the elders about requesting their council, for now we bide our time until we find a suitable solution, one where it doesn't end in bloodshed," my father tells me.

"And Sienna?" I ask, glancing at my mother.

"I will speak with her,"

"I don't want you near her!"

"Xandros, she can't make it up to the girl if you don't let her near her, your mother won't harm her,"

I scoff, she already has.

"I mean it, Xandros, I will make things right, I'll try with her," my mother says, yet I don't trust her, and right now I need Sienna to mark me. Because if Vin learns of me wanting to break the treaty, he'll come for her, and try to kill her, which in turn would force me to take his daughter as my mate or have the council take the kingdom and he knows this. Lycan's can't rule without a mate, and he can't touch her if our bond is solidified, or he kills me, which breaks any treaty we may have by forfeit. I need Sienna to mark me, to keep her safe, to stop the fall of my kingdom.

"Fine, can I go? I want to get back to my mate."

My father nods and I swiftly turn on my heel. As I step out of the door, Javier follows behind. "Xandros, are you really planning to break the treaty?" he asks me, his voice laced with concern.

I stop in my tracks and turn to face him. "I won't be forced into a loveless marriage, Javier," I say firmly. "Not when I have found my mate."

"Breaking the treaty will have consequences. It could mean war," he warns me.

"I understand that, but what choice do we have? I refuse to let Sienna get hurt because of our mistakes," I reply, determination in my voice.

"Then we need to find a way to negotiate with Vin without breaking the treaty, let me collect Carina; I will ask around to see what I can find out," Javier suggests.

"Fine, call her driver and tell her you will collect her; hopefully she chooses not to return," I mumble, not looking forward to having to deal with her. "For now, I need to focus on Sienna. I need her to mark me before it's too late."

Javier nods in understanding, and we make our way through the palace toward Sienna's room. As we walk, I can feel the weight of the kingdom on my shoulders. The future of our people rests on my decisions, and every move I make from this moment on will impact their lives.

All I can think about is Sienna: her safety, her happiness, and our bond. Yet as I unlock her door, I hear movement in the room just as I enter. She is opening the door to the hidden bar. In her hand is the phone. She stares at me like a deer in headlights.

"Fuck!" I hear Javier breathe out behind me, I kick the door shut, storming over to her.

I snatch the phone from her hand, hitting redial while she backs away from me. The phone rings when suddenly Toby's voice sounds on the other end. "Sienna?" Pulling the phone away from my ear, I hang it up, tossing it on the sofa.

"Why were you on the phone with Toby?" I ask her, stalking her around the sofa, her hair is still wet and clinging to her skin, the towel tucked tightly between her breasts. She shakes her head at me and nearly trips over the lamp table, barely catching herself with her outstretched hand clutching the armchair. With all the drama going on I had completely forgotten about her calls to Toby.

"Answer me, Sienna," I demand, my voice low and dangerous. She looks at me with fear in her eyes, and I can see the tears that are threatening to spill over.

"I just wanted to hear his voice," she admits softly.

"Hear his voice?" I repeat, my tone incredulous.

"I-I was just calling to check on him. Make sure he's okay," she stammers out, avoiding my eyes.

"You have no right to be calling him! He's not your concern anymore," I growl at her, my anger boiling over. In that moment, I want nothing more than to shake some sense into her. She is mine! I won't share her!

"He's my friend, Xandros," she argues weakly, yet I can see she doubts that, feel the flicker through the bond, she cares for him, and that thought makes me wild.

"He's nothing to you! You don't know him anymore, and you never will again," I snap at her, my temper flaring.

Sienna flinches at my words, and I can see the hurt in her eyes. I won't stop. I can't stop. The fear of losing her is too great, and I'll do anything to protect her.

"Xan—"

"Don't speak," I cut her off harshly. "Just mark me already so we can put an end to all this nonsense." Sienna backs away from me, her eyes widening in shock. "Xandros, you can't be serious," she breathes.

"I've never been more serious, Sienna. If you don't mark me, I will kill your precious Toby!" I tell her, my voice laced with fury. Yet she glares at me, the defiance obvious in her hardened gaze. "Is that a threat?" she challenges me, her hands balling into fists at her sides.

"Take it however you want, Sienna. I need you to mark me now," I demand, taking a step closer to her. She backs away again, shaking her head.

"Then do it, Xandros," she challenges, her voice firm and unyielding. "Know this, if you lay a single finger on him, I will never forgive you."

I feel the anger and frustration building inside me as I take a step toward her. "You have no choice in the matter, Sienna. You will mark me, or I will make sure Toby suffers," I say in a low voice.

Sienna backs away, her eyes filled with fear and anger. I take another step toward her, closing the distance between us.

"Xandros, please," she pleads with me, her voice barely above a whisper. "I don't want this."

"You don't have a choice," I tell her, my voice cold. "If you don't mark me—Then you leave me no choice," I reply sternly. "I will make you mark me."

I take another step toward her, my hand outstretched. She backs away again, and I can feel the tension building between us. Then, something changes in her expression. Her eyes narrow slightly, and she seems to harden. "You force me to mark you, and you force my hand!" she snarls at me when she suddenly smashes the bowl on the dresser. She grabs a chunk of glass, holding it to her neck. "I mean it, Xandros. You touch him, or try to force me to mark you..." tears stream down her face, her hand trembling as she presses the point against the vein that pulses rapidly beneath the soft flesh of her throat. I stop in my tracks and her voice trembles.

"I mean it, Xandros! I will fucking do it!" My blood boils in my veins at her words and I hear the door open behind me. Javier's scent reaches me, and her eyes go behind me, they widen slightly and she looks at me like a cornered animal, frantic and I feel him move closer assessing the situation.

"Put down the glass, Sienna. Killing yourself won't stop him from killing Toby," Javier tries to reason with her and he's right, her killing herself for that bastard will only ensure I make his death extra slow and torturous.

"He'll force me to mark him," she stammers.

"I'm your mate!" I growl taking a step toward her and she takes one back, the glass slipping down her neck, causing blood to trickle down as she nicks her skin. Yet she doesn't seem to feel it as she backs up into the dresser.

"I won't be your mistress, your little whore on the side!" she screams at me. I've had enough of her defiance.

"Xandros, calm down," Javier whispers. However, I'm past the point of reasoning now, my aura slipping out stuns her. Her hands are shaking when I grab her waist and her hand. "Drop it." I warn, my voice dangerously calm, Javier steps closer, hands out in some placating gesture that does nothing to soothe the anger writhing through me. Blood drips on the floor where the glass is clutched in her hand, her veins pressing against her skin from the tension and strain as she tries to fight the command. Within seconds, Javier snatches her hand, prying her fingers from the glass when she surrenders with a loud sob, her body giving up as she turns limp in my arms.

Javier tosses the glass on the floor. Her body stiffens at my touch.

"Look what you've done," Javier whispers in rage beside me, his eyes softening when they take in Sienna as she wraps her arms around herself, an involuntary shudder racking through her body.

"She's terrified of you! Can't you see that?" His voice is filled with worry. "Don't do this, Xandros, not like this," he tells me, but I won't lose her. Not to Toby, my mother or anyone else.

"Shift!" I command her, her marking me will make her as strong as me, solidify the bond so she can't fight me, fight my commands, but no one will be able to harm her, command her against her will, not with my blood flowing through her.

Sienna whimpers, her bones cracking and realigning. "Xandros!" Javier exclaims as her body starts to contort. She hasn't shifted since the first time therefore it might as well be just as painful, her body not used to it. "No, I need her to mark me!" Javier shakes his head, backing away while I refuse to let her go, knowing the moment she shifts she will turn savage and attack me. No sooner than I think it, she does exactly that, only I am not prepared for the fury behind her blow which sends me backward forcing me to release her.

My Lycan side loves a fight, loves her, and she just gave it two things it loves most by challenging me. I pounce on her and her claws rake down my face, as we hit the ground. I pin her, stunned by her Lycan; her fur is almost silver it is that gray, completely different from my black fur, her eyes a mesmerizing piercing blue, they seem to have no end as I stare into them, yet it makes my eyes go to the scar my mother gave her. It runs down her face and across her snout even in this form. A whimper escapes her when my blood drips on her, her tongue slipping out to swipe at my face. My hands clutch her furry arms, my knees digging into her thighs, yet my Lycan side calms some as she gives up, knowing it is pointless to fight me.

"Shift back," I command her, now she's shifted, she can mark me. My command to keep her Lycan side dormant now lifted, forced to shift back, she does, her fur replaced with her warm tender skin.

"Get out," I command Javier as the rest of her changes, not wanting him to see her naked. Javier complies. I know he doesn't agree with my treatment of her. What choice does she give me, though?

"I will stop talking to him, please," she whimpers.

"I don't trust you," I warn her.

"If our relationship is anything to go off, trust has nothing to do with it. You don't have to trust me. I just have to be obedient, right?" she asks, striking a chord with me along with her tone. I grit my teeth.

"That's what you want, right? Obedience, a toy?" she whispers, tears burn in her eyes as she lifts her head, her lips grazing mine so softly.

"I know what you're doing?" I warn her, knowing she is trying to distract me from forcing her to mark me.

"Is it working?" she asks.

"Yes." I state, her lips quirk into a small smile as her lips graze mine. "Seems I'm not the only one who's a slave to the mate bond," she whispers, kissing me. She nibbles on my bottom lip. I feel like fucking prey helpless against the urges inside me and she knows it, pushing herself up against me.

"I am not a slave to anything," I growl, my grip doesn't loosen as she tries to climb on top of me.

"What are you if you're not a slave?" she asks her hands on my chest, her pale soft skin tempting me.

Her body is temptingly warm and in spite of what she's done, what she says, I still want her more than any other woman I've ever touched. "A king," I state watching her. I groan when my eyes move down her body landing on her perfect breasts. Pushing my pelvis into hers, she moans and my lips crash down on hers briefly. Tearing our lips apart, I pant heavily at the sight of her nude body contouring mine. It is a sight that never fails to fill me with hunger. She squirms against my hold which brings us closer together.

"Sienna," I groan her name, unable to deny this sweet little temptress anything at this moment. She rakes her nails over my chest making small red marks on my skin, her hands continue downward until they come across the bulge in my pants. She teases me through them until I start to squirm at her touch. A low, guttural moan escapes me as she massages my length. Her other hand goes to my hair, she grips it, pulling me down to kiss her before letting go. My mouth consumes hers, my hips rocking against her when she turns her face to the side, giving me access to her neck. My lips and tongue trail across her skin, my touch featherlight.

She draws in a sharp breath, her body coming alive from my touch. As I glide across her skin, I'm captured by the captivating aroma that arouses me more. I move downward, my lips latching onto one of her nipples. I'm distracted by the taste of her skin and the way she squirms beneath me, proving she, too, is just as affected by this bond we share as I am. I peer down at her smirking up at me with those mischievous eyes,

"I guess being king means you're a slave to your own desires." Before I even realize what is happening, a painful boom erupts as the lamp that was knocked off the table during our struggle collides with my head. The impact causes me to see stars and her face blurs in front of my eyes, then everything fades into darkness.

Chapter Thirty-Six

Sienna

I gasp for air, my chest heaving as I fixate on the ceiling above me. Fury swells within me, consuming me with regret and shame for reaching out to Toby. I needed his voice desperately to clarify my confusion, to remind myself of why I despise him so much—when he's near, everything is foggy and unclear. My fists clench as beads of sweat drip down my temples and the heat of rage radiates from my soul.

I am buried beneath Xandros, my chest crushed beneath the immovable weight of his body. My mind races faster than my heart as I confront my regret in a wave of panic. How could I have been so foolish to alert Toby? Too late now; I hear a deafening knock on the door. The rapping on the door startles me back into reality, and I know if I don't act fast, Javier will come in and see the mess I've made. I have no time to spare.

Rolling Xandros off me, I leap to my feet. His groans echo through the room, along with the sight of blood streaming from where I have clobbered him with the lampshade. Adrenaline floods through me and I know I have mere seconds before Javier bursts in. Escape is my only option. Desperation claws at my insides as I throw on my clothes and frantically search for a way out.

I rush to the windows. My fingers desperately search each window.

None will open, no matter how hard I try, they're all locked tight. As Xandros begins to stir, getting to his hands and knees while clutching his head in pain, terror races through my veins like wildfire. Spotting a nearby stool, I grab it without hesitation and crash it against one of the windows. Surprisingly it smashes, the amount of times I have tried to break those windows, and it takes Lycan strength to do it. The glass shatters into a million pieces as a gust of fresh air rushes inside.

I scramble up the window frame and feel a chill run down my spine as I peer out at the sheer drop I must make. I stare down into the abyss below. The daunting jump seems to get further away as Javier's voice booms from behind the door.

"Xandros! What's going on in there?" Javier yells just as he groans, making me peek back at him to see him getting to his feet. I suck in a breath knowing I don't have time.

"Sienna?" he murmurs just as our eyes meet, his widen in shock briefly. "Don't you dare." I ignore him, tipping forward out the window.

A rush of fear engulfs me, and I take a deep breath before plunging toward the ground. The air whips past my face as I close my eyes, anticipating the searing pain that will follow impact.

My heart pounds in my chest like a drum as I open my eyes. Time seems to slow and the ground races toward me with astonishing speed. I squeeze my eyes shut once more, and brace for impact, but in surprise, my feet touch the edge of the roof below instead. Relief washes over me which is short lived as I tumble off the roof and crash onto the ground with an almighty thud, knocking all the air out of my lungs.

I turn and spot Xandros on the windowsill above me. Gazing up, Xandros's furious face pierces through me like a dagger. He roars with rage and takes off after me, his heavy footsteps land on the roof. He lets out an angry growl and starts to move toward me. Taking my chance, I sprint away, pushing through bushes and gardens until I reach the driveway. Thunderous shouts echo through the gardens as guards join in pursuit.

"Grab her!" Xandros yells to his men.

Desperation bubbles up inside me as I near the iron gates that will lead me to safety, but suddenly they start to close with a loud crunch. "No!" I scream out in despair, pushing myself harder than ever before.

It is too late; before I can get there, they slam shut right in front of me, trapping me inside.

I slam my hands against the gates, frantically searching for another way out. The world around me blurs as tears well up in my eyes. I refuse to be caught again, to be at his mercy. Just as I begin to lose hope, I hear a voice beside me.

"My son is willing to go to war for you, you aren't leaving, Sienna," comes Queen Adina's voice from the rose garden. She steps out of the shadows, her dress wrinkled and hair slightly out of place, yet she still looks picture-perfect. I back up, my hands yanking on the gates. As I lose hope, I hear his voice behind me.

"That was incredibly stupid of you." Xandros's voice booms like thunder, echoing through the air with an intensity that electrifies my skin. Rage radiates from him in waves, and I can feel the scorching heat of his anger. He moves closer to me with a slow, calculated stride. He touches his forehead and hisses before snarling, his fingertips covered with crimson blood from where I hit him.

A cold chill radiates off him and I can feel it sink into my bones. He stops just short of me and commands.

"Don't move." His voice pierces me like a knife, and any lingering thought to run evaporates from my mind. The pressure of his dominance holds me in place, like invisible chains. I know no matter what I do, I won't escape unscathed. He will always find a way to drag me back in.

Xandros grabs hold of me, his grip almost crushingly tight and fingers digging into my soft skin. His eyes blaze with a menacing darkness that sends a terrifying thrill throughout my body. His voice is low and intense as he speaks, seething with a mix of rage and ownership.

"Did you really think you could get away from me?" he growls, his words laced with betrayal and fury. "You are mine, Sienna. You have always been mine, and you will always be mine." I can feel the waves of energy radiating off him, a potent mix of danger and possessiveness. His voice is low and threatening as he speaks.

"Did you think you had the right to leave me for another?" he growls, his words sharpened by seething anger.

"Did you honestly think you could just run off into the sunset with him and I would allow it?" he hisses, his words laced with anger and betrayal. "You belong to me, Sienna. You always have, and you always will. I will kill you before I let another take you from me."

As he drags me back to the castle, his mother and the guards who caught up follow quietly. Not one of them utters a word as he manhandles me back down the driveway. Yet as we near the castle, lights on the driveway illuminate us, making Xandros stop. Adina also turns to look at the sleek limousine stopped at the gates.

"King Vin Dresdan, My King," a guard sings out. Xandros growls.

"What's he doing here?" he asks his mother, who seems just as shocked as Xandros. "He must have already been on his way here when he called." King Rehan growls, and Xandros curses under his breath. "Let them in, while I deal with my mate!" he orders one of the guards.

My heart races as Xandros's grip on my arm tightens, his black eyes glaring menacingly. Our footsteps echo down the hallway as he drags me down them before turning into my room, where he flings me through the door. A few maids cleaning up the shattered glass from a broken window glance at us. "Leave us!" With one powerful command, they scurry away like frightened mice. The door slams shut behind us and an ominous silence fills the room. Everything is still, even my breath.

I stand trembling before him, feeling the force of his presence like a physical force pushing down on my shoulders. His voice pierces through me, low and demanding, as he orders me, "Mark me." There's no escape from his command, and I'm fearful. There is a resignation, and something else as I take a single step toward him. Our bodies almost touch as my heart races in my chest, cold sweat beading down my body.

"Wouldn't that be considered me challenging Carina?" I murmur.

"I don't care, she accepted, therefore she won't challenge you, but you're marking me, Sienna." His voice is a threatening rumble as he looms above me. "Do this now," he snarls, his words thick with menace and power. Terror and acceptance battle within me, understanding I have no other option. I take another unsteady step forward until our bodies are almost one. Xandros sits in the armchair and motions with his hand to come to him, tears prick my eyes and I stand between his legs only for him to jerk me down, so I straddle his lap.

He grips my face in one hand. "There will be punishment later for your actions, for now I need you to mark me," he tells me, letting me go and turning his head to give me his neck. My canines extend like a reflex to his command. My heart races in my chest as I press into him, my razor sharp teeth graze his neck.

I lean forward, teeth extended with anticipation. With one bite, I sink into his flesh and an overwhelming rush of emotions sweeps over me.

The intensity of his emotions is overwhelming—his anger, his betrayal, and his deep, undeniable love for me. It's a tumultuous mix that threatens to consume me. The bond between us pulses with that moment in newfound strength, reminding me of the undeniable connection we share. At that moment, I can't deny the depth of his feelings for me, even if I don't fully understand them myself.

As I release him, I'm left breathless. Our eyes lock in a fierce and passionate gaze. There's a tumultuous energy between us—a collision of emotions that crackles in the air. I can see the conflict in his eyes, the war raging within him as he tries to reconcile his love for me and the anger he feels toward me.

"Sienna," he murmurs, his voice laced with vulnerability. A knock sounds on the door and Xandros sucks in a deep breath when it suddenly opens, Javier walks in and Xandros holds his hand out, his eyes trained on me.

"She marked you?" Javier asks.

"She did," Xandros tells him, using his other hand to wipe his blood from my lips, when Javier drops something in the hand he's holding out. Before I have a chance to even pull away, the cold metal is biting into my wrist. "You will not shift to break out of these, and you will do as you're told from now on," Xandros orders. His command strikes like an urge, yet is slightly different, strong and relentless, yet not painful like every other time.

I'm torn, caught between my anger and the undeniable connection we share. There's a part of me that wants to push him away, to protect myself from further pain. However, another part, a part that still loves him, can't ignore the depth of his emotions. He then stands, his arms slipping beneath my ass, and I thrash, realizing he is about to handcuff me to the bed.

He tosses me on the bed making me bounce before I can even think of moving, his chest is pressed against my back. "You will remain here until I say otherwise, you disobey me or try to run, Toby will die, and I will make you kill him while I watch, are we clear?" Xandros growls, and I nod, tears slipping down my cheeks.

He clasps the handcuff to the metal frame of the bed and rises. "King Vin and Carina are downstairs waiting for you," Javier tells him.

"Stay with her, don't let her out of your sight, and send for someone to fix the windows. I want everything in this room stripped out or bolted down," Xandros snarls before stalking out of the room.

My chest rises and falls rapidly with every ragged breath. I'm trapped here, with only my thoughts for company. Tears slip down my cheeks as I wait for Xandros to return.

The maids he chased out of the room earlier must have returned already because I don't see them anywhere, yet I hear the sounds of moving around the room while I lay on my side, my eyes trained on the ceiling above. From time to time someone looks in, but no one enters. Tired from all the emotions that keep swirling through me, I finally slip into a restless sleep.

For how long, I don't know, but the sound of someone talking is what eventually pulls me from my sleep. The voices are soft and muffled, so it takes me a few seconds to realize where I am and what happened. Sitting up, I lean against the headboard, as my eyes adjust to the sudden burst of light after having slept through the entire night.

Except for Javier, no one has ever been kind to me and that might be a reason why it's such a nice feeling to have someone be concerned about me, even if only for a short span of time.

"Try and eat something," Javier's voice says at the door, followed by a softer voice of one of the maids.

"We've removed everything and bolted the last few things down," she tells him, and I glance around to find most of the furniture gone, only the bare minimum, even the pictures have been removed from the walls.

Javier watches me for a few seconds.

"Why does he insist on keeping me here?" I ask him, my heart twisting in agony at being denied death, denied the right to live, denied everything. Javier sighs heavily. He steps in and moves to the other side of the room, gazing out the window. "You and I both know, Sienna. There's no escape from this," he murmurs.

He looks tired and worn out. Anger mixed with exhaustion and regret, and something else; acceptance if I had to guess. Slowly, Javier turns to me and smiles gently.

"I can smell his scent on your neck. Now everyone will know who you belong to just the same as him, the bond has fully merged." He peers around, still like through a fog. "King Xandros did this for yours and his protection, you must try to understand that..." he says softly, and I frown.

"I don't understand," I tell him, confused about what he means by protection. He shakes his head.

"Some believe only death can break a mating bond," he tells me, turning to stare out the window again, and for a moment I see the pain in his eyes before it's quickly wiped away by the mask Javier has on when he turns back to me.

"Xandros could kill you tonight, Sienna, but if you didn't already know, that would mean he is forced to mark Carina or lose his mind. He doesn't want her, he's been fighting this marriage since he found you. He is obligated to his kingdom, your kingdom once he figures out how to fix the mess this has become."

Javier glances at me with sad eyes. "As king, Xandros has responsibilities to his kingdom and his people. He must put their needs above his own desires."

I swallow hard, trying to push down my own desires and fears. "And what happens to me in all of this?" I ask, feeling small and insignificant.

"You are still the future queen of your kingdom," Javier reminds me. "Xandros must protect you for the sake of both kingdoms."

I nod slowly, feeling a sense of wistful resignation settle over me. "So, I'm just supposed to stay here and wait for it all to happen?" I ask, a sense of hopelessness washing over me.

My mind reels at Javier's words. Xandros could kill me? And all because of this supposed mating bond? I feel like I'm in the middle of a nightmare, one I can't seem to escape.

"Why did he mark me in the first place?" I ask, desperation creeping into my voice. "I never asked for any of this."

"Sometimes these things just happen," Javier says with a sad shrug. "And once the bond is formed, there's no going back. You and Xandros are tied together forever now, whether you like it or not. If it makes you feel any better, Sienna, you think he isn't fighting for you, but he just breached the treaty by allowing you to mark him, that in itself is a challenge against Carina," he tells me, and I gasp.

"Don't worry, Carina hasn't declared the challenge, she is aware you're his mate, and honestly, I don't think her vendetta is against you, something else is her driving force in all this."

The weight of this settles over me like a heavy blanket, suffocating me. I'm trapped, consumed by the tangled mess of emotions Xandros has stirred up within me.

"And Carina?" I ask, my voice coming out as a whisper. "What about her?"

Javier's expression softens. "She's just a pawn in all of this, too, like he is," he says, his voice filled with sympathy. "Xandros believes she is being forced. It's clear she loves him, she is just not in love with him, and the fact she refuses to agree to the divorce yet allows him to keep you says her hand too is being forced," he tells me.

"By her father?" I ask him and he shrugs. "She's scared of her father. I've heard them on the phone. She told me she couldn't go back home. She almost sounded sorry," I whisper, wondering what Carina means by all her cryptic conversations.

I nod numbly, not sure what else to say or do. The reality of my situation is starting to sink in; I'm trapped here with no way out, and the only person who has any power over my fate is the same man who marked me against my will.

Chapter Thirty-Seven

Xandros

My footsteps echo in the long, winding hallways, a reminder of my annoyance as I near the entrance into the new part of the castle. My heart races with a flurry of emotions; eagerness mingled uneasily with apprehension. Eagerness to get back to my mate, so I can punish her; love her. Yet, unease fills me with King Vin's sudden arrival. A crisp clean smell carries on the draft as I enter the main part of the castle, firmly driving home the reality of what awaits me beyond those doors at the bottom of the steps. I take one last deep breath before pushing them open to meet King Vin and Carina. Taking the stairs two at a time, I can see guards near the foyer doors leading outside, a few glance back at my approach before warily turning their attention to outside.

I head down to the front doors. I'm a mix of curiosity and caution. They pull up in a white limousine just as I reach the entrance, my mother and father, who are already engaged in conversation with the guards, wait patiently. As Carina steps out of the car, I notice an unfamiliar tension in her body language. She darts close to me, her delicate fingers latching onto mine with such force that it feels like a vice grip. The warmth of her skin against my own sends a rush of conflicting emotions coursing through me. Her sudden need, confusing and unnerving at the same time. The sound of doors closing as their entourage comes in the gates makes me glance around to see guards rushing about.

"Please, play along," she whispers, her voice filled with fear. I hesitantly glance at her, taken aback by the fear in her voice. She pleads with me silently, her fear palpable in the air that hangs between us. I take a deep breath and stare into her eyes, trying to decipher what she isn't saying out loud. An intense moment passes, and I can see a vulnerable side of her that wasn't present before. I feel pulled toward her, drawn to protect her from whatever danger she is facing. I may not love or want her, but she is my wife. This woman doesn't scare easily, so seeing her fear so evident, I know something is wrong. My arm gently encircles her shoulders, and I can sense a small wave of relief pass through her body as she leans into my embrace.

"I want an explanation," I whisper back, my voice low and filled with concern. She nods in response, and we wait for her father to climb out of the car. I clench my fists, aching to ask what has happened that has led us there. My whispered words are charged with annoyance as I ask for an explanation. The weight of her unspoken answer seems to press on me and fill the air like a storm cloud. We stand in silence as I take in the car, whose headlights illuminate the night. I feel my chest tighten as her father slowly emerges from the vehicle. His heavy footsteps and the creak of his leather shoes echo in the crisp night air around us.

"King Xandros, you gave me quite the fright when you left," he declares, trying his best to conceal his inner annoyance as he speaks. As if anticipating trouble, he has brought along his elite guard, their armor shoes shuffling along the ground and rustling clothes echoing off the castle walls, ensuring their presence is known as they wander checking perimeters and speaking with my guards. "I brought my guards in case you needed assistance; you left in such a rush I had no idea what was going on."

"Mate issues, but it's sorted now," I answer honestly.

"I can see that," Vin's eyes narrow on the bite mark.

My eyes remain on Carina's father, and I feel a chill spread over my body. His tense form and hard stare bore into me, as if he can see every secret I am desperately trying to hide. The heaviness of the silence that ensues makes it clear he has many questions burning through his brain. I have no answers, not ones he wants to hear.

His eyes flash with a cold hatred as he spits out the words, each syllable heavy with disdain. "I thought we agreed you wouldn't allow your mate to mark you." The words drip from his mouth with a thick, cream-like poison, corroding me from the inside out.

I grapple to maintain my composure wanting nothing more than to rip the man apart limb by limb while Carina steps in before I can utter a syllable. Her father's stern voice reverberates around us, silencing all other noise as if pressing an invisible mute button. His rigid body language and the feeling of contempt, clashing against mine, heightens the tension. I'm about to respond when Carina speaks up, surprising both me and her father.

"Xandros called me beforehand, Daddy. I gave him permission," she says, her voice steady. I cringe inwardly at her use of endearment. I nod in agreement, leaning down to kiss her forehead.

"Yes, she was fretting when I was away. She nearly died," I confirm, the weight of the situation heavy on my shoulders.

The air stills as her father studies us. His glare seems to bore into our souls, his menacing presence looming over us. He finally speaks the words that feel like daggers; "This won't affect our treaty, will it? Is this mate of yours intending to challenge my daughter?"

I can feel Carina's unease next to me and we both shake our heads in unison. I try to swallow, but my mouth has gone dry, time feels as though it has been suspended.

"I assure you, King Vin, that our alliance is secure. Sienna won't be an issue," I respond, my voice filled with false certainty.

Vin nods, seeming somewhat appeased. "Very well. I have spoken with the Elders recently, and they are somewhat placated now that you've found your mate. However, there is confusion regarding the alliances and treaties, and also the marriage to my daughter."

My mother interrupts. "I shall make some tea."

"Whisky would be better, Adina. I need a drink after that horrid drive," Vin requests. My mother nods, and my father leads Vin inside.

We move to the parlor, and I take a seat at the table, Carina shocking me further by sitting in my lap.

"Well, I might as well stay for the week," Vin announces. "I have business here with the seekers, anyway." As he speaks, guards enter the room, carrying suitcases and placing Carina's and her father's bags by the door. I watch them closely and notice one of the guards smirking at Carina, then winks at her in a way that makes her visibly tense. My blood boils as I watch the guard's gaze fall on Carina in such a lewd way. I can practically see what he is thinking.

Anger flares within me, and I instinctively place my hand over Carina's lap, shielding her from the guard's gaze. His eyes, black pits that seem to suck up all the remaining light in the room, travel up her legs, lingering on the hemline of her skirt which I tug down further.

Then they trail slowly up and quickly dart away when he meets my piercing glare. Vin backs away at the low rumble that has formed in my throat; his inquisitive glance replaced with disbelief at the raw power emanating from within me.

"Are you okay?" he inquires, the worry deeply creasing his features.

My lips are tight as I speak through gritted teeth, my voice trembling with barely controlled rage. "There has been a reprehensible breach of respect," I reply. "That guard must be removed from this premises or else face the wrath of my fury. If I spot him so much as winking at my wife once more, then his eyes will be plucked from their sockets." My words hang in the chilly air that has settled in the room, and my potent aura of menace rushes out.

Vin fixes his eyes on the guard, and it is as though he has been struck by lightning. A chill runs through the room, and a palpable tension surrounds Vin. The guard's face drains of color and he quivers with fear. "You heard the king," Vin says in a low, dangerous voice, his words carrying an invisible weight. "Leave immediately...or else." The guard shrinks away from Vin's presence, hastily exiting.

My mother arrives with a glass of amber liquid, a silent offering to Vin. My father refuses, preferring instead to sit and observe. The tension in the room is so thick, it seems like you can cut it with a knife.

"So, this mate business," Vin begins slowly, each word weighed down by its implications. "It won't hurt my daughter's chance of becoming pregnant, will it? I've heard stories that your kind can experience great pain when coupled, that your mate will be affected by you performing in the bedroom with my daughter." The air hangs heavy between us, this conversation is treading into unknown territory. The atmosphere in the room grows tense at the shift in conversation to more delicate matters.

I swallow hard, feeling a mix of nerves. "We will take measures to ensure my mate is comfortable. We are aware of the challenges, and we will navigate them together."

Vin gives me a satisfied smirk. "Excellent. I hope she will be expecting an addition before your nuptials. There is nothing more powerful than heirs when it comes to forming lasting treaties."

My mother's voice rings out, laced with curiosity. "You chose not to bring Anita here, King Vin?"

A sinister darkness sweeps over his face briefly. "Matrimonial struggles. Reassure yourself, My Queen, she is being suitably disciplined for her misdeeds, that I can assure you."

My mother's expression hardens at his words and Carina drops her gaze to her lap, a feeling of unease filling the room. I want to probe deeper into the underlying tension between them, but keep silent, knowing now is not the time. Vin stands to signal it is getting late.

"It is late indeed. You all must be tired from such a day. Let us continue our talks tomorrow morning," he declares in a booming voice as he gestures for a servant to show him to his quarters.

"Yes, we have much to discuss. We can chat after Adina goes into town?" my father suggests, looking at my mother.

"You're leaving in the morning?" I ask my mother, staring at her in confusion.

She nods. "Yes, I have my usual hair appointment tomorrow. Carina, you're welcome to join me, if you'd like."

Carina smiles politely. "Yes, I would very much like that."

"Good, bring your handmaiden, she can carry our bags; we might do a bit of shopping afterward," my mother says, and I cut my gaze across to my mother who smiles politely.

As everyone begins to disperse, the weight of the impending discussions settles on my shoulders, and I clench my teeth. Carina rises to her feet, staring toward where her father wandered off to with my parents. "Are you alright?" I ask Carina, and she glances back at me, nodding.

She peers up at me, her eyes filled with uncertainty. "I... I don't know. This is all happening so fast. And the way that guard looked at me..."

I squeeze her hand reassuringly. "Don't worry about him. He won't bother you again, not here at least. Have you had issues with your father's guard before?" I ask her, and she tenses.

"We should get to bed," she whispers, wandering off, and I rise to my feet. I want to go back to Sienna, but with Carina's father under my roof, I know I must keep up the façade of a happy husband.

As we make our way back to our room, I can't shake off the feeling of unease that lingers within me. I brush away these thoughts, forcing myself to focus on the present. Carina is quiet and subdued, the only sound that fills the corridors is the soft rustle of our clothes and the faint echo of our footsteps. When we reach our room, I close the door behind us and turn to face her.

"Are you sure you're okay?" I ask, searching her eyes for any sign of discomfort.

Carina slips out of my grasp, moving toward the wardrobe to change into a nightgown. As I stand there, watching her, I can feel the tension between us growing.

Carina turns to me, her eyes searching for answers. "Your explanation?" I ask her, and she chews her lip then changes the subject.

"How is Sienna?" she asks.

"Fine, she tried to run, I forced her to mark me."

"So, what happens now?" she asks.

I take a deep breath before answering her. "I don't know," I admit. "You can sign the divorce papers?" Carina rolls her eyes, bored with me constantly asking. "Exactly how long do you plan to keep this up?"

"As long as it takes until you realize I am not going anywhere," she answers, and I growl, turning for the door. "You can't leave, my father catches you sneaking off to her, you put her in danger. I know you don't want that, just as I don't want to be forced home."

"And why is that, Carina, what happened on the drive here?"

"Nothing, my father is overbearing, you know that, pressuring me to get knocked up, solidify the alliances, the treaty and all that crap." I curse. Yet something tells me she isn't being completely honest, she was scared when she arrived, now she seems more herself.

I cross the room in a few strides, pulling Carina toward me. "Tell me the truth," I demand, my eyes burning with intensity.

She stares up at me, her eyes flickering nervously. "I... I don't know what you're talking about."

"Don't lie to me, Carina," I growl, my grip tightening around her arms. "What happened on the drive here?"

Carina stands at that moment, an eternity stretching out between us. I can make out her harsh breathing and the rustle of her clothes as she pulls away from me. "Nothing, Xandros," she spits, her voice laden with venom. Fury burns in her eyes, like embers ready to consume.

I reach for her arm, and she recoils like a feral cat. "We've been together two years, Carina," I plead. "I know you're being forced into this. If it's your father, I can protect you."

Her laugh is a caustic bark, scraping against my skin like blades of glass. "You can't protect me, no one can," she sneers, fingers entwined in the hair at the back of her neck as if trying to strangle the fear away.

"What does he have over you?" I growl.

She closes her eyes briefly before slowly opening them again, a resolve now resting there which sends a chill through me. She takes a deep breath and speaks in hushed tones, as though afraid someone else might hear. "Let's just get this marriage over with, and then I'll go on an extended vacation." Her lips quirk up into a twisted smirk as she adds: "You can be with Sienna."

My blood runs cold. "I'm not sleeping with you," I say through gritted teeth, my fists clenched so tight my knuckles shine white.

Carina waves me off dismissively, her gaze still focused on some distant point beyond my shoulder. "Because you're incapable? Come on, we'll find another way." An unfamiliar darkness settles around us, filling the space with an air of sinister foreboding.

Carina stares at me for a moment before bursting into an angry, sarcastic laugh. "Oh come on, Xandros, what do you think this is? You have no choice in the matter, and neither do I," she says, her voice laced with bitterness.

I take a step back, still not believing what I'm hearing. "No, I won't do that either," I say firmly, shaking my head. "I am not having a child with you."

Carina's face contorts in rage, and she takes a step toward me. "It's not like we have any other options," she hisses, her words dripping with venom.

Carina's eyes flash with anger. "You don't have a choice in this, Xandros. You're my husband now, and you'll do whatever it takes to maintain appearances," she spits.

I can feel my temper rising, my patience wearing thin. Carina takes a step forward, her body presses against mine. "Things change, Xandros. You need to adapt if you want to survive in this world," she says, her voice low and dangerous.

"What, like forcing yourself on me?" I spit out the words, barely able to control my temper.

Carina's eyes flicker with something that looks like fear before hardening again. "I didn't mean it like that," she insisted. "I just... I don't know what else to do. My father is relentless, and I can't keep living like this."

I feel a flicker of sympathy for her, but it is quickly drowned out by my own feelings of frustration and helplessness. "There has to be another way," I say, my mind reeling as I try to come up with a solution.

Carina shakes her head, her hair tumbling around her face. "There isn't," she says simply. "Not unless you can convince my father to call off this ridiculous arrangement," she shrugs.

Chapter Thirty-Eight

Sienna

The following morning, I wake to Rehan entering my room. Javier instantly moves to greet him, and as I groggily wake up, I note it is still dark outside. Every muscle in Javier's body tenses up as he runs to greet him, and I can feel the confusion radiating off us both. "My King?" I gasp, jumping out of bed with a start. Confused, I look at Javier, who also appears perplexed by the unexpected visit. "My King?" I ask again, hastily wrapping my blanket around myself.

Rehan's normally thunderous voice is like a whisper, the intensity in his gaze creating an unbearable tension in the air. His words are like knives piercing my skin, as he growls, "None of this 'My King' business. I am not here as your king, I'm here as your father-in-law. Now, time to start your training." I glance nervously at Javier who stares at the king as if he has lost his mind. "Do you know how to throw a punch?" The pressure around us builds until it feels as if the whole room will explode.

I shake my head, a mix of curiosity and apprehension building within me. My heart hammers in my chest and I feel the first stirrings of unease. Javier yanks the king's arm, harshly jerking him away from me. I'm shocked by Javier's forcefulness, and the way he man-handles the king so roughly, yet the king doesn't seem fazed, as if it isn't the first time

Javier has laid hands on him. I stand awkwardly, clutching my blanket tighter, my arm straining under the pull of the handcuff where I am shackled to the bed. The two of them hiss in hushed whispers, sending me furtive glances as I strain to decipher their words. My apprehension grows with every passing second as I realize the gravity of the conversation upon hearing my mate's name.

"Does Xandros know?" Javier asks, his voice laced with concern as he casts a nervous glance at me.

"No, and you won't be telling him. She needs to know how to defend herself, especially while that snake is here," King Rehan asserts. My eyes widen at the mention of King Vin, the man who gives me an unsettling feeling.

"Now, give me the keys!" King Rehan demands holding his hand out expectantly to Javier. Javier presses his lips in a line. "You know I'm right, Javier," the king adds, and Javier reluctantly hands a set of keys to the king, who swiftly unlocks my handcuffs.

I flex my sore wrists, relief flooding through me as I massage feeling back into it, the cold metal having left indents in my skin.

~

"Let me guess, after last night's incident, he's forbidden you to shift?" Rehan questions, his eyes scanning me curiously. I nod, uncertain of where this is leading.

This is the first time I have really got a good look at the man, this close, he appears shorter than when I have seen him in the dining hall, not as intimidating. Maybe it's the royal red silk pajamas he wears and his matching slippers. His hair is dark, like black ink, perfectly combed back. He reminds me a little of his son, they share a lot of the same features.

Plump cheeks, feigned redness staining them and a sparkle in his eyes that seems too innocent for this man when his lips turn up in the corners cunningly.

"Well, we'll make do. Now get ready," he instructs, a mischievous glint in his eyes. "Now try to punch me, give it a good hard crack," he encourages, bouncing on the balls of his feet, looking absolutely ridiculous since he is in his pajamas, and the scuffling of his orthopedic slippers just makes it all the more bizarre.

"Excuse me?" I blurt in shock, my mind struggling to comprehend the request. He can't be serious.

"Come on, girlie, show me what you got!" King Rehan exclaims, his eyes twinkling with excitement. I hesitate for a moment, and Javier nods for me to do as the king asks. I cringe internally; who am I to deny the crazy king? Slowly lifting my arm and throw a punch at his outstretched fist. He dodges it easily, letting out a hearty chuckle, and motions for me to try again.

"I promise you, girlie, I may be old, but I'm still lithe on my feet," he says with a smirk, demonstrating some peculiar footwork. Javier snorts at the sight, shaking his head in amusement.

This time, when I throw my punch, he catches it midair and uses my own momentum to swing me around backhanded before releasing me. A thrill of surprise courses through me as I'm reminded that despite his age, this man can still hold his own in battle if necessary. I stumble back, trying to regain my balance, and peer up in surprise.

"What did you think of that one? Not bad for an old man." He grins mischievously and motions for me to come at him again. I shake my head, he's insane.

"You need to learn how to defend yourself. King Vin is in the castle for who knows how long," Rehan explains, his expression growing serious. My unease intensifies as the gravity of the situation settles upon me. Still, I hesitate to take action, this feels far too odd, and some part of me wonders if I am trapped in a dream, in some twisted alternate reality. This man has barely said two words to me since being here and suddenly wants me to punch him?

"Hit me!" the king commands, his eyes narrowing slightly. I look to Javier, hoping for some clarification on whether the king has lost his marbles.

"I always get stuck playing the guinea pig," Javier growls softly, reluctantly stepping forward and swinging at the king. In a swift and fluid motion, Rehan blocks Javier's punch and counters with a skilled strike, knocking Javier onto his back with a resounding thud.

My eyes widen in astonishment as I witness the king's agility and strength. A mix of fear and excitement courses through my veins. He turns his attention back to me, a challenging glimmer in his eyes. "Don't let the slippers fool you, Anna, I'm stronger than I look," he tells me, waving me forward. I chew my lip, glancing down at Javier who stares up at the ceiling almost bored.

"Now it's your turn. Don't hold back," The king says, adopting a defensive stance. I take a deep breath and cautiously step forward, attempting a punch. Rehan easily evades it, demonstrating his agility and quick reflexes once again. We continue the training session, with Rehan patiently guiding me through various moves and techniques, though I don't understand why, it seems pointless to me.

My muscles ache with each exertion, bruises forming on my arms and legs as I absorb a few accidental blows. The training is grueling, pushing me to my limits, and beyond. By the time we are done, the sun is shining outside, the morning birds chirp while I clutch my knees panting having had the wind knocked out of me again. "You're too frightened, how many times do I need to tell you to forget my status?" King Rehan states.

"This is pointless, I can't even shift! So what good would I be defending myself against him," I tell him as the session comes to an end. I collapse onto the rug, my body weary. Rehan wipes his head with a towel, his gaze meeting mine.

"That will do for today. Besides, I must get to breakfast before anyone notices, or Adina wakes up," he says, his voice filled with a hint of exhaustion. He leaves the room, and I find myself lying on my back, staring at the ceiling.

Javier stands over me, his expression a mix of concern and weariness. "Go shower, Sienna. I suspect the king will try to sneak off to see you, and you're covered in his father's scent. He'll ask questions," he tells me.

"So?" I respond, my voice laced with fatigue and defiance.

"So, in case you haven't noticed, your mate isn't here, and he forbade me from letting anyone in here with you. Meaning he doesn't know about Rehan's little training session. Now get up, I am not being skinned alive because you are too lazy to shower," Javier snaps at me.

I groan and roll onto my side, pushing myself up from the rug. With aching muscles and a heavy heart, I make my way into the bathroom, my mind filled with conflicting thoughts when I stop, turning back to face Javier.

"If I have to keep this secret, then you need to get me a phone," I tell Javier, my voice firm as I stand in the bathroom doorway.

"Excuse me?" he replies, surprise evident in his tone.

"A phone, or I tell Xandros you let his father visit," I assert, a sense of determination fueling my words.

"Are you blackmailing me?" Javier asks, his brows furrowing. "Why do you want a phone?"

I don't answer, it's clear he knows why.

"The answer is no. Xandros will kill me," Javier adds, his voice tinged with concern.

"Death is better than being skinned alive," I shrug, shutting the door. I quickly shower. The warm water cascades over me, washing away the sweat and grime of this impromptu training session. Once finished I make my way to the walk-in closet pulling my uniform from a hanger.

I dress in my maid's uniform, a sense of urgency pushing me forward. The castle is coming alive with noise, and I know I will be sent for any minute if Carina is back.

As I step out of the closet, I find Javier waiting in my room. Nervousness creeps up within me as I wonder why he has returned. "Ah, you're back already?" I ask, my voice tinged with a hint of anxiety.

"I mean it, if he catches you with this, he'll think you stole it!" Javier says, striding over to me. "And I won't be telling him otherwise!" He hands me a phone, his expression a mix of concern and uncertainty. "Now hide that and hurry up. Carina and Adina have requested your presence."

"Why?" I inquire, puzzled.

"Just get dressed!" Javier snaps, his patience wearing thin. He walks out of the room, shutting the door behind him. I let out a sigh, my mind reeling with questions and suspicions.

Quickly, I slip the phone into a hidden pocket of a jacket of mine at the back of the closet. Thoughts swirl as I hurriedly finish getting dressed.

I make my way through the corridors, my steps filled with apprehension. Carina and Adina's request is peculiar, and I wonder what lies behind their sudden interest in me. I navigate the halls, passing by maids and guards with a newfound sense of awareness. They are all watching me, and I can feel Javier behind me, following like my shadow.

As I reach the grand foyer, I find Carina and Adina waiting for me. Carina's smile is warm but guarded, while Adina wears her usual composed expression. "Sienna, so glad you could join us," Carina says.

"What is this about?" I ask, unable to hide the curiosity in my voice.

Adina steps forward, her eyes fixed on mine. "You'll be joining us in the city."

I take a deep breath, sensing the weight of their words. Great, now I have to survive not just Carina but also the queen, just my luck.

As Carina, Adina, and I prepare to leave for Adina's hair appointment, a sense of unease settles within me. I try to blend into the wall, becoming a mere shadow in the grand foyer of the castle.

Just as we're about to make our exit, we run into Vin and Xandros. When I see them, I feel the blood from my face drain, and I am unable to breathe.

The two men walk toward us, hands clasped behind their backs, powerful enough to bend steel with a single squeeze. My gaze instinctively locks onto Xandros, and I can feel my heart skip a beat. His presence still has the power to stir emotions within me, a reminder of the tangled web that binds us together. Trying to hide my apprehension, I wait for the interaction to unfold.

"What time do you think you'll be done?" Vin asks, his voice laced with an underlying tension. His arms are folded across his body as he stands with his feet spread apart. He wears his black hair loose, framing his porcelain white skin, highlighting the deep lines in his forehead and around his eyes. His face is devoid of expression as he stares at me, his eyes showing no signs of recognition or compassion.

"We should be back by 2 PM, though you're leaving a little earlier, aren't you, Carina?" Adina replies, her smile concealing any hint of the hidden turmoil within our lives. Carina nods.

However, when Vin's eyes land on me, he shoots me a glare, and I avert my gaze, my heart racing. The encounter is brief, but the weight of his disapproval hangs heavy in the air. As the queen and Carina stride away, I move to follow, desperate to escape the suffocating atmosphere.

I try to pull away from Xandros's grip when he clasps my arm tighter. He stares at me. "What happened to your cheek?" he whispers, his voice laced with emotion, he lifts his hand where Rehan accidentally got me when I didn't dodge fast enough. He brushes his thumb over the mark.

My gaze quickly shifts to Javier behind him, and Xandros questions me further before I can answer. "Did one of them do this to you? Tell me and I will handle it," he adds, his eyes searching mine for answers.

I shake my head, my voice filled with bitterness. "No, Xandros. The mark on my cheek is a result of your actions, of you handcuffing me to the bed!" I lie effortlessly.

Xandros looks taken aback by my words; he releases his grip on me and takes a step back. Guilt flashes across his face, and I can feel his remorse through our bond. "No more handcuffs," he concedes, his voice softening. "You must remain with Carina and Javier at all times. Promise me," he whispers.

Reluctantly, I nod, knowing I have no choice but to comply. The freedom I crave is still out of reach, replaced by the suffocating constraints of this new reality. The restraints of my mate and his family. Xandros leans down, pressing his lips to my forehead as he pulls me into his embrace. "Xandros!" I hiss at his actions, glancing around nervously for King Vin, thankfully, he has wandered off elsewhere.

"I missed you," he whispers.

"Funny, you handcuffing me to the bed says otherwise," I retort, and he growls. "You knew you'd be punished for running, what did you expect?" he hisses at me angrily.

"Not to be handcuffed to a bed like some bed toy," I growl. Xandros sighs when I hear someone clear their throat. Both Xandros and I tense.

"Sienna, dear, are you coming?" Carina's singsong voice calls out from the doorway, interrupting our conversation. Xandros turns to see her standing there, a picture of innocence. "I might be coming home earlier. Mom wants me to call her. Can you send the other car at 1 PM for me instead of 2?" Carina asks, her gaze shifting between Xandros and me.

Xandros nods, seemingly lost in thought and I step away from him, this situation growing more tense, yet Carina doesn't seem upset, more accepting of their strange relationship. I want no part in it. Glancing at Carina, she digs through her purse, retrieving her phone.

Carina's a vision in a white summer dress, its skirt a modest knee-length, and the neckline dips low between her ample cleavage. Her hair is tied into a high ponytail, and she's wearing a pair of silver peep-toe pumps. "I'll organize it," Xandros answers her, and she nods. "The car will be here in a moment, Adina already called for it," Carina tells me, and I nod, watching as she turns back to the door and steps out to stand with Adina.

"Go," Xandros tells me. I glance once more at the door leading outside, knowing I have to play my part in this intricate dance. With a heavy sigh, I step away from Xandros, not even slightly excited about being stuck with these two women all day. Javier follows silently, remaining close as I expected he would. Stepping out the door, I move to join Carina and Adina, and we head toward the waiting car.

Chapter Thirty-Nine

Sienna

The day unfolds like a façade, as Carina and Adina pretend everything is normal. We shop around for a while, and I watch as they try on clothes and admire jewelry, while I try my best to ignore them; yet Carina even forces me to endure their shopping spree, her and Adina forcing me to try on clothes.

However, I am shocked when Carina actually buys them, handing me the bag. I stare at her when Adina speaks. "These would go nicely with that dress you got her," Adina says, and I raise an eyebrow at the heels, turning my gaze to Javier, he shrugs, also confused. It makes me worry about their true intentions with me. They are both acting as if this is nothing more than a girls' day out, an afternoon of distraction and fun. I'm truly out of my element right now.

"Oh those are pretty, do you like this, Sienna?" Adina asks. I glance around, looking for the other Sienna, she may be speaking to when she thrusts them at me. "Try these on. Javier, help her," Adina nods toward me. Javier kneels before me, grabbing my feet suddenly, and I wobble back, gripping his shoulder.

"No, I am fine."

"Nonsense, they will look lovely with that dress," Adina waves me off while Javier slips one of my flats off. He buckles the sandal up that has a tiny heel. "Perfect fit," Adina announces, and I am quick to remove it. Adina pays for my shoes, and I lean into Javier.

"Maybe she is trying to make amends," Javier whispers to me. I almost scoff. Adina making amends with the traitors' daughter. He shrugs, nudging me to follow them as we leave, his hand on my lower back.

Carina then insists we have lunch together, leading us to a small cafe near the edge of the street. We take a seat in the sun, and Carina orders something for the both of us. Nothing fancy or extravagant, just a simple meal that might have been enjoyed by any trio of friends.

As the afternoon progresses, Carina cancels the driver who was meant to pick her up early. I try to shake off the unease, pushing aside the nagging sense that something isn't right. It's during the ride back home that the façade finally cracks.

Adina and Carina chat away, their laughter filling the car, when Javier's phone rings. Eavesdropping on the conversation, I can tell it's Xandros on the other end.

"I will head over there now. How long has he been there?" Javier's voice sounds urgent, his tone laced with a mix of concern and determination.

"He left twenty minutes ago. Just stay out of view. I want to know who he's meeting with," Xandros responds before hanging up. He taps on the driver's window, instructing him to pull over.

"I've been called away. I need to check something for Xandros. I will find my own way back," he informs Adina, who dismisses him with a wave of her hand. Javier climbs out of the car, disappearing down the street.

The chatter in the car gradually dies down as we leave the city and approach an intersection near the back road leading to the castle. Suddenly, the sound of a roaring engine fills the air, and within seconds, our car is violently struck on my side. The impact sends us rolling down an embankment, a cacophony of metal and glass crashing around us.

In the chaos, Carina is thrown out of the car, her body tumbling through the air. My world is a blur as the car tumbles down the embankment. I feel pain everywhere as I am jostled about, disoriented but thankfully seemingly okay. I am hanging upside down from my seat belt, the leather digging painfully into my shoulder and my head pounding from being tossed around. I hear Carina screaming in terror from somewhere outside of the car and fear grips me as I try to make sense of what just happened.

Suddenly, a bright light fills the air, and I squint against it. A loud crash follows and then complete silence. The car comes to a halt, and I slowly unfasten myself from my seat belt, dropping onto the ceiling of the flipped vehicle.

Everything is spinning around me and for a second all I can do is sit here, trying to catch my breath.

The sound of screeching metal and the roar of an engine racing away snaps me out of darkness. The air is filled with a choking blanket of smoke, and I am pinned in by the twisted wreckage of the car. With every ounce of strength, I claw toward the shattered window, desperately struggling to break free of the savage flames that inch ever closer. Peering around, my stomach turns as I take in the lifeless body of the driver, hanging like a rag doll from the crushed front window.

My gaze shifts to Carina's trembling form lying motionless on a nearby hill. Carina is lying on her back on the grassy slope twenty feet away from where we had been sideswiped by some unknown force or vehicle. I can't see Adina anywhere as I choke on smoke. Seeing Carina on the hill I realize something. I can escape, a chance to find Toby and get out of this cursed city; it's all within reach now! My heart races with anticipation at the thought of seizing this opportunity for freedom. With a sudden burst of energy, I wrench myself away from the car and run toward her, determined not to let this opportunity slip away.

A groan breaks through the chaos, and I turn to learn Adina is trapped within the burning wreckage. Adina's cries for help pierce the chaos like a gunshot. Halfway up the hill, I freeze in horror as her screams become muffled by the smoke. My steps falter, and I turn back, dreading what I'll find.

I cannot leave her to die such a grisly fate. Cursing under my breath, I race back to the car, crawling back into the inferno to reach Adina. Black smoke obscures my view as I listen for her cries trying to gauge whereabouts in the wreckage she is, getting on my hands and knees I peer into the mangled car.

The world around me grows darker as fire takes control of the car, the driver's body burns. The smell of burning hair and flesh make me gag and cough as the front of the limousine is engulfed in a cloud of smoke and flames. Desperately, I search for Adina, spotting her trapped beneath the mangled front seat. Crawling through the wreckage, I shove away the twisted metal to reach her legs. She stares up at me in shock, her voice slows with disbelief and gratitude.

Her legs are trapped, and the heat intensifies as flames lick up the side of the car. Choking on the thick smoke, I try to pry the seat away, my hands trembling with both fear and determination.

"You came back," Adina croaks, shock resonating in her voice. "Why?" she asks, confusion etched in her eyes.

I meet her gaze and respond, my voice filled with determination, "Because I am not my parents." Together, we struggle against the wreckage, the relentless heat threatening to engulf us.

With a final burst of strength, I manage to free Adina from the wreckage, dragging her out of the burning car. Coughing and gasping for air, we stumble up the hill to where Carina lies unconscious.

I roll Carina over gently, patting her face in an attempt to rouse her. Adina's voice trembles as she asks about the driver, and I can only respond with a grim shake of my head. "He's dead."

Adina's eyes widen in horror and we both look away, unable to comprehend the tragedy that has unfolded. Dropping next to Carina, I tap her face, then pry her eyelids open.

Suddenly, Carina jerks awake, grasping at her chest making me jump. She gasps for air, her eyes wild with panic.

"What happened?" she croaks, confusion and fear evident in her voice.

Adina and I exchange a fearful glance.

"We were in a car accident," I say softly. "The car flipped over and the driver...the driver is dead."

Carina's face goes pale. She pushes herself to a sitting position, wincing in pain as she does so.

At that moment, we hear the distant sound of approaching cars and emergency service sirens filling the air. I begin to fill with a sense of urgency as I help Carina and Adina to their feet and encourage them to climb the hill toward the main road. Once at the top, I help Adina sit on the guard rail. Adina rubs her wrist, panic creeping into her voice as she realizes her bracelet is missing.

It's just a bracelet. I think to myself, shaking my head at the triviality of it all.

With a heavy heart, I stumble back down the hill, leaving them by the roadside. As I make my way toward the burning car, the guilt consumes me as I leave behind knowing I can't do anything for them. When I reach the car, flames dance around its twisted frame. The fire is huge now, and I have to squint to make out any detail in the burning wreckage. I crawl under what remains of the car's passenger side, searching desperately for Adina's bracelet. The heat is unbearable, and the smoke stings my eyes. Still I keep going, praying I find it quickly as the fire grows closer to this side.

Finally, after what feels like hours of searching, I catch sight of a glint of metal in the rubble and reach in near where I found her, I snatch it out and quickly escape just as the flames eat the inside of the car. As I turn to leave, expecting an explosion that never comes, I hear a frantic voice calling my name.

Xandros's terrorized voice rings out, echoing off the trees, filled with despair and panic. His grip tightens around my arms as he pulls me into an embrace. His touch sends a jolt of energy through me, making me feel alive, anchoring me in the chaos that surrounds us. "You're okay," he whispers against my skin, a wave of relief washing over his features as our foreheads meet. Xandros pulls me to him, and I push him away, hearing the approaching emergency vehicles.

"Your wife," I point to the top of the incline. He looks at me in disbelief. "You're the one I'm worried about," Xandros murmurs, his voice filled with a mix of tenderness and concern. The sound of approaching cars and King Vin's enraged shouts echo in the background, making me peer up to see him rush to Carina. Dizzily, I turn to climb the hill when Xandros speaks again. "You didn't run," he states before kissing my temple.

"I wanted to run," I admit, my voice laced with both guilt and frustration. But I couldn't. I wouldn't. Even in the midst of my confusion and fear, I knew I couldn't leave his mother behind, trapped in the mangled remains of the car. I couldn't run away, leaving her to burn alive and die alone in the wreckage.

"I would have, your mother was trapped. I couldn't leave her to die," I whisper as I glance back at the burning car, smoke billowing into the sky, and I know I couldn't have lived with that guilt and weight on my conscience.

With Adina's bracelet clutched in my fist, I start climbing the hill. Now that the adrenaline has worn off, the pain is seeping in. My entire body seems to have its own pulse as it throbs, each movement suddenly stealing my breath and making me uneasy on my feet. I clutch my side where it hurts the most, only when I do, my fingers and palm brush something hard. I swallow, glancing down to see a hole in my uniform and the glint of silver poking out.

Using my hand, I cover the metal jutting out of me and stagger another step. Now I am aware of it, it's all I can think about, like seeing the wound has brought it to the forefront of my mind suddenly.

Xandros's grip tightens on my hips as he senses my pain and exhaustion. "You're hurt," he says, his worry evident. I try to brush off his concern, insisting I'm fine despite the piece of metal protruding from my stomach. The pain intensifies, making it clear I'm not as fine as I pretend to be.

Without hesitation, Xandros scoops me up in his arms, disregarding the presence of the king and the chaos unfolding around us. "The king is right there," I protest weakly, my voice filled with a mix of apprehension and vulnerability.

"Fuck the king," Xandros declares defiantly, his words laced with determination. He kisses my forehead gently, his actions a tender reassurance amidst the chaos. Carrying me up the incline, he settles on the guardrail with me next to his mother. Carina stares blankly ahead, her mind undoubtedly reeling from the events that unfolded, and I can tell she is in shock. "Show me?" Xandros fusses, trying to pry open my blouse. I slap his hands, and Adina turns to look at me. Her eyes go to Xandros's hands, and she gasps when suddenly King Vin's voice echoes around us in fury.

King Vin's demanding voice is loud above the chaos. "You need blood!" Vin tells her, and he motions to me. Carina shakes her head and Xandros's growl is menacing. "I'm fine, Father," Carina states.

"Nonsense. You'll heal faster!" he growls at her. Yet Carina's gaze hardens, her fangs baring at her father.

"I said no! Leave her be. She saved both our lives," Carina snarls, defending me. This is the first time I have seen her stand up to her father and over me, of all people —she is defending me? This day is just becoming weirder and weirder.

King Vin looks on the verge of exploding at her defiance but presses his lips in a line, turning to wave the firefighters toward the wreckage when he turns back to his daughter. Dirt and soot cover her face, her clothes filthy and her dress ruined.

"Why are you even here? Where is your car? I thought you were being picked up early?" Vin asks.

Carina seems taken aback by his question as she looks up at her father. "What?" she asks just as Xandros pulls my shirt up, and I hastily pull it down.

"No, you're bleeding," Xandros snarls in panic.

"It's nothing," I tell him. He growls, ripping my shirt open and gasping. "That is not nothing, Sienna!" he growls just as Javier and a few guards rush toward us, having finally arrived at the scene, but my attention is on Carina and King Vin.

"I canceled the driver; I wanted to stay. Why does it matter?" Carina asks.

King Vin scratches his chin, an air of curiosity mixed with suspicion hanging in the air. "Just curious," he mutters, his eyes lingering on Carina. Ambulances pull up and Xandros rushes me straight to the nearest one. I'm loaded into an ambulance, the paramedics attend to my injuries.

Just before I'm whisked away, I remember the bracelet in my hand. "Wait," I call out, holding the bracelet out to Xandros. "This is your mother's, I think?" I hope it is, or I risked my life going back for nothing. Confusion clouds his expression as he takes the bracelet from me, his gaze questioning my actions.

"You went back for this?" he asks incredulously, his voice filled with a mix of surprise, disbelief, and anger.

"Your mother seemed upset over it," I shrug. Xandros raises an eyebrow at me, shaking his head in disbelief.

"Mother!" he calls out to Adina, who limps over to us. He holds his hand out to her and her brows furrow, as she moves to take what he offers. He drops the bracelet into her open hand. "You found it?" she chokes on a sob, and I wonder what the story around it is, she clearly has some attachment to it. Maybe it's a wedding anniversary gift or something.

"I didn't. Sienna went back for it," Xandros states, and she looks at me. The queen opens and closes her mouth, her gaze shifting between me, the burning car, and the bracelet in her hand. Xandros climbs into the ambulance, shutting the doors behind him, and I find myself face to face with him.

"That was foolish going back for that," he tells me, and I know he is right. He bites his wrist, offering it to me, but I push his hand away. "No, I'll heal."

"Not fast enough once he pulls that out," Xandros states, and I look at the medic who nods.

"Please, Sienna," Xandros begs, his voice laced with desperation and concern. Reluctantly, I accept his blood, feeling a surge of warmth and energy flow through my veins. He pulls me into his lap, cradling me gently. "Ready?" the medic asks, and I am about to say for what when he rips the chunk of steel out. My scream is loud only to be swallowed by Xandros lips covering mine.

His blood rushes into my mouth, the pain dulling instantly, and I realize he cut his tongue with his teeth, feeding me more of his blood. His tongue demanding as his hand fists my hair, holding me in place, not giving me a chance to breathe while I feel the medic is prodding and poking me.

Finally, he releases me, pulling back and glancing down at my stomach. He exhales. "See, you're all healed, well, mostly," he murmurs, pressing his lips to my temple. His lips linger in the spot longer than necessary, yet I am too sore and tired to argue, instead relishing in his soothing scent and letting it calm my nerves.

Chapter Forty

Sienna

Once back at the castle, it doesn't take long before Xandros goes back to ignoring me, using the excuse it is for my safety when we learned King Vin would be staying longer than he initially claimed. The limousine was dragged off for examination, though I doubt they'll find much since there was barely anything left of it once the fire tore through it.

The driver was buried the day after the accident, and watching his daughter cry over his coffin as he was laid to rest was horrid.

Since then a few days have passed, which I believe has something to do with King Dresden, yet he is a good actor playing the role of a worried father and concerned king; no one seems to have noticed or seen past the façade, and I can't be bothered arguing it, what's the point; I am invisible until they choose to use me or request something of me.

However, things have since returned to a semblance of normalcy. Although, tension is still lingering in the air. King Vin remains at the castle, and I haven't seen Xandros for the past two days now. Surprisingly, I find myself not caring about his absence. Sitting in the walk-in closet, I dial Toby's number, my heart racing with the excitement of knowing I would hear his voice. Hiding in this closet has become the highlight of my days. For a moment, I can pretend I am not here but with someone who actually does care for me.

It has become a daily ritual in a sense; all day, I anticipate speaking with Toby. It's like a reward at the end of the day after playing handmaiden to Carina. Xandros sent word via Javier that he must keep his distance right now, that Vin has constantly been pestering him and pushing for the wedding. He thinks he is making progress with Carina signing the divorce papers. I believe otherwise; they seem the same.

Toby answers the call after the second ring, and I smile goofily, his voice filled with excitement.

"Hey, babe, I didn't think you'd call. I've been waiting by the phone for an hour," Toby tells me.

"I got caught up with Adina; she spotted me talking to Rehan in the halls."

"That old fossil still training you?" he asks, and I sigh, another thing that has become a ritual every morning at the crack of dawn. Rehan shows up to train with Javier and me, yet it seems pointless because Vin hasn't come near me since the accident.

"Yep, every morning. Adina asked if something was going on between me and Rehan." I chuckle at the thought.

"Like she wouldn't feel it if there was." Toby laughs.

I sigh; things have become comfortably miserable and normal to the point where I no longer care. It is what it is…

"So, any news?" I ask him nervously, praying he was able to get a hold of the seekers after the failed attempt. Security was heightened after the accident, making escape impossible, yet now things have died down. I'm hoping he has been able to reach out to them again.

"Actually, I do have some news. After our last failed attempt of breaking out, Sienna, the seekers have arranged an escape plan for Saturday. Tyra will sneak you out in the laundry hampers on Friday like originally planned, then you need to make your way through the old tunnel system to meet me. I will pick you up at the back of your old house. We will stay at a hotel until Saturday morning until the seekers can sneak us out the next morning." Toby explains.

"Xandros will be able to track me down; the bond will lead him to me if I remain in the city," I worry.

"Which is why I will be marking you before we leave. It will stop him from sensing you, it will tarnish the bond, and he'll be in too much pain to come after you. I've emptied out all my accounts over the past couple of weeks. Tasha will handle the club. We can finally get you out of the city, Sienna, and start a new life together," he assures me.

As I listen to Toby's words, it feels like a dream come true, a fairy tale unfolding before my eyes. I can envision a life of freedom and happiness, away from the constraints of Xandros, free to be with Toby.

"What about my mark?" I ask, my voice tinged with uncertainty. "He forced me to mark him," I admit.

Toby sighs heavily. "I have a plan for that, too; I know a witch who can break the bond. It may be costly, but there is a way to free you from the mate mark, allowing us to be together without any lingering ties to him." I chew my lip; despite hating Xandros, I still wonder what kind of effect that will have on him when we break the mate bond.

Just as I hang up the phone and hide it away, I hear Javier's voice calling out my name. Relief washes over me, and I rush to open the door. "It's just you, thank God," I breathe.

Javier has become my only friend in the castle. I don't really know what to make of King Rehan and my relationship; he now treats me like the daughter he never had, yet not at the same time since only I and Javier see that side of him, so I don't know whether to class him as a friend or a foe with an agenda which he is yet to reveal to me. I never know with this family; for all I know, he is probably hoping I finish my parents' job and kill off his son and wife to collect insurance money.

"Just bringing up your dinner," he says, moving toward the coffee table. He sets the tray down.

"Thank you," I tell him, and he nods once and turns to leave. Besides the morning routine we have, and when he follows me around like a shadow as I do my chores, I have no one else to talk to. Tyra slips in a hello or good morning when I drop the linens off each morning. We can't risk being seen talking. So, Javier is my only choice for friendly conversation. And this place is extremely lonely.

"Wait!" I call out to him as he reaches for the door handle. He sighs; I know he must get sick of babysitting me or standing outside my door.

"Please stay," I murmur, two simple words, and I can't even hide my desperation or the loneliness lacing my words. The empty castle walls seem to close in on me more and more each day, and I long for actual physical company. A friend.

"You know I am not supposed to; if Xandros finds out I spend the mornings in here or his father, he'd be mad, and he'd take it out on you, you know this," he tells me. I nod, a lump forming in my throat. I suppose I could stay on the phone with Toby until I fall asleep, yet I'd run out of credit, and that means asking Javier for more since I have no money or a way to recharge it. I hate asking more of him. He goes to leave again, and I turn toward my food, spotting the slice of cheesecake. I know Javier or Rehan is sneaking it up to me because I never used to get desserts.

"I'll share my cheesecake with you," I offer, holding out a small slice from the tray. Javier smiles, his eyes reflecting a genuine warmth while also echoing pity back at me. Am I really that pathetic that I've been reduced to begging for a friend? Javier bites his lip, glancing at the door.

"Only for a little while," he agrees, taking a seat in the armchair. He grabs the remote and flicks on a movie, creating a sense of comfort and distraction. I try to give him my cheesecake, he shakes his head.

"No, you eat it. I don't want anything from you, Sienna. You don't need to bribe me; I just don't want to get you in more trouble," he tells me. Trouble for wanting the company of an actual person and not the voices coming from the TV.

Sitting, I eat my dinner. I find the loneliness of being in this room a little less cold with Javier's quiet presence. He is also a welcome distraction from my bond that grows more haywire each day when left on my own. With nothing to do and no distractions, I find it becomes my sole focus, the longing, and pain of it so hollow and cold.

The bond between Xandros and me continues to grow stronger each day despite his absence. Now I can even feel when Carina brushes up against him and touches him in any way; it burns. I know they don't have sex; it's merely her touching him because I also feel his repulsion, his anger when she does, yet a few times I've also felt his protectiveness of her which leaves me confused.

Halfway through the movie, exhaustion takes hold, and I fall asleep on the couch.

When I wake up, I find myself in my own bed, the blanket tucked around me; the room is cloaked in darkness. The emptiness of the space feels suffocating, and my bond aches in my chest, a painful reminder of Xandros's absence. Javier must have put me in bed because I don't remember waking up at any point.

Once again, Xandros never came to see me, leaving me to face the cold night alone, leaving my bond in pain once again. Does he not feel its distress, or does he simply not care? I've tried to sense his yet I can't; as if he blocks me out sometimes.

Desperate for a distraction, I try to call Toby, hoping to find relief in hearing his voice. However, there's no answer on the other end. Wrapping my fluffy robe around myself, I attempt to warm up by the now extinguished fire. I know Javier won't be outside my door; he usually leaves once I fall asleep. I've woken a few times and called out to him or gone out into the hall to find him gone.

The unbearable ache of the bond intensifies, and I exhale, feeling defeated. With a heavy heart, I move to my bedroom door and open it, knowing I am never truly alone in the castle. The watchful eyes of the cameras track my every move. Driven by a mix of curiosity and desperation, I make my way to Xandros's quarters.

The hallway is empty except for a few stray servants and guards. Their heads are bowed, but their eyes glance up at the sound of my slippered feet scuffling along the stone floors. Some eyes glare at me, some are masked in indifference, yet all watch me. I wrap my arms around my waist, trying to ward off the cold that has seeped into my bones.

I pass the camera in the hall, and the light is now off, meaning they're not using it for the moment, or perhaps it's been overridden. I'm not sure, and I don't care. My need to be near my mate overpowers my curiosity, and so I continue on. I can see his door looming before me; I'm almost there. The wind howls outside, drowning out my footsteps as I walk the lonely castle halls.

Once there, I press my ear against the door; I hear no noise and sit outside his door for a while. It does nothing to stop the hollow ache in my chest. Even in this quiet solitude, no relief comes. About to give up and leave, I hesitate, my hand gripping the door handle. To my surprise, I find it is unlocked.

The door creaks open, and I cautiously push it ajar, just enough to slip inside. The room is dimly lit, the faint glow of moonlight seeping through the curtains. As I peer around, I'm instantly hit with Xandros's addictive, intoxicating scent and Carina's delicate floral perfume. It's a potent combination that makes my head spin. I carefully close the door and turn to look at the bed. The sheets are rumpled on the bed in the shape of two bodies; Xandros faces the door, arms folded in his sleep, while Carina presses against his back.

My heart thuds in my chest as I chew on my lip, my nerves gnawing at me. Slowly, I make my way to Xandros's side of the bed, lying down on the floor, trying to blend into the shadows. I know I shouldn't be here, but I can't resist the temptation to be close to him, even if it's just for a stolen moment. As I try to make myself comfortable, I turn to face the bed. Xandros's scent is thick in the air directly above me, like a heady incense that permeates my nostrils, making my head swim with wild thoughts. I breathe in the scent, trying to calm myself.

Suddenly, a deep, guttural groan breaks the silence, shooting my eyes open. The sound of fabric and shuffling on the bed makes my heart race. Peering up, I see Carina's perfectly manicured hand gripping Xandros shoulder, rolling him onto his back. Panic surges through me as I realize they're waking up when I hear Xandros muttering in his sleep. Then, I hear it—Xandros murmuring my name. My heart clenches, and a sharp pain shoots through my stomach, aching and cramping. I press my hand against my mouth, desperately trying to stifle any sound. I can't believe what I'm hearing—"Anna, sleep," he groans, and I hear Carina stifle her giggle.

I catch a glimpse of movement on the bed in the dim light. I can't tear my eyes away as I watch Carina. My heart stops as I see Carina straddling Xandros, her body illuminated by the moonlight. Every muscle in my body tightens, and I can feel an icy chill run down my spine. I want to scream, to shout at her to stop but my throat is too dry, and my tongue feels like lead in my mouth. All I can do is sit there, immobile and paralyzed by pain.

Carina gazes down at Xandros with a hungry look in her eyes before she leans closer to him and presses her lips against his. His hand slides up her back and fists in her hair as her lips descend on his naked chest. "Sienna, sleep. It's late," Xandros murmurs. Carina smiles cunningly while I remain frozen in place, knowing if I move, I will give myself away.

She frees him from his boxer shorts, and her lips wrap around Xandros's cock. Her head bobs up and down, and the sight tears at my heart. Xandros's hand is fisted in her hair, guiding her, and a moan escapes her lips at his touch. The feeling of betrayal churns in the pit of my stomach like bile as I watch them in bed. Yet I remain motionless on the floor beneath them, as if I were invisible or nothing more than furniture for their personal pleasure.

My world shatters at that moment, and tears blur my vision. The moment she moans, "That's it, baby," Xandros suddenly jolts awake. I duck back down, hiding beneath the bed, my body trembling. "What the fuck, Carina!" Xandros's voice booms and a thud follows. Carina groans, hitting the floor. Their voices grow louder as they argue, and I shrink further into my hiding place.

"You're my husband; I should be allowed to touch you!" Carina's voice trembles with frustration. "No, we had an agreement. I stay in this room so your father doesn't find out about us not getting married until after you've left. But I never agreed to you touching me!" Xandros's voice is filled with anger and resentment.

My heart pounds in my chest, fear gripping me as their voices grow louder. "Every damn time your father gets you alone, you revert to some desperate little girl trying to get his approval. What has gotten into you? What has he got over you?" Xandros's voice is laced with both concern and frustration. Carina remains silent, refusing to answer his question.

"I can't help you if you don't tell me!" His voice rises, desperation creeping into his tone. "If we just give him what he wants, he won't bother us again. I can remain here," Carina pleads. Xandros scoffs, clearly unconvinced by her reasoning.

"Please?" Carina's voice takes on a desperate tone as she resorts to begging. She peers out from behind the corner of the bed, reaching out to touch him. "Just close your eyes and pretend I am Sienna," she pleads, her voice cracking with vulnerability. Xandros grips her wrists, pushing her away. "You're not Sienna. She is in enough pain without us causing her more." Carina reaches for him, and he steps back.

"Why is he pushing so hard for this?" Xandros demands.

"The alliances," Carina answers, yet not even she sounds so sure of her answer.

Xandros scoffs.

My breath catches in my throat, and I struggle to comprehend what's happening.

Xandros really wasn't lying when he said he and Carina were working out the divorce, yet why has she backtracked. She lifts her hand, motioning for him to remain quiet when he goes to argue again with her.

"What is it?" Xandros asks.

"Do you hear that?" she asks, tilting her head to the side. I quickly duck back down, my heart pounding in my chest as her naked body moves toward the door. She tilts her head, brows furrowing as she strains to hear when her head snaps in my direction. She blinks rapidly, eyes roaming over me. "Well?" Xandros asks, and Carina wanders toward me.

"Seems you don't have to pretend since she is right here!"

I watch from my hiding place as Carina approaches me, her eyes locking with mine. My heart leaps into my throat, fear and anticipation intertwining within me. She tilts her head to the side, studying me with a mix of curiosity and amusement. I know the consequences of being discovered are severe, but I can't tear my eyes away from her piercing gaze.

Without warning, Carina reaches down and grabs my arm, pulling me up from my hiding place. "Sienna?" Xandros gasps, his eyes are wide in horror. A whimper escapes my lips as her arm wraps around my chest, holding me tightly. Xandros reaches out, his hand trembling with worry. I see the concern etched on his face, his outstretched hand a silent plea for her not to hurt me.

Carina runs her nose along the side of my neck, her breath warm against my skin. "Please, I'll go. I won't come back," I whisper, my voice trembling with fear and desperation.

The room is heavy with tension as Carina continues to hold me close, her touch both intoxicating and suffocating. I'm caught between the conflicting desires to stay and be with Xandros and the overwhelming need to run away from this tangled web of pain, betrayal, and his wife.

"How many times have you snuck into our room at night?" Carina's voice purrs with a mix of amusement and curiosity.

"Carina, let her go," Xandros growls, his voice laced with warning. Carina presses her nose into my hair, inhaling my scent as if trying to claim me.

"How many, Sienna?" Carina asks, her tone dripping with taunting delight.

Tears prick at the corners of my eyes as I try to find my voice. "Only this time, I never meant to intrude. I made a mistake, and I promise it won't happen again," I manage to stammer out, my words filled with both shame and regret. As Carina's hardened nipples scrape against my back through my cami, a shiver runs down my spine, both from the touch and the complex emotions swirling within me.

Xandros seems taken aback by my confession, his gaze avoiding mine as he swallows guiltily. The weight of his shock bears down on me, and I feel my face flush with embarrassment. Carina's touch continues to trail down my body, her hands tracing a path of ribs. "Well, I think we just found the solution to your incapacity to get hard for me, Xandros," Carina purrs, her voice laced with seduction and mischief.

"I bet I can make her cum," Carina purrs, her tongue trails along the side of my neck as her fingers push inside the waistband of my pants, sending shivers coursing through me. Despite my reluctance and the conflicting emotions churning within me, I can't deny the sensations that Carina's skilled fingers elicit. They expertly tease my clit, drawing out pleasure even as I resist her touch.

A warning growl escapes Xandros as he tries to assert his control. "Carina!" he warns, his voice laced with a dangerous edge. Carina only tightens her grip on my jaw, turning my face toward her. "What is it, Xandros? Jealous I'm touching your mate?" Carina purrs, her tongue gliding along my lips, leaving a trail of heat in its wake. And then, she pushes a finger inside me, eliciting a moan from deep within my throat.

I glance at Xandros, only to see his face twisted in pain. A part of me wants to revel in his discomfort, to make him feel the torment that has plagued me. Carina doesn't relent, adding another finger, intensifying the sensations. She turns my face back to her, her lips grazing mine.

"Want me to stop, Sienna?" she purrs, her voice dripping with temptation. The air becomes heavy with a dangerous allure, and I find myself hesitating. Did I want her to stop? Could I truly embrace this twisted game and seek revenge on Xandros?

At that moment, everything becomes too much to bear. The weight of my emotions threatens to drown me, and I succumb to the darkness surrounding us. The allure of revenge tugs at me, whispering its temptations. I can make Xandros feel the same pain I'm experiencing and make him understand the torment he's put me through.

I'm consumed by conflicting emotions as Carina's lips brush against mine. Her touch is electric, igniting a spark within me I can't ignore as she uses her other hand to hold my face toward hers. I want to hurt him the way he's hurt me, to make him question his choices and feel the anguish that has become my constant companion.

And so, against my better judgment and driven by a mix of desire, anger, and a longing for some semblance of control, I do something I never thought I would. I kiss her back. In that stolen moment of passion and rebellion, I allow myself to be swept away by the chaos and desire that entangle us all.

However, despite knowing what I'm doing is wrong, my body betrays me as I respond to Carina's touch, my mind clouded by a whirlwind of emotions. It's a dangerous game we play—one filled with power struggles, desire, and the desperate need to reclaim a sense of self. A desperate need to hurt the one man we both share.

But as the heat of the moment engulfs us, Xandros snarls, unable to bear the sight before him any longer. "Enough! Let her go!" he demands, his voice dripping with both anger and pain. Carina chuckles, her lips reluctantly leaving mine as Xandros hisses, his frustration palpable in the air.

Caught between them, I feel the weight of their conflicting emotions pressing upon me. It's a volatile situation, a whirlpool of emotions threatening to consume us all. I try to take a step back, my eyes darting to Xandros as I try to catch my breath and make sense of the chaos that surrounds us.

At that moment, I realize the gravity of the path I've chosen. This dangerous game is a double-edged sword. Yet seeing the hurt and pain in his eyes, the same hurt he must see in mine when he looks at me, that deep-rooted anger, deep desire to break him takes over me, and I relish it; it'll be worth the punishment just to watch him squirm.

Turning, I look at Carina, my eyes roaming over her naked body. She is gorgeous, her body slim yet breasts full, and her skin looks velvety smooth when my eyes trail down to take her all in. My eyes stop, noticing that she is shaven. I swallow at the thought. I kinda don't like the look of my own vagina, let alone having someone else's near my face, but hey fuck it, you only live once, right, and this may be my only chance to hurt Xandros.

My hand lifts and Carina smiles, her eyes burning brightly, and her lips twitch when she grabs my hand, placing it on her breast. The touch of her skin is like satin, soft and supple, and I'm tempted by Xandros's growl. Carina purrs as I feel her silky smooth skin beneath my palm, her hardened nipple grazing it. "Seems someone wants to play," Carina purrs, stepping closer to me.

Her lips slam against mine. Carina moans low in her throat as I kiss her, her finger gently tugging at my hair before she shoves me back. A shriek leaves me at the sudden motion when I land on the bed, the soft mattress breaking the shortfall. Carina stalks me toward the bed when she is suddenly hovering over me, her lips ghosting across mine.

"Carina!" Xandros snarls furiously.

"Either join us or watch, Xandros. If you won't give me what I want, maybe your little mate will give me something else." Her voice is seductive, hypnotic; her breath is a whispering breeze as her words caress over me.

"And what is that?" Xandros growls. Carina laughs, the sound is sadistically seductive.

"A taste," she moans. Her lips press against mine softly, and her hands go to the buttons of my top; she rips it open, her lips traveling down my neck, and I moan; my eyes roll as I peer up at the canopy headboard and push up on my elbows.

Carina's lips travel lower, down my neck and chest, before her tongue swirls around my nipple, making it harden. My breathing comes in short gasps at the feel of her soft lips exploring my body. When I feel her tear my pants, I stare at her; she seems completely lost to her own desire, her tongue tracing my thigh to the apex of my legs. When I spot Xandros, his eyes are glued to me, dark and stormy, and I can feel his desire to rip her off me. He growls, his eyes flicking to me.

"I know what you're doing, Sienna..." he speaks through gritted teeth. "I get it. You want to hurt me, but this isn't the way." He growls just as her tongue flicks over my clit. I moan at the feel of her tongue diving between my folds, her hands gripping my thighs. Xandros jolts, his eyes flickering as his claws extend. Fury boils in his gaze along with his pain, his hands twitching to relieve the agony he's in; I can feel it exactly. He is aroused because it's me he's watching, but the pain it causes him is horrendous.

"Fine, have your little revenge, just remember what comes with action is the consequence," he snarls, moving and falling into the armchair by the fire when Carina lifts my hips slightly, which forces me onto my back as her warm mouth and skillful tongue tease and taste me. My hips move against her mouth on their own accord as I become overwhelmed by the sensations.

I can feel Xandros's eyes on me, watching when I hear him groan before hearing him remove his pants before they hit the ground. Turning my head, his eyes are on me as he fists his cock, which is rock hard. I lick my lips, unable to help myself. Xandros raises an eyebrow at me. "Is this what you want?" he growls. Carina lifts her head and smiles deviously. Her lips are coated in my juices, her hand reaches out, and she brushes her thumb across my lips.

"So soft, so warm." Carina purrs before shoving her finger in my mouth; I suck on it while using my tongue to trace the side of it. Xandros groans while Carina licks her lips. "I want to watch you fuck her pretty little mouth," Carina purrs.

"Maybe it's not her mouth I want?"

Carina's brows furrow, and I gasp. My plan for revenge backfiring. Carina chews her lip nervously yet doesn't move from between my legs, not even when Xandros stops beside her. "Isn't this what you wanted, Carina?" Xandros practically sneers at her before turning his gaze to me. "Is this how you planned your petty revenge against me?" Xandros asks. I clench my eyes closed.

"No! You watch like you made me," Xandros snarls, and I glare at him defiantly. While Carina looks like a deer caught in headlights as to what she should do. I nod to her when she doesn't move, blinking back tears.

Her lips quiver, and she looks on the verge of apologizing, realizing the mess she just made for me.

"I'm... I..." Carina shakes her head, and Xandros grabs her hair, making her cry out. The moment she does, he jams his cock down her throat. She gags when he holds her head there, yet his eyes remain on me while tears slip down my face at the torturous agony it causes; it's like between my legs caught on fire. Just as quickly as he forced his cock into her mouth, he shoved her away, only to lean over me.

"The pain you just felt?" he questions, wiping my tears. Carina stares at us, horrified. "That is nothing compared to what I am enduring. Only I love you too much to betray you like that, but you can have your revenge. I will allow it. Just remember, I am choosing the agony you'll put me through, and I won't forget it, and later neither will you," he warns as his hand grips my throat before his lips crash against mine hungrily, furiously. He bites my lip hard enough I feel the tender skin break.

At the same time, Carina's hands grip my thighs almost eagerly. Xandros pulls away, his fingers pinching my cheeks as he pulls me up by my face, so I am forced to lean on my elbows. "Finish her, so I can punish her," he orders Carina. Carina obliges, and before I can protest, her lips are back covering my pussy, her tongue tasting every inch of me.

Xandros makes a pained growl, his fingers digging into my cheeks when I see him fighting the beast within from coming forward. He wants to kill her. Kill her for touching what's his.

"Open your mouth," he growls. When I don't, he tugs on my bond to make me compliant as I try to resist. Then he plays dirty; he drops his guards down protecting my bond from his, and only then do I feel the pure torment, self-loathing, fury, anguish, and so many other emotions, and then complete and utter torturous pain I'm causing his bond.

His agony steals my breath, and I haven't realized how much he is hiding from me through the bond we share. My lips part, and his thumb brushes down my cheek softly. When Carina sucks on my clit, Xandros looks on the verge of passing out, his legs shake, and he grips the side of the bed.

"How bad do you want to punish me because I am about to pass out?" he asks, his voice barely a rasp. My eyes roll into my head when she shoves a finger inside me, and I almost collapse against the bed at the pleasure she is building.

"How bad are you going to punish me?" I moan, my hips jerking when he suddenly grips my arms and pins me in place. "Badly, you'll be lucky if I let you walk afterward." I swallow at his words, knowing he means them. And knowing even if I back out now, he'll still punish me for taking it this far anyway.

"Well, then I better make it worth it," I growl back at him before leaning over and grabbing his cock in my hand. He makes a pained-filled moan before gripping my hair and forcing himself down my throat. I gag on his cock, only to moan at Carina's tongue swirling around my clit.

"Fuck, I think I prefer to pass out," Xandros groans thrusting into my mouth, trying to remain focused on me and not the pure torturous pain the bond is causing him. I moan around his cock when I feel Carina withdraw her finger, only to add another one. "Carina! Stop teasing her. Are you trying to kill me!" he growls at her.

I become a moaning mess as she chuckles before sucking hard on my clit. My walls flutter, my orgasm tearing through me painfully, harshly, as my legs shake. Xandros buckles under the weight of it, pulling out of my mouth and dropping on one knee. I collapse against the bed, panting heavily when Carina sinks her fangs into my thigh, the pained sensation only prolonging the crippling orgasm that tears through me.

Staring up at the ceiling, Carina moves above me, a devious smile on her lips. She kisses me, her tongue forcing its way into my mouth. I kiss her back, completely exhausted, and she laughs. She then moves to lean against the headboard. Xandros gets to his feet, his breathing heavy and his canines protruding as he glares at her, his tone ice cold.

"Are you finished now?" he asks her.

"Yes, she's all yours," Carina laughs. "Now let me watch you fuck her. I want to see if it's your name or mine she screams," Carina purrs. Xandros growls, turning his icy gaze on me.

"She won't make that mistake twice on the same night," Xandros snarls, and I try to get up, only for him to grab me. He flips me onto my stomach, dragging me half off the bed and entering me in the same motion. I groan at the way his cock fills me. Sparks rush over my body, only for the feeling to be destroyed when his palm comes down on my ass. My cheek burns fiercely, making me cry out.

"You were warned, love, actions have consequences," he tells me, pulling out of me only to thrust harshly back into me. Despite the brutal thrusts, a moan escapes, my inner walls squeezing his cock, making him groan. "Fuck, I love your tight little cunt," he growls.

I grit my teeth as he slams into me again. As he maintains the brutal pace.

"That's right, baby, beg for me," he tells me when the cock slides out of my pussy, leaving me hollow and crying out all too loudly. I know Carina is watching, so I try to keep it together; it's hard when I fail.

"Please, I can't... I need more," I whimper. Xandros grips my hips and flips me onto my back, his eyes on fire as he leans over me and slams into me from above. With our eyes locked, we kiss passionately, hungrily, almost killing each other with a fire-fueled passion as he pounds into me over and over, almost desperately. The sounds of our bodies slapping together fill the air, making moans escape my lips.

I cry out when he pounds into me; my inner walls tremble as his tip bumps against my cervix.

"Yes!" Carina shrieks. "Fill this pussy all the way with your cock; I want to watch it spread her lips wide for you." She moans loudly, her head thrown back as her fingers dance between her thighs. Xandros growls, saying something to her before driving into me hard enough I see stars as he swells inside me. "Cum!" he demands, snapping me out of my pleasure-filled haze. I open my eyes to see him glaring at me. Is this what the anger and brutality are about? The fact she made me cum faster than he ever did? A second later, I realize that is exactly what it is, the fact I gave myself to her willingly.

He growls, realizing I am being defiant. "Sienna!"

"What's wrong, Xandros? Can't finish off your own mate?" Carina taunts.

"She'll finish alright!" he snarls, his eyes flickering dangerously at her challenge. His lips crash down on mine, and sparks rush over my skin as his lips descend my neck, nipping and licking his way down before he sucks on my mark. My toes curl at the blissful euphoria rushing over me and I fight to keep my head, refusing to give him what he wants.

My defiance makes him growl; the sound vibrating against my neck sends a shiver down my spine. I know if I don't surrender to him, I will be leaving here quite uncomfortable. My breathing is harsh as I try to focus on the roof and go elsewhere in my mind. However, Xandros doesn't allow me to zone out, instead recapturing my attention along with my lips. His thrusts slow a little, drawing out slowly before slamming back in, making me gasp. Yet his annoyance grows. "1... 2..."

"Fuck you," I growl at him, and he pulls away; the furious glint in his eyes makes goosebumps rise on my arms. The next, a savage snarl tears out of him and his teeth are embedded in my neck.

The moment they do, I fall apart; my walls clamp down around him, squeezing and milking his cock. Xandros groans, his teeth slipping from my neck as I fall apart beneath him. Xandros follows at the same time, his cock twitching inside me as the warmth of his cum coats my insides.

"Boo, that's cheating," Carina whines. I blink up at him, my consciousness waning and slipping away. I giggle, and he peers down at me. "Carina was better," I murmur just before I pass out; the sound of his angry growl echoes around me, along with her laughter. His anger is bleeding into me. He can punish my ass all he wants; I won't be awake to feel it.

When I wake up, it is to the feel of water caressing over me, Xandros's enticing scent flooding my senses, and the warmth of his skin touching mine sending pleasurable sparks across my back everywhere his skin touches. His arms wrap around me securely, and we stay like that for a few moments as I wait for him to say something. I can practically feel his thoughts swirling, his underlying anger simmering beneath the surface.

"You ever put on a display like that again, I will—"

"You'll what, Xandros? Huh, what will you do? In case you haven't noticed, all you've done is put Carina on display in front of me, yet I'm not allowed to return the favor?" I try to climb out of the bath, when he jerks me back down, making water splash over the sides of the massive tub.

"I never touched her like that!" he growls angrily.

"Maybe not, but you've let her put her hands on you!" I retort. Xandros stands, pulling me up with him. He gathers both our clothes from one side of the room before setting them down beside us and motioning with one hand for me to get dressed without any other words needing spoken between us. I roll my eyes, not feeling the need to fight with him right now. Once clothed, he takes hold of my hand tightly, leading us out into the main pool's area, the room filled with steam and the air salty.

"Shouldn't you be with Carina?" I ask dryly, and he stops abruptly, making me run into his back.

"Vin left for the morning. We woke up, and he was gone, so I have the day free to spend with you! Not that you deserve it after last night," he growls.

Xandros squeezes my hand and jerks me to his side before dropping his arm across my shoulders. He is leading me out of the bathhouse, my reflection catches in the mirror, and I stop. Xandros also stops while I move toward the mirror, my fingers prodding my face. Xandros watches me carefully.

"It healed?" I murmured, tracing the spot that was marred by his mother's claws, the skin now smooth. "You've marked me."

"Ages ago, and it never healed," I tell him.

"You marked me, still it takes me marking you after you've marked me to heal you and give you—" he trails off, making me look at him.

"You're getting stronger," he tells me.

I swallow, remembering how he demanded I cum last night. "You're struggling to command me." I gasp.

"Because something is wrong, it shouldn't affect my command of you. You should be able to resist everyone else, except me!" he tells me, and my brows pinch.

"Pardon?"

"I have Javier looking into it, but something is not right. You should not be able to resist me."

Chapter Forty-One

Sienna

Xandros takes me back to my room, his grip on my arm firm. Javier is already waiting for us, sitting in the armchair by the crackling fire. A small smile tugs at my lips when I notice Javier's presence, but it quickly fades as Xandros glares at me, his eyes filled with suspicion and a hint of possessiveness.

"Did you find anything?" Xandros asks, his voice cutting through the tension in the room. Javier gets up from the armchair, a book in his hand.

Xandros points a finger between Javier and me, his voice laced with accusation. "Is there something going on between you two?" His demand hangs in the air, and Javier shakes his head, disbelief etched on his face.

"You can't be serious?" Javier mutters under his breath, clearly taken aback by Xandros's accusation.

"I'm very serious!" Xandros growls, his gaze shifting from Javier to me. I instinctively take a step back, my heart pounding in my chest. Xandros grabs my arm, his grip tight and possessive as he jerks me back toward him. "Xandros! Let her go, be angry at me, not her. She has done nothing wrong," Javier intervenes, his voice filled with a mix of concern and frustration. Xandros growls, reluctantly letting me go, and I fight the urge to check my arm, his claws having pierced through the thin fabric into my arm.

Javier moves toward the door, his body tense with the need to defuse the situation. Xandros growls in response, and reluctantly follows him, leaving me alone in the room. As they step outside into the hall, I can't resist the temptation to eavesdrop on their conversation. I press my ear against the wooden door, straining to catch their words.

A thud resonates through the door, making me gasp. "Do you like her?" Xandros demands, his voice heavy with accusation.

"We are friends, it's not like she has many in this place because you don't allow it! Now get off me, you should know me better than that," Javier retorts, his voice laced with frustration.

"I'm going insane, she is driving me insane. This bond is!" Xandros rambles.

"You're not insane, you're just jealous because she gives you the cold shoulder," Javier tells him.

"Of course I'm jealous, she'd rather fuck my wife than me!" Xandros booms, his words hitting me like a dagger to the heart. Silence falls and I wait, listening intently.

"She'd rather what?" Javier blurts out, his disbelief evident in his voice.

"Never mind, I'll tell you later, or maybe she will since you're her 'friend'," Xandros replies, a bitter edge tainting his words. Javier sighs heavily, the weight of the situation seems to be getting to him. "Just tell me what you found," Xandros finally asks.

"This. Found it in the library," Javier replies.

"What does it say? I don't have time to read an entire book," Xandros snaps, his impatience seeping through his words. Javier takes a deep breath before responding while I hold mine, also wanting to know the answer.

"It says the only way she can resist your command after you've marked her is if the bond is breaking," Javier explains. My brows furrow, taking in his words. I didn't know that was possible, Toby never told me a bond could break on its own.

Xandros scoffs at the words, his disbelief evident and rippling through the bond. I can feel his curiosity and worry at Javier's words.

"Impossible, you can't break a fated mate bond," he retorts.

"Actually, you can. If you kill it," Javier states, his words hanging heavy in the air, confusing me even more.

"What do you mean?"

"You're a king, Xandros. Your aura, your command, is stronger than anyone else's. She now holds a part of it. Your constant rejection of her is tarnishing your bond, weakening it. It is possible to break a bond. Witches have done it. And you are doing it by rejecting her," Javier explains, his words resonating with a deep sense of truth. My bond pangs painfully at his words. I shove it aside, trying my best to ignore it.

"I haven't rejected her," Xandros argues.

"Maybe not in so many words, but in your actions. Her bond is protecting itself, so it doesn't kill her. It's rejecting you."

"Excuse me?" Xandros sounds outraged at the thought of me rejecting him. And it makes me worry if that will be another thing I am punished for, my unruly bond.

"When a bond is broken, it can attach itself to someone else. You're a Lycan King. You can't go on without your mate. She was human before being infected and changed, therefore she can. You need her to stop from going crazy, yet you're the one driving her crazy, so her bond is protecting her by rejecting you," Javier explains, his words echoing in the air, carrying with them a sense of revelation and consequence. Well, serves him right, maybe there is a way out of the bond after all; he will cast me aside once he is done breaking me.

"So what happens if it breaks?" Xandros asks.

"It doesn't say, just that you'll both live. No one knows in what state you'll be in when it does. Eventually, though, your ability to heal her and command her will stop, and her ability to shift will stop. She'll pretty much return to being human, only with immortality," Javier reveals, his voice filled with a mix of caution and concern.

"Well, I guess I do have time to read this stupid book then," Xandros says dismissively. "Are you doing anything tonight?"

"Watching Sienna's door, like always," Javier replies.

"No, I need you to do something else. I want you to go into the city and monitor Vin. I would like to know who he's going to meet," Xandros commands, his voice carrying an air of command.

'Very well," Javier tells him.

As the door handle twists, I quickly move away from the door and take my place in front of the fire, trying to appear like I wasn't eavesdropping.

Xandros enters the room, clutching the book in his hands and moves to the armchair. He says nothing and I reach for the TV remote. I spend the day watching TV, trying to distract myself from the weight of Xandros's presence. Hours pass, and boredom seeps in as I keep a watchful eye on the alarm clock resting on the bedside table. I steal glances at it, my mind filled with thoughts of Toby. The anticipation of hearing his voice gnaws at me.

"Why do you keep staring at the alarm clock? Do you have somewhere else to be?" Xandros's voice cuts through the silence, his eyes trained on me. I feel a surge of panic rise within me as I try to come up with a plausible explanation. "No, I... I was just... wondering about the time," I stammer, my voice betraying my unease.

Xandros places his book down, his gaze fixated on me. The intensity of his stare makes me shrink under his scrutiny. I can feel his suspicion and possessiveness weighing heavily upon me, suffocating me. The room feels smaller, the air thick with tension as I wait for him to speak. "You were wondering about the time?" he asks, his eyes narrow slightly.

"Yes, I'm just bored, okay?" I mutter under my breath, my fingers fumbling with the remote as I change the TV channel. Xandros chucks the book onto the coffee table with a frustrated sigh. "Come here," he tells me. He clenches his jaw, the tension in the room palpable. "Please," he adds, his voice softer this time.

I chew on my bottom lip, my eyes darting between him and the TV screen. Reluctantly, I get up from my spot on the floor and move closer to him. He reaches out, his strong hands pulling me onto his lap, enveloping me in his warmth. I sit awkwardly on his lap, wanting to hop off him. When I try to move his arms wrap around me, holding me tighter.

"What do you want to do then?" he asks. My heart pounds in my chest as I battle the conflicting emotions swirling within me.

Call Toby, I think bitterly, the desire to reach out to him consuming my thoughts.

"Surely there is something you want to do?"

"What is there to do? Besides playing maid, all I do is rot in this room," I retort, unable to suppress the anger that simmers just below the surface. The weight of my words hang heavy in the air, yet he doesn't acknowledge my bitter tone.

"Come on then, let's go for a run," Xandros suggests, tapping my thigh gently. He gets up from the couch and moves toward the walk-in closet, and I follow him to see him grab a bag and some warm clothes for both of us. When he emerges, he nods toward the door, a glimmer of excitement in his eyes. "Come on, do you want to shift or not?" he asks, his voice tinged with anticipation.

"You'll let me shift?" I ask, confusion clouding me. He holds out his hand to me. I hesitate, and when I don't move to take his, Xandros reaches down and clasps my hand firmly, his touch sending sparks up my arm and lacing my skin with goosebumps. I follow him, letting him lead me through the castle toward the back gardens.

We step outside, the cool breeze sweeping across my skin. The scent of earth and nature fills my senses, grounding me in this moment. Xandros guides me toward the dense forest that surrounds the castle, and for a fleeting moment, panic surges through me. Is this a trick? Is he leading me to the dungeons to punish me for what happened with Carina? My steps falter, my body tensing, and my feet stop. Xandros also stops, glancing back at me and tugging on my hand. I step back, jerking my hand from his grasp.

"Sienna?" Xandros's voice breaks through my racing thoughts, and I shake my head, trying to back away. He sighs, a mix of exasperation.

"Fine," he huffs, moving towards me with purpose. I raise my hand instinctively, ready to protect myself if necessary. Instead of lashing out, he swiftly wraps his arms around my waist, lifting me effortlessly and tossing me over his shoulder.

I thrash in his grasp, my muscles tense and my heart pounds with a mix of fear and anticipation. The world spins in a dizzying blur as Xandros takes off with an alarming speed that makes my surroundings a mix into a wall of brown and green. Nausea churns in my stomach from the sudden motion, my senses overwhelmed by the rush of wind against my face. My grip tightens on his back, my fingers digging into his shirt as I cling to him, worried about him dropping me at this speed.

Within moments, we arrive at our destination. Xandros sets me down gently on the forest floor, and I stumble slightly as I find my footing. Glancing around, I take a deep breath, filling my lungs with the earthy scent of the forest. I'm not at the dungeons, instead deep within the forest.

As my eyes adjust to the dim light filtering through the trees, I take in the beauty of the surroundings. Towering trees stretch toward the sky, their branches intertwined like a protective canopy. The soft rustle of leaves and the distant call of birds echo around us, soothing my senses and easing the tension that has coiled within me.

Xandros stops, dropping the bag on the ground and unzipping it. He then starts removing his clothes, placing them in the bag. I watch him undress, nervously. He strips off his shirt, revealing a smooth chest and abs. His gaze fixed on me. The contours of his muscular torso are well sculpted, his abdomen a mountain of firm muscle. He is grace personified—the embodiment of perfect masculine beauty.

Before I realize what I am doing, I step toward him. My fingertips brush against his forearm. His skin is warm and soft, smooth to the touch. His shoulders are broad and sturdy, and his muscles ripple with each movement. His broad chest is covered in silky hair that trails down to where his pants hang low on his hips. "Are you going to undress, your clothes will rip if you don't," Xandros speaks, breaking me out of the bond induced trance I became absorbed in.

Glancing around nervously, I remove my clothes until I am just standing in my bra and underwear. Xandros however sighs, stepping closer to me. His hand grips my hip, tugging me to him, while the other slips behind me, unclasping my bra. He tosses it near the bag before gripping my underwear and crouching. He pulls them down, and I grip his shoulder, stepping out of them, feeling extremely exposed to his wandering gaze. "Do you need help to shift?" he asks me, and I hesitate, wondering how he can possibly help me to shift. At the same time I also don't know how to just shift on my own; both times I've shifted it was forced.

I nod slowly, my gaze fixed on him. Xandros nods in return, his

Lycan King's Captives

fingers trailing over the skin of my hip as he circles around me. His touch sends shivers down my spine, and I can feel the heat of his breath against the back of my neck.

"Close your eyes," he murmurs, his voice low and hypnotic. I do as he says, my heart thumping with anticipation and a hint of fear. His fingers trail down my spine, and I can feel his warm breath against my skin as he whispers. "Now picture your Lycan form," I try to do as he says. "Focus on the memory of when you shifted, what it felt like." My body tenses remembering the pain, the way my bones stretched and moved, the feeling of my skin burning and rippling as it too stretched. I take a deep breath, focusing on the innate animal within me. My bones ache as they elongate, my muscles contracting and expanding as they transform. My skin tightens as fur sprouts from my flesh, covering me in a soft coat of fur.

I feel Xandros's hand on my back, grounding me in the present moment. His touch is electrifying. He guides me through the transformation process, his voice soothing and calm. My senses heighten as I shift, my vision turning to black and white as the world takes on new shapes and forms. The forest is more vibrant now; every scent more vivid, every sound crisper. Xandros is beside me, still in his human form but with an energy rippling off him. He moves to stand in front of me, while I stare at my hands and the sharp claws that split my nail beds. I giggle and then jump at the sound when I find I can still talk and make noise in this form.

Xandros snorts, making me look at him, and for once I am taller than he is. Though not for long because he quickly shifts into a huge black Lycan. I peer up at him, and he steps closer, sniffing me before nipping at my now pointy ear. I shake my head at the feel of it before scratching my ear, only to remember my claws when they slice through it, making me hiss. Xandros makes a weird noise. "Gentle, you need to remember you're stronger in this form," he tells me, grabbing my hands and holding them up. "And claws are sharp," he tells me. I nod, knowing exactly how sharp claws are from when his mother slashed my face. Yet, my body buzzes, making me feel giddy with anticipation. "Go on then, I'll follow you," he tells me, and excitement fills me.

I take off running through the forest, darting between trees with ease. Xandros follows close behind me, his own form moving with grace and speed that matches mine. We run for hours, exploring every corner of the forest. The world around me is a blur of colors and smells—a wild and untamed place I become distracted by as I explore. As the sun begins to set, Xandros grabs my tail, making me stop. My clumsy Lycan isn't exactly balanced well when it comes to stopping and turning.

As I pivot, Xandros is jerked forward, knocking into me, and I am suddenly falling. My eyes widen as I see the canopying trees and then dirt. I clench my eyes shut and toss out my hands just as I feel him grab me. With a soft thud, I land on top of him, and he groans. Opening my eyes, I see my claws piercing his chest like hooks and my eyes widen in horror. "Sorry," I blurt, pulling them out. Blood spills out of the holes and on instinct I lean down, running my tongue over them. His clawed hands brush my fur gently and tug on my ears, making me stop and sit upright, realizing my own actions. As I peer down, I realize my saliva healed him, the wounds now closed.

"I didn't mean to startle you, I forget you're new to this," he tells me, tugging on my tail that he seems to like playing with. Only then do I realize it is wagging from side to side, his eyes tracking it as his other hand grabs it. He chuckles. "So weird seeing you with a tail, yours is so fluffy," he laughs as it whips out of his hand only for him to snatch in his other. I try to make it stop moving only to find it impossible.

"It's because you're happy, and excited to be free. Don't be embarrassed. We are part animal," he tells me, sitting up and making me straddle his lap. I hastily climb off him, wanting to run some more, when he grabs my hand, tugging me in a different direction. As we step out of the trees, I find one of the maids setting up a picnic. She nods when she sees us and disappears into the treeline. Xandros leads me over to it and I gasp at the view. Had we really run to the top of the mountain? As I step closer to the edge, Xandros snatches my tail, distracted by the breathtaking view. I hadn't realized I nearly stepped off the edge of it. He jerks me back, not letting me.

"You're so easily distracted in this form," he tells me, shifting back and sitting, I shift back too, finding it easier to shift back than into my Lycan form. I look for something to cover myself when Xandros grabs my wrist, pulling me into his lap. Up here and naked, the wind is like ice. Goosebumps lace my skin, and Xandros rummages in the basket, pulling out a blanket, and wrapping it around us. With the blanket and his body warmth, I eventually stop shivering enough to eat as we watch the sunset.

The world around us is bathed in shades of orange and gold, nature's canvas painting a serene backdrop. However, my heart is anything but calm. Unresolved emotions churn within me, tearing at my very core. I long to be back in the safety of the castle, away from the torment of conflicting desires.

Right now, Xandros is far from the man I'm so used to.

Xandros sensing my unease, his keen senses attuned to my every shift in mood. He comes to a halt, his eyes fixing on mine with unwavering intensity. "So, what do you want to do next?" he asks, his voice a deep rumble that sends shivers down my spine. His concern is evident, yet I can't bring myself to share the true turmoil that plagues me. And If I did, it would only get me punished.

The truth is, I want to hear Toby's voice, knowing this is around the time I would sit on the phone with him. I can't make that call with Xandros by my side, his piercing gaze burning into my soul.

Instead, I muster a tired smile and feigned exhaustion. "I think I'd like to go to bed," I reply, hoping he will accept my excuse and grant me the solitude I crave.

Xandros, however, has other plans. He reaches out, his fingers brushing against my arm in a gentle, possessive gesture. "It's still early," he states, his voice laced with a mix of curiosity. "Surely there is something you want to do?" His question hangs in the air, waiting for my response.

The memories of a life before Xandros flood my mind, though now they feel distant and hazy. What did I enjoy doing? I searched my thoughts, realizing my previous existence had been devoid of many options for leisurely activities. However, a faint spark of recognition flickers within me. "I used to enjoy reading," I admit, a glimmer of nostalgia in my eyes.

Without hesitation, Xandros takes my hand in his and leads me through the corridors of the castle, guiding me toward the heart of knowledge—the library. As we step into the grand room, I am enveloped in a sense of awe. Towering bookcases reach toward the ceilings, their shelves cradling countless volumes of literature. The warm glow of a chandelier bathed the room in an ethereal light, while the setting sun cast golden rays through the large windows.

Xandros gestures toward the shelves, his voice filled with genuine interest. "Take whatever books you want," he encourages me. I scan the titles, my gaze darting across rows upon rows of books. War stories, westerns—genres I expected from a man like Xandros. I bite my lip, hesitant to voice my preferences.

"They're not really the sort of books I usually read," I confess, hoping he won't judge my tastes.

Curiosity dances in Xandros's eyes as he presses me further. "What sort of books do you like, then?" he inquired, his voice filled with genuine curiosity. I take a deep breath, summoning the courage to share my guilty pleasure.

"I enjoy romance," I admit, my cheeks flushing with embarrassment.

A mischievous grin tugged at the corners of Xandros's lips. "A romantic at heart, are you?" he mused playfully. "Well, then let's go find a bookstore."

"None would be open at this hour," I remind him. He raises an eyebrow at me. "You forget who you are speaking to, nothing in this city is closed for a king," he tells me.

A quick call later, and the store owners were preparing to welcome us despite the late hour.

As we enter the quaint bookstore, the scent of old paper and ink fills the air, and my heart quickens with excitement.

The shelves are a treasure trove of stories waiting to be discovered. Xandros and I wander through the aisles, exchanging whispers and laughter as we explore the world of literature together.

He plucks books from the shelves, reading their synopses aloud to me with a twinkle in his eyes. The titles ranged from historical romance to modern-day love stories, their intriguing plots enticing my imagination. Amidst the banter, his gaze falls upon a book with a slightly provocative cover, adorned with the promise of dark romance.

A playful smirk curves his lips as he thumbs through the pages, raising an eyebrow suggestively. "Hmm, this one looks interesting," he murmurs, his voice laced with an amused undertone. He stares down at the title, and his face erupts into a wide grin.

"Erotic Hysteria: A Tale of Forbidden Love," he reads out loud. I lean closer, catching a glimpse of explicit illustrations inside that make my cheeks flush.

"Or maybe not," Xandros chuckles, handing the book to the store clerk as he catches my glare.

His interest for the book is obvious.

"I might read this one myself." He flicks through the pages and waggles his eyebrows.

"Definitely keeping this one," he tells me enthusiastically as he takes in all its juicy details with childlike excitement as he flips the page, tilting his head. "Now that is an interesting position," he hums, eye dancing with excitement.

"Or maybe not," comes his lighthearted comment when I glare at him accusingly, he passes the book to the girl.

A mischievous glint dances in his eyes as he attempts to defend himself. "What? You can read book porn, but I can't appreciate the art?" he teases, his arms wrapping around me from behind. His lips brush against my ear, sending a shiver down my spine.

"I'd be more than happy to provide a real-life interpretation for you," he purrs, his breath warm against my skin.

"This is not book porn!" I tell him, waving my book at him. He raises an eyebrow at me, plucking the book from my hand while I try to snatch it back.

"I'll be the judge of that!" he states. He holds it out of reach.

"Now, let's see what my little hussy of a mate is into?" he says, intrigued while flicking through the pages.

"Not porn, huh?" he taunts. My face heats when Xandros suddenly clears his throat, glances at the cover. "Her Fae lovers...!." He arches an eyebrow.

"Now, let's see who this adulterer of an author is! This Jane Knight." I try to snatch the book, knowing what he'll find. I know her books far too well. "No, this is meant to be about a tantalizing plot line, we'll see now," Xandros mocks.

Nervously, I glance at the girl waiting patiently, my face heating.

Great, she'll think I'm a deviate. Yet nothing prepares me for Xandros to test his narrator skills.

"He sucked in a deep breath as he brushed his thumb over her clitoris. Working two fingers inside of her, marveling at the tight wet heat that surrounded his digits. Her soft gasping moan made him smile as he worked his fingers in and out of her."

My eyes widen when he starts to read it out loud, my face flushing hot. I try to grab the book, and I am one step from tackling him to the ground. Xandros laughs but keeps reading in an overly feminine voice, adding in extra dramatized moans.

"Loving the way she moved her body against his, Merrow's hand moved over Lola's hip. His fingers brushed against Lu's wrist. Smirking, he met the other man's eyes. "Couldn't wait, could you?" "Shut up," Lola growled as she wrapped her hand around the back of Merrow's neck and pulled him closer..." Xandros stops. "Wow, she is one frisky lady, there are two men!" he states.

"It has a good storyline," I cringe at his facial expression.

"I fail to see this storyline between all the cocks she is taking," Xandros growls, he flips through more of the pages. "Yep, more cocks, ooh what a surprise more cocks, she is one cock hungry lady."

"Stop," I snicker, trying to reclaim my book while the clerk laughs. "No...no...I am trying to emphasize this storyline, we are just getting to the juicy bits." I lunge for the book and nearly trip and Xandros catches me around the middle tugging me against him while holding the book out, so I can't reach it.

"See right here. Merrow brought his hands up to tease her breasts as she moved her other hand past the waistband of his shorts. Her fists wrapped around his cock, stroking him in a jerky motion. Her body started to shake from the stimulation, and Lu's voice was husky in her ear as he spoke. "The way ye move against me, Lola," he said as he thrust against her again,"" He states with a fake feminine moan added to the end.

I playfully elbow him and push him away, refusing to indulge his teasing. "Is this seriously the type of books you read, with multiple men?"

"No, Xandros. I prefer to focus on the storyline," I reply with a coy smile, determined to redirect the conversation. Just because I read it doesn't mean I want to be with multiple men. I roll my eyes at the thought.

"Ah, so it is the plot line?" he chuckles, playing along.

The store clerk joined in our playful banter, adding her voice to the mix.

"Oh, that's one of my favorites, too," she chimes in, winking at me.

She straightens. "And the plot line is good, too," she quickly adds. "But the spice," she fans herself. Xandros turns his attention to the clerk, feigning a dramatic sense of shock.

"You've read this, too? I feel like I need to wash my mouth out, maybe even my eyes," he quips, pretending to be scandalized.

I seize the opportunity to snatch the book back from his hands, determined to put an end to our playful back-and-forth.

"This is what you're into? Wanting all holes filled?" Xandros whispers in my ear, his arms wrapping around me once again. He nibbles gently on my neck, causing a shiver to run down my spine. I push him away. "No!"

"Good, because I am not a man who likes to share, though I am more than happy to fill you," he growls and I sigh.

I am definitely not that sort of girl, one asshole is enough to try to survive, let alone finding two Xandros', I think to myself.

"The storyline seems intriguing, I only read half of it before you kidnapped me," I retort.

"Storyline? What storyline, the discovery of her gagging on cocks, or are we talking about the tantalizing storyline of counting foreskins?" he mocks and I roll my eyes.

"Nope, if you're reading that I am keeping my picture book, it has a good storyline, too."

"Hmm, so what's the story about?" I ask Xandros.

"Ahh, about... I'm sure it has one," he tells me, and I smile deviously.

"So you want this one?" the store girl asks.

"Yes," Xandros states.

"Sure, the storyline, I will pretend that's the only reason you want to read it." I laugh.

The store clerk chuckles at our exchange, clearly amused by our banter. I take the book he chose back from the clerk, holding it up.

"Well, if you're interested, you might as well grab book two as well. I devoured both in two days," she tells him.

"Oh, I liked book 2 better," I tell her, shoving the book with erotic pictures into his chest before wandering off.

Xandros whirls around to face me, feigning outrage. "You've read it already?" I laugh softly while he points an accusing finger at me.

"And you're complaining about my book tastes when you've read it? Unbelievable," he teased, a playful glimmer in his eyes.

I held his gaze, my smile widening. "You don't want to read it; you just want to admire the pictures," I reply, teasing him in return. He sputters in mock offense, attempting to defend his intentions. We both know the truth: he wants some images for his spank bank!

"Fine, I expect a full rundown of the book," I tell him. For a few seconds, I'm not certain what he'll do. Xandros narrows his eyes as he glares at me. It's like an intense stare-down between two street cats, each one waiting for the other to look away first. Finally, I break the silence by laughing, knowing damn well I won't get a full run down but seeing him squirm is worth it in itself.

His eyes sparkle deviously. "Fine, I'll read it from front to back, only if we reenact the raunchy bits," he purrs. I shake my head, following the girl to the counter, while he chuckles, following me.

Chapter Forty-Two

Xandros

Seeing Sienna genuinely smile is something I haven't seen before. And all it took was a book? I shake my head, watching as she reads, her eyes glowing in the darkness as her vision adjusts.

She said she was just reading the first page, but I have noticed she is a good fifteen pages into the book already. As we pull into the driveway, she still does not look up. Or when the car stops, for that matter.

I'm wondering how long it will take for her to notice we are back at the castle. Glancing at my watch, I see I've been waiting five minutes for her to notice we've stopped, so I clear my throat. She jumps at the sound, and I raise an eyebrow at her. Sienna quickly glances around, snapping her book shut, and I see the slightest tinge on her cheeks.

"You've ignored me this entire drive," I chuckle. "Why do I feel like I am going to regret allowing you to have books?"

Her fingers grip it tighter, like she believes I truly would take it from her. The small motion stings for some reason. Have I really reduced the woman to someone who would rather be off with the fairies with her nose in a book than be present in the real world with me?

Before I can ask any questions, car lights heading toward us on the driveway catch my attention. My grip tightens on the steering wheel as the vehicle comes to a stop beside us. The door opens, and Vin steps out, wearing a smug smile.

King Vin opens my door, and I grit my teeth.

"You're back early?" I tell him, not looking forward to this argument, which is no doubt coming.

"A little birdy saw you in the city. Without my daughter, you must understand how bad that looks for my son-in-law to be running around with another woman on his arm?"

"What I do is none of your business. Carina is okay with it," I tell him, holding my hand out for Sienna to take. She does, hesitantly, peering up at Vin as she slides out of the car. The moment she does, Vin blocks her path and I sidestep getting between them.

"What do you want, Vin?" I growl in warning before my jaw clenches.

Vin's smirk widens, his gaze flickering between Sienna and me. "Ah, Xandros, you know what I want. I was just intending to have a little chat with your precious concubine."

My blood boils at his words. He's intentionally provoking me, trying to undermine my authority. Sienna remains silent, her eyes focused on the ground.

"What's the meaning of this, Vin?" I demand, my voice sharp and commanding.

Vin's gaze narrows as he locks eyes with me. "I would like to ensure Sienna isn't challenging for your hand. You've spent the entire day together and night." I open my mouth to demand to know how he knows that, but he keeps speaking.

"I have eyes everywhere, you know this. The wedding is to go ahead next week, Xandros. You will marry Carina, or else—"

I interrupt him, my voice dripping with anger. "Or else what? What kind of leverage do you think you have over me?"

Vin leans in, his voice low and menacing. "I have so much dirt on your family, Xandros. Don't forget that. I will have your kingdom dismantled in the blink of an eye. Your people will become slaves to my kingdom."

My patience wears thin, and I grab Vin by the collar, yanking him closer to me.

"You think you can manipulate me? Threaten me?"

He smirks again, unfazed. "Is that what you want to be known for, Xandros? The king who let his people suffer?" he asks before he peers at Sienna behind me.

"And are you planning to outdo your parents' reputation? It's bad enough the Lycan population hates you. You don't want to be responsible for the deaths of your own people, do you?"

"They're not her people anymore; she is no longer human," I state.

The threat hangs in the air, igniting a fire within me. I release my grip on Vin, taking a step back. His words hit a nerve, reminding me of the precarious position I am in.

"And what about your family, Vin?" I retort, my voice dripping with venom. "How would they fare if the council were to find out about your own dirty secrets? Let's not forget the skeletons lurking in your closet."

Vin's eyes widen for a split second before his crooked smile returns. "Ah, you're quite the cunning one, Xandros. Rest assured, I have my ways of keeping the council at bay. They won't dare touch me. But you... I wonder what the council would have to say if they learned your mother killed one of their own?"

A growl escapes me, and Sienna grabs my arm, halting me. I clench my fists, fighting the urge to lash out. This game of power and manipulation has gone on long enough.

"Don't forget the only reason your little mate is alive, Xandros, is because of my daughter," Vin says, his voice dripping with contempt. "Your mother wanted her dead, along with her parents. You will marry Carina, or I will let the world know exactly what sort of traitor you have for a mate. I wonder if Elder Alaric would be pleased to know whose daughter she is? Or what truly happened to his best friend?"

"I'm sure he'd be interested to learn you helped cover that up."

My fury reaches its peak, and without thinking, I grab Vin by the throat, slamming him onto the roof of his limo, the bang of his body hitting the metal is loud, the thud echoing around me as his body crushes the roof inward. Moments later, my mother's voice breaks through the tension as she steps out of the castle.

"What's going on?" she asks, her eyes scanning the scene before her.

I glare down at Vin, who wears a triumphant grin on his face. Just then, Carina rushes out, her voice filled with concern.

"Dad?" her voice rings out loudly, and I turn my attention to her.

"Xandros, what do you think you're doing? Let my father go!" she snaps at me.

With a growl, I shove Vin off, his body tumbling to the ground. Carina rushes to his side, and I turn toward my mother and Sienna. Grabbing Sienna's arm, I pull her toward the castle where my mother is waiting. Sienna's eyes remain fixed on Vin, a mix of fear and betrayal in her gaze.

"What happened?" my mother asks, grabbing my arm, her voice filled with urgency.

"Later," I reply, my tone cold and detached. "Let me get my mate back to her room. Where is Javier?"

"With your father," she answers.

"Send for him," I tell her.

The weight of the situation hangs heavily upon me as I lead Sienna away, my mind racing with the knowledge that the stakes have been raised. I can't afford to lose control, not now.

Chapter Forty-Three

Sienna

As Xandros leads me to my room, a heaviness settles in the pit of my stomach. His grip on my arm is firm, and there's an underlying tension in his touch. As we approach my room, Javier is waiting already, having beat us here. We enter the room, and Xandros releases me, his gaze lingering on mine for a moment before he speaks.

"I'll be back soon," he says, his voice filled with a mix of exhaustion and concern.

"Javier will stay here to watch over you."

I nod, my eyes darting to Javier, who stands waiting for a command. The entire time, my mind races with questions, before I can voice them, Xandros is gone, leaving me alone with Javier. I turn to him, my eyes pleading for answers.

"No, don't look at me like that, Sienna. Any questions need to wait for Xandros," he states, moving toward the armchair. He grabs the remote, flicks on the TV, and makes himself at home like he always does. I follow and sit across from him in the other chair. "What did Vin mean about Carina saving me?" I ask, my voice trembling.

Javier sighs, his eyes filled with a mix of sadness; it's rare that Javier denies me the answers I ask, and this time is no different as he gives in, knowing I will keep pestering him until I have the answers I need. "Carina refused to hand you over when she turned your mother and father in," he explains. "Instead, she gave you to your uncle, pleading with Adina to listen. Carina believed you were just a baby and shouldn't be blamed for your parents' mistakes."

Confusion sets in, and I struggle to comprehend Carina's actions. Why would she go to such extremes to save me? What did I mean to her?

"When she returned them to the castle, she had her guards take you back to your uncle. Your mother and father, when they fled, took you thinking King Vin would protect them from their crimes."

"Why would they think that?" Javier shrugs. "No idea, but when they were returned for punishment, Carina pleaded with Adina to leave you out of it. She copped quite the scolding from her mother and her father for having you sent to your uncle. She disobeyed a direct order."

Why would she risk punishment for her handmaiden's child?

Before I can delve deeper into my thoughts, Javier turns the volume up on the TV, providing a distraction. I take the opportunity to retreat to the walk-in closet to retrieve my phone before escaping into the bathroom, taking it with me. I dial Toby's number, my heart pounding with anticipation.

Toby answers after just one ring. His voice filled with relief. "I was so worried when I didn't hear from you," he says.

"I can't speak long, I am just calling to say we need to push things along. I need to get out, Toby. The city is going to war, and I'm afraid I'll be caught in the middle of it," I tell him, desperation seeping into my voice. I know no matter what, Xandros is not getting out of this marriage, and I have no intention of watching him be with another woman. Or get caught in the crossfire if he refuses the marriage.

"Why?"

"King Vin is pushing for the wedding to be next week, I have a feeling something will happen before then. I think he is planning something," I tell him.

"Fine. We'll figure it out together, I will speak with Tyra and see if we can find a way out tomorrow for you. We'll have to hide out until the seekers can get us out," he assures me.

A knock at the door interrupts our conversation. I quickly end the call, promising to speak again soon. Opening the door, I find Javier standing on the other side. Relief washes over me, knowing it wasn't Xandros.

"I need to duck down to check the cameras for Xandros. I'll be back. Don't answer the door unless it's me or Xandros. Not even for Queen Adina or King Rehan," Javier instructs me.

I furrow my brow in confusion. "Why not them?"

"Xandros is paranoid. Just do as I say," Javier says, his tone grave. "And stay off that phone. Xandros catches you speaking with Toby he'll have both our heads," he warns, and I nod. He turns to leave then stops.

"Sienna." I peer up at him. "Whatever you're planning with Toby, don't. You run, and Xandros will hunt you down. That won't end well for your friend or you," he warns me.

"Yet you haven't told him," I tell him, and his brows furrow. "Because you're my friend, Xandros is too. He's my boss. I'm charged with keeping you safe, though sometimes I wonder who I am trying to keep you safe from..."

"What do you mean?"

"I don't know. I know he won't kill you; I know I can't do much, though I am not blind to your suffering. I'm not blind to his, either. You think he doesn't want you, I promise he is doing everything he can to be with you."

I swallow.

"I know you hate him, royal politics isn't just some argument between rivals. Lives depend on it, more than just yours and his. His kingdom, everything his family has built here, he's risking it all for you. It may not seem like it, but he is."

I nod. After hearing Vin threaten the human populace, I understand the severity of the situation. Javier leaves, and I'm left alone once again, anxiously awaiting his return or Xandros's. Time seems to stretch endlessly, each passing minute fraught with uncertainty.

Finally, an hour later, the jiggle of keys in the door has me sitting up in bed. The door opens, and Xandros steps into the room. His face is etched with anger, his eyes burning with intensity. He silently wanders around the room before moving to the bathroom and shutting the door.

Around ten minutes later, he steps out of the bathroom, followed by the billowing steam. Without a word, he climbs into bed beside me, and I instinctively keep my back turned to him. The tension in the room is riddled with his burning anger.

Whatever happened, he is not speaking about it or taking it out on me, so I suppose I should be happy about that. My body tenses when I feel his hand grip my hip. He tugs me closer, spooning me tightly. His touch is both possessive and comforting, a tumultuous mix of emotions coursing through me.

My heart races as I feel the heat of his body against mine. My mind is filled with questions, and I can no longer keep them at bay.

"What did Vin mean about the council and your mother?" I whisper, my voice filled with curiosity and apprehension.

Xandros's grip on me tightens slightly, his voice laced with bitterness. "My mother's father was the head council member," he reveals. "They believe he died when my father's kingdom was attacked, and his parents were killed. What they don't realize is that he was the attacker, and my mother was merely defending herself and her sister."

I take in his words, the weight of the truth settling upon us. It's a burden we both carry—the dark secrets and hidden truths that threaten to tear us apart.

"But it was self-defense," I answer, and he presses his lips to my shoulder. "Doesn't matter. He's a council member; he has immunity. Also, the council was aware of the conflict between her father and mine."

"What do you mean?"

"My father challenged her father, threatened to oppose him on the council if he didn't give my mother to him. They would have assumed my father killed him to take his place."

"And this Alaric person?" I inquire, my voice soft and filled with curiosity. When he doesn't answer, I glance at him behind me.

Xandros's gaze softens, and he presses a gentle kiss to my shoulder, then sighs. "Alaric had just discovered my aunt was his mate," he explains.

As I absorb his words, I realize the intricate web of fate that binds us all together. Everyone is connected to some of the things my parents did. We are intertwined in a story that goes far beyond our own desires and choices.

"I thought she had no mate?" I ask him.

"She was pregnant, technically, until he marked her they weren't mates. He couldn't because she was carrying my sister. Also, my aunt wasn't of sound mind, so Alaric knew he had to take things slow with her."

"That's why your mother hates me so much; your aunt was her surrogate."

Xandros nods.

"Javier... he," I stop, wondering if Javier would get in trouble for telling me.

"What did Javier tell you? You can tell me, Sienna; I know you two are friends," he answers.

"He said you blame yourself because you gave my mother the key. I don't understand. Wouldn't you have been a child?"

Xandros laughs. "We are immortal, Sienna. I'm over 200 years old; I was an adult. My aunt was actually younger than me. Lycans age a lot slower. When my mother helped her sister escape their father, he retaliated, which cost my mother the ability to have any more children. She thought she was done with me, but having the ability to have more children taken from her seemed to make her want another child right away. Her sister felt guilty, so she offered to be a surrogate for her. It sounds odd, I know, but Lycans aren't human. We have time, endless amounts of time."

"Your mother killed her father?"

"Yes, protecting her sister; they were close, and she was the only reason she remained in contact with her father. When she learned he had another child, she stayed close, trying to prevent her from having the same upbringing. They don't share the same mother, and her father raised them both alone."

"He never found his mate?"

"He did. My grandmother was his true mate, and he killed her."

"Don't Lycans go crazy without their mates?"

"Males, yes, but only those of royal blood. Her father wasn't. He was head of the council. He oversaw the supernatural kingdoms and helped create the laws. He was a man of power, even above the royal families. Just because I am king now doesn't mean I don't have to answer the council. The council is basically the twelve kingdoms' advisors, they're in-between. So when treaties are made, alliances, the council is the one that oversees and governs them to try to prevent wars. They were brought into place after the war—one from each kingdom. My mother's bloodline was royal on her mother's side, her father wasn't. When her kingdom was dismantled after she rejected him, he waited for my mother to be born and killed her."

"Why was her kingdom dismantled?"

"Because my grandmother rejected him."

"Why?" I ask.

"He marked her against her will. She was only sixteen when he discovered her; her parents refused him and said to wait until she was of age. My grandfather didn't like that, so he had her parents killed, he kidnapped her and raped her. She rejected him, not realizing that once marked, you can't. Since she refused to back down to him, he waited for my mother to be born, then killed her. Unfortunately, she never stood a chance. He killed her on her seventeenth birthday, the same day mother was born, he slit her throat the moment she gave birth." Bile rises in my throat, hearing the tragic tale. His grandmother was killed so young.

"And the council didn't care he killed his mate, a child, and killed her parents?"

"No, no one was game enough to go against the head of the council. Everyone knew he was corrupt; he always has been."

"Isn't the council formed to stop that sort of thing?" I ask; I see no point to a council if they're all corrupt.

"The council was formed after the wars. Too many humans were killed off. The Lycan kingdoms were blamed, and a lot were at fault. The lack of humans meant a lack of blood source for the vampire kingdoms, which in turn caused more wars, so the council was formed—a member from each of the founding kingdoms, initially—then it became a voting system or passed down when council members retired. Mostly, it's a corrupt system. Very few remained neutral within the council; it just became another power play, a way to dictate the kingdoms." It is all too much for me to comprehend. Power is the biggest source of evil, along with greed. Only now am I realizing to what extent power can be abused.

Chapter Forty-Four

Sienna

The following day, I opened my eyes to find Xandros absent from the room. However, Javier is sitting on the couch, engrossed in the television. I stretch my limbs, feeling alert and awake for the first time in ages. "When did you get here?" I ask, my voice still laced with sleep.

"A few hours ago," Javier responds, his eyes fixed on the screen.

"Where's Xandros?"

"Working," he replies before a knock on the door cuts off his words. Javier swiftly moves to answer it, revealing King Rehan standing there.

"Morning," he greets, stepping into the room and shutting the door behind him. Javier sighs in response, a subtle sign of annoyance. However, Javier makes no comment as Rehan enters in his stripey pajamas and his slippers like he does each morning.

Rehan moves around the room, pushing all the furniture out of the way to clear space while Javier finishes his coffee. "Some help you are," Rehan whines at him.

"Coffee comes first," Javier replies, holding up his mug. King Rehan shakes his head while I move to get into different clothes; my nightie is definitely only appropriate if I intend on flashing the king, which I don't.

Grabbing some clothes, I slip into the bathroom and change before coming back out, only to have a surprise attack launched on me.

My breath catches in my throat, and for a moment, I can only lay there stunned. As I lie on the ground, gasping for air, Rehan stands above me with his arms crossed over his chest and a smug smirk on his lips.

"Cheap shot," I groan, struggling to get up again.

Rehan and I engage in our morning training session. We spar, exchanging blows and blocking each other. In a surprising turn of events, I manage to knock down Rehan for once, a burst of pride surging through me. I do a little happy dance. However, my celebration is short-lived as my feet are suddenly kicked out from under me. I fall to the ground with a thud, the air knocked out of me.

Rehan swiftly moves to stand over me, pinning my wrists down. "Don't celebrate too early," Rehan scolds. I lift my leg, using my strength to push him off before swiftly pinning him back down. I open my mouth to reply when the door swings open, freezing us where we stand.

We freeze in panic as Queen Adina steps into the room. Her hair is black and straight, pulled back into a high ponytail. She wears a black dress, with a black belt and black stiletto heels. The queen's eyes widen as she takes in the scene. I quickly realize how bad this looks, with both of us drenched in sweat and me straddling the king, her mate. Especially when the queen already hates me.

"What the hell!" Queen Adina snaps, and I immediately jump off King Rehan. Adina pauses as she steps forward, her eyes lingering on Rehan before darting to me. Her fists clench at her side as she takes a deep breath. Javier reacts quickly, placing his body in front of me as a protective shield. King Rehan scrambles to his feet, attempting to explain.

"Love, it's not what you think," he insists, however, she is livid.

"What do I think? What do I think, Rehan?" Queen Adina's voice trembles with anger.

"I've spent the last hour looking for you. Can you imagine my horror when I asked a maid where you were, and she said in Xandros's mate's room! Do you have any idea how angry he'd be if he caught you in here wrestling his damn mate?" she snaps; Javier's hand moves to my hip, pushing me further behind him.

"Training his mate. That's all. Nothing sordid is going on," Rehan insists, his voice laced with desperation.

"Sordid? I know that. I would feel if you were sleeping with her, Rehan. I'm angry because you've been doing this behind my back, and Xandros he'll be livid if he finds out. Did you think of how much trouble she would be in if caught in here with you two all sweaty!"

I remain silent, watching the heated argument unfold between Rehan and Queen Adina. Javier stands resolutely in front of me, acting as a buffer between them. I do my best to ignore their words, knowing I shouldn't be a witness to their quarrel. Queen Adina's accusations cut deep.

"What have you got to say for yourself, Rehan? Sneaking into her room each morning. I thought I was going crazy and imagining things. I even accused her of hitting on you!" Queen Adina's frustration is evident in her voice.

"Well, I couldn't exactly train her in the hall. Let's not pretend that you would have agreed to that, Adina. I had no choice. Xandros definitely wouldn't have approved, with Vin's presence, she needs to know how to defend herself. I know what her parents did, and I know—" Queen Adina abruptly cuts off Rehan's explanation.

"She isn't her parents, Rehan. I know that now. This little scene would have put her at risk if Xandros had walked through that door. Not from Vin, but from our son. Not in her room. Somewhere more public. If Xandros catches you training her in her bedroom, he will be furious. It doesn't look good, and it seems like you're sneaking around behind his back. Hall or not at all," Queen Adina snaps before storming out of the room, slamming the door shut behind her.

Rehan and Javier exchange a bewildered expression.

"Did she just give me permission?" Rehan asks, his voice filled with surprise.

"I think so," Javier admits, his tone tinged with uncertainty.

After Queen Adina is gone, Rehan quickly follows, and Javier goes to get me lunch, leaving me alone in the room.

I decide to take a shower, hoping to wash away the tension that hangs in the air. However, when I'm in the shower, I hear a noise in the bedroom, causing me to freeze. I listen intently, my heart racing when suddenly Tyra's voice reaches my ears.

"Sienna?"

I quickly turn off the water and wrap a towel around myself before stepping out of the bathroom. Tyra is standing there, peering around nervously. "How did you get in here?" I ask, surprised. She holds up a key.

"Master key. Got it copied," she replies, glancing nervously at the door. "I have to be quick. Toby called me. I need you to meet me in the laundry room at 2 PM. I've organized an additional pickup; I lied and said it's extra laundry from Vin's guard and the extra guests. Luckily, I was stockpiling extra laundry in case I had to get you out early."

"Wait, today?" I ask in shock; that is very little time for me to prepare.

"Yes. The king isn't due home until tonight. 2 PM, no later," she warns.

"How am I supposed to slip away? Javier is watching me," I say with a surge of anxiety.

Tyra rummages in her pockets and produces two pills. She drops them into my hand. "Put these in his drink. They'll dissolve and knock him out. We'll only have an hour max, before he wakes. Sleeping pills don't work on Lycans as they do on humans," she explains. I nod, understanding the gravity of the situation. Also, how would I manage that without him noticing? Tyra quickly leaves, and I stare down at the dissolvable pills.

Quickly rushing back to the shower, I wash the soap that is still in my hair out. By the time I come out, Javier has returned with lunch. The tray sits on the coffee table while he sits in his favorite armchair, sipping his bottle of lemonade.

"Sandwiches," he points to the coffee table. I nod, moving to the walk-in closet and getting changed; glancing at the two pills in my hand, I chew my lip, trying to figure out how I am going to get this in his bottle of lemonade. When I come out, Javier is sifting through the DVD collection he snuck up here a few days ago.

"Which one?" he asks me, holding up the folder full of DVDs.

"You pick; I'll probably read," I tell him, moving to the coffee table. I sit beside his drink, which luckily still has the cap off. I grab a sandwich while he flicks through his folder. Finding one he likes, he gets up, moving to the TV and DVD player.

While his back is turned, I drop them into his drink. My heart races the entire time as I watch them sink to the bottom. They fizz, making the bottle cloudy as they do so. I glance at Javier, who is setting the DVD in place, and my heart rate picks up rapidly as he grabs the remote and turns. I quickly grab his drink, moving to take a pretend sip of it.

"That one is mine. It's sugar-free," Javier tells me.

A bead of sweat runs down the back of my neck as I set it down before I finally inhale. The fizz has stopped, and the pills wholly dissolved.

"Sorry," I tell him, and he shakes his head.

"It's fine," he tells me, taking a sip of his drink. At the same time, I take a bite of my sandwich and sip my drink. Javier and I eat, watching the previews on the DVD. I then grab my book when Javier comments. "It tastes different," he mumbles, swirling the bottle. "Did it taste strange to you?" he asks.

"Tasted bitter; I suppose it would with no sugar," I shrug, dropping onto the couch.

"I hate when they change it; I'll have to ask Mari what they changed," he sighs.

I was two chapters into my book when I noticed Javier jolt; peering over my book, I watch him fight against exhaustion. "Are you okay?" I ask him, and he yawns.

"Yeah, the movie is boring," he states, then shakes his head. I return to my book, occasionally glancing at Javier; eventually, his head falls forward, and I get to my feet. Walking over to him, I tilt his head back. He mutters something unintelligible, and I rest his head back on the couch. Moving to stand before him, I rummage into his front pockets while my heart thuds rapidly.

No excuse would be good enough if he woke and caught me with my hand in his pocket. Grabbing his keys. I quickly put on my everyday uniform and grab the bathroom laundry basket. I stuff a bag with a change of clothes in it under the dirty towels. Moving to the door, I glance once more at Javier before carefully unlocking the door and slipping out into the hall.

I make my escape to the laundry room, where I meet Tyra, who is glancing around nervously. "Finally!" she whispers, moving to shut the door. She locks it and helps me climb into the massive hamper with my bag. She covers me with linen, wheels it outside to the waiting truck, and whispers the final instructions.

"Stay down, and when the truck stops, you must be quick. Don't let the driver see you. Toby will be waiting for you in a black van." she tells me. "Good luck," she says when I hear a man's voice before I can reply. "Just the one?" he asks.

"Yep, extra guests; thanks, Patrick," I hear Tyra tell him.

"Any time," he replies. As the hamper rolls away and is lifted into the truck, my heart pounds with fear but also excitement. This is my chance for freedom, to break away from the web of deception and danger surrounding me. I take a deep breath; I am finally going to be free. Finally free of Xandros and this luxurious prison.

∼

The bumpy ride in the huge laundry hamper leaves me feeling queasy. Despite this, I am filled with a mix of excitement and worry. I'm excited because I'm finally escaping the castle's confines and my overbearing mate. Also, worry because I can't help thinking about its impact on Xandros. The pain he'll feel when we manage to break the mate bond. Some part of me also wonders if the side of him I've recently seen is legit. The words he spoke, did he truly mean them? Despite my conflicting emotions, a sense of freedom washes over me. Freedom to be with Toby, to explore a different life without having to peek over my shoulder every few seconds, hoping not to be scolded or punished.

As the van slows, I brace myself, ready to move, while praying I am not caught by the driver. Quietly as possible, I climb out of the laundry hamper, my heart pounding as adrenaline courses through my veins. Listening intently, the van stops, and I hear the driver fiddling with his paperwork. I crack the rear door of the van open, listening for footsteps.

I hear the driver climb out of his van and quickly jump out, closing the door at the same time he slams the driver's door shut.

Peering around, I find myself standing in the loading dock of the laundromat. Not wasting any time, I quickly slip out of the dock and up the side of the building. The hum of machines and the scent of detergent fill the air, along with chatter from inside the building. A few people stand out in front of the laundromat, smoking.

I swiftly blend into the small crowd, scanning the surroundings for Toby's car. Luckily, no one pays attention to a woman in a cleaner's uniform. My clothes are bland, just like the laundromat staff. Striding to the corner of the building, I spot Toby's car. Toby has his back to me, staring in the opposite direction.

My escape is parked near the bakery across from the laundromat. The parking lot on this side is empty except for his car, a black van that glistens in the fading sunlight. I breathe a sigh of relief upon sighting his car.

Yet standing here, I am a sitting duck and a sense of urgency pulses through me. I hurry toward the car, my steps quickening with anticipation. Toby stands by the car, his presence a beacon of familiarity and comfort. The moment Toby hears my rushed footsteps, he turns, a huge grin on his face.

As I reach him, Toby immediately pulls me into his embrace. The warmth of his body envelops me, and for a moment, everything else fades away. "Thank the Goddess, I was starting to worry," he whispers, squeezing me tight. I hug him back, enjoying his embrace.

"I've missed you so much," he whispers, his voice filled with longing. I can feel the sincerity in his words, and the depth of his emotions. He presses his lips to my temple. "Come on, before we're spotted," he whispers, turning and nudging me toward the passenger door.

He guides me around the car and opens the passenger door. As I settle into the seat, I notice the back seat is packed with suitcases. Toby, anticipating my needs, leans over me into the back, tugging a tote bag into my lap. He opens it, handing me a pair of jeans and a hoodie to change out of my maid's uniform.

"Quick, get changed," he tells me, helping me unbutton my dress while using his body to help shield me from people outside. I tug it down to my hips, and Toby immediately pulls the hoodie over my head. He glances around nervously before gripping my dress.

"Lift your butt for me," he whispers, and I do as he says before ripping the jeans up my legs. He shuts the door, casually walking around the car while I do up the zipper and buttons. Toby climbs in, reaching into the backseat again and handing me some socks and sneakers. I pull them on while he starts the car. "Ready?" he asks, and I smile before nodding.

Once we're on the road, I toss my old clothes into the backseat, and notice two duffle bags filled with cash in back there. Toby glances at me before returning his eyes back to focus on the road ahead. "What did you do, rob a bank?" I ask him. "Sold my house. We'll stay in a hotel near the entrance to the tunnels until the Seekers call," he explains, his voice laced with excitement. Yet guilt gnaws at me with how he has just tossed the life he built here away for me.

On the drive, he tells me about a cabin in the woods he's purchased, a place where we can truly be free. It sounds like heaven, an escape from the bonds that have held me captive. Escape from Xandros, though I wonder how Toby feels about tossing everything away and starting again.

However, as the distance between us and the castle grows, a wave of nausea washes over me. The bond that connects me to Xandros tugs at my core, the pull becoming stronger and stronger. I clutch my stomach; the pain intensifies until it becomes unbearable. "Sienna. Sienna, are you okay?" Toby gushes, reaching over and gripping my shoulder. He pushes me back in my chair.

"Crap, hang on," he murmurs, and I feel the car jerk to one side. The world blurs and Toby's voice fades into background noise, and the next, my ears are ringing. Darkness steals the edges of my vision when I feel his hands on me, tugging the seatbelt away. "Hold on," he tells me before I feel a pinch in my arm just as I succumb to darkness.

ABOUT THE AUTHOR

Fueled by caffeine, barely-contained sanity, and the chaos of raising five kids, along with a penchant for the wicked. Jessica Hall is an international best-selling author from Australia. Her writing spans a few genres, from dark and seductive paranormal romance to gritty contemporary mafia and the dark and taboo that push boundaries.

Known for writing stories that ignite desire and stir the soul, Jessica Hall invites readers to explore a world of forbidden fantasies, emotionally charged twists, and characters who don't just break the rules—they shatter them. Whether it's commanding Alphas, morally gray antiheroes, or heroines with more bite than their enemies, every page promises a thrilling escape into the deliciously dark and dangerous.

If you crave stories that toe the line between love and obsession, innocence and sin, you're in the right place. Just don't expect happily-ever-afters to come easy—or without a fight.

After all, a mind like hers can only create magic—or madness.

CONNECT WITH JESSICA HALL

- 🌐 *Website:* www.jessicahallauthor.com
- **f** *Facebook:* facebook.com/jessicahall91
- 📷 *Instagram:* instagram.com/jessica.hall.author
- ♪ *Tiktok:* tiktok.com/@jessicahallauthor

Printed in Great Britain
by Amazon